THE PUZZLING MIRROR

CW00880945

MIRROR

Croft Frances
The Puzzling Mirror.

DRAGON

© 2005 Frances Croft
Second edition © 2009 Frances Croft
The Puzzling Mirror

ISBN 978-0-9541119-0-8

Published by Dragon Smoke
8, Lower Fairview Road
DARTMOUTH
Devon
TQ6 9EE

A CIP catalogue record of this book
can be obtained from the British Library.

Book Designed by
Michael Walsh at MusicPrint, Chichester

Printed in England by Short Run Press Ltd., Exeter

Cover design by Kirsty Race

CONTENTS

Dedication

For Alan, my brother, and for all the children
I have taught around the world.

There are more things in heaven and earth, Horatio,
Than are dreamt of in your philosophy.

Hamlet – Act 1 Scene 5

An adventure to follow

On this planet of ours that we call Earth there are many worlds existing in different planes, side by side with each other.

For the most part each one is completely unaware of the others.

In the Sparkat trilogy the world in which we live is called Bioworld.

The puzzling mirror of the title of this first book guides the children and their animal friends in their quest to regain control over stolen DNA, and so prevent the destruction of Bioworld.

The travellers visit seven worlds before reaching their ultimate goal of Creation world.

Follow the work of the mirror in:-

Rainbow World

Frost World

Lost World

Technoworld

Youth World

Land of the Masai

Star World

When you have finished reading the story, see if you can remember:

the clue that gave entry to each world

the treasure found there

the colour of the jewel appearing in the frame of the mirror.

The Sparkat Trilogy

Book jackets for this trilogy designed by children
in Dartmouth Community College, Devon.

1 Monkey

The long tail swung slowly, backwards and forwards. Furtively, Monkey glanced to right and left, up and down, his piercing gaze missed nothing – he knew he was where he shouldn't be, and was watchful. Absentmindedly, he picked a flea from his chest, examined it and ate it. The stiff grey fur along his back stood erect with expectation. His bead-black eyes opened wide in his furry face, and the long white fingers clasped each other in glee. He chittered in excitement.

Nowhere could there be another forest such as this! He peered upwards through the motionless branches of the nearest tree but saw no sky beyond – just leaves, each one composed of tiny leaflets of luminous green, arranged around a central spine. Monkey stretched out a skinny arm and touched one lightly. It shrivelled back – its tender feelings displayed genuine alarm. Monkey laughed mischievously and threw himself onto the gnarled trunk. Light though his touch was, it drew from the wood the cloying scent of the tree's sticky resinous blood. He skittered out onto a branch, swinging his long, prehensile tail for balance; his were the movements of a graceful and much practised acrobat. The leaves shuddered as he passed. Monkey laughed again – this was fun! He peered through the foliage to the next tree. He raced to the end of a bough and soared over to it, scattering alarm and confusion among the fern-like scarlet leaves as he went. He moved on, leaving them in quivering disarray from his touch.

Monkey opened his mouth, revealing strong pointed teeth and a bright pink tongue, and screamed with delight. Then he was off, leaping and scampering in this endless playground, yanking protesting leaves from their secure hold and scattering them onto the mossy earth below. He ran down the trees headfirst. He hung by his tail and watched the ground sway beneath him. He chattered and gibbered as he went.

Monkey was happy.

Suddenly he stopped. His fine white fingers flew to his gaping mouth and his round eyes stared.

Why was he here? Boss had put him here. What was it Boss wanted?

Monkey scratched his head. A frown joined the lines of his wrinkled face.

A seedpod! Yeah! That was it!

Well – Monkey knew about trees. The best pods would be near the top. He scrambled to the canopy above, where it seemed many of the trees mingled together. Monkey could have his pick. But which to choose? Boss had said any pod would do, just so long as it came from this forest. He began plucking flowers and fruits at random and examining them closely. As he scrutinized each one, he shook his head, shouted 'Nah!' very loudly and tossed it over his shoulder, enjoying the way it rattled through the branches to the ground below.

Finally his gaze settled on a large flower with five ragged orange petals – white round the edges as the bloom shed its life, its function over. There, in the middle, was the mature seedpod – small, round and golden. It was flat on top, a circle with a frilled edge, and across this disc ran a number of straight lines. And, in the angles where these lines met in the centre were strange markings, each one different from the others. Underneath the disc was a circle of silver pinpoints that would later open to set forth the precious seeds.

Monkey's long, dextrous fingers reached towards the prize. He cupped the golden orb in both hands, and pulled. It didn't yield. He pulled again and again. Monkey was a creature with little patience. He chattered angrily to himself and rubbed his chest with the back of his hand. His face puckered into a frown as he examined the pod from all sides. Then a cheeky grin spread between his pointed ears. He bent down to where the pod joined the stem and began to chew. Ugh! A strange musty taste, and full of sticky prickly fibres that stuck between his teeth. Monkey pulled them out and spat them upwards, watching to see which carried further – spit or fibre. His good humour returned with the fun of the new game. But, his concentration quickly deserting him as it always did, he crunched and chewed and spat haphazardly; and at last had the treasure in his grasping paws.

"Gotcha!"

Monkey liked to be smart, and now he felt and looked scruffy. His long grey fur was matted with yellow sap and his elegant hands and feet were sticky and smelly. Using his rough and powerful tongue, he set about straightening himself out. He did so meticulously, starting at his chin and finishing with the tip of his long, muscular tail. Monkey was proud of his tail. He was proud of the whole of himself – he was a cool, clever monkey, he thought. He was also full of devilment. He examined the little orb he had taken from the tree.

So this is what Boss wants! I wonder what for? He scratched the golden surface and delighted in the shine it gave to his fingernails.

"Well, it's mine!" he called out to the forest. "Boss is not having it!

It's mine! It's mine! It's mine!" he shouted ever louder to the trees; and grinned as they rustled in reply.

Monkey hid the treasure carefully in the long white hair of his armpit – the place he always used for carrying things. He took a last look round, seeking to remember landmarks among the foliage – he would like to return some day. He glanced above him. He was still not at the top of the trees. They can't go on for ever. I'm going higher.

So on he climbed, his curiosity giving him strength to venture, with leaps and bounds, ever upwards.

Then, at last, a gap among the trees – a blackness.

"I knew it! Night sky!" exclaimed Monkey smugly to himself.

But the black hole that appeared among the foliage wasn't waiting for Monkey to approach. It all happened the other way round.

The black hole came down through the trees in a rushing howl. There was nothing to see but much to feel as it swept up terrified Monkey and whirled him round and round, and up and up, until he lost consciousness in the frantic maelstrom.

Then came the silence and the stillness. Tumbling over and over, falling, falling, falling – arms and legs and tail angling themselves strangely in a spontaneous, unconscious, desperate bid to cling onto whatever might be there in the nothingness.

Until finally the black hole tired of its game and spewed Monkey out.

Monkey regained consciousness in the canopy of yet another tree, in yet another world. He was stiff and sore in every bone. He rubbed his head and arms and legs and inspected his tail for damage. He felt the warm, kindly sun on his back, and the soft air on his fur. He looked around. These kinds of trees he recognized: jungle trees, homely trees, trees full of colourful parrots and snakes and things he understood. Then he remembered his seedpod – yeah, it was still there – tucked in the hairs of his armpit.

Must hide it from Boss.

Monkey chuckled. He felt his old self again.

Gingerly now, he climbed further down the tree. He explored the cracked trunk until he found a small hole in the wood. The edges seeped resin. Monkey drank in the sweet scent of it with pleasure. He pushed his precious prize into the hole and covered it with moss and, on top of that, bark, fixing it skilfully so no prying eye could see there was a hole beneath. His secret was safe.

Pleased with himself, he skipped off through the jungle until he was stopped for ever by an arrow from the bow of a wandering bushman. Monkey screamed in pain and fear and anger, and was still. That night the bushman's wife and children had monkey stew for supper, and the bushman's little girl cut off the long tail and made herself a skipping rope.

As for Monkey's prize, it remained hidden for hundreds of years until the tree was felled to make room for farmland, and a talented young man carved from its trunk and branches, statues of giraffes and rhinos and lions and elephants, to sell to the tourists.

2 Tom

Eagerly, Tom's eyes scanned the notice board. There it was – the team for tomorrow's match.

Substitute! Always substitute! Mr. Taylor had promised him a game. He'd promised a game to anyone who attended all the practices, and Tom had been to every single one since he joined the school, a year ago now. Tom knew well that subs often had half a game, but Tom didn't want *half* a game. He could feel the anger welling up inside him. He knew that would lead him into trouble and fought to control it. He must get out of here – fast – before it spilled over. He pushed into the overcrowded cloakroom, forcing his way past other children, all desperately trying to reach their bags quickly and gain the freedom of after school hours.

"Hey! Watch where you're going!"

"Don't push!" yelled Kayleigh, and shoved him back.

Tom dragged his bag over the head of Tim, the smallest boy in the class, and knocked his spectacles to the floor.

"Be careful!" protested Tim, scrabbling around amid the sea of legs and muddy shoes to retrieve them.

Tom didn't care; he didn't care about any of them. He hated them all. He hated the children. He hated the teachers. He hated the school. He knew he often behaved badly. He knew no one would like him if he wasn't pleasant to them, but he'd tried being nice and that hadn't worked. Grandma – he lived with Grandma – had said he must be patient. It was difficult for someone coming new into the village, especially at the top of the primary school when so many of the others had been together all their lives. Tom really had tried – to start with – but they made remarks behind his back, just loud enough for him to hear. And then, one day, they found out about his temper...

He knew they thought him odd. He lived with Grandma – they found that odd. And Grandma had no idea about football strips and trainers and computer games, nor the money to pay for these things.

At Grandma's suggestion, he had asked a couple of the other boys to the house on his birthday. They had ridiculed the sandwiches Grandma made and the silly old-fashioned games she wanted them to play. And he ended up hating Grandma.

He was good at lessons but the other children laughed at him when the teachers praised him. He quickly learned that it wasn't cool to be good at schoolwork. Well, it didn't take him long to sort that out; he found it quite easy to become disruptive. Why was being disruptive considered cool by the class when James and Matthew did it, but irritating and silly when it was Tom?

He knew he was good at football but the other kids had the team all worked out. Mr. Taylor must be afraid of them, thought Tom. Well he, Tom, wasn't afraid of them. Although sturdy Tom was not particularly big, but he knew, when it came to a fight, he could get the better of any one of those other kids. That had more to do with his temper than his fighting skills. He would lose all control, and then his punches landed hard and heavy. No one else knew that his temper frightened him more than it did them. He struggled hard to master it, having sufficient intelligence to realize it brought him mega problems.

He had a great deal of success modifying his behaviour, as teachers put it, at his other school, but here the provocations were just too great. He knew well that the other kids enjoyed goading him but he just couldn't help himself. It was as if something inside him that wasn't part of his own body was screaming to be let out. So, whenever possible, he avoided confrontation and spent playtimes in the classroom, working on his endless drawings and designs. One or two of his classmates would show an interest in what he was doing but none dared befriend him, for fear of being rejected themselves.

It was a dreary day in early October but Tom decided to take the long way home, over the cliff path. He didn't want to face Grandma yet, not before he had cooled down.

His bag was heavy, full of the homework he didn't intend doing, and his football kit, and the giraffes he always carried everywhere.

He loved his giraffe statue. Skilfully carved from hardwood, it came from Africa. It was a present from his father who treated him so badly but whom he dearly loved. Made from a cylinder of wood, the statue had a central tree, and around it curved three giraffes; these stood free of the tree except for the joins of heads and feet at canopy and roots. Tom thought it quite exquisite. He would like to have shown it at school – one of the dinner ladies had been to Africa – but feared for its treatment in insensitive hands.

Tom stopped at the bend in the cliff path and sat down in the scratchy bracken. He took out a somewhat flattened sausage roll left over from lunch, and chewed on it thoughtfully. The comfort of the food and the cold, grey drizzle from the autumn sky quelled his anger and replaced it with a deep sense of friendless misery and self pity. Tears rolled down his face.

Then Tom saw them. Three boys from his class: the captain, the goal-keeper and the best striker. Tom didn't move as they closed in on him from different directions.

"Taking a break, eh?" sneered James. He grabbed the sausage roll from Tom's hand and threw it into the bracken.

"What d'you keep in this then?" jeered Matthew, making a grab for Tom's bag.

"Leave that!" shouted Tom, as homework and football kit spilled to the ground. For once his temper wasn't there. It was a surge of injustice he felt. "Why don't you leave me alone? I haven't done anything to you."

"Oh, yeah! So telling isn't anything?" scoffed Philip.

"When did I tell on you?"

"You told Miss Sykes that I took sweets off Sophie."

"Well – you did – and she's much smaller than you."

"You don't understand a thing, do you? Sophie's my little sister, and she's too fat, that's why I take her sweets. She shouldn't have them in school anyway. What else is in the bag, Matt?"

"Some kind of totem pole."

"Give that back to me!"

"Come and get it!"

Tom sprang to his feet. He could feel the fury rising from his stomach, but too late to save the precious statue from clattering down the rocks to the beach below.

Blinded by his tears, he scrambled after it, the jeering laughter of the bullies ringing out behind him.

Slipping, sliding, covering himself in mud from the soaking drizzle of the last few days, Tom finally landed at the bottom of the cliff. His statue was lying on the sand.

Thankfully it was still in one piece. Closer examination revealed a few knocks but they would polish up with care. A smile spread across his tear stained face and he wiped his eyes with the back of a grubby hand.

Then he noticed the crack just under the canopy. Gingerly, afraid of spoiling the statue further, he pulled at it. Part of the statue came away in his fingers. Something bright fell to the sand below and disappeared between two pebbles. A knot from the original wood, perhaps? Tom rolled the wet pebbles to one side and picked up a tarnished yellow orb, like a ripe seedpod from some exotic African plant. It was deeply rounded and had a flat, circular top. Lines crisscrossed this, and the edge of the circle was frilled. Just underneath the rim was a series of pinpoints of a silverish colour. Tom looked at it with admiration. He had a great appreciation for beautiful things. He wondered at how long it must have lain buried inside the wood. Then, fearful that the bullies might still be about, he returned it carefully to the hole as being the safest place to keep it.

I'll glue it all together when I get home.

Home! What's Grandma going to say? I'm dirty and I'm late. But I don't care, he thought. I don't actually care about anything very much. And that gives me power, he grinned to himself. No one can hurt me if I don't care.

He clambered slowly up to the path, retrieved his belongings and stuffed them back into his bag. He made his way lazily to the village main street where Grandma lived in one of the terraced houses. There was a car outside the house. Grandma didn't have a car – another point of ridicule. The car belonged to Aunt Jane who was standing on the doorstep, impatiently waiting for him.

"Where've you been? You're late. And you're filthy dirty." Aunt Jane glared at him in disapproval. "Oh, never mind that now." Her harassed expression softening a little, she urged Tom inside. There she told him that Grandma had fallen on the back step, had broken a hip and been taken to hospital.

Tom was genuinely concerned, and immediately sorry for all his unworthy thoughts about Grandma.

Over tea, Aunt Jane explained:

"Grandma won't be able to look after you anymore. Even when she comes home a small boy will be too much for her. And Uncle Richard and I can't make that kind of commitment; the business takes all our time. There's no one else to look after you, so you'll have to go to your father in Africa."

Tom's mind struggled to take in this sudden and momentous change in his young life. His mother had died when he was two years old. By that time his father had already disappeared, some dark secret that no one ever talked about sending him half way across the world to Africa. He showed little interest in the toddler left behind.

And so Tom went to live with Nana in Birmingham. Tom had been happy there and stayed with his first grandmother until she too died, a year ago now. That was when he came to live with Grandma by the sea.

I don't seem to have much luck with my relatives, Tom thought to himself, only half listening to Aunt Jane, who was obviously keen to get rid of him as soon as possible.

Africa! Tom's mind started to race as the new concept sank in. He was going to live in Africa with his father, the father he adored.

He knew so little about his father. He had asked very many questions over the years, but these were always met by silence from the adults, and knowing looks would be exchanged across the room. His persistence was such, however, that he did gather some scraps of information. Tom's father had clearly done something horribly wrong. The family was both afraid and ashamed of him, and his move to Africa had been an escape from his past. Tom wondered what his crime might have been. Was he a burglar, or a swindler, or even a murderer? When Tom lost his temper, he was told he was like his father – the only time they ever mentioned him – and Tom had therefore come to the conclusion that he must have done something very violent. Nevertheless, he adored this man, who wouldn't even recognize him. That thought brought Tom up with a jolt. He wouldn't be welcome there either. And maybe his father had another wife, and maybe children – his brothers and sisters. Tom gulped. What would they all think of him? Suddenly, Grandma's cosy little house seemed more attractive than it had ever done; at least here he knew where he fitted in.

Aunt Jane was still talking. A flight next Monday. "We'll have to spend the rest of this week getting your belongings sorted out, and making sure you have all the right injections."

A week! Less! Just five days. And no more school. What matter the football team now! Tom knew there were things here he would miss. The rugged coastline, the soaring gulls with their wild mocking cries, and the caves and the rock pools, and the strange creatures to which they were home. And his crabs – he'd have to let all those go. Tom was fascinated by crabs, and kept a number of them in three buckets, just outside the back door.

Aunt Jane had the coming days completely organized. Tom was hustled here and there, told to pack this and that, and bare his arm for the many injections – tetanus, TB, yellow fever, polio, typhoid, cholera, hepatitis, rabies – until he felt like a pincushion.

He visited Grandma in hospital. She cried at the thought of her grandson's departure. She had enjoyed the freshness of youth and the future in her old house, so full of the past and its memories. She had been kind to Tom, and he promised to send her letters and photographs.

The little free time he had, Tom spent down on the beach. There he released the crabs. Carefully, one at a time, he carried the heavy buckets down the winding rocky path. Some of the prisoners he took to the rock pools, choosing the largest ones so they would have plenty of room to move around. He watched them scurry, swimmingly, under sheltering fronds of seaweed or overhanging stones, and laughed at the urgency of their movements. The others he took to the edge of the sea where small waves slapped against the rocks and frothy white bubbles curled and hissed onto the sand. Tom delighted in the salty tang, as did the crabs. They skittered sideways through the foam and shuffled under the floating network of plant life at the base of the rock. Tom felt sure that under that crusty ugliness lay intelligence, for the crabs were at home in two worlds: they knew about land and about sea in a way that most creatures couldn't.

As Tom watched until all his pets had found security, and the marks of their passage had been covered by the progress of the incoming tide, so too did Nerissa, hidden under the overhang of a pool, watch the release of her friends.

Old and barnacled beyond the normal for crabs, she had lived on that coastline all her life, and had watched, as she had been instructed to do. Of the reasons for what she was doing, she had no understanding. But she had seen and reported: the flash of light that had been awaited for so many years had appeared suddenly, and as suddenly been snuffed out. But she knew, with a certainty that reached into her whole being, that she had been aware of that for which she had been waiting. She knew that Tom would soon be involved in things that he didn't at all understand, and neither did she. And that to her was frustration; she realized all over again, how much harder it is to know there are things you cannot know than to think there is nothing else to know at all.

3 Africa

And so, less than a week later, Tom found his life packed into a small suitcase and stacked away in the hold of a BA jet. Clutching an old, faded blue rucksack that contained items for the journey, he climbed the steps that would take him to Uganda. The roaring that issued from the heart of the plane and the wind that stood his hair on end excited him with the momentous change that had overtaken his whole being. He stopped on the top step to wave a jaunty farewell to all he had ever known, and turned to embrace the stillness of the cabin.

His insides churning with excitement, anticipation and worry, he was quite unable to sleep during the long flight, and very grateful to the kind hostess for the many drinks and other treats she plied him with during the hours of darkness.

Red fingers reached out from the blue line on the edge of the horizon to peel the night away, and the fiery sun pulled itself over the edge of the world in a blaze of heat and light. Tom pressed his face against the window and peered down to see a map of Africa spread out before him: mountains, ravines, plains and rivers, different shades of brown and grey, were all clearly identifiable.

And there are people and animals down there although I can't make them out. I'm going to see lions and elephants and hippos and giraffes. He laughed out loud. The passing steward smiled.

The plane droned on, slowly it seemed from that great height, covering the motionless land below with its single shadow.

Then, at last, it started its descent. Green and blue were added to the spread below that had suddenly gained in speed. Forests and swamps, rivers and lakes were all brought to Tom's view as the plane rolled slightly from side to side. He craned his neck further. How green it all is, he thought. Films always depict Africa as hot and dry, and full of deserts. And all that water – like the sea – that must be Lake Victoria. He had read about Lake Victoria from the pamphlet in the back of the seat in front of him.

The jumbo jet touched down at Entebbe with a good ten minutes to spare. Tom had left England on one of her very worst autumn days – cold, dreary and wet. What a contrast awaited him when he stepped into the searing African heat. The wall of hot air that met him and the glare of the sun quickly persuaded him to put down his rucksack and struggle free of his jacket.

There were people watching from all sides. Black men and women. Tom had seen black people before, but never in such large numbers. My father's wife is black – Aunt Jane had discovered that much – my stepmother. Will that be good or bad? He really couldn't say.

He followed the stewardess through Immigration and Customs, and then out into the noise and the dust of shouting taxi drivers, all vying for a fare. Tom waited patiently as the eyes of the stewardess anxiously scanned the crowd of seething humanity and finally landed on what she was looking for – a thin young man holding a placard on which was written, in bold irregular letters: MASTER TOM.

"Here you are," she said, leading Tom towards the sign. "Good luck." And then she disappeared. Tom suddenly felt very alone. But the young man picked up his suitcase and gave him a broad smile. With his free hand he grasped Tom's, shook it vigorously and said,

"Good morning. You are most welcome. My name is Muramuzi. You come with me."

Muramuzi guided Tom through the car park of coughing engines and flying dust, to a battered vehicle that seemed to be held together by rust and determination. He beamed at Tom who cheerfully sat inside while he roped the door closed; its handle had fallen off some time ago. Still beaming, he took the driver's seat, and the old car sped, rattling, into Kampala, banging and jumping as it attacked the many potholes along the way. Tom gulped in warm air through the open car window. There was no way he could have closed it even had he wanted to; the mechanism for that had long since disintegrated. He felt free and very alive.

He drank in the many impressions surrounding him.

Along the sides of the road grew beautiful flowers in great profusion – orange, red and purple. Large and gaudy, they added sweetness to the warmth. Behind them were banana trees with their rough circled trunks and large, broad leaves. There were great throngs of people everywhere – sitting, standing, walking, cycling – the place was a hive of activity.

Ugandans like cheerful, colourful clothes, Tom decided. The men wore bright shorts and patterned shirts. Most of the ladies were dressed in western style skirts and blouses in a variety of materials, and a few wore traditional dress of rich brocade.

Everywhere there was talking and laughter and smiles.

There was a railway line, but people were walking along it, just as if it were a street, carrying great bundles on their heads and backs.

All along the sides of the road were houses, no more than shacks. Tom could see into many of them where wood turners and carpenters were at work, making bowls and tables and chairs and endless piles of coffins.

Where there was space, and sometimes spilling out onto the road itself, were market stalls, piled high with a great variety of fruit and vegetables: huge red tomatoes, great green cabbages, heaps of pineapples and oranges, and much that Tom had never seen before.

As they drew nearer to the city they passed sumptuous houses – ornate buildings with archways and pillars and balconies surrounded by huge gardens. But all were in ruins, with flaking paint and walls pockmarked by bullets and shells. Their former owners had long since fled from the cruelty and barbarism of Idi Amin, and they were now home to numerous squatter families who decked the huge windows and doorways and verandas with endless strings of washing.

Then they reached the heart of Kampala city. Tom was spellbound. Shops and market stalls jostled for room beside each other. Sellers shouted their wares across the street. There was an endless clutter of items for sale, all lovingly laid out to best effect. And those who found no room on the pavements used themselves as display cabinets; young boys draped their bodies in watches and trinkets and packets of biscuits.

Behind them was the matatu park. A chaos of barked commands, revving engines, diesel fumes and swirling dust, it nevertheless had its own order. The rules of its well-hidden efficiency evident to only a few, it served the travelling public very well. Some time, Tom vowed, he would try out the system for himself.

Muramuzi stopped his car beside a collection of round tables, set out on the uneven pavement. Huge umbrellas protected customers from the fierce sun. Here people ate and talked and enjoyed being alive, and here, it seemed, Muramuzi knew everybody. Many of these places, mimicking the European style, had opened up in recent years, and were very popular.

"Many muzungu here." Muramuzi pointed to the white people, and laughed.

A coke and a pizza, and they were on their way again. As they travelled the crowds lessened, the heat diminished, and it seemed to Tom that the countryside grew steadily more beautiful. The vegetation became more luxuriant and the ground more undulating with every kilometre that passed.

Even here there were many traders who had set up business by the roadside: to sell woven mats and multi-coloured baskets and stools, the motifs that adorned them vying for brightness with sun and flowers.

Eventually the tarmac road came to an end and Muramuzi's old car turned onto the murram – very red and dusty and full of holes. Muramuzi took all the dips and humps in his stride, wrenching the steering violently from side to side, throwing his passenger back and forth, and covering the many pedestrians and cyclists in choking red dust. Muramuzi laughed, and Tom did too, as they roared up the slopes and raced down the other sides like some crazy fairground ride.

They passed small groups of houses, and seemingly endless banana plantations that stretched up the slopes on either side of the road. They stopped to buy a bunch of kabaragara, a small yellow variety. Muramuzi handed one to Tom.

"I think I could live on these," he declared, as he sank his teeth into the soft flesh of a third.

"Many of us do," laughed Muramuzi.

And then, quite suddenly, they came to a sign declaring they had reached the Highland Tea Estate. Tom gazed at the sea of small regular bushes, and the big white building to one side of them, and took a deep breath.

They drove slowly up the drive to the house and the long journey was over.

Two small children, playing on the veranda, raced inside and returned, pulling their mother behind them. Priscilla's smiling eyes met Tom's and he knew at once that this at least, was going to be all right. The dark and beautiful girl with the welcoming face was his father's wife – his stepmother. She came forward to grasp his hand and then gave him a spontaneous hug. The baby, strapped to her back, grinned over her shoulder as she did so.

"Meet your brother and sister, Oscar and Rebecca," she invited, pushing the twins forward. The two little ones, lighter skinned than their mother but with the same dark eyes, touched him with nervous fingers, giggled and ran off to play. Priscilla ushered Tom into his home.

It was a sturdy, brick-built structure with a tiled roof. The floors were made of russet-coloured stone, and there were big doors and windows so that the place was constantly airy and light. Beyond the sitting room was a long wooden veranda with a small rail, painted white. From this, steps led to the garden – an extensive lawn surrounded by white and purple bougainvillea and orange hibiscus.

Tom quickly learned about his new family. As well as the six year old twins and the baby there was another brother, just four years old. And then there were Betty and Agaba. Betty was the housekeeper and helped Priscilla with cooking and cleaning. She was immensely fat and very jolly, and Tom warmed to her. Agaba was the house girl, a cousin from the nearby village who took care of the children. Not much older than them herself, she had only been with the Anderson family for three weeks. Desperately shy of strangers, none of which ever came to her village, she took one look at Tom and, like a startled young deer, ran to seek security at the bottom of the garden.

Outside, Tom met Moses and Isaac. Isaac, whom everybody called Mzee because he was so very old, introduced himself. He explained, in perfect English, that he was the caretaker and watchman for the family, and was also an excellent handyman.

He informed Tom that Moses didn't speak any English but was a very good worker who did many of the heavy jobs around the house and garden. Tom looked at the young man who stood grinning at him. He was broad and strong with firm muscles that rippled under his skin. He wore a pair of old red shorts and nothing else.

Mzee was still talking.

"Moses fetches the water from the well," he said.

No taps? wondered Tom, amazed.

"Come," he went on, "I show where I live."

Tom walked beside him across the lawn. The old man was tall and very thin; he had grey hair and kind eyes and Tom took an immediate liking to him. He led his new friend to a tiny mud built hut with a roof of grass. Inside there was a single room with an earth floor. A mattress had been rolled out in one corner. There were a few clothes hanging on the rafters that supported the roof and a paraffin lamp on a small table.

Mzee cast around for something to interest Tom.

"Look," he said and, from behind the mattress, he brought out a bow and some barbed arrows. "I made these myself," he added proudly. "Come, feel." He placed Tom's hand on the smooth wood of the bow and the sharp, deadly barbs of the arrows. "With these I guard your father's property," he announced proudly. Tom just couldn't imagine so warm a person directing so lethal a weapon at anyone, and he smiled uncertainly.

Oscar and Rebecca were keen not to be left out and they came to claim him from Mzee's home. They showed him the chickens and the goats and the young calf and tried to explain, in their halting English, how they helped care for them. They showed their new brother the cookhouse and the food store and the latrine.

Tom realized there were a number of things he was going to have to

15

get used to. One was the lack of running water, and another the electricity supply that was more often off than on. But he had already decided that there were plenty of other things to compensate for these minor inconveniences.

It was three hours later that Tom's father put in an appearance at the end of his day's work. Tom saw him approach across the lawn – a stocky figure with a shock of black hair, not unlike Tom's own, and a full, bushy beard.

"Come on," shouted Rebecca, "race you to Daddy."

She and Oscar set off across the daisied grass. Reaching the veranda, they threw themselves into his widespread arms. He chortled deeply as he swept them both off their feet.

Then he caught sight of Tom and, pensive now, put the twins down. He looked across at the boy standing unsure, at the bottom of the steps. For a moment his dark brown eyes settled on an identical pair in Tom's face. His gaze examined the tousled black hair, the square obstinate jaw, the swarthy skin, the sturdy body and the large feet; in this ten year old boy he saw himself quarter of a century ago.

"So you're Tom," he said awkwardly. "You are welcome here." He turned, walked across the veranda and into the house. Nervously Tom followed. He was grateful for the chatter of the children that helped along the meal that followed.

That night, lying in his own bed in his own room, he mulled over the events of the day. He decided that, apart from the austere presence of his father, things were going very well indeed. He looked at his statue that had made the trip to Africa in the safety of his rucksack.

I wonder if he remembers sending it to me all those years ago?

He stroked the smooth surface of the wood. The piece that had cracked open – was it only a week since? – came apart in his hands despite the glue, and the golden seedpod fell out as before. Tom looked at it wonderingly, and then carefully replaced it in its hiding place. He had other things to think about tonight.

4 Lucifer

Lucifer lifted his paws one after the other, shook them and examined them gently. Then he checked his magnificent coat, from the end of his long fluffy orange tail to his tufted green ears – no damage there either.

I seem to be in one piece, he reluctantly acknowledged to himself, apart from a few blunted claws. He inspected his strong curved talons, usually so razor sharp, with some distaste.

But what a ghastly place to land!

Lucifer shook himself and looked around.

He was stretched out on a flat and very solid rock that was damp and covered in moss; it smelled vaguely of peat and stagnant water. All around the rock were huge tussocks of tough dead grass, bent to the will of the cool moist wind. Lucifer looked further. A vast empty moor stretched in every direction with little to relieve the monotony. Only the occasional hill or splash of purple heather, or a solitary hawthorn bush, bowed and crooked after years spent fighting unfriendly elements and now crowned in its glory of autumnal red berries, relieved the bleakness of the landscape. Above, grey clouds scudded freely across a pale and watery sun, birds of prey running before them, dipping and gliding, using the thermals with practised skill and shrieking their enjoyment as they did so. Lucifer watched them in bad-tempered admiration.

Lucifer was a sparkat. He was something like a domestic cat in shape but bigger and heavier. His splendid tail was the length of his body and very bushy. It had a pronounced knob at the end that trailed the ground as he walked. His whole body was covered in deep thick fur that accounted for much of his bulky appearance. His coat was bright orange, patterned with luminous green rosettes. Green banded his chest and the fronts of his legs, and tiny flecks of it showed among the orange, giving the rest of his body a speckled tinge; except for his tail that was bright orange, and his tufted ears that were green. He had a black nose and thick white whiskers. His eyes were pure emerald. He knew he was most handsome. In his home, in Rainbow world, he was well camouflaged among the bright and varied plants that grew there.

But here, he thought, here I stand out most conspicuously.

He had already caught the attention of a surprised eagle, searching for rabbits to feed its young. It swept low to inspect the new creature but was unprepared for the snarl and drawn back lips displaying sharp and pointed teeth that met its interest. It quickly soared to realms where it knew it was safe.

Like all sparkats, Lucifer was a shape shifter. By emptying his mind completely, and then filling it afresh with images solely of the shape he wished to assume, he could shift into it simply through the power of concentration. This he now did.

Starting at the tips of his pointed ears, and moving along his head and body, and then down his legs, and finally to the end of his glorious tail, he turned himself into a large and ragged tabby cat. Just his tufted ears and long knobbed tail and a hint of orange in his brindled fur betrayed his origins.

The golden eagle, mystified, watched the change from hovering wings but decided against making this unkempt moggie into breakfast for her ever hungry young. It may be too tough and gristly for their small and very delicate digestive systems. Better to be sure and stick to lamb or rabbit!

Cautiously, Lucifer climbed off the rock, slowly for fear of falling in a place so bereft of footholds. He landed on the soft springy turf below. Immediately his paws became aware of the unpleasant cold wetness of that marshy terrain, and his ears twitched their protest at the keenness of the wind brought by encroaching night.

"Miaow," he uttered pitifully, his annoyance at the whole situation increased by the pathetic voice. No sparkat ever sounded like that.

Fancy being dumped in a place like this!

Lucifer was beginning to regret his agreement to take part in this important mission. Wandering around in a cold bog disguised as a tabby cat wasn't what he had in mind when he signed up. But Nerissa, the crab, was a good watcher, and she had signalled that, after remaining hidden for hundreds of years, the secret had surfaced near here. Her report had travelled to headquarters in Spy world. The signal had been faint and had quickly disappeared, but it had originated somewhere in this part of Britain where Scotland meets England on a wild coast, she had assured Control.

And he, Lucifer, had been brought by the star ship to the exact spot. Well, more or less. Stars aren't that brilliant at navigation, Lucifer grumbled to himself. I remember that mission to Pluto when I travelled on a star ship – no, better not think about that.

I need to call in for more information. They must have some by now.

But I can't do it out here, too much wind and water to interfere. I need to be somewhere warm and dry and hidden, and I need something to eat.

He made his way carefully from one tussock to another, cursing under his breath their insubstantial footholds, and cursing out loud every time he slipped from a grassy summit to the wet and freezing bog between it and the next.

But his passing didn't go unnoticed. Laura, on her way home from school, heard his calls that came to her as miserable wailing, and her warm heart responded.

"Kitty, where are you? Kitty, come here!"

"Miaooooow!"

And then she saw him, standing atop a mound of rough grass in the middle of a swamp – a large fiery tabby cat with dense coarse fur, obviously confused and distressed.

"You poor thing," soothed Laura, putting down her schoolbag. "You must be lost. Here. Come to me." She crouched and stretched out a welcoming hand. Skilfully she clambered over the uneven ground and lifted the poor cat out of its wretchedness.

Settled in the farmhouse by the comfortable fire of blazing logs that spluttered and sparked merrily and filled the room with the smell of wood smoke, Lucifer began to feel lazy and content and extremely grateful to this young girl who had fed him and warmed him and showered kind words upon him. He nuzzled her feet where she sat at the table with her schoolwork.

"That manky cat goes in the morning," grumbled her father from behind the newspaper.

"Yeah Dad," smiled Laura.

Pushing homework to one side, she pulled Lucifer onto her lap. She stroked and stroked him until his coarse fur lay smooth and gleaming, and she stroked him again until he couldn't help himself – he purred, and that caused sparks to fly from his coat like mini-fireworks – part of his sparkatality that couldn't be repressed.

"Look Dad," exclaimed Laura, "when I stroke him sparks come from his fur!"

"Really?" replied her father disinterestedly, not looking up from the paper. "Maybe we could use him for our electricity supply? And save a bit on the bills."

Lucifer snarled. Dad put down the paper to glare at him, and then picked it up again.

Left on his own by the dying fire while others went to bed, Lucifer dragged himself from the delicious warmth and remembered he had work to do. After all he wasn't an ordinary moggie, or even an ordinary sparkat, if indeed there was such a thing. He was agent number Zero One Zero. That meant there were only nine more important than he, and many hundreds less. Lucifer intended climbing that ladder even higher. He knew he could never make Double O One – that position was only a few moves from the Creator himself – but Double O Two might be within the reach of a creature as talented as he. What as yet unimagined power would come with that! He was proud of his achievements in the Intra Galactic Intelligence Service where he worked.

This business of the seedpod for Bioworld had been on file for some time now but Nerissa's report meant that it could be nearing its conclusion. Now it was out in the open it had to be found and used properly before any dark forces hijacked it for less worthy purposes.

"About time," muttered Lucifer. "Too many open files in the office at the moment."

Lucifer went to the window and sat on the sill to search the night sky. There were a few stars that might give a signal. With a gentle paw, he carefully rubbed at the furless patch immediately behind his left ear. So thick was his fur that this patch was quite invisible to anyone who had no knowledge of it. Back and forth he rubbed with his soft pad until the mobile phone came free. Lucifer angled this at one of the few stars appearing in this rather gloomy night. To his relief the signal came across strong enough. Messages were sent by him and reached down to him by means of energy akin to the forces of magnetism that amplified hearing a thousandfold.

He learned that there had been another, more recent sighting of the seedpod, the 'ody' as Control called it. This had occurred halfway across the planet Earth, but still in Bioworld, in the middle of a place called Africa. Lucifer cursed. The 'ody' had been moved. That meant he was behind in the chase. The others may get there first, he thought. Whoever the others may be, I don't even know that yet. He took details, forgot his own discomforts, and planned to leave.

The window was shut, and so was the door. Locked all too probably. Well maybe a few hours wouldn't make any difference? And the embers of the fire were so seductively warm, and smelled so inviting, and he was so tired, and there would be breakfast tomorrow …… He slept.

20

"Good morning my little electric cat."

It was Laura with a saucer of milk and tender caresses. Lucifer purred and arched his back. He would have preferred something more substantial than milk, but he politely lapped it up and then made for the door.

"Don't be too long," shouted Laura, "I have to go to school."

Lucifer crept round the back of the house, laying flat his ears in distaste as the cold air hit them and blew his fur awry. He would get to Africa by shifting himself to a migrating bird. That way he would be able to use his instincts to take the correct route.

This was far more difficult than shifting to another member of the cat family, and would not last nearly as long, and would require much more energy, but do it he would. He needed spy credits if he was to move up the ladder.

5 New Faces

Duncan Anderson had already left for work when Tom got up next day. Tom felt uneasy about his father. Did he really want him here? Probably not. But the rest of the family was all that he could have wished for, he tried unsuccessfully to console himself. And what about school? he wondered. Nobody had said anything about school. Well he certainly wasn't going to remind them about that!

Breakfast over, Tom quickly learned that everyone, from youngest to oldest, was expected to take their share in the running of this house. Betty had plans to make a cake for the twins' seventh birthday party.

"We need some sugar and flour from the trading centre," she instructed Tom and placed a woven basket and a purse in his hands, pushing him out of the door as she did so.

"We'll show you." Rebecca and Oscar came to his rescue. One on either side of their new found brother, they walked the few metres to the T junction and crossed to the trading centre on the other side of the road.

This hub of activity consisted of several mean shacks, quite unpainted, most with metal roofs, but a few with straw or turf. In the front was a grassy verge, worn away at the edges by many bare feet. Everywhere there were people and all, it seemed to Tom, were staring at him.

"A new muzungu," explained Rebecca knowingly, nodding her head.

Many of the locals were sitting on benches in the sun, playing cards and drinking; all men, noted Tom. The women were working in the fields and plantations.

In front of two of the houses were older men busy with sewing machines – just like Grandma's, painted black with golden flowers. But these machines had no power at their command other than the tailors' feet that busily worked the treadles while hands and eyes dealt with the cloth and thread. Never, it seemed, did they look up or take a break from their work.

On the path near the road was a group of youths standing around a pile of bicycle parts, working as if at a jigsaw puzzle to make two healthy machines out of them.

At one end of the row of buildings was a flimsy structure made from sheeting stretched across poles. On this covering were the letters UNHCR. Outside was a big notice declaring a barber's shop, and a large board displaying pictures of many extravagant hairstyles. Tom peered inside and saw a couple of men covered in protective capes who sat on chairs while other men snipped with scissors. The ground was deep in locks of black curly hair. Noticing Tom staring, one of the barbers stopped work and cheekily snipped the scissors in his direction. Tom withdrew his head quickly and gales of laughter issued from under the sheeting.

Behind the barber was the butcher. A whole cow hung just inside the doorway; it had been skinned except for the tail. For a reason he found hard to explain Tom found this disturbing. On the path outside sat the bloodied head of another cow that had just been slaughtered. Covered in buzzing flies it presented a grotesque sight, but was there for a good purpose. It kept the flies occupied and persuaded them to leave the meat in the shop behind alone. The stench of offal and sawdust assailed Tom's sensitive western nose as the trio passed the opening.

Oscar walked in stolid silence but Rebecca was keen to show off her knowledge to Tom. She explained brightly that the little shops were called dukhas, and led her brother past the rows of staring eyes to the one at the furthest end from the butcher.

Outside were heaps of very large tomatoes and bunches of kabaragara. As the three entered through the open doorway, the young boy who had been lounging beside a pile of cabbages, chewing lazily on a piece of grass, leaped to his feet. He pulled a baseball cap backwards onto his head, spat out the piece of grass and dodged past his customers into the recesses of the shop.

It took Tom's eyes some moments to become accustomed to the gloom, such a contrast did it present to the glare of the sun outside.

The shop had a barny, pleasant smell to it, from the husks of the many varieties of grain that had occupied its floor. In the centre was a rough wooden table. On this were more tomatoes and bananas, a wooden cabinet with a glass front that housed a pile of doughnuts, and a box of eggs. In front of the table, on the earth floor, was a heap of fresh pineapples. To one side were sacks containing sugar, flour and salt, and drums of cooking oil. On the rickety shelves behind was an assortment of articles: cans of drink, pens, packets of biscuits, tubs of margarine. All were covered in the dust that permeated the air. The large, curious eyes in the boy's face were turned expectantly on Tom.

"Agandi," said Rebecca.

"Good morning," answered the young shopkeeper.

The transaction was conducted in a mixture of English and Runyan-kore, Rebecca being determined to show off her competence with the latter in front of Tom, and the African boy equally anxious to practise his English.

Rebecca put the flour and the sugar and the biscuits into the bag. She assured Tom that Betty would be all right about the biscuits, and they left the obscurity of the dukha for the bright sunshine and red dust outside.

"Let's go back the long way," encouraged Rebecca, pulling Tom in the opposite direction to home. She was thoroughly enjoying being in control of the situation.

As they turned a corner in the road, a great cheer erupted from the other side of a small clump of banana trees. It seemed to overtake the whole sky with sound.

"What's going on?" asked Tom.

"Come and see," smiled Rebecca.

They climbed the bank beside the road and took the short path through the plantation. In the field before them was a group of about twenty boys. Tom thought them probably a little older than himself. They all had bikes. They were the black heavy Chinese bikes that are seen everywhere in Uganda. All but one. That was a mountain bike, a bright red Saracen N-Zyme, and the boy who rode it was white.

Tom stared in amazement. The other boy was too absorbed in the fun and being the centre of the group, to notice him for a while. When at last he did, he came over to introduce himself. He removed his baseball cap and shook Tom's hand. Pushing his sweaty brown hair from his eyes, he gave him a wide, generous smile and said,

"Hi, I'm Alex. You must be Tom. I've heard about you."

And then he was gone, answering a shout from his band of followers.

Tom and the twins sat down with the huge crowd of bikeless children.

The field was set out as a dirt track. Two thirds of the way down one side of it the bikers had built a great triangular mound of earth, steeply sloping on one side, sheer on the other, which they were using as a jump. There was a smaller jump opposite, by the trees. One at a time they took their mount to a far point the other side of the field. Pedalling furiously on the downward track, head low over the handlebars, shirt flying, they approached the mound at great speed, shot up it and soared over the launch lip into the sky. They landed with a thump on the back wheel on the other side. The front wheel hit the ground and the bike skidded to a halt to the cheers of their friends.

Rebecca explained that only a very few African children have bikes of any kind, certainly not mountain bikes. Tom was amazed at the enthusiasm with which these less fortunate children were content to watch their wealthier friends; they showed not a shred of jealousy. But then Tom discovered that some did indeed have a turn, even on the mountain bike – in the end.

Tom looked out over the mass of curly black heads. All so similar, he thought, until his eyes fixed on a curly red head sat among them. Tom approached the girl with the long auburn curls that framed a freckled face, and sat down beside her. She wore a simple green cotton dress. Her arms and legs were deeply tanned and her feet were bare like those of the African children. Idly she plucked loose grass from the field with her slender hands.

"Hi, I'm Tom."

There was no response from the girl who stopped pulling the grass and held a hand to shield her eyes from the sun as she strained to see what a particularly loud burst of cheering might herald.

Tom continued. "Who are you?"

"I'm Megan," she said without turning round. "That's my brother with the mountain bike. He's always showing off. And that's his new bike." She laughed infectiously. "But now I have his old one. It's an Emmelle Ascent, and it's black and yellow. There are two other boys with mountain bikes," she added, "but they're not here today. They're Ugandans, and sometimes they have to work on the farm."

As she spoke a crowd of bikers sped past, leaving the field, Alex in the lead, laughing and scattering dust over the onlookers who didn't mind at all.

At last Megan turned her gaze on Tom. She fixed him with wide grey eyes that seemed to take in every bit of him. And then she smiled, a warm generous smile just like her brother's.

"I'll show you something else," she said, and the smile challenged him.

"Not just now." Tom excused himself with genuine regret. "Maybe later. I have to get back to Betty, I think she has more jobs for me."

"Suit yourself." Megan shrugged sending her curls bouncing, and she ran off with the other girls.

Back at the house, Tom realized that he was going to be given little time in which to be idle. He swept the veranda with a stiff yard brush that Moses provided, and collected the warm eggs from under the sweet smelling chickens whirring contentedly in their pen.

"Would you fetch some water for me please, Tom," came Betty's voice. "Moses usually does it but he's busy chopping wood. Take the smaller jerrycans."

Overcoming his shyness, Oscar explained that men carry the large jerrycans that hold twenty litres each, and boys the smaller ones.

Tom picked up two cans and followed Oscar down to the well. Not really a well, he thought. An underground stream had been channelled into a pipe. It was from this pipe that the villagers collected water, the residue flowing on down to join the stream below. The well was crowded. There was much laughter and joking at a place used as much for social gatherings as collecting water. A temporary silence fell as the newcomer approached. But that was short lived and the boys and girls soon resumed their excited chatter. Tom sat on the warm stone steps and patiently waited his turn, idly listening to the rise and fall of the Runyankore of which he understood not a word. It was heavy work carrying the water back up the hill and he was pleased with himself to do it without stopping. He knew all eyes would be on him, weighing up any strength there might be in his meagre figure.

6 Party

The twins' birthday party was awaited with great anticipation by all the children of a like age from the village. Birthday parties were rare in this part of Uganda. Few families could afford to go to such expense, certainly not for children. But it was a western idea that Priscilla adopted with great enthusiasm. All her children had birthday parties every year, and other families in a position to do so followed her lead.

The party for the twins was always special. Enough enjoyment for two had to be crammed into one. Crisps and ice cream were brought from Mbarara, and there was Ugandan fare also – roast goat on sticks and passion fruit juice. Best of all was the cake, made by Betty and iced by Priscilla. Priscilla had quickly caught onto the craft of decorative icing and on top of this cake were elephants and giraffes, all carefully sculptured out of sugar. The twins were enthralled. Far too excited to settle to anything, they spent the waiting hours chasing each other around the garden.

Daddy came home from work early and organized boisterous games on the lawn for the twenty young guests.

Tom looked on; he felt uncomfortable. He was far and away the oldest child here and he didn't know any of these other boys and girls. And there was his father, playing quite openly and happily with them, while with him, his eldest son, he was stiff and formal. Duncan's deep laughter rang through the garden as he and his children's playmates romped with each other.

Tom was jealous and could feel a dark mood coming on. It was almost as if the sun itself was shining for everybody except him. He fought to control his anger and fixed his face with a false, forced smile. I mean, his father didn't even encourage him to join in with the others; he saw him there and just ignored him.

After the games and the food came the present giving. It seemed that even the smallest child had made or found something for the twins. The gifts were inexpensive, some of them costing nothing at all, but carefully chosen. There were books, pens, a belt, coloured stones and beads, a painting, a picture made from banana fibre and feathers, even an egg, and two small chickens.

Nobody told me about presents, thought Tom sourly. They're my brother and sister, and I have nothing to give.

As if echoing his thoughts a small voice, whose owner was no more than half Tom's height, piped up,

"What's your present going to be?"

She had clearly been dared to ask the question by a group of watching friends, and chosen for her command of English.

"I haven't got anything yet," replied Tom evasively.

The little girl returned to her friends and whispered something behind her hand. They all started to giggle and glanced at Tom. Then they huddled together over some other secret, heads close, bottoms up in the air.

I didn't know about the presents! Tom wanted to yell. I don't seem to belong to this family. I might as well not be here.

He knew he had to remove himself from the situation – and fast. He strode across the lawn and into the house where he deliberately kicked over a jerrycan half full of water, knowing how much the precious liquid was valued. He stomped into his room and slammed the door. Betty, who was witness to all this, followed his movements with wide-eyed amazement.

It was Duncan, his father, who found him a couple of hours later: still there, sitting on the bed, staring into space. His eyes were red and swollen, but he had stopped weeping long ago. Without speaking, Duncan sat down beside Tom. Tom didn't move or acknowledge his presence in any way. After a while, Duncan broke the silence.

"I'm the same, you know."

There was no response from Tom.

Duncan went on. "You're just like me. I have a temper exactly like yours and, even now, it takes some controlling. I thought you controlled yours very well today."

He paused. Tom still said nothing, so he went on.

"You did better than I did all those years ago."

Despite himself, Tom was interested. Was he going to find out something about his father's past?

"What do you mean?" he asked, and turned to look into his father's face.

"Did you ever wonder why I left England?"

"Yes, of course I did." Tom was all attention now. "But no one would tell me."

"I'll tell you now," said Duncan, "because I hope you and I are going to be mates." Tom gave him a wan smile.

Then Duncan told his son about how, because of his violent temper, he

28

felt he had to leave the home he knew and loved, and his young wife and baby son.

"Everything I did turned out wrong," he said. "I had this dreadful temper that kept letting me down. It was always getting me into trouble. And I blamed the temper, not myself, claimed I couldn't do anything about it.

"And then, of course, the inevitable happened. I was accused of something I didn't do. There was a burglary on the estate, and the shopkeeper was beaten up by a friend of mine. I wasn't even there but Jake, the other bloke, framed me very cleverly, and I was arrested. I was so angry at the injustice of it all that I hit a policeman and that made matters worse.

"None of my family or friends would believe my story, I had no proper alibi, and Jake had never been violent before. I was tried and found guilty and sent to prison for something I didn't do. I can't tell you how that makes a person feel Tom." Duncan shuddered at the memory of it. "The whole business made me madder than I had ever been and I became a difficult prisoner.

"But a lawyer was working on my behalf all the time. I suppose that was a lucky break: to have been given such an obstinate young barrister to defend me. Finally forensics proved that it was Jake who had committed the crime, and not me, and I was released.

"But for me it was too late. I had nothing but contempt for those so-called friends who now wanted to make up with me. I felt they acted purely out of guilt and, even then, didn't believe in my innocence. I couldn't see my way to trusting the legal system any longer. I couldn't stay in a place that had so let me down.

"And so, and I'm not proud of this, I ran away. I left you and your mother who, by this time, was already very sick, too sick to embark on a new venture. I came on my own to Africa to start a fresh life here. And that part of the story is good, very good. I met Priscilla. She is strong and loving. And she has helped me master my temper – she and the other people here who are so accepting and trusting of us with all our faults. Something I hope you will find out for yourself.

"So you see, it can be done. That temper can be overcome. I want to help you, Tom, and dull the memory of the bad parent I have been so far. When your mother died, I wondered if I ought to send for you, but I was in awe of my new happiness. I thought of it as a fragile thing; I didn't want to risk spoiling it by bringing in someone from my past. But now I realize just how secure my new contentment is. You have shown me that Tom, by coming here and taking your place in my family without causing a ripple. Priscilla and the children all love you already. I know I can never make up for the lost years, but I can hope to make the ones that are still to come full of joyful companionship between us."

That was a long speech for Duncan. There was a silence. He laid his big hand on Tom's shoulder and Tom let it stay there.

"You are already better at controlling your temper than I ever was at your age. And you knew to distance yourself from the problem. Let me into your secret."
Tom turned to look at his father, and smiled.

"It's not a secret really. It was the headmaster of a school I was at in Birmingham. He gave me three steps to take when I start feeling angry. First I *stop*," Tom held up one finger, "and then I *think* for quite a while, and only after that, the third thing which is *act*. And it works in a way; that and getting myself out of the situation for a time. But," he added spontaneously, "what will really help is knowing you are on my side, and you understand." And father and son smiled the same smile.

"And what was the trigger this afternoon?" asked Duncan.

"I didn't have presents for Oscar and Rebecca, and nobody told me ....."

"Come with me," said Duncan.

Duncan led his son out into the star-filled darkness, across the lawn noisy with the many sounds of the African night, to the wooden work-shop beyond. Holding a flashlight he unlocked the padlock on the door and ushered Tom inside. The smell of bruised wood and sawdust met the two of them. Tom trod the soft shavings underfoot as he took in the atmosphere of his father's workshop. In the middle was a workbench, complete with lathe and other tools, and around the sides were shelves laden with bowls and dishes and lamps, all beautifully turned. Tom knew he was privileged to be in this private place. He picked up a bowl and ran his hand over the smooth surface admiringly.

"I come here often," said Duncan, "and always if I feel anger coming on. The wood works out any tensions I may have. You can come here too if you like, and I will teach you to work with wood."

Tom beamed with delight. He was good at anything artistic; something else he must have inherited from his father.

"Now, how about presents for Oscar and Rebecca." He took Tom to a shelf laden with carvings of animals.

"Did you make these?" gasped Tom, enthralled.

"I did indeed," replied Duncan, pleased at his son's admiration. "You can take two, one for each of the twins."

Tom handled the animals, felt their curves, and finally chose an elephant and a giraffe to reflect the theme of the birthday cake.

"A good choice," agreed his father.

"The best presents they'll ever have," was Tom's delighted opinion.

"And now I have something for you," said Duncan, and he pulled aside a piece of old sacking to reveal a superb mountain bike, a dark blue Raleigh Stonefly.

"It's not new," he added hastily. "I did it up myself when I heard you were coming."

"It's magnificent," was Tom's verdict. "Oh thank you, Dad. I can't wait till the sun comes up tomorrow, and I can join the others at the race track."

Duncan laughed and ruffled Tom's thick black hair.

"Come on, let's go and help clear up."

7 Treasure

It was the middle of the afternoon. The twins lay on the veranda, rejoicing in the heat on their bare limbs. Tom sprawled on the grass; he was busy sketching his bike propped against the railing.

The peace was shattered when Alex swept into the drive, his tyres sending small stones in every direction as he braked hard. Megan, also on her bike, almost piled into the back of him.

Alex threw himself onto the grass beside Tom.

"What you drawing?" he asked, pulling the paper from under Tom's hand.

"Hey, that's pretty good. And that's some mean machine. It did well on the track this morning."

Tom felt himself glow at this praise from the older boy.

"We've come to invite you over to ours for a barbecue," interrupted Megan. "Remember I told you I had something to show you."

"First let's see what *he's* got," suggested Alex, rolling over onto his back and scowling at the fierce sun.

What've I got? thought Tom, unprepared for the suggestion. He had arrived in Africa with one small suitcase and an old rucksack.

"Come on," said Alex, "show us your room." He leaped up, hauling Tom to his feet. "You have got one of your own, haven't you?" he asked, sensing the younger boy's reluctance.

"Of course," replied Tom. He very much wanted to make friends with this tall, gangly lad with the open friendly face and the laughing blue eyes. Everyone liked the extrovert Canadian in spite of his boastful ways. He continued to talk as they made their way to the house.

"Have you got a computer?"

"No …."

"I've got two. You can borrow one of mine. And I've a whole pile of Play Station games. And my uncle in Canada has promised to send me a Dreamcast magazine, to choose one of them."

It was hot inside and all the windows of the house had been thrown open to let in what air there was. Tom looked despairingly round his room for something to interest his new friends. Megan sat expectantly by the window, and Alex on the end of the bed.

Of course he had something to show them. He dived under the bed and brought out his old rucksack. He pulled out the torch that Grandma had given him that gave off light of different colours, and a compass

32

from Aunt Jane. Alex looked at both briefly and put them aside. Then Tom found the book of stars, the present from Uncle Richard. His uncle had spent some time in Africa before he married Aunt Jane and had said, mysteriously,

"When you get there you will understand why I have given you this book."

And Tom already knew what he meant, from the very first night he spent in Uganda. The stars here were much brighter and more numerous and seemed nearer than they did in Europe. Maybe that's because of our position in the Milky Way, he wondered. He would look it up some time. He was fascinated by all things scientific.

Megan soon became absorbed in the book but Alex was looking at him, wondering what else he had in the bag. He put in his hand and brought out his statue.

"My father gave me this a long time ago," he said, proudly running his hand down the smooth wood, and holding it out for their inspection. Megan looked up from the book. She and her brother said nothing. You could buy statues like that all over Africa. Realizing they were unimpressed, Tom went further.

"This isn't just any old statue. Look, there's treasure buried inside it."

Carefully, he pulled at the crack and brought out the golden seedpod.

"Hey, now that *is* something," exclaimed Alex admiringly as the colour of the little seedpod picked up the sun's brightness. "Looks like real gold."

"Let's have a proper look." Megan took the treasure to the light of the window. "Where did it come from?"

"I don't know. It was stuck in the wood. Could've been there for hundreds of years."

"Must be very special," mused Alex, peering over Megan's shoulder.

Sharp little eyes in the bush caught the glint from the window. Tom was suddenly unaccountably afraid for his treasure's safety.

"Let's put it back."

He took it gently from Megan's hand and pushed it into the wood. He placed the statue on the table beside his bed.

"Are you hungry?" Tom wanted to distract his friends. "There's some cake left over from the twins' party."

"Sure am," said Alex. "Betty's cakes are always good."

They entered the kitchen to find Betty piling up a tray with delicious leftovers. She had seen the Martyn children arrive and knew it would only be a matter of time before they came looking for something to eat. Alex crept up behind her and snatched a cake from under her nose. She slapped his hand and laughed; you couldn't help but like this charming, over-confident young man.

They took the tray out into the garden. Megan allowed herself to be pulled into games with the boisterous twins, while Alex and Tom talked 'bikes'. None of the children noticed the crowd of baboons that had gathered in the trees at the bottom of the lawn. Their approach had been silent, and now they sat quite still. All gazed at the little party by the house, gleaming eyes wide in their dark grey faces, dog-like muzzles sniffing the air.

Suddenly they pounced. Two small baboons loped across the grass towards the cakes and began stuffing them into their mouths, using both hands and allowing no time at all to swallow in between. But this was merely a diversion for something more sinister. While the children tried to chase off the smaller baboons who determinedly held their ground, a large male, working under cover of the distraction, crossed the lawn in a few huge bounds and leaped in through the open window of Tom's bed-room. And then he was out again, the statue clasped firmly in his hands.

"Hey! What you doing? That's mine. Put it down."

Tom scrambled to his feet and made off after the baboon, Alex and Megan and the twins close on his heels. The big baboon made threatening growls as it bounded lightly across the grass without a backward glance, growls echoed by the whole troupe that now ringed the garden and snarled unpleasantly.

"Put it down!" shouted Tom helplessly.

The baboon's clever fingers worked eagerly over the statue, even as it ran down the path that led away from the Andersons' garden, towards the bush. It crossed the open ground, leaped into the trees and bounded along the edge of the forest, the panting children in pursuit. And then it had the crack open. A horrid snarl of triumph escaped its mouth as it drew out the seedpod and cast the statue aside. The children stopped to retrieve the statue. Above them, high in a tree, sat the baboon, the treasure glinting in its left hand. It watched them from gleaming red eyes, a malevolence in its look that drained the blood from their faces, and then it was gone, and the treasure with it.

Tom was appalled and sank to his knees. He could feel tears of frus-tration welling up inside him and he knew the anger would soon follow. Megan picked up the statue, secured the crack, polished the woodwork with the hem of her skirt, and gave it to Tom.

"There," she said, "the statue isn't harmed."

He took it, not trusting himself to look at her.

"But what about the treasure?" Tom's voice came uncertainly.

"You didn't know it was there until a few days ago," Alex observed sensibly, "so you'll hardly miss it."

Tom wasn't at all sure that was the end of the matter, and neither was Megan. There had been something so menacing in those red eyes.

"That's baboons for you." Alex shrugged it off. "Pretty dangerous animals."

"Don't forget you're coming over later," shouted Megan as she and her brother disappeared down the drive, pedalling hard. Both raised a hand to wave farewell as they turned the corner of the road.

And then his anger was on him. Tom started to take it out on the railing of the veranda but, catching sight of the twins' worried, puzzled faces, he thought better of it and made his way over to his father's workshop. There, the smell of the wood and the presence of beautiful things had a calming effect.

"Stop. Think. Act." he muttered to himself.

"Would you like to try making something?" Duncan stood behind him.

"Yes," said Tom suddenly. "I'd like to carve something very special for Megan."

"Would you now?" said Duncan seriously. "Anything particular in mind?"

"I'd like a box with animals all over it."

"How about we start with a basic box and see how we go from there?" suggested Duncan.

And the two set to work.

8 The Martyns

Alex and Megan lived with their parents in a large house on the other side of the tea estate. Their father, Steve, worked there as an engineer, as did Tom's. They had arrived from Canada seven years ago when Alex was five and Megan three. Parents and children had quickly adapted to life in Uganda and had little intention of ever returning to Toronto.

Tom got off his bike and walked slowly up the drive, as always nervous of meeting new people. What would he say? What would they think of him?

He spotted Alex before Alex spotted him. He was alone on the veranda that overlooked the riotous colour that was the garden. He was strumming a guitar, softly and with feeling. His wavy brown hair fell over the instrument and his tall body seemed to be curled into it; he was completely unaware of anyone or anything outside his music. The sight took Tom by surprise. There was a quieter side to Alex that it reassured him to discover.

"Hi," said Tom gently, not wanting to disturb the playing.

Alex looked up, startled. "You came. Great!" he exclaimed and put the guitar to one side.

"Do you play?" he asked.

"A bit," admitted Tom. He had taken lessons for a while but Nana had run out of money to pay for them.

"Would you like a go?"

"I'd rather listen to you."

Hearing the voices, Megan joined the boys on the veranda. Her animated face displayed her pleasure at seeing their visitor, her grey eyes smiled gently at him.

"Megan wants to show you ...." teased Alex.

"Shhh..! I want it to be a surprise. Come on."

Grinning indulgently, Alex followed the other two round to the back of the house.

"There!" she said. "My pet rabbits."

Tom saw before him an intricate arrangement of hutches, all set out round three sides of a rectangular wooden platform about a metre above the ground. There were ten adult rabbits of various colours and sizes, and a number of babies. Some were out on the platform, munching their way twitchingly through a pile of greens; others preferred the shade of the hutches.

Tom did his best to look impressed. The only pet he had ever owned was a hamster and that had died when he had only had it a week; he never found out why. He had never thought much about rabbits.

"Ugandans keep lots of rabbits," Alex informed him, "but theirs all end up in the pot. Onion sauce! Onion sauce!" he chanted provokingly to the captives in the hutches. Megan scowled at him.

"Mine are all counted and named," she said. "No one would dare harm one of them. Let me introduce you to Peter; he's the most handsome of them all," and Megan was away on a favourite subject.

She reached up and caught hold of Peter, her arms disappearing into the thick coat.

Peter was a large black rabbit with unusually dense, long fur. The weight of him was almost too much for Megan and Tom gallantly grabbed hold of Peter's ample hindquarters to help. Safely on the ground, Peter lolloped contentedly around Megan who sat down to fondle him. Politely, Tom crouched beside her and tickled Peter behind the ears.

"You might as well have a word with Snowball too," laughed Alex. He brought a second rabbit down from the platform. Snowball was smaller than Peter; he was completely white except for the black tips to his ears.

Megan spent many hours alone with her rabbits. She meticulously cleaned them and fed them, but mostly she enjoyed playing with them. The reason for her adoration was simple. She had once been into another world, a world creatured with rabbits. She had told Alex about it and had been pleasantly surprised that he hadn't made fun of her, little knowing that the reason for his acceptance was that he, too, had been in another world, but not a world of rabbits.

"Are we allowed to meet the visitor?"

The booming voice sounded from the house.

Steve Martyn was big in every way: big in body, big in voice, with a big mop of red hair just like Megan's, and big in friendship.

Mrs Martyn was pleasant and kind, dark-haired and pretty; she was yet overshadowed by her larger than life husband.

Tom already knew he would always be welcome in this house, and accepted just as he was. He wouldn't have to prove anything.

Steve Martyn wanted to know all about Tom and his life in Britain.

"We're Brits too you know," Alex told Tom.

"Speak for yourself," laughed Steve in his North American drawl. "I'm one hundred percent Canadian."

"Mummy's from England," explained Megan, "but we've never lived there."

Tom had questions for all of them about Uganda. And finally he dared to ask,

"Do children go to school here?"

This evoked a guffaw of laughter from Steve that shook the chair in which he was sitting.

"They most certainly do. But it's holidays at the moment. They have lots of holidays. They're late starting back this October. The Government completely ran out of money for the teachers. It's all sorted out now, and the schools will open on Monday." He grinned broadly at the dismayed look on the children's faces.

"School's not bad," volunteered Alex. "The teachers think they're strict but we do pretty much as we like most of the time."

"Some of the lessons are really boring," protested Megan, "and sometimes the teachers don't show at all."

"What do you do then?" Tom wanted to know. He could imagine the anarchy that would reign in his old school if the teachers didn't show up.

"Muck around." Megan giggled. "That's quite good fun."

Holly, her mother, glanced at her sternly.

"Alex and Megan go to the local primary school," she explained to Tom, "although we'll have to think of something else for Alex fairly soon." Alex made a disapproving grimace. "We don't really hold with boarding school, that's where most white children go."

"I hope I'll be going with you two," declared Tom.

"Course you will," said Megan confidently. "You'll be in my class, P5. Alex is in P7, the top class."

9 Sparkats

Things had not gone according to plan for the migrant sparkat in his guise of house martin. The other birds quickly sensed he was not one of them, and it was late in the year for migration, so his instinct apparatus was imprecise. He reached Uganda by way of America, and arrived at his destination completely exhausted. If he wasn't so convinced that these endeavours would be well received back at Control, he would begin to have serious doubts about the whole project. But then, he always was something of a cynic.

At least he was here, he thought. Probably too late. Others undoubtedly knew of the existence of the 'ody'. But he was convinced that he was in exactly the right place. He had plotted his position carefully once he had spotted an elephant and knew he was in Africa, and he didn't make mistakes over that kind of thing. Now to get out of these dreadful feathers!

Gleaming eyes watched feathers turn to fur, wings become legs and the beak disappear into a black nose surrounded by white whiskers. It's always easier to shift back to one's original shape, and Lucifer soon returned to his sparkat glory, from the knob on the end of his orange tail to the tips of his tufted green ears.

Unaware of the intense baboon gaze fixed unblinkingly on him, Lucifer pampered himself with a few moments of indulgence in which to admire the bright handsomeness of his pristine fur. He lay on the warm African earth and licked himself all over with his coarse, rasping tongue. Then he allowed himself some minutes flat on his back, all four paws up in the air, soaking the heat into his furry tummy.

But he was a conscientious spy who knew well the importance of remaining undetected. With a sigh of regret he shifted again, from his ears to his tail resuming the identity of the unkempt tabby befriended by Laura. He looked down at himself. What a mess! Should be able to tidy it up a bit. And he began licking into shape his rough coat, trying to bring out what highlights it had; he was pleased to note it still retained the orange flecks.

Something hard and heavy stung his back. He jumped up, startled, as small missiles rained on and around him, thrown by a group of noisy children who laughed every time he winced. To avoid his tormentors he ran into the nearby bush. The mocking laughter of the youngsters and their falling stones accompanied him. Not quite the same as Laura's reception, he thought sourly.

The children in the village didn't have pets. In their world animals were for eating or putting to work. Anything that was no good for either was at best tolerated, at worst driven away. Lucifer's present dishevelled appearance fitted in perfectly in this land where cats and dogs fended for themselves.

He looked up from the bush to which he had fled and noticed a large house, some distance away across a patch of open ground. Slowly, he made his way towards it. Maybe .....

"Now where did you come from?" exclaimed Megan in delight.

She crept closer cautiously, so as not to alarm the sudden arrival. Lucifer backed away. What kind of a child was this one? A 'Laura', or one of the other kind? He judged from the tone of her voice and her gestures that she was a 'Laura', so he stretched up his head to meet the hand put out to caress him and arched his back contentedly as her stroking fingers passed along it. He brought his head back and pushed his nose against her hand again, urging her to repeat the performance.

"You look thin and hungry. I don't suppose you belong to anybody. Cats here never do. Maybe you could be my pet?"

Lucifer smiled his catty smile. That would do very well. He needed a base where he could relax and be fed. He must be in the correct place. His own navigation had brought him here, and he was an excellent navigator; he had won several competitions back in Spy School, all those years ago.

Holly came across the lawn, her arms full of sweet smelling bougainvillea.

"Mummy!" cried Megan. "Look what I've found! He's hungry. He must be lost. Can I keep him?"

Holly looked at Lucifer with disapproval. She didn't like cats. They caught birds, and she was very interested in those. She put out food for them and counted the numbers of the many different species that visited every day. She took herself for walks, especially by the lake, to discover which varieties might be found there. All of this information she marked off in a big book.

So now she said,

"You've got enough pets, dear. Look at all those rabbits. He's probably got fleas. Anyway, he's a tabby. If I had to have a cat, I'd have a black and white one; they're much more intelligent."

Lucifer pricked up his ears at this extraordinary piece of information.

40

Well, madam, he thought, colour really is no problem. I can be black and white in a trice, if that's what you want. Actually, I could shift into anything. Perhaps you'd prefer a dog? But animals in the cat family are always much easier, same genus as a sparkat you see. So how about a lion or a tiger? He'd love to have made such a shift just to see the expressions on their faces. But now was not the time. He was on serious business.

Lucifer stopped his own reverie to realize that Megan was still arguing with her mother, and rapidly losing the fight. The woman was obviously made of steel under that soft and gentle exterior, he thought.

Then Megan had a brilliant idea. "I know. I'll take him to Tom. He doesn't have any pets – yet."

"I'm not sure what Duncan and Priscilla will have to say about that," began Holly, concerned that she was transferring a problem onto friends. But Megan wasn't listening. She scooped Lucifer up into her arms and set off down the track at a run that shook Lucifer's brain inside his head and made his teeth knock together.

"Tom!" called Megan from the road.

Tom was sitting on the veranda, deep in his own company. The other children were out with their mother, and he and his father were alone in the house. Tom was working on possible designs for Megan's box. He had decided the sides were to be embossed with rabbits. There was to be a tail at the back, a friendly rabbit face at the front, and ears to lift the lid. Hearing her voice, he quickly tucked the paper under a cushion and rose to greet the smiling freckled face of the girl who stood before him, her arms full of cat that by now was becoming rather too heavy.

"I've brought you a present," she gasped. "Everyone needs a pet, and you haven't got one."

Tom stepped down off the veranda and tickled Lucifer behind the ears. Yes, he would like the company of an animal. Out loud he said,

"I don't know. It depends on Dad. I'll have to ask him."

Tom was still not quite sure of his father. He now knew he was wanted and loved. But Duncan had long moods when he was silent and emotion-less, and then it was best to keep very quiet around him.

"What depends on Dad?" asked a deep voice behind him.

Tom turned to look up into that dark, bearded face. Megan's grey eyes gazed seriously at him. Lifting one knee after the other in an attempt to shift the burden in her arms that itself was becoming uncomfortable and beginning to struggle, she explained about her find in the garden, and her mother's rejection of it.

"Why don't you put him down? He needs to get used to his new home," replied Duncan.

"You mean I can keep him?" asked Tom, disbelieving.

"Yes," said his father. He smiled at Tom's delighted face and rubbed his hand over Lucifer's tabby back. Megan grinned impishly at him; she knew how to soften that stern countenance.

"Wow!" exclaimed Tom. "Cool! Thanks Dad!"

"What are you going to call him?" Megan wanted to know.

Duncan looked into the penetrating gaze of the emerald eyes.

"Lucifer," he said, and returned to his paper work.

Lucifer watched Duncan back into the house, and then turned to the children and gave himself up to their caresses.

All seems to be going well enough, thought Lucifer complacently. In the depths of his self-congratulation, he completely failed to notice the constant presence of a number of baboons that watched continuously from spy-holes in the leafy trees. The mission is on the right track. I have a secure base. Time for reinforcements. Two spies were always appointed for these 'other world' ventures. He wondered idly who would be sent to assist him.

That night, out on the veranda, he used the mobile phone he carried behind his ear to contact Control and inform them that the time was right for a co-spy to join him. Back came the reply that Zero Six Six was ready to leave.

Jessica! He knew her well, of course. She would fit in admirably. At number Zero Six Six she was well down the order of importance, but she was a pleasant enough sparkat, sufficiently bright to be useful to him and yet not bright enough to challenge him in any way. He would have to do most of the work as she had far less experience than he. A great sigh escaped him. Ah well, these youngsters have to learn somewhere; but training them can get a bit tedious.

Many animals, that night, saw a beam of energy in the form of light leave a bright star and reach Bioworld. Just a few saw the energy that had been spread throughout the beam materialize, on landing by the veranda, into a glorious creature that glowed orange and green. But only the group of red-eyed baboons knew what it was all about.

"Too late! Too late!" chanted their leader, grimacing horribly. Playing with Tom's golden seedpod, it sent the treasure triumphantly from paw to paw.

"Good to see you, Jess," said Lucifer, heartily welcoming. He had decided to do his very best for the young spy. "It's lonely work down in Bioworld. But get a move on, Jess. Sparkats aren't common round here. You're beaming like a lighthouse. Shift yourself into an insignificant moggie before anyone notices you. Make it fast, and make it black and white."

"Why black and white?"

"Just do it!"

And, from the tip of her nose to the end of her knobby tail, Jessica turned from orange and green to black and white. And what a pretty cat she made. Even Lucifer had to concede that. She had a broad white circle round her black neck and two large white patches either side of her nose. Three of her paws were white and so was the tip of her tail. The rest of her was jet black.

Mzee, on his way home, did think he saw something strange on the veranda that night, but then he had drunk a great deal of waragi at his brother-in-law's party.

"Look Mummy, she's black and white, she's intelligent," shrilled Megan from the garden as Holly prepared breakfast. "You said if she was black and white I could keep her!"

"I don't think I exactly said that, Megan."

"Oh Mummy, please can I keep her."

"Course you can, Sunshine," said Steve, seating himself at the table.

"Daddy, I love you," shrieked Megan, and she flung her arms round her father's neck before rushing back to her new pet.

"Steve!" Holly pulled an angry face at her husband.

"Oh, come on Holly, pets are no trouble in this country. It'll stay outside and find its own food. We may even get rid of some of those rats in the store-house."

"That's not the point," protested Holly. "Anyway, where are all these cats coming from?"

"Daddy, what shall we call her? You can choose a name." Megan emerged through the doorway, carrying her prize.

The amber eyes of the cat met Steve's gaze.

"Jessica!" he said thoughtfully. Jessica nodded her head in approval.

10 School

Tom's stomach turned over. The first day of school.

He had met many of the children already, lots of the boys and some of the girls, when out biking with Alex. What fun that was, not just the track and the jumps, but the long rides on roads that had so few vehicles.

"Nervous?" asked his father, at breakfast.

"A bit," agreed Tom, understating the matter.

"You'll be all right."

Those few words meant a lot to Tom and made him feel much better. His respect for his father deepened by the day. Even in his dark moods, he liked to be near him.

As he left the table, Duncan rubbed his hand over his son's tousled hair making it even more untidy than it already was.

Priscilla was the authority on school and Tom had all the right gear: white, short-sleeved, open-necked shirt, grey shorts and trainers. What would they have said back in Ilpington? He shuddered to think. Priscilla beamed at him. She said he looked splendid and he decided to believe her. Oscar wore the same as he did, and Rebecca the uniform green-checked dress. Tom packed his rucksack with exercise books and pens; these weren't provided by the school. In his pocket was an envelope with the school fees; there was little free education in Uganda.

"Come on," shouted Rebecca, "let's go!"

She bounded in front of Tom down the drive.

Children were already passing the gate, at 7.30 in the morning, on the three mile journey to the primary school. Many had already walked several miles to get this far, and most didn't have the luxury of shoes on their feet. Tom realized, with relief, that here it didn't matter in the least what make your trainers were.

They rounded the corner and Alex and Megan joined the group that grew in size as they passed each isolated house.

Dust and chatter were Tom's companions on that first walk to school – and laughter – always laughter in Africa. But he understood not a word of any of the conversations, and looked on incredulously as Megan joined in with the rattling Runyankore. Several of the children, he noticed, were trudging under the weight of bundles, items asked for by the teachers. Many had younger siblings hanging onto both hands.

The path wound across dried grassland. The Ankole cows, wide heads swaying under the weight of their commanding horns, grazed conscientiously, and took no notice of the passing children. But the youngsters guarding them, standing with legs apart, leaning on strong sticks, gazed fixedly at these other children who led a life so very different from their own. All had large, staring eyes in wide grimy faces; their clothes were dirty and ragged – scraps of material hanging on with reluctance to their owners. They immediately noticed Tom, the one strange face in all that crowd. Over and over again they shouted out, 'Muzungu, what time is it?' practising the little English they had picked up from those whose parents could afford the school fees.

The road crested a hill and then wound down into the valley.

The school comprised three blocks of mud-walled buildings with metal roofs, forming three sides of a square. Each block was divided into a number of rooms. There had been some attempt at painting the buildings in the past but most of this had now flaked off, leaving large off-white patches on the brown mud. There was no glass in the windows, not even shutters, and the doorways were open entrances. In front of the blocks were rough paths and flowerbeds, their edges outlined by bricks slanted to form triangles. These were well tended and full of colourful blooms that did much to lighten the otherwise dreary outlook. In the centre, between the buildings, was a worn, dusty area. In the middle of that, on a small patch of grass, stood a flagpole surrounded by a circle of large stones, painted in the red, black and gold of Uganda's colours.

Tom took in the busy scene as children shouted greetings to each other and clasped hands in friendship. Quite suddenly the buzz of excited arrival was broken by a loud metallic clang. Tom looked in the direction of the sound. A large boy in trousers that were too tight for him had picked up a stone from the ground and struck the rusted metal hub of a wheel that hung from the branch of an old tree. As Tom watched, he struck with the stone again and the clang reverberated round the playground. The children scampered in all directions, making lines in front of classroom doors. Rebecca shouted a cheerful 'bye' and she and Oscar made for the doorway that had Primary 2 written above it. He could see Alex's tall figure outside Primary 7 and was surprised to notice that he was far from being the biggest there. Very many of the children looked much older than he.

"P5 for us," hissed Megan. "Come on."

Tom found himself standing in an extraordinarily long line of black, woolly heads. They're all different sizes, he noticed. Indeed, a great many of the African children were several years older than the two muzungu.

Ugandans only attend school when they have the money and can be spared from work at home. The boy behind Tom was stepping on his heels. The children made their way into the gloomy classroom.

The mud walls were battered and pictureless. There were great holes in the wall at the back, through which Tom could make out other figures moving in the room next door. A pock-marked blackboard swung unevenly on a string. There was a list of some kind pinned beside it, but otherwise the room was bare of decoration. Tom looked up to the exposed beams that held the metal roof; there was no ceiling.

"Sit beside me," said Megan and Tom was pulled down onto a rickety bench seat to which was attached an equally rickety bench desk. This was made to accommodate six children, and did so with difficulty. The four on the other side of Megan all peered past her to size up the stranger. Tom shuffled his shoes over the uneven mud floor. There were dents where the feet of other children had fidgeted over the years.

Suddenly all whispering ceased as Mr Karumu made his way to the front and solemnly wrote the date on the board. He turned to face his class, his piercing eyes swept over the charges before him. He had a long, gaunt face to match his long, gaunt body. His clothes exuded dusty shabbiness. His spectacles fell half way down his nose as he seated himself at the table from where he called the register. It took a great deal of time on this first morning of term, not only because there were very many names to be called but also because there were fees to be collected. Some children didn't have the right money, some none at all. To Tom's amazement, they were sent home to fetch it and told not to return until they had the correct amount. And so, at a stroke, Mr Karumu's overlarge class was brought down to a more manageable size. Three children disappeared from Tom's bench, leaving it to him and Megan and one other. After chatting to Megan for some time, this boy leaned across in front of her, grasped Tom's hand and gave it the traditional Ugandan handshake, saying solemnly as he did so,

"You are most welcome. My name is Asiimwe."

His serious face was overtaken by a brilliant warm smile, and Tom was pleased to have made another friend. Tom watched Asiimwe as he resumed his conversation with Megan. He recognized him as a friend of Alex. He was the same age as Alex but still in P5 because he had started school late. He was occasionally in the crowd at the bike track, whenever he was not required to help with chores at home or on the farm. He was also a close friend of Megan's, Tom noticed. He wondered at the strange, unpleasant feeling that came over him as the two of them whispered happily in Runyankore while Mr Karumu took time to organize the day's lessons. Why couldn't the teacher have done that beforehand? Tom wondered resentfully. He noticed that Megan listened attentively to everything Asiimwe said, and gave him many of her impish smiles that set her eyes sparkling. Tom wished Mr Karumu would hurry up and start the lesson and so stop this conversation that so clearly excluded him.

MATHEMATICS

The word appeared in capital letters on the chalkboard. Tom gulped. This is it, he thought.

Everyone obediently pulled out maths exercise books and pencils from their bags and waited for the next move. Asiimwe took a pencil from his thick curly hair and, seeing that Megan was having trouble finding hers in the bottom of her bag, provided one for her too. Tom was impressed. What a great place to keep a pencil. He noticed many of the children used their hair for this purpose. My hair's pretty thick, he thought. But when he tried to anchor it there, his pencil slipped to the floor. He stooped to retrieve it and earned a glare from Mr Karumu.

Another word in capital letters.

FRACTIONS

Good, we did 'fractions' last term. Tom was not at all bad at Maths.

Mr Karumu wrote some figures on the board.

$1/4 + 1/8$

"Now, class," he said, "who can do this sum? Who can do this sum?" Tom was to learn that Ugandan teachers always say everything at least twice.

Hands shot up all over the classroom.

"Yes, Mugisa, you come here," said Mr Karumu. He threw the piece of chalk on the floor.

Mugisa picked it up, and wrote $2/12$.

Stifled cries and waving hands sent the embarrassed Mugisa quickly back to his place.

As the lesson progressed, so Tom relaxed.

I can cope with this, he thought.

After Maths came English. Mr Karumu read a story about the lost city of Atlantis. All the people and their city were destroyed by a volcano and plunged under the sea for ever. In the beginning, Mr Karumu's pupils concentrated very hard but, as the story went on and on, one after the other they switched off. But they all sat still and quiet, their bodies totally obedient, even if their minds were elsewhere. A good story, thought Tom, but he wished he could have had his own book to follow it. There are few books in Ugandan schools, and only the teacher has access to those. At the end of the story Mr Karumu asked some questions. Failing to get a satisfactory response from the class, he answered the questions himself.

"Mwayetegyereza?" he asked.

"Do you understand?" Megan giggled the translation to Tom.

"Twayetegyereza," replied the class in unison.

Then Mr Karumu wrote the questions on the board, requesting the children to copy them into their exercise books and write the answers beside them. At this point Tom found his classmates craning their necks to see what the new muzungu had written.

After a while, "Mwaheza?" asked Mr Karumu.

"Twaheza," all replied.

Tom looked inquiringly at Megan.

"Have you finished?" she said, slamming her book shut with relief. Tom, with the other children, closed his book too, and passed it to the end of the row.

Tom was getting restless. Never, at school in England, had he been required to sit still for such a length of time.

It must surely be playtime now, he thought. But no, there were forty minutes of Social Studies to follow, during which he learned the names and positions of the countries of Africa, and the capital cities too. He really couldn't concentrate on this as well. When he thought Mr Karumu's eyes were elsewhere, he allowed his gaze to rove the classroom.

There were as many girls as there were boys, he noticed. He had seen several of them watching at the bike track. They didn't have bikes of their own but hung around hoping that friends and brothers would allow them a turn, which they usually did.

Altogether his classmates, he thought with some relief, were very much like a class at home. There were the clever ones who always had their hands up, the quiet ones who had to be asked a question directly, some who never concentrated. There were even a few who chattered while Mr Karumu was speaking, but not so loudly that it disturbed anyone else. If by chance they did so the result was a resounding thwack on the legs from Mr Karumu's cane. It pleased Tom to see that everyone seemed genuinely happy when a classmate got an answer right; encouraged by Mr Karumu they would break into enthusiastic applause. He wasn't so sure about the derisory laughter that often followed a pupil who made a mistake, but the wrongdoer seemed to take it all in good part and often laughed with the others.

At last it was playtime. Tom thought his legs had grown so stiff they would never move again, but they managed to propel him into the playground with the other children. Here, all English was forgotten in a babble of Runyankore. Tom couldn't follow a word; everyone spoke together, and everyone spoke so fast. But all wanted the new muzungu to join in their play, and he soon found himself in the middle of a good-natured game of football. Tom noted that the players were all sizes, girls as well as boys. Many had nothing on their feet and the ball was made of banana fibre; yet still the game was played with all the intensity of a cup final. Asiimwe joined in the football for a while but, when Megan dropped out, so did he. It was then that Tom, taking his frustration out on the ball, scored his first goal. The adulation that followed restored his good humour.

Back in the classroom, he learned a few more names. School was going to be OK.

11 Storm

The days became hotter and hotter. The smell of dust laid an odorous blanket over the land; a harsh dry wind blew it into faces and clothes, and filled the creases in exposed skin. The ground was stiff and broken; from the depths of the cracks, it seemed that parched voices cried for water. Everything green turned feeble and yellow, its dry carcass lacking any nourishment for the wandering cattle whose ribs showed through taut, stretched skin. The blue sky and glaring sun were relentless. Rays of heat stabbed the earth with burning fingers and refused to answer its prayers.

Just when life thought it could take no more, a small cloud appeared on the horizon. Like a living creature, it pulled itself up over the curve of the earth. Slowly it dragged the fullness of its body behind it, until it formed a great tower stretching ever upwards. It began to mushroom sideways with exponential speed. As it did so, it thickened and darkened and developed an awe-inspiring menace.

A restlessness came over the village as people and animals and plants felt their stupor leave them. A welcome coolness blew along the huddled tracks, and the smell of dry, scorched earth developed freshness and energy. Clothes flapped round rapidly cooling bodies as the wind caught them. Children, looking up to the sky, laughed at each other in excitement.

The greyness of the heavens advanced, covering the brightness of the sun, stealing its power and direction, breaking it into tiny bits of gold that tinged the newcomer's edges, and the sun lost the battle for supremacy.

Thicker and thicker grew the advancing storm, piling cloud upon cloud, like the building of some great castle of the heavens that advanced over the world. Then began the roaring, and the cloud took on life. The battlements of the castle grew teeth and became a monstrous living wolf, engulfing all and bringing blackness as it piled on layer after layer of resistance to the sun. Shafts of light, like the edges of celestial daggers, tore across the wolf's fur, and were met by the threatening roar of his thunderous growl.

The wind grew in audacity, first turning leaves and snapping twigs, then twisting trees and catching the loose corners of metal roofs so that they rattled, demented.

Then the wolf was overhead. One or two huge drops, saliva from mighty jaws, banged on the corrugated roofs like bullets from a gun. Falling slowly at first, their pounding grew to a great frenzy so that nothing could be heard of any conversation taking place below.

In the schoolroom it went completely dark. There were, of course, no lights of any kind. Mr Karumu could no longer make his voice heard so he wrote some sums on the board and departed. Left to their own devices the children pleased themselves what they did. Some put their heads down on the desks and slept. Some chalked a design of triangles on the floor and began to play the traditional game of stones, variations of which had amused youngsters for generations. Small, roundish pebbles were tossed into the air, and points allotted as to how they were caught on the back of the hand, or how they fell within the triangles. Some children even did the sums on the board.

Many rushed to the doorway and windows to witness the drama of the storm. The rain became a wall of water, creating lakes around the playground. A stream rushed past the classroom door, making a barrier between it and the path beyond. Where there was concrete, the huge drops bounced back up again, creating a park of mini-fountains. Leaves were ripped from trees, young saplings bent right to the ground, and flowers were battered, their petals torn and cast aside.

Standing in the doorway, the children caught excitement from the skies. They turned laughing faces to each other and held out their hands to the cool, refreshing flood. They looked up to feel the storm splash on their faces and peered through the dizzying maelstrom of falling water. They shrieked with glee at the coldness and wetness of it all and then, becoming more adventurous, left the comparative shelter of the doorway and jumped back and forth over their new stream. Their sodden garments outlined their skinny bodies and the wind tugged at skirts and shirts in an attempt to remove them altogether.

The two sparkats stared into the fury from the shelter of the veranda. Like many members of the feline race, they felt an aversion to water. They stood with their ears flat against their heads, tails lowered. For company they had a group of striped swallows.

These perched huddled together on the rail, peering out into the deluge. Their heads twisted from side to side; their bodies were quite still among the noise and drama of the elements. They were aware of the two animals behind them but knew, by a wild thing's instinct, that, at this moment, they posed no threat whatsoever.

Lightning ripped through the heavens and the thunder caused the boards of the veranda to bounce, and the cats shrank imperceptibly in distaste. But they continued to watch, their concentration absolute on the mayhem of the skies.

A bolt of lightning flashed across the back of the wolf and tore into a tree but two fields away. It struck through the trunk and entered the heartwood. Groan followed crack and the great tree lurched and turned black. Flames and smoke belched from it. It twisted and screamed in its dying agony as the trunk wrenched from the roots and fell in a spray of water and mud and leaves and broken branches.

The swallows, alarmed, rose and circled the veranda once, before returning to the safety of their sheltering perch. Jessica and Lucifer stood back on their haunches, stunned.

"There," exclaimed Lucifer, "look where the lightning struck the ground! See that shining point, the silvery gold bit? For a moment it was magnified by the lightning. It was round with a flat top. Did you see it had lines and figures on it?"

Beneath her coat Jessica felt her skin prickle.

"The 'ody,'" she whispered. "Those creatures in the tree, they're baboons. Baboons were ever his slaves. They're using the storm to seize power over the 'ody'. They've beaten us to it!"

"Well they won't get power like that," scoffed Lucifer. "They need to read the signs, not smash it to pieces!"

"They're not far away. We could take the 'ody' from them," suggested Jessica.

"Brilliant!" snarled Lucifer. "And exactly how do you propose we track down a tribe of vigilant baboons and steal a treasure from them?"

Lucifer felt disgruntled. So the baboons had the 'ody'. They had one up on him, and Lucifer never liked that. True, it was not a mega set-back. They might have the 'ody' but they clearly had no idea at all what to do with it. And they wouldn't know how to read the clues even if they knew that 'read the clues' was what you had to do. *He* knew how to read the clues of course. But how could he do that if he didn't have the 'ody'?

"And I wish this rain would stop," he snarled from sheer bad temper.

Lucifer and Jessica crumpled together in a miserable furry ball. They hid their faces for they had seen what they dreaded to see. They did their very best to shut out the outside world and return to a better place.

The swallows started to shuffle on their perch. A few preened themselves carefully.

As suddenly as it had started, the pounding rain ceased. The wolf's anger spent, he withdrew to the horizon and restored the sun to power. Rivers still gurgled past doors. Flowerbeds remained sodden heaps. Trees were bent and bruised. But the land started to steam as warmth returned. Below the surface seeds drank in the life-giving nourishment and began to swell with fertility. Insects, imprisoned under stones for months, stretched their wings for flight and became lunch for the group of hungry swallows.

Zero One Zero spread himself out in the sun and proceeded to sort out his fur methodically, starting at the tail. He paused to roll over and expose his tummy to the heat and allow the delicious warmth to seep down into his bones. He purred to himself. His bad temper had vanished with the pounding rain.

Not at all a bad place for an assignment, this. Well, he had chosen it himself. Being one of the most battle-tried agents, he had earned that privilege. Lovely place. Just a pity Zero Six Six messed up with the actual mission. Fancy allowing the 'ody' to fall into *their* hands at the outset! He'd have to report it back to Control. They probably wouldn't be too hard on her. He genuinely hoped not. After all, they would get it back sometime. He had never been beaten before and he didn't intend to start now. His eyelids slowly closed and he fell into a deep sleep beside Zero Six Six.

For any outsider it would be difficult to see how Zero Six Six could possibly be blamed for the loss of the 'ody'. But Lucifer had that most useful asset in his sparkatality, a supreme conviction that nothing was ever his fault and that therefore some other creature must be to blame. This confidence had given him an arrogance that had already brought him far. He told everyone that he was infallible and spoke with such assurance that they believed him.

12 Baboons

The smell of baking that wafted from the cosy kitchen attracted Megan to peer round the door. Looking up from the hot stove and wiping sweat from her eyes with the back of her arm, Betty's rotund figure responded to the laughing smile in the freckled face of her visitor. She uttered a squeal of delight and gave the girl a floury hug.

"Tom's out at the front. He and Asiimwe are working on their bicycles," she said. "Here, take these mendazi with you."

She put a plate of the soft doughy cakes on a tray, and then added three glasses and a large jug of obotunda straight from the fridge.

Both boys were kneeling before an upturned bicycle, completely absorbed in mending a puncture. Asiimwe looked up at Megan's greeting, his hands covered in grime and a smudge across his face where he had wiped away the sweat. He picked up a rag and hastily cleaned himself up, passing the rag to Tom when he had finished with it. They greeted each other in Runyankore.

"Come and have a break," invited Megan. "Betty's been making mendazi. They're still warm." She set down the tray and started to pour the obotunda into the glasses.

The boys needed no second bidding and eagerly took the offered drinks. Asiimwe spread himself out on the grass and grinned broadly at Megan. This was a bonus, to have her unexpected company.

"What are the drawings?" she asked, indicating the papers lying beside Tom.

"We're creating a design for my bike," explained Tom.

All the children in the village who had a bike decorated it lavishly.

"He wants stars and moons, like me," added Asiimwe. "He doesn't have a mudguard, so it'll have to be on the frame."

"But we've got to mend the puncture first. I got the puncture last night," he explained to Megan. "I must have gone over a thorn from the acacia."

Megan laughed, all the bikers knew about whistling thorn trees.

"I'll remember to avoid those in future."

Tom smiled ruefully. There was an acacia bush at the corner of the garden. As well as beautiful creamy white flowers, it had thick thorns, at least two centimetres long. Tom had been quite amazed and almost disbelieving when his father had told him that giraffes actually eat from acacia trees, choosing the topmost branches where the younger thorns are softer and more pliable.

Megan went across to inspect their work.

"I wouldn't touch anything," warned Asiimwe. "The grease won't go too well with mendazi."

Megan said something in Runyankore that made him laugh.

So full was the scene of happiness and warm contentment that the arrival of the baboons came as a brain-crunching shock. Two of them, half grown, had been at the side of the garden for quite some time, idly picking parasites and dirt from each other's fur. The children were aware of them but they were of little real interest; such a sight was very common. But they looked up, intrigued, when the baboons started to cross the lawn, playing tag in an amusing manner as they did so. It was unusual for baboons to come quite so close to the house. And what they did next brought all three children to their feet. As if at a signal, they stopped their play and sped at full tilt across the remainder of the lawn towards the upturned bicycle. Each grabbed one of the tools that the boys had been using and that now lay scattered on the ground, and made off with it.

The three children jumped up and set off after the thieves, shouting at them to come back. Normally this would have been pointless; baboons move at great speed. But this time it was different. The baboons kept just out of reach of their pursuers, as if taunting them. The children followed, quite unthinking of the possible significance of what they were doing.

Asiimwe was in the lead, his long legs putting a gap between himself and his two friends, and the baboons kept just ahead of him. Gibbering and screeching as they went, and waving their prizes in tight little hands, the baboons made their way lightly across the grassland, among the cows, and into the bush beyond. As if wanting their pursuers to catch up, they waited for the children. Asiimwe reached the forest first, followed by a panting Tom and Megan.

"Where are they?" demanded Tom angrily.

"Look, there, just up in that tree."

"Have they still got the tools?"

As if in answer to the question, the two baboons cheekily waved their new possessions at the indignant children.

"All we have to do is wait," said Asiimwe very knowledgeably. "Pretend we're not interested, and they'll probably drop them."

"Well that's OK," said Megan. "I need a rest," and she flopped to the ground. Hugging her knees, she watched the trees.

The baboons laid the tools down carefully between their back feet and spent a few minutes picking fleas from each other's coats. And then, tools in hand once more, they were on the move again.

"Come on," said Asiimwe, pulling Megan upright.

"Does it really matter?" she protested.

"Course it does," replied Tom, feeling the anger rise. "Those are my dad's things."

The baboons were moving more slowly now. They made their way along a narrow animal track into a denser part of the forest.

"They're playing games with us," complained Megan, "and they're going to win."

"Oh, don't give up," despaired Tom. "We've got to get those tools back."

They followed the young baboons along the winding track. Then the shrubby trees became more thinly placed and the baboons broke through into a clearing. They climbed onto a rock in the centre where they stopped. The children emerged from the trees.

"Wait here," said Asiimwe. "I'll see if I can persuade them to give up their prizes."

On silent feet he crept nearer to the rock, holding out his hand in what he hoped was friendship. The baboons allowed him to come close, and then hissed and spat, clutched their trophies more tightly and moved further up the rock.

Then Asiimwe tried something else. He picked up a small stone and threw it at the obstinate animals, with the intention that they would throw a tool back at him. He hit one of the thieves on its nose. It squealed but then put down the spanner it was carrying, picked up a fistful of gravel and hurled that at Asiimwe instead. Asiimwe ducked, the gravel rattled to the ground behind him. The baboon picked up its spanner and smirked at him.

"It's no good," sighed Megan. "They won't let go." She sank down beside the huge stone, Tom joining her, his face crumpled in despair.

The two baboons looked down triumphantly from their perch, and continued to tantalize the children by waving their tools at them.

"Don't look," said Megan firmly. "They're just trying to provoke us."

It was Asiimwe who noticed it first. In the trees all around them, were rustling sounds and patches of grey fur flitting between branches. Baboons, hundreds of them.

"They're surrounding us," he despaired, looking behind and to the sides. He felt a stab of fear plunge through him. The normally expressive little faces of the baboons had become inscrutable with charged malice. Megan and Tom were on their feet, their backs against the rock. Dread coursed through them as more and more of the animals joined the first-comers. The gibbering and screeching that suddenly ensued was terrifying. All three put their hands to their ears, and creased their eyes closed to blot out the sight of those cavernous pink mouths with the pointed teeth and protruding tongues.

As suddenly as the noise had begun, it stopped. The children opened eyes and ears to see a baboon of vast proportions move from the trees. It had gleaming red eyes that were almost purple. Its gaze never wavered. Its grey fur shone silver. The children instinctively turned from that penetrating stare that reached into their souls. It beckoned with its left hand, its bony fingers curled towards the palm, and its lips folded in a snarl. Other baboons left the density of the forest and crept forward. Asiimwe stamped his feet in a futile effort to scare them. A few hesitated, but only momentarily.

"Come on," said Tom. "There are fewer of them over there. Let's break the circle." He grabbed Megan's hand.

The roar sounded from one of the tallest trees. The baboons stopped in their tracks, as did the children. A magnificent leopard stepped out onto one of the branches. Muscles rose and fell under dense fur that had perfect markings – brown spots and rings on a sea of gold. Its flowing movements were a stream of molten liquid. Its perfectly proportioned head twisted gracefully towards the largest baboon. Its golden eyes glowed with powerful contempt. It thrust its white chin forward as another deep-throated snarl rumbled from far inside its cavernous frame. It raised a heavy paw in a gesture of dismissal. The baboon leader looked up, made a feeble growl, thought better of it and bounded into the forest, followed by the rest of the pack, all gibbering and screaming and pushing to be first.

The children stood motionless, gazing at the great leopard. Asiimwe had never seen one so large, and all three were paralysed with fear.

"Run," suggested Tom, the first to break the silence.

"No! No!" said Asiimwe. "It's important not to show any fear."

The great beast slowly rippled down the trunk of the tree and, swinging its heavy tail, padded on massive silent paws towards them. It was the closest Megan had ever been to a leopard and some of her fear evaporated in admiration of the wonderful markings and thick fur. Instinctively she put out her hand. The leopard came closer, licked it with a rasping tongue, and then licked her face as Tom and Asiimwe watched mesmerized.

The leopard fixed Megan with its golden eyes and lay down before her. Megan put her hands in the thick fur and climbed onto the broad back. She felt a thrill of exhilaration as her bare legs hugged the silkiness, and the great beast rose to its feet and started to pad slowly through the forest.

Tom hesitated for a moment and then pursued the disappearing tail. Asiimwe delayed only to retrieve the tools the young baboons had dropped in their fright, and joined them.

They wound their way back along the track by which they had come that seemed so much longer now than it had on the outward journey. Just before they reached the open grassland the leopard lay down for Megan to dismount. She slid to the ground, falling beside the great white paws that were almost as big as her head. She whispered an awed 'thank you'. The leopard inclined its head in reply and then, in one great bound, was gone. The children gazed at each other. None said anything. The boys, on either side of Megan, joined hands with her. They raced across the grassland to the house.

Jessica was curled in Megan's lap. She loved the way she stroked and petted her. And tonight Megan told her a story – a story about spanners and baboons and a magnificent leopard. Zero Six Six pricked up her ears, wound herself free of Megan's grasp and made off into the night.

"So what did the baboons want with the children?"

"Oh, come on, Zero Six Six, work it out!" replied an exasperated Lucifer. "Surely you remember one of the first lessons in Spy School – 'how to gain power over a treasure'?"

"There are always tasks to be done," Jessica ventured. "And items to be collected in order to perform the final act."

"Yes! And who has to perform that act?"

"Some creature from the world to which that treasure belongs." It was coming back now.

"And?"

"It should be the first creature or creatures to have touched the treasure."

"So?" Lucifer encouraged.

"And so – the children must have been in contact with the 'ody'! That's why the baboons want them. To perform the final act to release the DNA. We know the baboons already have the 'ody'. We saw them trying to master it in the storm!"

"Exactly. You're catching on fast, Zero Six Six."

Jessica looked concerned and a frown appeared, creasing her black forehead into three parts.

"Then the children are in danger."

"And they also know something about this 'ody'. For their own safety they must be told about the mission. 'Knowledge is power. Knowledge is safety'." Lucifer quoted a much-expressed opinion of one of their former teachers, now deceased, in Spy School.

13 Revelations

Very often in an evening, Tom and Asiimwe would join Megan and Alex on the veranda of one of their homes. Together they absorbed the sights and sounds of an African night. They watched the darting diamonds that were firefly tails in the bushes. They listened to the powerful, rasping song of cicadas that grew louder with the gathering darkness. Sometimes Alex had his guitar, his gentle strumming carried to those sitting quietly outside their houses in the village. Asiimwe too had a good ear for music, and between them they lulled their neighbours into a relaxing evening.

While Alex and Asiimwe tried out a new song, Tom found himself gazing, enraptured, at the stars that were taken for granted by the others who had never known any other sky. There were so many of them, and so intensely bright. Some were so vibrant and close together that the individual pinpoints joined to form a dense white swathe across the firmament. Megan idly stroked Jessica's fur as she too studied the sky, while Tom tried to interest her in the names of the stars and the legends behind them.

"However hard I look," Megan protested, "I just can't see the shapes you're talking about."

"Look at Jess's fur!" interrupted Alex. "She's like a silver firework!"

They looked towards Jessica, purring contentedly in Megan's arms.

"She makes sparks when I stroke her," explained Megan, as if there were nothing so very extraordinary in that. "Just look!" She pressed more firmly with her stroking hand. Sparks of silver flew in all directions and turned to nothing when they landed on the children's clothes and skin, just like sparklers on bonfire night.

Alex put his guitar to one side, made a grab for Lucifer and immediately started to stroke him. Lucifer gave a faint mew of protest at the rough treatment. But Alex's firm stroking had the same magical effect – silver sparks shot everywhere. Both cats remained quite still. Both wore the same inscrutable expression of self-satisfaction, and emitted deep purring sounds that challenged the crickets for supremacy of the night.

Asiimwe hung back. First strange baboons and an unusual leopard. Now this. It looked too much like magic to him. He had always been taught to fear and avoid magic. Forcing his reservations deep inside himself for he knew the others wouldn't share his concerns, he said, in an almost off-hand way,

"There must either be something strange about the night, or about the cats themselves."

"Jessica, tell me," joked Megan, looking straight into the wide amber eyes of her beloved pet. "Is there something strange about you, Jess?" she whispered into her ear.

"Not really," replied a furry voice. "It's just that I'm not an ordinary moggie. You see, I'm a sparkat."

"Did that cat say something?" asked Alex, stunned that he should even contemplate such an absurd idea.

Megan stopped stroking. Asiimwe backed away. Only Tom saw nothing out of the ordinary in the disclosure.

"Is Lucifer a sparkat too?" he enquired.

"Indeed I am," replied Lucifer. His voice was deep, rough and gravelly. "A leading sparkat," he couldn't resist adding.

"So what is a sparkat?" Alex always needed an explanation. Even with the evidence in front of him, he remained sceptical.

"Shall we show them or tell them?" asked Lucifer mischievously. He was never happier than when he had an audience. As he spoke his lips hardly moved, but every word was perfectly articulated. He turned to Jessica.

"One, two, three ..."

The cats stood nose to nose. They closed their eyes. First a glow, an orange light, appeared and expanded at the extreme tip of each tail. This light crept the full length of the tails and then raced across the cats' bodies, turning their fur thick and glossy and very orange. Bands of green spread up their orange legs. Green rosettes mingled with the orange fur on their backs. Orange raced over their heads to black noses and dense white whiskers. Above their glowing eyes tufted green ears twitched back and forth. The sparkats looked at each other and a big grin split each face. They shook themselves. The long hairs of their fur stood on end, and from each hair came a silver spark that together covered the two animals in metallic brightness.

"You're beautiful," breathed Megan softly, her grey eyes wide with pleasure.

A smile of sheer delight swept across Tom's face.

He and Megan struggled to scoop their much changed and much larger pets into their arms.

Asiimwe, confused and doubtful, stood to one side. He wanted to join in but didn't quite dare let himself. Alex's expression was sheer question. There must be a logical explanation.

"Behold, two sparkats," announced Lucifer, pleased with himself and the reaction he had caused. "It's easily explained," he continued. "We are shape-shifters. All sparkats are. We can take any form we like."

"So, the leopard ...." began Megan.

"No," Lucifer held up a paw. "Not so fast. That was Jasper. One of us. An 'other worlder', but not a shifter."

"An 'other worlder'?" repeated Tom.

"Yes. A creature that is able to move from one world to another, either on the same planet, or among the worlds in space. Sparkats are the most experienced at it, but many others can do it too."

"I've done it!" breathed Megan. "When I met Peter. In a world of rabbits."

Alex's face expressed his confusion and frustration.

Lucifer read his dissenting thoughts and had more to say.

"Most animals are 'other worlders'," he explained. "They have open minds, you see, and can therefore move between worlds. We call these creatures with open minds quite simply 'thinkers' and those with closed minds who cannot move between worlds we call 'nothings'. Most adults and a few children of your species are 'nothings'. The possibilities of all the wonderful experiences that come to 'other worlders' are closed to them. Sometimes this is because of their culture; sometimes because they have become over committed to the affairs of one world and leave themselves no room for another. They become the 'non-thinkers', the 'no-thinkers', the 'no-thingers', the 'nothings'," he finished dramatically.

Alex and Asiimwe looked at each other, Asiimwe contrite, Alex defiant; he knew what Lucifer was saying and he wasn't having any of it.

"So," he demanded, "where do you sparkats come from?"

"Our home is in Rainbow world," began Jessica.

"I know about Rainbow world," interrupted Megan. "Peter told me."

"Oh, stop talking nonsense!" Alex rounded on her, angry because he didn't understand.

Lucifer grinned a catty, knowing grin at Megan that urged her to silence for the time being. He was used to sceptics and enjoyed the challenge of confronting them.

"So," Alex continued, "what are you doing over here?"

All the time he was edging nearer to the two cats. He felt if he could just touch them he might understand how the deceptions of colour and voice were assumed.

"We're here because we are members of the Intra Galactic Intelligence

Service, and we're on a mission."

"Course you are," sneered Alex under his breath.

Asiimwe was fascinated in spite of himself and his inhibitions began to creep away. Alex was ever more impatient for the resolution of this puzzle. He pulled at Jessica's sparkling fur. The sparkat turned and nipped him lightly on the finger. Alex looked down at his hand and could see clearly in the moonlight the deep puncture wounds, and his dark red blood dripping freely from them to the ground. Jessica came to face him. She fixed him with her inscrutable amber eyes. She put out her rough tongue and passed it just once over the marks that her sharp teeth had made. Alex looked down. The blood had ceased to flow. His hand was whole as if no wound had recently disturbed the skin. He felt the frowning lines leave his face, and a deep content passed from Jessica into him.

When very much smaller, Alex too had been to another world. He had never admitted this to anyone. It was a world of reptiles and amphibians and huge dinosaurs; some friendly, others so fearsome they had given him nightmares long afterwards. Worst of all was the tiny raptor that for years he had imagined lived in the folds of the curtains in his bedroom. Although he had been sure it was real at the time, he had since convinced himself that it was all in his imagination.

But really, he had always wondered, why shouldn't there be other worlds? It seemed unlikely to him that our tiny planet, inconspicuous in the great scheme of things, was the only place in the entire universe to support life. And why shouldn't these worlds be all around us? We have, after all, only five senses. Five isn't very many when most of Nature works in millions. How can we be so certain that anything we can't see or hear or feel or touch or taste doesn't exist? What arrogance! Maybe these sparkats did have something to say.

Alex settled down to listen.

14 Mission Ody

"I'll simplify this as much as can," Lucifer began, in a superior manner and casually inspecting the claws of his right front paw; he enjoyed being the one with all the answers. "But it is a bit complicated," he added patronizingly, "so settle down to listen."

Megan immediately sat cross-legged on the boards of the veranda, chin in hands, gazing fixedly at Lucifer. Tom, equally intrigued, knelt down beside her. Asiimwe hung back at the edge of the circle, so he had an escape route should this magic get out of hand. Alex leaned on the railing of the veranda, pretending nonchalance but concentrating all the same.

Lucifer warmed to his theme.

"The universe," he said, "as all intelligent beings know," and here he shot a catty glare at Alex, "houses millions and millions of different planets, and on each of these planets are very many different worlds. But we are concerned solely with those of our own galaxy.

"Now, at the centre of this is a very special world indeed. It's called Creation world and is found on a planet at the end of a black hole. In this world grows a mighty forest. Within its depths is a single tree for each world in the galaxy; and for some not yet born. The trees grow DNA which they store in their seedpods. These seedpods are harvested and transported across space to their allotted planet where they are carefully emptied to a certain format to create a new world. The released DNA shapes plants and creatures which, in their turn, change and mutate to form other plants and creatures."

"Evolution," added Alex knowingly. Lucifer ignored him and carried on.

"The trees continue to produce fresh seedpods because extra DNA is frequently required by established worlds that are running short of species, usually because a dominant race has made them extinct. A top-up you could call it. And sometimes we just think a world could do with more variety.

"The trees that grow this DNA are formed by the Creator, the essence of goodness and intelligence. But, in order that good might exist, its counterpart, evil, must also be there. Nothing can be without its opposite."

At this point Jessica joined in, reciting a mantra learned at Spy School,
"Up has no meaning without Down,
"Right has no meaning without Wrong,

"Good has no meaning without Evil."

"Quite," Lucifer silenced her. Turning to the children, he asked, "Do you follow me?"

Tom and Megan nodded their heads vigorously.

"Good."

"When you talk of the Creator, do you mean God?" Asiimwe interrupted.

"Not exactly. No."

The sparkat's furry brow creased in puzzled thought. His green eyes held Asiimwe with suspicion and denied the boy further questions.

Lucifer paused for a few moments while he glanced all round, his emerald gaze penetrating the darkness, as if he thought others might be interested in what he was saying. All appeared still. Lucifer knew they would be out there. But probably they couldn't hear, and certainly they wouldn't understand. He pulled his mind back to the matter in hand.

"Now," he went on, "the Creator put in charge of this forest the spirit of a great cat called Gabriel. Naturally he looked to our species to fulfil this important task." Lucifer swelled with pride. "But," he sighed, "few things are that straightforward. Gabriel has a brother, Cassius, who became jealous of what he saw as favoured treatment."

"Not exactly a brother," Jessica interrupted him. "Spirits don't have relations. Rather a soulmate."

"Thank you, Zero Six Six," retorted Lucifer impatiently. "I was just trying to make things more understandable for our friends. Brother will do for now. This brother …"

"Soulmate," muttered Alex, grinning cheekily.

Lucifer glared at him.

"As I was saying before I was interrupted, Cassius became envious of Gabriel's power. He wanted to overthrow him and take all power for himself. Hence evil was born. But his coup, for that was what he planned, was thwarted, and he was banished from Creation world for all eternity. Ever since then he and his followers have been causing mayhem throughout the galaxy. Most of this we have to let go. We just don't have the resources to cope with it. But when something extremely wicked and dangerous is about to take place, then we send out secret agents to try and prevent it.

"The Intelligence Service, with its hundreds of agents, is based in Spy world. It was established by the Creator to combat the evil of such as Cassius and his gangs."

He paused and then added, "This is my forty-sixth mission." Lucifer preened himself. "Jessica has so far clocked up ten."

Big-headed cat, thought Alex sulkily.

Lucifer twitched his nose angrily, as if reading Alex's thoughts. The withering glance quite unnerved the boy who had thought his mind open to himself alone.

"So – to our present mission." Lucifer was keen to move on. "There has been concern for some time about the number of species in this Bioworld of yours that are so rapidly becoming extinct."

"Bioworld?" queried Alex. "What do you mean? Bioworld? We live on Earth."

"Of course you do," soothed Jessica. "But only a part of it. Earth is the planet. The planet Earth supports many worlds. You can't take the name of the whole planet for your world which is only one of many."

"So, you live in Bioworld," said Lucifer firmly. "It is typical of the arrogance of the human species that they take the name of the whole world for themselves, just as if you were to claim that Uganda is the whole of Africa. But let's get on.

"The Creator decided that more Bioworld DNA should be released to start off new species.

"Cassius heard of this and it gave him an idea. He would steal a seedpod full of DNA. He would then harm and change this DNA and so mutate and deform the new plants and animals that evolved from it; possibly even create some terrible disease that would spread throughout Bioworld. At least that's the gist of his plan. I don't suppose even he has worked out the details yet."

"How?" It was Alex's question. "How could he do that?"

Lucifer sighed. "It's really quite easy to destroy and harm things. It's the creation of them that's difficult."

Alex nodded. That was true enough.

Lucifer grew tired of explanations and questions and turned his furry back on the others. Jessica took over.

"So Cassius needed a seedpod from a tree in Creation world. He couldn't fetch one himself. He would have been recognized had he stepped anywhere near the forest. So he sent Monkey, innocuous little Monkey, to do his work for him. But Monkey was as deceitful and untrustworthy as he, and stole the seedpod for himself. What he planned to do with it no one knows. Probably he had no plan. Monkey delighted in devilment, and simply enjoyed upsetting the plans of others. So, fortunately for your world, he didn't deliver the seedpod. He hid it somewhere in Bioworld. We couldn't track it down. By the time we knew it had gone, it was hidden from sunlight and impervious to our searching rays, and also to those of Cassius.

"Then suddenly, thousands of years later, the seedpod came to light."

"My treasure!" breathed Tom.

"Ah," said Lucifer, "we knew it had something to do with you when the baboons tried to kidnap you. Tell us about your treasure."

And Tom told them the whole story from the moment he received the statue as a small child.

"Now we're getting there," said Lucifer, beginning to show signs of excitement as he turned to face Tom. "Your treasure is most certainly the seedpod, the 'ody' for which we are searching."

"Ody?" queried Asiimwe.

"You know that word, don't you?" asked Lucifer knowingly.

"Of course," replied Asiimwe warily. "In my culture, an 'ody' is a magic object."

"Exactly. So, we know the baboons have the 'ody'. They are undoubtedly in thrall to Cassius. But they can't activate the DNA yet. To achieve that, a number of steps must be taken. First there are instructions on every seedpod that must be followed in order. Tasks they are. 'Labours' Control calls them. These labours lead to items, items that must be collected, each one from a different world."

"Like the labours of Hercules," exclaimed Tom.

"Now there's a boy who's read some good stories," approved Jessica.

"Just so," continued Lucifer. "Once all the items are collected, they must be taken to Creation world and placed in a furnace where will be forged the power to release the DNA. This final act must be made by the first members of the world concerned to hold the treasure."

"So that's why they led us into the forest." Megan shivered in the night air that was going chill. An owl hooted mournfully as if in sympathy with her mood.

"But," said Tom, "Monkey was the first to touch the 'ody'."

"But Monkey is dead," Megan pursued his thoughts.

"So, if we died …"

"Yes, a baboon would do, those baboons were after your lives."

Tom went pale. "But they will come again."

"Worry not, we will keep you safe," said Lucifer dramatically. "They won't dare approach a sparkat, and you have one each to guard you. Now their first assault has failed they will forget you for a while and set about collecting items; that is if they can work out how to do so. After all you are of no use and therefore no real interest until all parts of the puzzle are in place. And baboons are single-minded and not very clever in these things. They have already tried to gain power over the 'ody' and surely failed because they don't know what they're looking for."

"It all sounds rather complicated to me," protested Alex.

"It has to be that way to make it as difficult as possible for anyone to gain power over the seedpods."

"So," asked Tom, "how do we stop them collecting all the items and then killing Megan and me?" He stared into the darkness. "Where's the list of items?"

"The list as you call it is found in tiny dots on the disc at the top of the 'ody'. The baboons used the lightning of last week's storm to try and magnify it and so make it more intelligible." He laughed, and his laugh was a choking gurgle deep in his throat. "As if making clues larger would make them easier to understand! Now they will watch and try to intercept us as we follow the clues."

"But," said Tom, puzzled, "we don't have the clues. They have them."

Lucifer was thoughtful. "Maybe we will find a print from the disc inside that statue of yours? The 'ody' itself we will forget for now. Cassius probably has it already and he will guard it well. When all is gathered together and we are back in Creation world, then we will take it from him."

Alex stared at Lucifer, more questions churning up inside him. He was about to speak when there was a shout from the house.

"How much longer are you four going to spend out there?" It was Holly's voice. "It's time Tom and Asiimwe went home."

Colour drained from the sparkats with lightning speed, to the very tips of their tails. They bounded off the veranda and into the night.

In bed Megan lay sleepless, going through the events of the evening, hardly able to believe what had occurred. She trembled when she thought of the fierce-eyed baboons, and smiled at the remembered feel of the leopard's soft, spotted fur. And it was with relief that she felt Jessica at the end of her bed.

"Oh, Jess," she said, and her arms went out to her, "I'm so glad you're here. But please could you shift into a sparkat. I'd feel so much safer if you did."

68

Jessica was more than happy to oblige. So the two curled up together, only Jessica's orange tail showing above the duvet.

"Megan! Megan!" Her mother's voice broke through her dreams. "Time to get up."

A few minutes later Holly was in the doorway.

"What have you done to Jessica's tail?"

"What?" replied a sleepy voice. Then Megan noticed the orange tail lying exposed beside the duvet.

"Oh, Mum." She feigned surprise.

Her mother, hassled as always first thing in the morning, had already jumped to her own conclusions.

"Alex," she shouted, "what have you done to Megan's cat?"

"Me? Why's it always me?" Alex spoke through his cereal but didn't look up from his football magazine.

Megan stifled a giggle, shook her beautiful sparkat awake, and told her to get shifted quickly.

Hieroglyphs

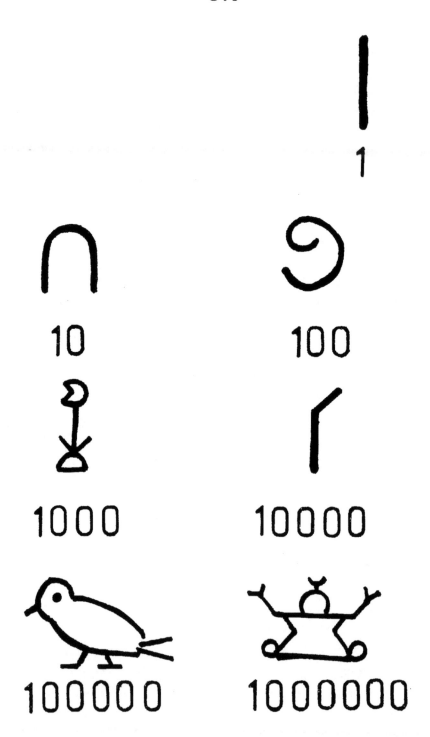

1

10

100

1000

10000

100000

1000000

15 Puzzling Mirror

Alex plucked a deep chord from his guitar and then, putting the instrument to one side, turned to Asiimwe beside him.

"What do you make of all that then?" He indicated two sleek-furred mongooses performing acrobatics on the railing of the veranda.

As they spoke Tom and Megan emerged from the house behind, Tom carrying his old blue rucksack.

"It's magic, isn't it?" replied Asiimwe, "I don't want to get involved in anything of that kind."

"I don't know," said Alex. "Clearly it's real enough. You only have to look at those two mongooses to know that. But whether or not it's magic … ?"

For a while Alex watched the little group on the veranda, and then continued. "Perhaps such things are magic if you don't understand them and science if you do."

Asiimwe pondered this explanation for a while. It certainly seemed true that the more science there was in the world, the less magic was around. If this should all be science and not magic…well then…. Finally he said, "Let's go and see what they're up to."

"Great!" Alex pulled his friend to his feet.

Lucifer had been watching the boys out of the corner of one eye, and addressed them as they came across the lawn.

"So, you've decided to join us." A smirk of triumph crossed his face and revealed needle-sharp mongoose teeth. "Now let's have a look at this statue."

Tom pulled the precious possession from his rucksack and, taking a quick look around for inquisitive baboons, he gave it to Lucifer who took it with paws that had become as dextrous as human hands. Lucifer prised open the crack and held the empty space up to the radiant sun, and was so enabled to see right inside.

Asiimwe's anxious eyes searched the dark bushes. He felt sure he saw red points, gleaming in the undergrowth.

"The baboons," he ventured, "I think they're watching us."

"Probably," replied Jessica. "We can't avoid that. As long as all they do is watch we needn't be concerned."

"Just as I had hoped. The disc of the 'ody', the part with the map of instructions, has left an impression." Lucifer was jubilant. "Come and see. The wood must have moulded itself round it quite perfectly as the tree grew."

"We could do with a mirror to look at it properly," suggested Megan.

"And not just any mirror," added Jessica.

Lucifer glanced across at her questioningly.

"Double O Four has a mirror in his office which gives information about the reflected image."

"Double O Four?" Lucifer was deeply suspicious. "What do you know about Double O Four?" he rounded on Jessica.

Jessica looked confused for a moment. Tom saved her further explanation.

"Can you bring that mirror here?"

"I've done it already," Jessica announced to an amazed Lucifer. "I asked for it last night when we reported back on the day's work."

"Apparently Zero Six Six can fix these things." Lucifer was contemptuous. He didn't like to be outsmarted.

"But how did it arrive?" Alex wanted to know.

"Same way as we did. Same way as you will when you start to travel through the worlds. Let me see ….." Lucifer was happy again now he had his audience back. "Think of it like television or radio waves. The person or object is broken down into tiny pieces, and then reassembled in the new location."

"But where does the power come from to do that?"

"Electricity of course."

"From your coats," exclaimed Megan.

Lucifer beamed at her.

"And how do you communicate with Spy world?" Asiimwe was determined to understand the scientific aspect of it all.

"By mobile phone of course," said Jessica.

"Of course," mimicked Alex. "How else would a cat send messages?"

Jessica noticed Betty come out from the house to collect in the washing. Fortunately, she didn't look in their direction.

"We'd better get shifted," she said. "There are too many people around."

That done, Alex proposed they find a more private place in which to use the mirror. The little party made its way to the lake.

The lake was a few kilometres from the school, so they travelled on their bikes, moggies trotting beside them. It was well hidden, round a couple of bends in the bumpy road, and surrounded at one end by thick trees and bushes.

Not for the first time Tom marvelled at the freedom allowed to children here. They went off on their own about their own concerns, and nobody worried about them or needed to.

They hurtled down the hill, rejoicing in the wind on their faces and the rutted road beneath their tyres, and slammed on their brakes at the bottom to avoid plunging headfirst into the still water.

They gazed out over the serenity of the lake, its surface gently broken by a lone young man in a dugout canoe, patiently searching for fish on the other side. In most places small bushes grew right down to the water's edge, and above them was farmland, cultivated in terraces to prevent erosion. Far away, like matchstick people, two men were digging drainage channels to keep the land from being stolen by the relentless rains.

The place was a haven for wild birds. They amazed Tom with their abundance and variety.

There were the menacing fish hawks that circled in the azure sky, lifting themselves to catch the wind beneath their wings. In contrast, he admired those smallest of all birds, the humming birds with a metallic sheen – red and green and blue. Stationary on suspending tiny wings, they fed with their long tongues from the hibiscus flowers that grew in great profusion on the banks.

But, of all of them, his favourite was the pied kingfisher that dived like a spear after fish seen from a tremendous height. It made not a sound, not even a ripple, as it broke the surface. It fished with unerring accuracy. Never once had he seen one come up empty beaked.

"Well, let's have the statue." It was Alex's impatient voice that broke into his reverie. Tom swung his rucksack onto the ground, took out the statue and placed it on the bank. As he did so, he was aware of a scurrying sideways motion, and a plop into the water. Surely that was a crab? Crabs don't live in fresh water. He smiled to himself. Such details were scarcely relevant any more!

From the thick fur beneath her chin, Jessica pulled out a mirror the size of a small human hand. It was set in a heptagonal pewter frame, heavy with strange symbols. At one edge was a jewel that shone with all the colours of the spectrum. She handed it to Lucifer who took it casually, pretending to be unimpressed. He turned his attention to the statue.

"I'm sorry, we're going to have to chip away at some of the wood, to see the impression more clearly," he told Tom.

"That doesn't matter." Tom sought to hide his concern.

A pungent smell of resin wafted past his nose as Lucifer carefully scraped the wood with razor sharp claws. He worked slowly for fear of inadvertently damaging the impression. Megan watched him, grey eyes intent. So did Asiimwe. Like all African children he seemed to experience no problem in sitting still for great lengths of time. Tom tugged heedlessly at tussocks of grass and threw them into the water, to see them sail away like boats, catching a current where none seemed to have been. Alex rode his bike a short way along the track, to practise sudden emergency stops, thoroughly enjoying the way the small stones flew and jumped to one side when he skidded among them.

"There we are!" said Lucifer at last. "Come and look."

In the top of the gap where the 'ody' had been was the reverse diagram containing the instructions they wanted. The children saw a frilled disc, from which ran lines to the centre, making seven sections, like the slices of a pie. In each of the sections was a series of tiny dots. And, in the angles at the centre, were a number of squiggles.

"Now let's put the mirror here," said Lucifer, placing it some distance from the impression. "What do you see?"

Megan looked first. She saw the disc with the dots and the squiggles, spinning slowly and, beyond it, a mass of formless gliding shapes – coming and going, growing and fading, changing colours – just like the screen savers on a computer.

"Those spirits will help us decipher the clues," announced Jessica proudly.

"Spirits?" asked Alex.

"Perhaps not exactly spirits," explained Jessica. "More streams of consciousness. But spirits is easier to understand."

"Is it?" wondered Tom.

"I prefer to think of them as screen savers," said Asiimwe. "It's more scientific."

"Call them what you like," shrugged Lucifer. "It doesn't alter what they do."

"Zero Six Six, you should be able to make a start," challenged Lucifer. "Remember that lecture we had from Mr Doubletalk, back in Spy School."

Jessica looked puzzled.

Lucifer sighed with impatience. "So, how many sections do you see?" he asked.

The children peered and counted, and all agreed that the answer was seven.

"I remember this bit," said Jessica. "These things always come in sevens – it's the magic number, you see." Asiimwe winced at mention of the word 'magic'. "And they must be followed in order. See the squiggles in each centre angle? They are the numbers."

"Those squiggles are Egyptian hieroglyphs," marvelled Tom who had studied Ancient Egypt back in England. "They're not in the correct order," he noticed, "but if you start at one and multiply by ten each time, they're all there."

"Exactly that," agreed Jessica. "So we start at segment number one. Which is, Tom?"

That was easy. Tom pointed to the 1. He wasn't quite sure whether Jessica was testing him or whether she didn't know herself and needed his help.

"But why Egypt? Why hieroglyphs?" Tom muttered to himself more than to anyone else.

"Because Egyptians show due respect for cats, of course." Lucifer clearly thought the answer an obvious one. "They worship cats as gods. Plus Egypt is in Africa, as are we." He gave Tom a look that brought the matter to a close.

Jessica brought everyone's attention back to the mirror.

"So we start here. The dots translate into a clue. Each clue will lead us to an item for the forge in Creation world. The clues will only reveal themselves one at a time."

"So how do we read the first clue?" Alex was restless. He peered down over the handlebars of his bike, alternately squeezing and releasing the brakes with rising impatience.

"Water," droned Lucifer, repeating another lesson, "is the element that magnifies and reflects and clarifies. We will always need water in some form to help read the clues. The baboons even got that bit wrong. They tried to make use of the fire in the lightning." He laughed, uttering a rattling, choking sound deep in his throat.

"Tom," he said, serious now, "put the mirror on the ground."

"But if I take it away from the statue," Tom protested, "the reflection will disappear."

"How very Bioworld bound you humans are," growled Lucifer with exasperation. "The reflection will stay there as long as we need it. The disc with its clues has been permanently transferred to the mirror." He gave Tom a withering glare.

"See, when we move the mirror the disc disappears as you would expect. But," and he held up a paw, "the screen savers are still there and they have stored the image like you would in a computer. To bring the disc back we press this multi-coloured jewel." He did so and, brighter than before, the disc spun into view.

"Now Megan," he said, "cup some water from the lake into your hands." Megan did so.

"Pour the water onto the mirror, carefully, just on the section with the number 1."

Megan steadied one hand with the other, to ensure she dripped the water in exactly the right place.

The children craned their necks to see. The segment they needed had expanded to fill the entire mirror. The eight dots within it took over the whole surface and grew to form hollow circles. The screen savers soared and fell between them, colouring each one a different colour, and then each circle of colour elongated itself at one end to become a raindrop.

"The colours of the rainbow," breathed Megan.

"There're too many," said Alex. "There are only seven colours in the rainbow."

"The savers haven't finished yet," interrupted Tom.

Nudging and pushing, the ethereal movements arranged the drops in sequence.

"They're making the right order," observed Megan. "But there's an extra one, between the blue and the green – the turquoise one. That doesn't exist."

"That's it then," exclaimed Lucifer triumphantly. "A raindrop from the turquoise band of the rainbow. And the world must surely be Rainbow world!"

"An excellent place to start," declared Jessica with relief. "We're going home!"

Tom put the statue in the rucksack and stuffed the mirror into one of the numerous pockets of his jeans. This particular pair had seven, and Tom kept something in every one of them. He felt sure the mirror would be safe in the one on his thigh, from which he removed the screwdriver.

"Shoo! Go away!" Megan was on her feet, waving at the baboons in the trees. They sloped off.

"Don't worry about them," Jessica assured her. They may watch what we do, and know what we're about, but they won't do anything to stop us just yet. Their power is minimal, and Double O Three won't show himself at this stage."

"So, where is Rainbow world?" wondered Asiimwe.

"Rainbow world is here of course, though most don't see it, so to get

76

there is no problem at all. We'll travel electrically."

"We're going now?" asked Megan, suddenly nervous. "Will we be long?"

"I'm not really sure," said Lucifer. "Time is a relative concept."

"And what about our bikes?" she persisted.

Lucifer looked at the four machines dismissively.

"I suppose they can come too."

"Well we can't leave them here," declared Alex.

"You go first, Jess," suggested Lucifer.

Jessica breathed in deeply. The fur all over her body, from her little black face to her long black tail, stood on end. Sparks flew from it as it turned bright orange. And then she was gone.

"Now you, Megan. Let's log on and surf this planet of ours. Never mind a mouse, click onto a sparkat! Stroke my fur!"

Megan did as she was bid.

"Harder!" urged Lucifer.

She stroked vigorously until the sparks flew. These shot up her arm and covered her all over. The boys watched in amazement her disappear. When Tom's turn came and he felt the sparks flow over him, he had a sensation of leaving the ground and flying through a tunnel of searing heat, before returning to earth just a split second later. Alex and Asiimwe, each harbouring his own reservations, logged on and got stroking.

16 Rainbow World

"Welcome to Rainbow world, surfers in the galaxy!" declared Jessica proudly.

Here, Lucifer and Jessica's sparkat brightness fitted in with everything around, so that they were virtually camouflaged.

There were trees and plants, in shape not unlike those of Bioworld, but the colours were more intense and varied. The children's minds struggled to make sense of purple trunks and orange leaves and many more unfamiliar colourings, all faintly luminous. The plants had more flowers; the trees had more leaves; everything it seemed was unusually large and brilliant. Megan noticed blooms of all the colours of the rainbow growing together all on one tree. Many coloured snakes with curious friendly faces hung from the branches like vines. The air was filled with noisy chatter that came from foliage thick with colourful birds. And then they looked at each other. Megan gasped in amazement.

"Oh, Alex!" she laughed at her brother. His hair and skin were light blue, and his bicycle was green.

"Never mind me, you're orange!" he exclaimed. "The colour of your hair has spread all over you!"

Asiimwe was inspecting arms and legs that had turned indigo, and Tom's hair flamed like fire.

Zero One Zero and Zero Six Six stood before them in all their sparkat magnificence, enhanced by their return to Rainbow world. Clearly delighted to have shifted to their familiar form, they surveyed the colourful children with approval. The cats' faces were so thick with fur it puffed out their cheeks and gave them a perpetual grin – like the Cheshire Cat in Alice. But the eyes told a different story. Lucifer's, deep emerald, were keen and searching with a touch of ruthlessness. Jessica's more mellow amber eyes, while full of kindness, had a hardness and determination in them too.

"So, how do we find the turquoise raindrop?" Tom, anxious to get on, broke the colourful excitement.

"Refreshment first," exclaimed Lucifer. "We're calling in at home."

He set off at a swift trot, closely followed by an equally excited Jessica. The children quickly mounted their strangely coloured bicycles and followed close behind, pedalling furiously to keep up with the cats' ever increasing speed.

Their noses took in the heavy scent of the bright vegetation through which they passed. But they were too busy with the mechanics of cycling along the path deep with ruts that flowed with pale green water to notice, among the trees, baboons with gleaming eyes – strangely coloured baboons, pink and lilac and yellow.

At last the two sparkats slowed and turned to face the cyclists who braked and dismounted.

"I've been to very many worlds," declared Lucifer smugly, "but this Rainbow world is surely the best of them all."

Megan opened her mouth to ask a question when her attention was taken by the two girls who ran across the bright green lawn to meet them. The leader was tall and slender and violet with long purple hair that fell to her waist, silky and smooth and quite straight. Her lilac face was serene and unsmiling, and very beautiful. Her large eyes glowed amethyst, and showed no interest at all in the four strange children and their highly coloured bicycles. Her attention was totally on Lucifer whom she scooped up in her lilac arms and pressed against her chest and caressed with her cheek.

"My Lucy," she crooned, "where have you been? I've been so worried about you." Lucifer did wish she wouldn't call him Lucy, but he purred politely and responded to her tenderness by looking adoringly into her lovely face.

Her companion, a younger girl of about thirteen, was green and, like her sister, delicately built. Her hair, too, was straight and shining and hung about her pale, aquamarine face like a dark green curtain. While a hand went out to stroke Jessica, her smiling eyes that were the colour of jade rested on the visitors.

"You are welcome to our home," she said formally. "I'm Klara. My sister, Simone, and I live over there."

She pointed to a small semi-circular house built entirely of branches; the colours of the wood arranged to make a design like the rays of the sun, from dark red to palest yellow, the door forming the sun itself.

"Come with us."

She led the little party through the shining garden to her home. Simone glared at her. Megan thought how the two girls reflected the sparkatalities of the animals; the one severe and haughty, the other warm and friendly.

A small dog ran from the door. He was brilliant white but covered in spots that were all the colours of the rainbow. His feathery tail arched over his back. Barking with delight, his tail wagging, he greeted the strangers with happy bounds.

"What are you like?" cried Megan, enthralled. She knelt on the grass so the little dog could lick her face.

"That's Plato. He belongs to everybody," declared Simone scornfully.

"He's called Pluto?" Megan was delighted.

"Not Pluto. I said his name is Plato. Our dog is a thinker."

"So, who's Plato?"

Simone gave Megan a withering look. Megan glanced questioningly at Tom who shrugged his shoulders. Megan and Plato were instant friends. He bounded by her side, trying to come between her and her bicycle so that they fell in a tangled heap on the lawn. Asiimwe gallantly came to their rescue. He picked up the bicycle, and the dog and the girl scrambled to their feet, laughing.

The inside of the little house was bare of furniture. Woven red and orange carpets lay on the wooden floor, and on these were scattered colourful cushions. To one side there was a large wooden chest. There were windows in three directions so that rainbow light flooded into every corner. In this world there was a rainbow permanently in the sky. Sometimes the colours were strong, sometimes, as now, very faint, but they were always there.

Klara indicated the cushions and, with Jessica purring round her legs, she left the room. Simone stood in the doorway. Lucifer, too large to succeed, was nevertheless endeavouring to curl himself round her shoulders.

"How is it that you speak our language?" asked Megan.

"You mean how is it that you speak mine?" replied Simone, and said no more.

"Oh Simone, stop being so grumpy," laughed Klara who had returned with a large rainbow cake. "I don't know how it works. Perhaps it's in the hearing. Perhaps we just hear in our own language?

"I wonder what would happen if I spoke Runyankore?" Asiimwe whispered to Megan mischievously. But then he looked at Simone's arrogantly beautiful face and thought better of it. Simone dropped Lucifer who complained loudly. She brought a knife and some plates from the chest.

"What colour?" she fired at Megan.

"Orange, please." Simone handed her a thin slice on an orange plate. Then she served the other visitors with equally meagre pieces.

"It tastes of real oranges," exclaimed Megan.

"Of course it does," snapped Simone. "It's orange isn't it?"

"And my blue piece is blueberries," declared Alex laughing.

Tom was sure his red slice was strawberries, but Asiimwe had problems identifying the green; he had never tasted limes. Simone looked at them all in astonishment, wondering that they should make remarks about such obvious details.

Simone picked up Lucifer, pulled him to her lap and stroked him furiously until sparks flew in all directions. Lucifer closed his eyes in ecstasy. Tom felt a stab of jealousy as he watched her. Then she beckoned, with a beautifully manicured lilac hand, to the trees. Three gaudy parrots flew down to perch beside her, allowing her to feed them with different coloured crumbs. A pink baboon looked in through the window. Megan shivered.

"So, what are you doing in our world?" asked Klara.

Megan was unsure how much to tell these strange girls, but the sparkats were clearly at home here, so probably they were OK. The boys were still busy filling themselves with cake, so it was she who spoke.

"We're here to find a turquoise raindrop," she began. "I expect it's in the rainbow. Perhaps the easiest part to look would be the rainbow's end," she added, thinking aloud. "That's it. I think we need to know the way to the end of the rainbow."

"You think you need to know," scoffed Simone. "Either you do or you don't."

"Well yes, we do need to know. But the sparkats can show us. We don't need anyone else," she added defiantly.

"I see." Simone's cold and haughty voice sent a chill through Megan. "And how do you propose to find the end of the rainbow when it keeps moving on?"

"Simone, stop trying to be difficult," laughed Klara. "Of course the sparkats will guide you."

The sparkats, at this time, were feeding on rainbow sardines and taking no notice of the conversation at all.

Simone disliked being challenged, and glared at Klara.

"They will follow the parrots," she announced. "Only the parrots really know where the rainbow ends. And they know because they roost there every night." The three parrots at her feet cocked their heads, listening attentively. "And, as the parrots know the way, the sparkats don't need to go," she insisted, cutting herself another large slice of yellow cake with unnecessary vehemence. "Lucy stays here," she declared.

Tom would have liked to challenge that decision but it was clear that Lucifer wasn't going to support him. Lucifer, now satiated with sardines, was licking his lips and cleaning his fur, and his smug look expressed satisfaction.

"Then Jess will go with you," Klara assured the bemused children.

Asiimwe and Alex would have liked some more of the fruity cake, but it clearly wasn't going to be offered.

"Off you go then," said Simone, abruptly standing up, ruffling the feathers of the parrots who protested at the rough treatment, squawking. "Follow the parrots. If you don't go soon they will all have disappeared for the night already."

Unceremoniously, she urged the four visitors out of the door and closed it noisily.

Even Alex was too stunned to counter this rudeness.

"Now we're in a mess," he remonstrated. "How are we going to manage without Luce?"

"Miaow," wailed Jessica protestingly.

"Sorry, Jess." Alex gave her a pat.

"Let's just follow the parrots," suggested Asiimwe. Jessica nodded agreement.

As they cycled along the jungle path, keeping their speed in time with the sparkat's gently loping gait, the sky turned from yellow to green. Before the surfers could articulate the question, Jessica answered it.

"The sky tells the time of day," she said. "It becomes red at midnight and follows the spectrum until the end of violet shows midnight again."

"So now it's just before the middle of the day," said Megan.

"Well done," beamed Jessica.

Code

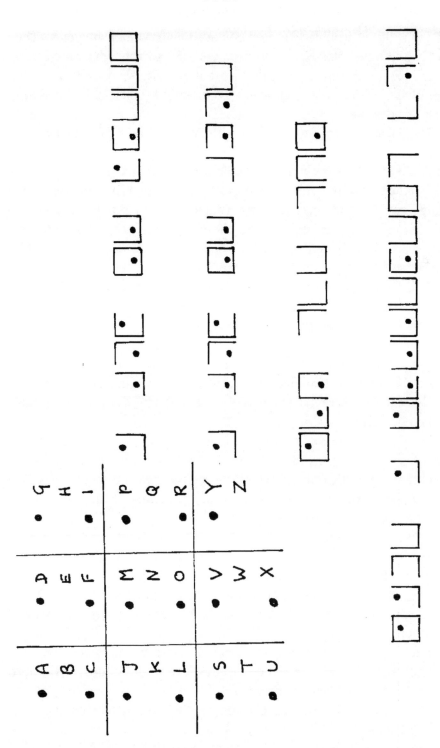

83

17 Water Drops

The children wobbled along the uneven path on their bicycles. They had to travel slowly now to keep with the parrots who were clearly in no hurry and were frequently diverted by tasty seeds hidden among the foliage of the trees. Jessica ambled lazily by their side, pondering Lucifer's desertion.

The parrots seemed to multiply with every metre of ground they covered, as more flew in to join the daily migration to the roosting places. Soon the air was thick with their colour and raucous cries. Some rode the handlebars of the children's bicycles, and Megan was pleased when a large one decided to take a ride permanently with her. He had a green back and a long green tail, a blue chest, a golden head and bright red, very sharp claws. The white circles round his beady black eyes gave him a surprised and questioning expression.

And so the strange party made its way through the primeval jungle, and baboons and snakes marked their passage and communicated what they saw to friends down the line.

"So, my special sparkat, have you news for me?" crooned Simone in Lucifer's ears as she rubbed them gently from behind. She turned her lovely head to ensure that she was not overheard by Klara who was busy in the kitchen.

Lucifer knew he was playing a dangerous game, but then danger was what his ambition thrived on. Simone and Klara were the daughters of Double O Five, the only humanoid in the Service. In themselves they had no power, but they had access to much, and Simone knew how to get it, and Lucifer was greedy for power.

He knew Simone loved him, and he knew he could use that. Simone would give him power if he gave her information that would fuel her own ambition. But he was Zero One Zero. He had sworn oaths and allegiances that he must avoid breaking at all costs. Any traitorous activity, however small, would be punished with unbelievable severity; were of course it discovered.

Each was wary of the other. So now Lucifer prevaricated.

"You know my position," he purred. "The whole future of Bioworld depends on the success of this mission"

"But you and I have a special relationship," persisted Simone, tickling Lucifer's chest. "I just need to know the nature of this mission that has brought those coarse children from Bioworld," and she wrinkled her sensitive nose, "to this lovely land."

Lucifer's emerald eyes glowed; he snuggled up to his mistress, but he said nothing.

"Look! Just look at that!" cried Megan from her position at the head of the line of bicycles. The boys had been diverted by snakes in the undergrowth and almost seemed to have lost interest in the original quest. Megan's shout brought them back to the task.

Before them was a huge fountain in the middle of a raindrop shaped pool, shooting up jets of water to mingle with the rainbow above it, creating spectra within spectra. As each spout moved skywards it formed an arc of light, a bunch of rainbows held at one end in the pool, the other end of which stretched to earth many kilometres away.

Surrounding it were many smaller fountains, and the water from these cascaded back into the pool moistening the multi-coloured rocks at the edge.

Round the rainbow circled thousands and thousands of colourful parrots; they spiralled up and up until they were out of sight, leaving the children to continue their mission alone. Only Megan's parrot still perched on her handlebars.

Megan moved into the spray. Below were water lilies and glittering fish, and above that kaleidoscope of liquid colour. She held up her hand.

"This must be it. Now we need a turquoise drop."

"And how are you going to carry a drop?" asked Alex, leaning on his handlebars.

"And where's the turquoise?" wondered Megan.

"Should be between the blue and the green," suggested Asiimwe, stretching out his hand from behind her to catch the spray.

Alex looked on, supercilious and indulgent. Tom paced around the pool looking for clues, although he had no idea what shape these might take. And then he noticed them. The salty smell drew his attention. Crabs, many of them, half-hidden in the reeds that lined the edge of the pool by the stones: spotted crabs, coloured crabs, watchers all of them. This must be the place if the crabs are here. Tom began turning the stones carefully, one by one.

Megan pulled her hand away from the rainbow. Clear water poured between her fingers. A scarlet bird in the trees above laughed raucously, as if making fun of her. A small pink baboon concentrated carefully.

"Well done, Tom," said a deep and familiar voice behind them. "There

85

is often a puzzle to solve at this point. I think I'm getting a bit long in the tooth for this secret agent stuff. It's all so predictable." Lucifer yawned, opening his mouth to reveal a perfect set of sharp white teeth.

"So you've turned up at last," Megan rounded on him. "Why did you desert us like that?"

"I knew you wouldn't need me for a while. There were enough parrots for you to follow. I see you have one with you still." He glanced disapprovingly in the direction of the bird on the bicycle. "And you had Jess," he went on. "Besides, I was still hungry. You must agree Simone does make the most delicious cakes."

"I can cook too," said Megan, feeling aggrieved. Then, after a pause, "Do you belong to those two girls?"

Lucifer laughed, long and throatily. "I don't belong to anybody," he assured her.

"Now those boys have the right idea. Why don't you join them?"

Asiimwe was with Tom, circling the fountain and examining the stones round the edge. They all got very wet in the search, and caused great confusion among the poor crabs who were trying to guide them. Alex decided three was more than enough for this task and enjoyed himself hugely, weaving his bike in and out of the spray.

Asiimwe stood back and it was then he noticed that one of the stones looked as if it had recently been moved, and not by them; the moss holding it in place was disturbed. Tom went over to help him lift the stone. On the underside were some letters, carved into the rock.

"Yess!" he shouted. "Over here!"

"Oh, well done," said Megan, still in a bad humour over Lucifer's perceived disloyalty. "Now you've told the baboons all about it."

Indeed, there were many curious faces in the leaves above them.

Megan moved nearer to take a look. Even Alex got off his bike and joined the others.

"What does it say?"

"It's some sort of code."

"Come on Tom, you've got brains," teased Alex.

"Not specially," retorted Tom. Ever since that school in Ilpington, he didn't like people to refer to his brains.

"Well, each symbol must stand for a letter," suggested Megan.

"Probably," agreed her brother, "but which letter?"

For some time they surveyed the symbols in silence. It was clear the sparkats weren't going to help. Both had fallen asleep beside the pool.

"I think I've got it," said Asiimwe. "It's based on a pattern. I saw something like it in one of Mr Karumu's old magazines." He explained how the squares and dots were arranged.

"You make a noughts and crosses grid, like this." He drew one with his finger in the sand at the edge of the pool. "Add dots to each square. And each letter is represented by a dot in a different part of the grid." Asiimwe continued drawing and talking while the others looked on, puzzled expressions on all their faces. Pleased with himself, Asiimwe decoded the clue and read out the answer.

"A cup of green, a cup of blue,

"Mix the two, make a different hue."

Tom took a couple of beakers from his rucksack. He held the first under the blue spray.

"It's just ordinary water," he complained.

"Try the green one."

"Again, just ordinary water."

"Now mix the two," said Alex, suddenly seeing the solution.

As soon as the two liquids combined the water took on a deep aquamarine colour. Megan put in her hand and brought out a perfect turquoise raindrop that turned to crystal in her palm. A broad smile spread across her freckled face.

"Well done," beamed Jessica. "You have the first item for Creation world. Keep the treasure safe."

Megan placed the crystal in the deep pocket Holly had made in her favourite skirt.

"What about the baboons?" protested Alex.

The animals were all around them, watching, looking confused. Clearly they had no idea about codes.

"Let's leave them a false code," grinned Tom. "It'll keep them busy. I know one with letters. You use the letter two places in front of the real one." He started scratching the message onto one of the stones. "The answer's purple," he laughed.

They turned to pick up their bicycles.

As they did so a commotion erupted behind them. A gaggle of disorganized baboons descended on the fountain, squabbling. They overturned rocks and hefted them heedlessly into the surrounding bush. For a few moments the surfers watched in amazement the coloured disorder.

The parrot that had previously been on Megan's handlebars now flew from the trees to alight on her shoulder.

"Could you shift into a baboon?" laughed Megan, addressing Jessica.

"I could if I wanted to," said Jessica disdainfully.

"Can you shift into anything?" persisted Megan.

"Well yes, in theory." Lucifer joined in. "Anything too big or too small can be very painful. All that stretching and shrinking." Lucifer shuddered at remembrance of the house martin episode. "As I said before, we shift best into different members of the cat family."

"Could you do a lion?" Megan was wide-eyed.

"Easy," replied Lucifer. His face became longer and squarer. He grew a ragged mane and the shifting spread to his tail. He let out a fearful roar. The surfers took a step back.

"But no tigers," Jessica reminded him firmly.

"Why no tigers?" Tom wanted to know.

"Because Double O Four is a tiger, and it would be disrespectful."

Lucifer sneered, and his lion lips curled down. He would like to have shifted to a tiger. He realized, with a jolt, that he didn't really respect any creature. He quickly shifted back to a sparkat.

"Hey you, stop, come back here!" Alex was on his feet, and Asiimwe right behind him, racing along the path where four baboons, on the bikes, disappeared round a bend, gibbering their delight.

"Come on you two, after them!"

The baboons had little idea how to manage a bicycle, especially at high speed, and Megan's was soon discarded by the wayside, its yellow rider nursing an injured arm and sobbing.

"Give it to me," shouted Alex to his sister. Mounting the machine that was far too small for him, he set off in pursuit of the other three baboons.

One by one, these abandoned their steeds and made for the forest where they felt on safer ground. The last to give up was a larger, violet, more adventurous fellow, but even he finally came to grief on Tom's bicycle. Looking back at his pursuer, he hit a rock in the path and sailed over the handlebars. Landing in the soft earth, he quickly scrambled to his feet and leaped into the nearest tree from where he watched the scene below. Chortling excitedly, he pelted the surfers with small hard berries and mocking laughter. They, panting with exertion, picked up their bikes while trying to avoid the missiles hurled in their direction.

"Look at my wheel," shouted Tom. He held up his hands in despair. "Just look what they've done to my bike!"

Fury etched in every line of his face, he hurled rocks and stones and twigs at the colourful baboons which were convulsed with laughter. His frenzy grew and he kicked at the base of the tree where they had taken refuge.

"Hang on," said Alex, "they're only baboons."

"They broke my bike, the bike my dad gave me." Tom's anger turned to sobs. He sat down and wept, his head in his hands. Megan picked up his bike. She and Asiimwe tried, without success, to straighten the wheel.

The sky was turning from blue to indigo as the subdued party made its way home to Bioworld.

18 Back Home

"What's that parrot doing in this classroom?" bawled Mr Karumu. Megan shook herself. "I'm sorry sir, I'll take him outside. Come on Percival."

She suddenly made up the name, hardly able to conceal her delight that he had returned from Rainbow world with her.

It was lunchtime, and the class dismissed.

"We're back."

"How did we get here?"

"No idea."

"It's only lunchtime. It was early evening when we left."

"Can we have gone back in time?"

"Unless we're in a different day."

"No, it's still Friday. Look, they're taking the desks out of the classrooms."

"So, we *have* gone back in time?"

"Why not? Time can work either way."

"That means we have to do the smearing all over again. Oh no!"

On Friday afternoons the upper classes had no academic lessons. Instead the time was spent preparing the classroom for the next week.

First the room was swept with branches taken from the leylandii trees that marked the boundaries of the school grounds. The choking, sweet-smelling dust permeated clothes and hair, making the sweepers sneeze and their eyes smart.

Next the children went outside to the land where the contented Ankole cows with their wide horns roamed free. They collected large banana leaves from the nearby plantation. They piled the cattle dung onto the leaves and folded them over it. They carried these parcels back to the classroom. Using their hands, they smeared the dung all over the floor. When dry this would create a seal to lay the dust.

Percival, perched on Megan's shoulder, became disorientated when she bent down to pick up her bundle. He squawked and fluttered his wings, and grabbed for support in Asiimwe's curly hair. His feet became entangled and Asiimwe fell forward, sending his sloppy, smelly load flying in all directions.

"You stupid bird!" he shouted at Percival, but there was so much laughter as he stooped to regain his slippery prize that he too joined in. The laughter brought Mr Karumu to the spot where he soon restored order with a few well aimed thwacks on legs.

Finally, it was the turn of the chalkboard. Megan and three other girls mixed together charcoal and leaves, beating them to a pulp with a pestle, before adding water. Two of the younger boys plastered the resulting mixture all over the board to create a fresh new blackness for Monday morning.

Grubby and giggly, they made their way home. Percival, now rather subdued after the fracas he had caused, was back on Megan's shoulder.

"I suppose we're going to meet at the lake again, like we did before," she suggested. I mean, if you live the same time again, it can't have different things in it, or can it?"

"I don't know," said Asiimwe, thoughtfully. "But, if that's true, then we're going to be caught in an endless cycle. An endless cycle of smearing," he repeated with dismay. "Presumably, if we go to Rainbow world again, we'll come back a few hours earlier and do the smearing again and again and again."

A look of horror spread across all three faces.

"Asiimwe!" It was one of his small sisters who called. "Asiimwe, you're needed for chopping wood."

With her was Rebecca.

"Tom," she said, "remember, you're going to supper with Mr Katembe. Mummy says to get home quickly and clean up."

They looked at each other in relief. Time second time around was not going to be the same again.

Tom found his bicycle at home. No longer bright purple, it had re-assumed its standard blue.

I'm glad about that anyway, he thought sulkily. I prefer it blue.

It was with dismay that he noticed the wheel still buckled. He felt the anger rising in him again, this time at himself for having made such a childish scene in front of his new friends. But Dad had given him some good tips. Cleaning up for Mr Katembe would have to wait.

He made his way to his father's workshop and immersed himself in carving the rabbits on the box he was making for Megan. He rubbed his hand over the smooth wood and felt its serenity pass into him. He looked at it lovingly, admiring the different shades of brown that made up its individuality. A smile came to his strained face when he thought how pleased Megan would be when the transformation into rabbits was complete. He was determined that she would be able to recognize Peter's unique features immortalized in a beautiful piece of wood.

There, his father found him. He knew what was wrong, for he had seen the battered bicycle outside. Tom didn't tell him what had really happened. Instead he said another boy had been riding the bike.

"And then, Dad, I just lost it," moaned Tom. "And now, Alex and Megan and Asiimwe, they'll all think I'm a baby who has temper tantrums and not be friends with me anymore, and …."

There was a crunching sound on the gravel outside as three bikes swerved to a halt.

"We've come to see what can be done with your bike." Alex's tall frame with its cheerful grin filled the doorway.

Alex and Megan and Jessica sat round the dying embers of the fire that Steve had lit for the barbecue supper they had all just enjoyed. Megan pulled out the turquoise coloured crystal from her pocket.

"It's beautiful." She held it up in front of her.

"Watch out the baboons don't see it," warned Alex, amazed at himself for the enthusiasm he was beginning to show. He pushed his hand through his brown hair and tossed it from his eyes.

"I think I'm finally in on this," he said, and smiled.

"You see, Jess," said Megan, squeezing her far too hard, "Alex really is an OK brother."

"I wouldn't worry about the baboons." Jessica peered out into the night. "They'll wait until we have all seven treasures before they strike. Until then they'll simply watch. After all they have the 'ody' itself, and that's very much in their favour. We only have an impression of it. In the end we will need the real thing. We will have to take it from them." For a moment, Jessica looked worried.

"I wonder if they managed to break our code," mused Megan.

"I doubt it," smiled Jessica.

"But I hope they did," went on Megan. "Then they'll have a purple crystal!"

"We need to keep our treasures somewhere safe." Jessica was thinking aloud.

"I know," said Megan, "I've got a money belt that I could wear all the time."
She ran inside to fetch it.

"That's just the thing." Jessica was pleased.

Megan clipped the belt round her waist, put the crystal carefully inside it, and zipped it shut.

Jessica went to the edge of the veranda where she had the clearest view of the stars. She rubbed gently behind her left ear until she had the phone in her hand. She dialled Control and reported the success of the mission in Rainbow world. The message that came back made her blush so that the white fur of her face went quite pink.

"Well," declared Steve, putting down the barbecue tools he was carrying, "that's a natty little phone." He picked up the instrument that Jessica had left on the veranda, intending to charge it later from the stars. Megan and Jessica froze in horror. Jessica cursed her carelessness.

Fortunately Percival saved the situation by creating a diversion. He flew onto Steve's head of thick red hair and squawked with all his might.

"Get that parrot out of my hair!" roared Steve.

Megan leaped to her feet and retrieved both parrot and phone.

"The phone belongs to a friend," she said, pushing it hurriedly under a cushion.

Her father looked at her suspiciously and picked up the tools again.

"Oh, Jess," said Megan when he'd gone, "we must be more careful."

The two clung to each other in happy relief.

19 Supper with the LC1

The LC1, Local Councillor 1, was an important man in the village, and Duncan was pleased to have established already, a good rapport with the one recently elected. He very much approved of this system of local government. A group of households got together and elected an LC5. From their ranks were elected the LC4s, from them the LC3s, and so on up the scale to the top man, LC1, who in this case was Mr Katembe.

When he heard of Tom's arrival, he insisted on holding a welcome supper for the boy in his own home. He told the family that one of his sons would arrive at 6pm to escort them to his house. Under Priscilla's supervision, Tom scrubbed the smell of dung and charcoal from his body as thoroughly as he could, and put on fresh clothes. At 7pm Deus arrived and chattered amiably about his studies at Makerere University as they walked the length of the village to his house.

Tom was a little in awe at his first experience of formal Ugandan hospitality, and honoured too. He was the only child invited. The twins and the others remained at home with the house girl.

Round the door of the Katembe home grew passionflowers and trumpet shaped blooms of which no one seemed to know the name. They were welcomed on the threshold by Mr Katembe, a somewhat stern-faced man, and his very large and jolly wife, wearing colourful traditional dress. They moved inside, into a big square room.

It had a small table in the middle, covered in white cloths, decorated with hand-embroidered flowers. Round the edge of the room were easy chairs with blue cushions. Across the backs of each one were blue and white crochet squares.

"Please sit." Mr Katembe indicated the chairs. "You take soda?"

"Thank you," said Duncan.

There was a scurry outside and a teenage girl entered the room. She carried a tray laid out with five bottles of soda, a bottle opener and a packet of straws. She distributed these to the visitors, and to her father, and to Deus.

While they drank Mr Katembe talked of the village which he served and the people who lived there, and of his business. He was a small trader in the town and also had interests in a construction firm. Many of his remarks he addressed to Tom who did his best to appear knowledgeable and interested. But soon, to Tom's great relief, he lapsed into discussing tea estate matters with Duncan.

A young girl in a red dress came into the room and knelt on the floor before her father. Tom recognized her as one of his classmates. She said something in Runyankore to which her father replied, and then she was gone.

"Now I would like you to meet my children," announced Mr Katembe. "You will surely have met some of them already at school," he added, turning to Tom and smiling for the first time.

In filed eight young people, with Deus making nine – five boys and four girls. They graciously introduced themselves, the girls giving slight curtsies to the adults, and the younger ones giggling at Tom who smirked back, embarrassed. Deus was the second oldest. There was a girl before him. She held a baby in her arms; at twenty two already married and widowed.

Immediately they had finished speaking they disappeared into another room. But one of the boys came back with two photograph albums that he placed in front of Priscilla. Mrs Katembe was a cousin of Priscilla's. On most occasions Priscilla would have retreated with her to the cook-house to help prepare the meal and chat happily while the men discussed business; but this was a formal occasion and she knew that Mrs Katembe would want her to play the visitor.

Tom soon grew tired of wading through pictures of people he didn't know who all seemed to look the same, standing or sitting in similar postures, wearing their best clothes. His gaze began to stray around the room. There were three pictures on the unpainted walls. One was an old wedding photograph, a very much younger Mr and Mrs Katembe. Then there was a picture of the Pope. And lastly there was a calendar, the dates on the lower half, the upper half taken up with a photograph of a beaming Yoweri Kaguta Museveni. Tom had no problem at all in recognizing him. His face could be found smiling broadly in very many places, public and private. Tucked in behind the calendar was a small flag: the black, red and gold of Uganda with the crested crane in the middle.

Suddenly everything burst into life.

A procession of children brought in the meal.

There were dishes, topped with other dishes; and enamelled red cooking pots; and cleverly patterned African baskets with lids.

One of the older girls spread a papyrus mat at the far end of the room. She laid some plates and forks on the mat, and placed others on the table. She hurried to ask something of her father, down on one knee to make the request.

The older boys and girls sat at the table, with their parents and the guests. The four younger children and the two house girls knelt on the mat. Tom was relieved to have beside him Tumwesigye, a boy from his class whom he already knew quite well through football and from visits to the bike track.

One of the smaller children came round with a jerrycan of water, and a bowl, and a piece of soap. Visiting each one in turn, she poured water onto the hands of her parents and the guests and her older brothers and sisters while they lathered the soap. There was no towel so Tom wiped his hands on his shorts.

Lids were removed from all the dishes to reveal a sumptuous feast. There was meat, always a sign of a special occasion. What kind of meat? wondered Tom.

As if reading his mind, Mrs Katembe told him it was goat.

There were all sorts of bits and pieces in the meat pot, floating around in the water in which they had been boiled. Tom didn't quite like the look of some of them. He picked out a few that seemed to be slightly more meat than gristle and put them on his plate. There was rice and sweet potatoes and matooke. Tom was already very familiar with matooke – plantains, peeled and steamed in banana leaves; it was an everyday food in this part of Uganda. In the baskets there was oburu, a real treat. Brown in colour, it was millet and cassava flour mixed with water to form a kind of bread. It was sticky and warm; you pulled off a piece with your fingers and rolled it into a ball. Then there was cabbage and tomatoes, and more soda, and beer for the adults.

On a small plate was a pile of rock salt that Mr Katembe spread generously over all his food. Although those at the table were given forks, much was eaten with fingers. Tom soon discovered that was the only way to tackle both oburu and meat. He grinned at a little boy on the mat who grinned back at him.

After the meal the children were lined up to sing a song of welcome for Tom, each voice perfectly pitched and in no need of accompaniment. Tom stuttered his embarrassed thanks.

Next came the speeches. Mr Katembe welcomed Tom and quickly moved on to talk about his new position as LC1. He hoped the village would continue to have good relations with the tea estate, and he looked forward to working with the organization, in the person of his friend, Duncan Anderson. Duncan replied by saying how pleased he was that Mr Katembe had been elected and he hoped for continued harmonious relations between village and estate in the future. He thanked Mrs Katembe for the wonderful meal, and the whole family for their hospitality, and the children for their singing.

Tom felt Priscilla nudge him. Tumwesigye caught his arm and pulled him to his feet. He couldn't escape from the realization that he too was expected to make a speech. After all he was the guest of honour. Although he couldn't help thinking that he was the excuse for his father and Mr Katembe to get together.

He looked at the sea of faces, expectantly turned towards him, and mumbled his thanks. And then he said what he truly meant, that the few weeks he had already spent in Uganda had been amongst the happiest in his life; everyone had welcomed him with sincerity and he had made many friends of all ages. Duncan led the applause that followed, and that was clearly the signal for formality to cease.

The adults abandoned themselves to further talk and beer drinking. Tumwesigye retrieved a football from under the table and went outside, Tom and the rest of the children following him.

Much later the family made their way home, all content that everyone had enjoyed a good evening. Their path was illuminated by a full moon that dimmed the stars and turned the trees into dark green giants. An owl hooted, and far off a fox cried.

Lucifer watched the family return as he had watched them leave.

Just before they reached the gate to the garden, Mzee appeared to bid them good night. Tom noticed he had the bow and arrows in a quiver on his back. Tom wondered again if he had ever actually fired one of those arrows, at a person or even an animal, and he knew he had.

20 Snowflake

Asiimwe's family was a large one; he had two sisters and three brothers. Like so many others in the village, they were orphans. AIDS had stolen their father and mother soon after the youngest was born. But these orphans were luckier than most. Asiimwe and his brothers and sisters moved in with their grandparents who cared for them.

Their grandfather, Amos, still strong at sixty years old, not only oversaw his own small farm, but also held down a good job as manager of the tea estate. His two sons did much of the work on the farm, helped at times by the younger children.

Amos dearly loved his busy, happy wife, Perpetwa, who cared so generously for her huge family. Unusually, she was not from these parts; she was a Masai from Tanzania. It had been hard for her at first, very hard, settling down in a strange land with different customs and ways; but she had never regretted it, and thought herself the luckiest woman alive to be married to Amos.

Their large, rambling house had an extensive garden, full of fragrant bougainvillea and hibiscus and many other plants that had found their way there from the bush behind. Beyond the flowers were the crops – beans, millet, cassava, sweet potatoes, cabbages, tomatoes – and behind them the banana plantation and the pineapples.

The family owned twenty cows and a number of goats and chickens. Favourite of all, with Perpetwa, were the ducks. She kept them for their eggs and, when they became old, they finished up on the table.

On the other side of the house was a yard and, across that, the cookhouse. This was where Megan loved to go and help Kukunda, Perpetwa's housekeeper, prepare the many meals amid the wood smoke. Two of her young granddaughters helped her for there were many mouths to feed.

She cooked in the traditional way, over open wood fires, each set in a ring of three stones. The smoke from the blackened pans curled out through the holes just below the darkened thatch roof. Pieces of burnt thatch would sometimes fall into the pot below and be stirred into the meal by one of the girls. This caused Megan some concern that highly amused Kukunda.

"It tastes better that way," she vowed.

Kukunda and the girls were always pleased to see Megan's freckled face, surrounded by its fiery curls, peer round the door.

"Come to help, have you?"

Megan left the sunshine where she had been playing with the younger children and took a ladle from its place on the wall. She surveyed the array of pots already being prepared, so early in the morning. Somebody special must be coming for lunch.

Always welcoming, Perpetwa said,

"I'm so pleased you've come, Megan. Amos' brother and his wife will be visiting for lunch, so we're making a few extra dishes. Could you help peel the matooke?"

Megan picked up a sharp knife and sat down beside Toppie, Asiimwe's twin sister and the recipient of many of Alex's songs. Together they worked on the pile before them. With practised hands they used the knives to peel the stiff green skins from the plantains. These they packed tightly into a large pot that they covered with banana leaves. They added water to the pot and heaved it onto one of the fires and so set the matooke steaming, which it would continue to do until it acquired the consistency of mashed potato.

Next, Megan turned her attention to the rock salt, an expensive and much prized addition to the meal. She picked up the biggest chunk, placed it in a small wooden bowl and attacked it with a large hammer.

"Make sure you get it good and fine and even," Kukunda called out to her.

Megan knew that you rarely see a Ugandan man in the kitchen, but young boys are always made welcome and set to work. One of Asiimwe's younger brothers was pounding the millet in a mortar with a huge pestle. The dust wafted into his nose and made him sneeze. Asiimwe was too old for kitchens and of him there was no sign.

But no one was too old to fetch water.

It was down by the well that Asiimwe and Tom bumped into each other. Asiimwe had a couple of heavy pails that Tom helped carry up the hill to the house.

It was still early and fairly cool, and a thick mist reached down into the hollows. Soon the sun would burn it off and send its scorching rays to parch the land but, for now, the earth rested in the gentle fresh damp-ness of early morning. Half way up the hill the boys stopped to rest. Tom looked out across the misty valley and thought again how beautiful this land was, with the rolling unspoiled hills and endless unpolluted sky.

He peered into the bucket of water. It was so clear you almost couldn't see it was there. Only the moving ripples from the struggle up the hill betrayed its presence. His reflection looked back up at him, slightly wavy at the edges.

"Asiimwe," he began warily, "what did you make of our visit to Rainbow world?"

His friend was thoughtful.

"I'm not sure. I know it was real. I know we couldn't all four have dreamed the same thing. It's not that I don't believe in other worlds and such like. I've always believed in them, most Africans do. It's just I'm not sure we should meddle with them. Magic can bring harm to ourselves and to those we love. That is what our culture teaches." He paused to gaze out over the countryside, and then turned back to Tom, "But, if it's science and not magic, well then ......" and his eyes twinkled.

"There was certainly no harm in Rainbow world," Tom remembered. "All those colours, and that beautiful fountain."

"But Rainbow world is only one. There are other items to be collected."

"But what we're doing is important. We're trying to prevent some terrible disease from overtaking our world. We're on the side of good."

"Are we?" Asiimwe was surprised that anyone could be so very confident about it all.

"Surely you don't think the sparkats have evil intentions?"

"No, of course I don't." Asiimwe was reassuring. The wide grin that always encompassed his eyes spread to the rest of his face.

"So, you're still with us?"

"Course I am!" he grinned. "Come on. Let's get this water to the top of the hill."

"Remember! Water is the element that magnifies and reflects and clarifies." Tom mimicked Lucifer's gravelly voice almost perfectly, so that they both laughed. "This water's so clear. Let's use it for the next clue."

"Shouldn't we wait for the sparkats and the others?"

"Don't see why. We can read the message as well as they can, and I've got the mirror in my pocket." Tom chuckled at his own arrogance.

Glancing round for baboons and seeing none, Tom took the beautifully framed mirror from his much pocketed jeans.

"Look, the screen savers are still in the mirror, as the sparkats said they would be."

The two boys concentrated on the restless spirits swaying up and down the glass.

"That's strange," muttered Tom, "there are two jewels in the frame. There was only one before. There's a turquoise one as well as the rainbow one."

Curious, Asiimwe peered over Tom's shoulder. He pressed the rainbow jewel.

Nothing happened.

"Obviously we must press the new one," he decided. "The one from the world we've just visited."

He did so and the slowly spinning disc, that now had only six segments remaining, swung into view, in front of the screen savers.

"We need the second hieroglyph," said Tom. "They're still in the wrong order. I suppose that's to make it more difficult," he grinned. "One times ten, that's ten of course – the upside down horse shoe." He pointed to the symbol. "I wonder what the spirits would do if we put the water in the wrong place?"

"Don't call them spirits," objected Asiimwe. "They're screen savers."

Tom grinned at him and carefully dropped a small amount of water over the part with the horse shoe. As before, that segment increased in size, sending the others out towards the frame and into oblivion.

"Eight dots, same as last time."

"Yes," agreed Asiimwe, "but they're in a different order. The first group were scattered at random; these are arranged in a hexagon, just two floating free."

Silently, chased by the screen savers, the two free dots did their work. They moved with great sweeps from one side of the mirror to the other. As they crossed their paths over and over again, they left behind them trails of white dust, until Tom exclaimed excitedly,

"A snowflake! They've made a snowflake!" He turned to Asiimwe. "Do you know about snowflakes?" he ventured.

He didn't want to patronize his friend, but surely it never snowed on the Equator? Asiimwe smiled patiently.

"What's that over there?" He pointed to the Mountains of the Moon in the massive range of the Rwenzoris. Their jagged heights rose to split the clouds. They were capped with glittering snow. "But," he admitted, "I've never seen a single flake on its own, not even in a book. Do they really look like this?" He was amazed.

"Well, yeah, but only under a microscope."

The two boys watched the snowflake move to the top of the mirror.

"What does it mean for us?" wondered Tom.

"I've no idea. We're going to have ask Zero One Zero after all." They laughed. "But come on, they'll be waiting for the water at home."

They arrived at Asiimwe's place to find Alex, beneath the bougainvillea, serenading Toppie with his new song. Everyone else was working at preparing lunch and setting out furniture, activities of which the couple seemed quite oblivious. Tom made a move towards them.

"Let them be," said Perpetwa, "and help me with these chairs."

"But I've already done it," complained Jessica. "I did it last night."

"And you shouldn't have done without me." Lucifer was quite put out. "Anyway that was in the dark. You need to learn to do it in the daytime when there are no stars to guide you. I've things I'd like to add – about the parrots," he said unconvincingly. "So try again."

Zero One Zero was on the veranda, busy instructing Zero Six Six on how to communicate the details of what they had already achieved back to Control. Jessica was having problems with the calculations she needed to do, to work out where the stars that sent the signals would have been had they been shining.

"You need the practice," said Lucifer. "And if we keep in close contact with Control, it shows them that we are still around and working, and ensures that everyone will be duly appreciative when it's all over and rewards are distributed."

The sparkats were interrupted by the excited chatter of three children.

"Tom and Asiimwe have already looked in the mirror and seen a snowflake," panted Megan.

"Have they indeed?" Lucifer was feeling prickly. "And what do they make of that?"

"Nothing yet. We thought you could help."

"That's what we're here for, after all. I might add that it would have been polite to wait for us in the first place. But now you've done it, let's see what we have."

He took the mirror from Tom's hands.

"Just suppose," suggested Tom, "we couldn't sort out the meaning of the snowflake. Could we go for the third item first? What would happen if we sprinkled water on number three?"

"Nothing. Nothing at all. Remember, the mirror belongs to Control." He shot a questioning glance in Jessica's direction. "Control kept the second clue hidden until we reported success with the first, and they'll hide the third until we register success with the second, and so on. Everything must be done in the correct order. It sometimes seems to us that the universe is chaotic, but that's only on the surface, the superficial things like man's moods or the weather. Deep down there is a fierce order that permeates everything. And we are dealing with the DNA of life," he finished mysteriously. He meant to subdue them and, looking at their faces, saw that he had succeeded. His good humour returned.

"Where's Alex?" Jessica wanted to know.

"He's singing love songs to Toppie," volunteered Megan, giggling.

"Maybe he's not very committed to our cause?" wondered Lucifer.

"Oh yeah? Who says?"

Hot and dishevelled, Alex jumped from his bike and approached the veranda. At the same time Percival flew from the top of the roof to land heavily on the railing beside Megan.

"I see you've still got that parrot," observed Lucifer disapprovingly.

"He's my new pet," said Megan, stroking his golden head. "I'm going to teach him to talk. Why, don't you like him?"

"He's OK I suppose. It's just that I'm a cat and he's a bird."

Megan smiled and winked at Percival who bent down to pull pieces of fluff from between his claws, mumbling to himself as he did so.

"Well, what do you make of this snowflake then?" asked Lucifer, turning his attention back to the mirror.

"That's what we're asking you!"

"Lucifer, stop teasing them." Jessica frowned at him. "It's a cold symbol so we're going to Frost world. Not my favourite place at all." She shivered.

"You've been there before?"

"Just once. That mission went all wrong. I was a very new agent then," she added reassuringly, seeing Megan's worried face.

"Is it as easy to get there as it was to get to Rainbow world?" Alex wanted to know.

"Oh yes, all these worlds are easy to get into because they're all on the same planet – Earth."

"Will we go to any other worlds, beyond Earth?" Tom was curious.

"Only at the end. You see this 'ody' is to do with life on Earth so most of the solutions will be here. Now, how do you think we could best enter Frost world?"

"Go somewhere very cold," suggested Megan.

"The Rwenzoris," declared Alex. "But that's a long way, and the mountains are steep and dangerous."

"We don't have to *go* there," explained Lucifer. "Remember we didn't *go* anywhere last time. We simply use the Rwenzoris as an entrance to Frost world. We'll travel by energy as we did before. Energetically, you might say." He smirked to himself. "Let's go one step further. Let's do it all at once." As always, Lucifer revelled in the attention of his audience. "Jess, time to shift ourselves."

And moggie fur turned orange and green.

"Quickly now. Before anyone notices. Hold hands and we'll log on."

Tom and Asiimwe both made a grab for one of Megan's hands and Alex attached himself to Asiimwe.

"Now Tom, you stroke Jess, and Alex stroke me. Remember, do it hard."

The boys stroked firmly over and over again. Expressions of ecstasy passed over the sparkats' faces until sparks shot in all directions, dazzling the eyes.

All went silent. Gone the sound of Moses' axe on logs. Gone the sound of lowing cattle and mocking, chattering birds.

21 Frost World

Tom felt the cold wind on his cheeks and opened his eyes into the vast expanse of silence. He was standing in snow that sparkled and glittered like myriad sequins, far into the distance under an intense blue sky. Behind him were towering fir trees covered in the same silver white glitter. He looked at Megan and the other boys in a line beside him. All were dressed in thick fur coats and boots and hats, and their faces glowed with the cold. They looked each other up and down approvingly.

"Not real fur, I'm thankful to say." The voice came from behind them. And there stood a huge snow leopard.

"Jess?" Megan asked uncertainly.

"That's me. How do you like my new shape?"

"It's brilliant," she exclaimed in delight. She rushed up to the leopard and pushed her fingers deep into the spotted fur. So thick was it, her whole hand disappeared and became deliciously warm. She looked along Jessica's back to the massive tail that trailed on the snow behind her, and then down to the huge heavy paws. Megan turned to see her brother and the others admiring Lucifer.

It seemed they were totally alone in this vast whiteness, until they heard a far off roaring that gradually became louder. Out of the distance, in perfect formation, swept four powerful skimobiles. They threw up clouds of churning snow behind them. Riding these were four burly polar bears, each sporting a colourful scarf and a pair of goggles. In the middle of them was a sleigh; it moved swiftly, gliding over the top of the snow and disturbing it not at all; in stark contrast to the noise and clatter of the snowmobiles.

The sleigh drew to a halt just beside the surfers. It was gunmetal grey, and the cushions on the seats inside were silver and white. Harnessed to it were four shaggy brown ponies with long black manes and tails, which lifted their feet and snorted with impatience as they drew to a halt. Megan stroked the first of the ponies, enjoying its warm breath on her cold hands.

"How beautiful you are," she whispered. The pony whinnied its appreciation. Never one to leave anyone out, Megan greeted the other three in a similar fashion.

Then she thrust her hands inside the sleeves of her beautiful grey fur coat to keep them warm, and found there colourful woolly gloves that she pulled over her freezing fingers.

Alex and Asiimwe were fascinated by the skimobile outriders, and seemed to be about to persuade a polar bear to let them have a ride, when Lucifer interrupted,

"The days don't last long here. Let's get started. Climb into the sleigh."

Asiimwe shivered. He was not used to the cold.

"Where are we going?" he asked, pulling the collar of his coat up round his ears. If Frost world is as big as Bioworld, how do you know which part to go to?"

"Do you remember the position of the snowflake in the mirror?" Lucifer asked him.

"Yes, it moved near the top."

"Exactly. So we're going to the top of this world. It's the only part that is really inhabited anyway. Have faith. Once we get there it will become obvious how we must proceed." He spoke with all the conviction of a veteran of many missions.

Alex glanced towards the polar bear to whom he had been speaking, and then back to Lucifer.

"I'd like to ride a skimobile instead."

"Me too," added Asiimwe enthusiastically.

"I suppose that'll be all right," growled Lucifer, clearly wondering why the request had been made when the sleigh was so comfortable. Alex and Asiimwe struggled through the powdery snow to the skimobiles. The polar bears helped them up behind, passed back goggles, and indicated they hold on tight.

"Now I hope you two aren't going to be difficult as well," remonstrated Lucifer, turning to Megan and Tom.

"Well," declared Tom, "I was wondering if I could ride one of you."

"You'd better get this out of your system," decided Lucifer wisely, and not at all displeased at the interest his leopard shape was causing. "Megan, you mount Jess. Tom get up on my back." He lay down in the snow to enable Tom to climb into the fur. It was so thick that he couldn't feel the body beneath, and was quite insecure.

With a great bound, Lucifer set off, racing across the snowfields, his paws hiding himself and his rider in a flurry of whiteness. Tom could see nothing but blinding snow and ice particles that cut and stung his face and hands. He clung on for his very life as the ride became ever faster. Mounting the top of a ridge, Lucifer jumped, and they were flying through the air. Tom lost his seat but hung onto the fur. He and the snow leopard landed in a heap at the bottom of the jump. They rolled over and over in the snow and lay there laughing. Jessica followed him with Megan aboard. Asiimwe and Alex climbed down from their skimobiles to join in the fun.

When everyone had had their turn and pelted each other with snowballs, Lucifer became serious again and suggested they get on with the mission. Tom and Megan allowed themselves to be ushered into the sleigh, while Alex and Asiimwe returned to their skimobiles. Megan was surprised to find there was already a passenger aboard the sleigh. A penguin sat on one of the seats.

"That's Percival," explained Jessica, "I taught him how to shift."

"I wish you hadn't done that," retorted Lucifer. "The fewer creatures who know what we're about the better."

"He's pretty harmless," protested Jessica.

And indeed he did look very docile, hanging his head beside Megan. Lucifer scowled beneath his fur.

He opened his mouth and snarled. This was clearly a signal of some kind.

The driver for the sleigh appeared from the surrounding pine trees, looking very flustered.

"I'm so glad you delayed your departure," he panted. "I was so sure I was going to be late. Couldn't get out of bed this morning, and I've been behind all day. It's the worry you see. And my brain is so flustered by all the talking. And now I'm not even sure I can remember the way."

Lucifer's emerald eyes were full of disdain. They roved over the large white rabbit with his watery blue eyes and droopy ears. The rabbit flinched under the gaze of the powerful cat.

"The way to where?" asked Tom.

"The way there," explained the confused rabbit. "So I've asked pine marten to help with the driving."

From the same opening in the woods emerged a long, thin, very white and sleek pine marten with intense busy eyes and twitching whiskers. His head bobbed from side to side as he looked the party up and down.

Ever since his appearance, Megan had been gazing at the rabbit in disbelief; examining, in particular, his ears that had black tips to them.

"I know you," she said slowly, with increasing delight. "You're Snowball, aren't you?"

The pathetic creature looked thankfully in the direction of the kind voice.

"He's about three times the size of Snowball," laughed Alex.

"He's Snowball all the same," insisted Megan. She put out her hand to stroke the agitated animal that shrank from her touch.

"Don't be afraid of me," she soothed. Gradually the rabbit became calmer, looking up at this hint of kindness in a cruel world, gratitude in his unhappy eyes.

"Do let's get on," growled Lucifer.

"There aren't any humans here?" observed Megan to the pine marten driver.

"They got rid of those a long time ago in this world; destroyed their habitats; made them extinct."

"How dreadful."

"Just about as dreadful as what humanoids are doing to other species in your Bioworld."

Megan grew thoughtful.

"But deep in the caves …," the pine marten continued. "But then you'll find out about them when you meet them," he finished mysteriously.

The runners of the sleigh hissed as it sped across the snow. The four ponies cantered in unison, their feet skimming the surface, and the ride was smooth. The two massive snow leopards loped behind, the pace of the ponies slow and easy for them. On either side the skimobiles roared furiously, in a mechanical effort to keep up with the flowing gait of the animals.

Megan couldn't take her eyes off the rabbit beside her. He was clearly extremely distressed. She put her arms around him in a gesture of comfort.

The pine marten proved himself an excellent driver and used the reins to coax the ponies as if he had been doing so all his short life.

The terrain changed. Open snowfields gave way to trees that stretched so high they left only a narrow strip of sky above. It became intensely cold. The ponies' hoofs thudded on. Megan lost her high spirits and began to feel prickly and uncomfortable.

"We're being watched," she said.

In the trees were crows that looked down from the topmost branches, but it wasn't these that disturbed her. It was the squirrels, lots of them. They kept up with the sleigh, jumping from tree to tree and peering at the travellers from behind the trunks. Occasionally, they chattered to each other and ground their teeth.

"Perhaps they're baboons?" suggested Tom. "They want to find out about the second item."

"Can baboons shift shape?" wondered Megan.

108

"I expect so. If they're working for Cassius, I expect he'll have taught them that trick. It doesn't seem to be such a big deal for most of these animals."

Eventually the trees thinned out again and the travellers found themselves in an open hilly landscape that climbed with every step. At the top of the rise Lucifer called a halt. He instructed the driver to unharness the ponies. From underneath the sleigh, he took out bales of hay for them to eat.

"Look under your feet," he said to Megan.

Megan pulled out a large metal box. Inside were some biscuits and a bottle of what looked like water. There were also cups and plates.

"How thoughtful," she exclaimed. "Was that you, Lucifer?"

"No, not me," he laughed.

"Well, it was in a way," explained Jessica. "We ordered it all when we reported in to Control this morning."

Tom held the glasses while Megan poured the liquid. Asiimwe and Alex, covered from head to toe in fine white powder so that they resembled abominable snowmen, were famished with the cold and already helping themselves to the biscuits. These were white in colour and felt to be frozen solid but, when they sank their teeth into them, they melted and hot soup warmed their throats and stomachs. They drank the water but it was hot chocolate that coursed through their bodies.

"This is wonderful," sighed Megan, happily feeding bits of biscuit to Percival. "But what about you?"

"Oh, we'll sort out our own lunch, won't we, Jess?"

"Yes, right away."

Jessica lolloped over to a group of trees to their left. There was a scuffle and a scream that stopped the children in mid-bite. Then Jessica emerged with two grey squirrels hanging from her mouth.

"Those'll do for starters," said Lucifer.

Megan stared at him in horror.

"Do you really expect big cats to live on biscuits?" he snarled, tearing at the flesh of a dead squirrel where the red blood was mingling with the white snow.

"Come on Megan, get real." Alex gave her a good-natured prod. He watched the cats, fascinated. There was something pink and sloppy stuck in the fur on Lucifer's chin. Megan turned away until the crunching should be over. She pulled her hat down over her ears. The whole scene had quite put her off her soup and chocolate.

"Those squirrels," Tom wanted to be quite sure, "are they baboons from Bioworld? They have the same gleaming eyes."

"'Fraid so." Lucifer spoke between mouthfuls. "They probably plan to follow us until we find the next item, and then try to steal it from us. They're an intrusion, nothing more."

"Apart from a remarkably good lunch," added Jessica.

"Perhaps we should eat as many as we can, eh Jess? Sort of meals on wheels for us."

"Or meals on paws."

And the two big cats laughed throatily at their own jokes.

"Time to move. There is much darkness in this world. And that brings with it intense cold." Lucifer looked around. "Where's that rabbit?"

Snowball appeared from the trees, panting and confused as before, the pine marten following him.

"Where've you been?" Lucifer was suspicious. "Don't you understand the importance of this mission in which you're involved?"

Snowball wrung his paws apologetically and climbed into the sleigh, mumbling about important business.

"This is the only important business of the moment," said Lucifer firmly. "Now, for the last time, let's get on."

The convoy moved along a wide track with trees on either side.

Suddenly there was the sound of a scuffle, muffled shrieks and thuds. Lucifer and Jessica stopped, snarling to the pine marten to do the same. The skimobiles braked hard and toppled over in a flurry of whiteness. Alex and Asiimwe were hauled from their seats by two brown bears who dragged them through the snow, kicking and struggling, towards the trees. The polar bears onto whom they had been clinging were on their backs in the snow, their skimobiles on top of them.

22 Rabbits

L ucifer and Jessica raced for the trees but could see nothing. They returned to ensure that Megan and Tom, at least, were safe. Indeed they were. The pine marten, as instructed, had pulled the sleigh to a halt on hearing the scuffle, and was now guiding it back to the dismounted outriders. Percival peered cautiously from under the hem of Megan's coat.

"What's happening?" asked Megan, horrified.

"You might well ask," snarled an angry Lucifer. "Why do we have outriders? To protect the vehicle in the middle. So what is the point of those being protected riding with the outriders? You humanoids, always have to do things your way." Lucifer's green eyes glinted stonily.

"Don't worry, Megan," said Jessica. "It's not your fault. Nor Tom's," she added, looking at his concerned face. We should have insisted that Alex and Asiimwe ride in the sleigh."

Lucifer was growling deep in his throat, his frustration clear for all to see.

"But where are they?" Megan sounded desperate. "Are the bears going to eat them?"

"I doubt it," said Jessica. "Humanoids are usually pretty stringy."

"How are we going to get them back?"

"First of all we need to work out *why* they were taken," said Jessica. "Then we'll find it easier to work out *where* they've been taken."

"Are the squirrels involved in this?" wondered Tom, hunching his shoulders and stamping his feet against the biting wind that had suddenly blown up.

"Probably not. They are content to watch. And bears and squirrels don't make for a good partnership."

Lucifer suddenly stopped growling and looked up to the sleigh where the pine marten and the rabbit were still holding the reins. His emerald eyes covered them. The pine marten did his best to stare back squarely at him, but the rabbit's eyes roved everywhere in desperate confusion.

"You know something about this, don't you?" Lucifer snarled.

He leaped to the sleigh in one huge bound and pulled the hapless rabbit by his neck into the snow. Then he laid the trembling creature between his paws and, looking straight at him, growled, "Tell me."

"Don't hurt him," shrieked Megan, sending Percival flapping as she leaped from the sleigh. Tom was already in the snow beside the terrified animal, stroking and comforting him.

"All right, all right, I'll tell you," sobbed the rabbit. "They won't come to any harm. We've only borrowed them. We didn't have any choice."

And the whole sorry story, mixed with heartrending sobs, poured out of him.

"It's the trolls you see. They're digging a huge underground chamber for the bride of their new king, Stefan. She's coming from beyond the glacier, a troll princess. But their workers are refusing to do the digging because they don't like their new king. He's cruel and mean and greedy. And he's banished his brother, Boris, to the deep forest so he can be king. He shouldn't really be king because Boris is the elder. Do you follow me?" Snowball stuttered to a halt.

"Yes, go on," urged Lucifer, his patience fast running out.

"They needed some new diggers, so they stole our youngsters from the cabbage patch." Snowball's voice rose to a high pitch. "Surrounded it; overcame the mothers and took the youngsters and no one stopped them."

I can well believe that, thought Lucifer, rabbits are so very indecisive.

"And now our babies are held captive down there, locked in an underground dungeon when they're not digging." Here Snowball broke down completely. Lucifer closed his eyes in disgust and it was left to Tom and Megan to reassure and compose the distraught animal. "The king will never let them go. There will always be more digging to do." Snowball turned away to wipe his nose with the back of a paw. "The troll king always teases his enemies horribly. We sent this pine marten here, who is our friend and braver than we are, to ask him to release them. Of course he said 'no' but, to tease us, he said he would give the key of the dungeon to two children of men, and allow them to unlock it. And then he laughed and laughed so that the whole forest shook because, of course, there are no men left in this world; they are all extinct.

"And then brown bear who is so kind .. the brown bears are always good to us rabbits because we saved them once from bears of another world. Do you want to hear that story?"

"Not now," said Lucifer firmly, flexing his claws against Snowball's neck. "Let's get on with this one."

"Well, brown bears are our friends, and when this brown bear...."

"I can guess who that is," said Jessica. "Three Five Seven."

Lucifer glared at the interruption.

"...told us about the sleigh and the human children from Bioworld, he said he didn't think it would matter if we borrowed a couple, just to release our youngsters, and..."

"Why didn't you tell us? Of course we'd have helped you," said Megan gently.

"We didn't know what to do," grizzled Snowball. "We spent the whole night talking. And those snow leopards are so fierce."

Lucifer growled his agreement. Snowball shuddered under Megan's hand.

"We couldn't take the chance," went on Snowball. "So we stole the human children. But we'll bring them back."

"You'll do better than that," snarled Lucifer. "You'll take us to them right now."

"They might even have rescued the little rabbits already," the pine marten tried to reassure Snowball.

"Whether they have or not is immaterial," snarled Lucifer. "You rabbits have too many babies anyway."

"Why do you have to be so mean!" shouted Megan, cuddling the finally released Snowball. "Of course we'll get your little ones back."

"Polar bears, you stay with the sleigh; pine marten too. We'll return very soon," ordered Lucifer. "Come on, Jess, and you two." Lucifer indicated Tom and Megan. "I don't want to lose any more children."

Percival cuddled into pine marten's soft coat. Even in his penguin form he disliked the cold.

Snowball loped at the front. Leopards and children followed him into the darkness of the forest. They soon came to a wide hole in the ground with mounds of freshly dug soil covered in light frost on either side. Snowball led the way downwards, first through layers of earth held rigid by ice, and then through damper, mustier regions that even dripped water from muddy roofs. The tunnel ended in an underground chamber, bordered on all sides by the roots of ancient trees that held the room together in knotty strength. Megan touched an old, gnarled root, and imagined the tree above to which it was giving life and support.

Then she saw them, in the darkness of an annexe to the main room, made up of yet more roots – Asiimwe and Alex held by two brown bears – and in front of them was a group of rabbits. Seated on a dais at the far side huddled the ugliest troll the children had ever seen. His completely round head sprouted black bristles, his eyes bulged and his grey skin was covered all over in warts. He had a large mouth but few teeth. His nose was curved and reached almost to his chin. His hands were small but his nails long and pointed. A stale smell surged in great waves from his body across the airless room. He was flanked by hundreds of smaller

113

trolls, all armed with deadly knives. And he was laughing.

"So, you have brought two men children to unlock the door." He was convulsed by so much laughter that, for a few moments, he couldn't go on. He held his huge stomach and gurgled. "Do you really think I'm going to release my workers so easily? I've changed my mind. I am a king, I can do that. But, seeing as you've brought these children to me, I think I'll keep them. I don't suppose they're much good at digging, but somebody might pay a price for them. It's just a question of finding out who. Maybe...."

He got no further.

With a terrifying roar that brought chunks of earth scattering from the ceiling to the floor below, Lucifer leaped at the ugly little troll. With one lunge of his powerful jaws, he broke his neck and stifled his laughter for ever, in a choking gurgle that shouted his fear. Then, to the horror of all spectators, he pulled off the head, took it in his great mouth, chewed it twice, and then spat it out across the room, shaking his ears and whiskers at the disgusting taste it left in his mouth. Gore and filth spattered everywhere, and a vile stench pervaded the space where the troll king had been sitting.

"Now," he said, "no messing about. Which one of you cowards has the key?" He indicated the hundreds of trolls that lined the room. None spoke. All their goggle eyes displayed fixed terror. "Now," Lucifer repeated. "Or do I have to eat you all?" and he killed the troll beside him with a single blow of his paw.

"Here it is," said the troll next to the one that had died.

"Give it to him," Lucifer indicated Snowball, "and show him the door. Now, you trolls," he said, "get out into the forest and find your rightful king. He will surely serve you better than that heap of foulness."

Relieved, the trolls made to depart.

"Not so fast," warned Lucifer. "Young rabbits first."

The troll wisely showed Snowball the correct door and hundreds of tiny rabbits of all colours teemed out, blinking and twitching their whiskers.

"Ah, look at them," cried Megan, and she and Tom made to move closer.

"Leave them," snarled Lucifer, and they stepped back. "Take them away," he said to Snowball.

Eagerly, Snowball raced back up the tunnel, the young rabbits bounding behind him, tumbling over each other in their eagerness to gain the upper air.

"Now, you trolls, you may go. But not that way." He snarled as the trolls made to follow the rabbits. "Find a different route out of this miserable hole in the ground."

And soon the chamber was empty, but for the children and the leopards and the bears.

"So, Three Five Seven, you decided to use your position for work of your own," Lucifer began. He fixed the grubby creature before him with emerald eyes that bore into his soul. "That is against the rules. Your motives were kindness and friendship but, good though these undoubtedly are, there is little room for them in the Intelligence Service. You will be demoted for this action. Your number will climb to over a thousand." His message finished, Lucifer turned his back.

But the bear had something to say.

"You can keep your Service. I want no part of it any more." His voice was deep and husky. "I would rather be an ordinary bear, and a kind one, than a ruthless agent with no time for friends. I hand in my notice. I resign from the Service."

Lucifer sneered. Megan ran to the bear and gave him a hug. His coat was smelly and greasy, and his breath was sour, but she didn't care.

"You did the right thing," she said. "I'm glad you rescued those rabbits. And I'm glad that evil troll king has gone." The bear stroked her face with a gentle paw and turned away.

"Come on everyone," urged Jessica, "we've important work to do. This was an unnecessary diversion."

Back in the open air, Alex and Asiimwe looked shaken and dishevelled and made no protest when Lucifer insisted that they travel the rest of the way in the sleigh. Percival was still sleeping under the seat when they all climbed in. The pine marten took the reins on his own. The polar bears positioned themselves on their skimobiles, ready to depart.

23 Playing the Game

The blue sky had become black while they were underground, and was covered in a multitude of stars that turned the sequins of the snow to diamonds. The children huddled in their furs; the intense cold bit into their bones. They were silent as they sped across the frozen ice fields, sleigh runners hissing in the frosty air that carried sound far across the frozen solitude.

And then, before them, the night sky erupted in a blaze of light. Great curtains of colour swept from zenith to horizon, fading and deepening by turns.

Like the spirits in the mirror, wondered Tom. He felt in his pocket beneath his furs. The mirror was still there, safe through all the activity. With numb fingers, he pulled it out.

"Look," he called to the others, "it's just the same."

Reflected in the mirror were the silent dancing lights.

The journey over the ice fields seemed unending to the freezing children but eventually their way took them along a sheltered tree-lined track to a narrow gully between high cliffs. The route began to climb, the ponies strained in their harnesses, until their way was barred by a massive door of solid ice. This was the entrance to a huge palace of ice and snow whose conical rooftops extended into the lights above, and disappeared into their swirling splendour. The children gazed up in awe to windows hung with icicles and decorated with enormous snowflakes.

To one side of the door stood a gigantic snowman. His face was creased in a huge friendly smile made of glittering jewels, and his eyes were chunky black coals. The pine marten climbed down from the sleigh and pulled a bunch of cards from under his fur. His brow furrowed in thought, he shuffled through these until he found the one he wanted. He looked intently at this, as if trying to memorize something, and then re-placed all the cards safely under his fur. Next he scrambled up the side of the snowman and onto his shoulder. From that position, he pressed the jewels in the snowman's mouth in turn, clearly following a code. At the sixth press, the decorated ice window above swung open, and a face peered out. It was a lined and friendly face with a long white beard.

"Hang on a minute," it said, and disappeared.

There was the sound of boots on stairs, a key in a lock, and then the heavy door swung open. Framed by light behind stood a tomten. Delighted,

Megan recognized him from a book of Finnish stories her great grand-mother had sent her. The old lady was a native of Finland and was keen that her descendants should know something about that country.

The little man stood about a metre high. He was very round and had short thin legs. He had bright red cheeks, a broad pudgy nose and bushy eyebrows. His untidy beard tumbled down across his bulging tummy. On his long white hair he wore a red pompom hat that fell behind him almost to the floor. He carried a large bunch of keys in his wide rough hands. At his side stood a small barred cat with curious eyes.

"Welcome to the ice palace," he said. His voice was full of friendship. He smiled merrily from sparkling dark eyes.

The travellers, cheered by the warmth of his presence, alighted from the sleigh. They bade farewell to the polar bears and the ponies and the pine marten. Together with Percival and the leopards, the surfers passed through the open doorway that crunched shut behind them. The tomten hung behind to lock it and then made his way to the lead.

"That should keep out the squirrels," remarked Asiimwe with satisfaction.

"Hardly," retorted Jessica. "There are many entrances to this palace, near the roof, that would present no problem to nimble, climbing animals."

"Was that how things went wrong for you before?" Tom wanted to know.

Jessica grimaced in a way that said, 'I'd rather not talk about it'.

They passed along a wide corridor, hung with portraits of spiky characters that looked like variations of Jack Frost, into a high vaulted room. The floor was packed snow that squeaked to the pressure of their boots. The walls were of shining ice – blue and green – and the window was hung with a silver curtain that drooped icicles. The ceiling was compacted snow and from it swung chandeliers, each one a perfect snowflake.

Curious, the children crossed to the window made of transparent ice. They looked through it onto an amazingly reassuring scene. There were small wooden houses, their roofs laden with snow, and fences dividing the land into fields. The many trees were hung with white lights.

"My home," declared the tomten proudly. "Maybe you will visit with me afterwards, but, for now, come this way."

He led them across the floor to an archway cut into the wall beyond. Passing through, they emerged into an enormous hall.

"Here you are," he said. "Here you will find your answer."

"Cool!" squawked Percival.

Everyone turned to stare at the parrot in amazement.

"Percival, you've got it at last!" shrieked Megan in delight. "I've been teaching him that word for days," she explained to the others.

"What else does he know?" asked Alex.

"He should know 'brilliant'," declared Megan hopefully.

"Brilliant!" repeated Percival.

They all laughed and looked to see what it was that had caused Percival to reveal his talents.

The hall was crowded with creatures, the like of which the surfers had never seen. They were made of ice and shaped like snowflakes, each one slightly different from its fellows, just as two snowflakes are never exactly the same. The creatures were animated by little faces in the middle and had six hands, one at the end of each spoke. They talked in high crackly voices in a language the surfers didn't understand, and they were playing board games.

"How cold it is in here," declared Asiimwe. There was a chill beyond what they had experienced outside.

"Of course it's cold," responded Jessica. "If it wasn't cold the ice creatures would melt and die."

"Now," said Lucifer, "as you see these creatures are all of a different design. Find one that looks exactly like that in the mirror."

Only Asiimwe and Tom had actually studied the design. Although they described it to the others, it soon became obvious that they were the ones who would have to make the identification: the designs were all so similar.

Tom took the mirror from his pocket but the snowflake had long since faded. How he wished he had taken more notice when it had first appeared. He pressed the turquoise jewel but nothing happened. Clearly the mirror gave only one chance.

Megan took Percival by the flipper and stared thoughtfully at each group of snowflakes. Some were playing chess, she noticed, some draughts; yet others were busy with ludo or snakes and ladders; but many more were engaged in games she had never seen before.

What had Asiimwe said? 'Basically a hexagon with feathery bits along each spike'. Well, they were all hexagons, and the feathery bits were all different.

Tom and Asiimwe wandered, confused, among the players who never looked up from their task. It was Asiimwe who eventually succeeded.

118

"Come over here, Tom. Isn't this how it was? The arms covered in feathers getting smaller towards the middle?"

"Well, yeah, but there are many like that."

"But this one has those two hooks at the end of the longest feather. Those were definitely in the mirror. Oh, I do wish these creatures would keep still."

"Yeah! You're right! Over here everybody."

All crowded around the two little creatures who were busy playing chess.

"There must be a clue somewhere. Maybe under the board?"

"Come on, Jess," said Lucifer. "Let's leave them to it. Maybe we have time to finish that game we started all those years ago. Can you remember where we were up to?"

"Excuse me. May we just have a look?" Tom asked politely, indicating the board in question. The ice creatures clearly didn't understand.

"I'll lift the board and you look underneath," suggested Alex.

The board was made completely of ice, with some colouring in shades of blue to differentiate the squares. Because of the extreme cold it stuck to Alex's gloves as he lifted it.

"Look, there's writing on it."

Tom bent down and read.

"'Regardez les nombres'. It's in French."

Alex carefully put the board down. He smiled at the two creatures who scowled at him and continued playing with their ice figures.

"Who knows any French?" asked Megan.

It was not a subject taught in rural Uganda. They all looked at Tom.

"We did some French at school in England. This sentence is easy. It says, 'Look at the numbers'."

"What numbers?" asked Megan.

Asiimwe picked up a pawn discarded by the players.

"They have numbers underneath," he declared.

The others crowded round him and picked up other figures. The two ice creatures, thoroughly exasperated at these huge persons spoiling their game, squealed in a high-pitched manner and spat at the intruders.

"Yuk," said Alex, wiping the spittle off his fur.

"What are they all playing games for anyway?"

"Because it's cold outside," suggested Megan, teasing him. Alex pulled a face at her.

The ice creatures sat broodily and icily contemplating the destruction of their chess game.

"They must put numbers on the bottom of all the pieces so they don't get mixed up. This chess game must be game number 7. Look, all the pieces have a 7 underneath. If the numbers are all the same, which one do we take?"

"I wonder." Tom looked carefully at all the 7s. "Yess! The white queen! Look at her seven. It has a cross on it. That's how the French do their sevens."

They quickly checked to ensure this was the only seven with a cross. Abandoning any attempt to limit their interference with the ice creatures who ran round trying to set right the order of everything they put wrong, they decided this indeed must be the answer.

"Isn't she beautiful," said Megan.

"What? Who?" asked Alex.

"The queen. Look at her solemn face. She looks as if she's carved from ice, but ice shot through with ivory."

"She'll turn into quartz," remarked Jessica, "once she warms up."

"Did you know it was the queen all the time?"

"Sort of," replied Jessica, enigmatically. "But we knew you'd manage the clue for yourselves in the end; and we had our unfinished game to deal with. We thought you would enjoy the challenge," she teased.

Megan grimaced. "So who won?" she asked.

"She did," said Lucifer sulkily.

He quickly changed the subject before anyone should chance making a clever remark.

"Let's think how we might fool those squirrels before we leave this place. They'll be right behind us."

As Lucifer spoke, there was a rustling sound from the roof as if some creature were trying to get in.

"I know," suggested Tom. "Let's add a cross stroke to one of the other sevens."

"Try it if you like," said Jessica. "But I don't think the squirrels will get as far as numbers in French. They'll find it easier to rob us later on. I suggest we take a second piece; perhaps the other queen, the blue one. Then, when they come stealing, we can put that in their path."

"It seems such a shame to make a mess of their lovely chess set," sighed Megan, looking over to the two ice creatures who were now scratching figures on the frozen floor, their expressions angular and glum.

"Don't worry about them," smiled Jessica. "They'll soon make new

120

ones. It's part of what they do."

"But why are they playing all these games?" Asiimwe wanted to know.

"That's how the future of some worlds is determined. It's all to do with the moves the ice creatures make."

"So," wondered Tom, "by interfering with a game, we have changed the destiny of a whole world?"

"Probably," acknowledged Jessica.

"For better or for worse?"

"Who knows?"

"So, Megan, put the chess pieces in your money belt, and we'll be on our way."

Megan struggled to do so, under all her furs.

The friendly tomten reappeared and led them back the way they had come. A deafening noise erupted behind them. A group of squirrels had overloaded a section of the ceiling that fell away, scattering frozen snow and ice among the players beneath. The ice creatures squealed and spat as the squirrels turned the boards upside down and threw the pieces aside, looking for they knew not what.

Lucifer laughed. "They'll never find what they're searching for because they haven't a clue what it is. They'll just cause mayhem while they look."

"Poor little ice creatures," said Megan. "We've made an awful mess of their day."

"They'll soon have things sorted." Lucifer dismissed them. "They're used to interruptions."

"But it won't be the same as before, will it?" Tom was trying to make sense of things. "Because the games have changed, so too have the futures of many worlds. And all because of the capricious actions of a group of squirrel baboons."

The tomten guided his friends to a much smaller door than the one through which they had entered. He selected another key from the bunch at his wrist and the door creaked open to reveal a narrow path they had seen from the window in the palace. The sky was iridescent with stars, white lights glowed in the trees and the tomten and his barred cat led their visitors across the frozen ground to the wooden hut with the windows of yellow.

"Cool!" exclaimed Percival. "Cool!"

"Welcome to my home."

Proudly the tomten threw open the door of the little house.

Megan was delighted to see the cosy inside just like the picture in her book at home. The heavy wooden table and chairs, the colourful rugs and cushions, the cheerful pictures on the walls. A log fire roared in the big grate. Half finished wooden toys lay to one side of the hearth.

The surfers shuffled out of their fur coats and boots. The tomten urged them to sit on the cushioned chairs.

He set a bowl of steaming liquid on the table and, using a heavy ladle, scooped it into glasses for each of them, and two very large bowls for Lucifer and Jessica.

The liquid was red and spicy. It sent a glow all the way down to their stomachs, and left their cheeks shiny and burning.

"Gloggi!" declared Alex. Holly had introduced the children to gloggi at Christmas time, using an old recipe handed down from the Finnish side of the family. It was warm spiced wine, and tasted very fruity. In no time at all it had everyone relaxed and happy, especially the big cats, and Percival it sent straight to sleep on the floor.

"This puts us in the mood for talking and telling stories round the fire," explained the tomten.

"First of all, tell us about when you come to our world at Christmas time," requested Megan.

"Only too happy to oblige," declared the tomten, who had been going to do that anyway. And he told the visitors how tomtens make and distribute presents in Finland and, more importantly, help with jobs around the farm on Christmas Day so that the farmers and their families can have some time off. He told how they feed and milk the cows on that day, and collect the eggs from the chickens.

Then it was the turn of the children. Each told a story with much laughter and joking. Only when the big cats had lapped up the very last of the gloggi did Lucifer say,

"It's time we were getting back."

The surfers climbed into their fur coats once more before meeting the cold air outside. Their breath froze in white clouds before them, and the hairs inside their nostrils stiffened with frost.

The tomten led them through the palace grounds, unlocked a gate in the great wall, and there was the sleigh.

With the pine marten was Snowball. Megan threw her arms round his neck. This was a different Snowball from the one they had seen before. Now he was confident, almost jaunty; his blue eyes no longer watered but sparkled with happiness; and the black tips to his ears stood erect. He twitched his nose in Megan's face, and she delighted in the tickle of his whiskers.

"Did the young rabbits get home safely?" she asked.

"I'll say they did. And you should have seen the joy on the faces of those mothers and fathers …."

Lucifer held up a paw to silence him.

"Snowball will see you home by a different route," he explained. "Jess and I will pass through Rainbow world. Remember to keep the white queen safe. The darker one – let whoever take that." He laughed, and they were gone.

With an unexpectedly smooth motion, the sleigh rose into a sky now thick with stars, so that it seemed there were more stars than there was sky. The sleigh pulled away beyond them and behind the curtain of moving light. Megan put out her hand to touch that curtain but it swayed just beyond her reach and tantalized them all with its bending shifting colour.

"It feels almost as if we're in the mirror," wondered Alex.

As they travelled the air became warmer, the lines of the sleigh and Snowball became indistinct, and then were nowhere at all. Megan who had been grasping the rail of the sleigh, found herself hanging onto the veranda of her home in the darkening African night.

24 Home Thoughts

"Snowball!" Megan's cry almost made Percival lose his perch on her shoulder. He dug in his claws and, for once, Megan didn't protest.

She ran to her pet rabbit; there he was, small and white except for the pretty black tips to his ears. His size apart, he was exactly like the rabbit in Frost world. Megan spoke to him. There was no light of recognition of a shared experience in those blue eyes, but Megan knew that Snowball knew that they had been somewhere else today.

"So you're back, Lucy," said Simone, rather sourly. "I don't know where you've been but I know you've been on a mission. I can smell other worlds on your fur. I must know all about it. You will tell me in time. We are one."

And her purple hair fell over the sparkat as she stroked him until sparks flew from his fur.

But I think I would be wise to keep you in darkness, purred Lucifer to himself. You shall know just enough, my darling, to keep your interest alive.

So, for the time being, he succumbed to her caresses. Lap cat had a certain appeal as long as it was lap cat on his own terms.

It was dark on the veranda. Megan unzipped her money pouch and took out the blue queen. She passed it round to the others. They glanced into the bushes, hoping that the baboons were there and would fall for their trick.

"Don't look," said Tom, "they're coming." He held the queen out in his hand so they could see it clearly. Then,

"Hey, stop thief!"

A baboon had crept up behind him and wrested the blue queen from his hand. It raced across the darkened lawn in the beam of the security light, the four children after it. Out in the open grassland, the baboon quickly lost its pursuers and the children panted to a halt. They looked at each other and burst out laughing.

As they ran back to the garden, among the many noises of the night, they could make out the threatening roar of a leopard warning away all other predators.

Back in the house, Megan took off her money belt and placed the turquoise crystal and the white queen on the table.

"Look," said Alex, "if I hold the queen up to the light, there's a heart of red fire deep inside her; it's moving slightly like flames."

"Let's see." Asiimwe took the figure from his friend.

"It's beautiful," he breathed, and passed it on to the other two who were impatiently waiting by his side.

"I wonder if the crystal does the same?"

Asiimwe held that too to the light. Sure enough, right at the heart of the stone was a shifting core of deep turquoise, and it was that which gave the colour to the entire crystal. He passed it to Alex so he too might have a look, and at that moment the lights went out.

"Power's gone," announced Tom unnecessarily. He set about lighting the paraffin lamps.

Carefully, Megan replaced the two treasures in her money belt and fixed it round her waist.

Eyes on the lamps, Alex was pensive. He looked at his watch. "It's eight o'clock," he said slowly.

Tom thought again how wonderful it was that, in Africa, no one worried about where children were. If they weren't at home, everyone assumed they were being fed elsewhere. But all I've had for a very long time is gloggi. I'm hungry.

Alex hadn't finished. "We left for Frost world in the early afternoon and got back in the evening so time has been moving forwards; although not as fast here as it did in Frost world."

"That depends," said Asiimwe thoughtfully.

"On what?"

"On whether or not today is the same day as the day we left. I mean, it might be tomorrow, or it might be yesterday."

"How are we going to find out?"

"Wait and see which day's lessons Mr Karumu gives us next time we're in school!"

Percival was grateful for the variety of seed that Klara put in his dish. She and Plato watched with fascination as he cracked the kernels with his strong beak. He knew they were pleased with him tonight, and he knew that was because he had remembered every detail about the happenings in Frost world.

Double O Four looked closely at the message sent in by Zero One Zero and Zero Six Six earlier that night. Good that they had the second item. But what had caused Three Five Seven to resign? Strange that there was nothing of so important a matter in the report. The big cat was suspicious.

Something needed investigation. He must keep a closer eye on things.

Zero Six Six was uneasy. She would have liked to include the affair of the rabbits in the report. But Zero One Zero was adamant.

"What rabbits?" he had asked when she had mentioned it. Zero One Zero didn't create mess-ups. There were no rabbits.

25 Bikes and Cows

Moses and Mzee were digging a new latrine. The process fascinated Tom. Such a huge excavation was required, about six metres deep and two metres square. A concrete cover would be placed over the pit. In this was a hole and two indentations to hold the feet.

Moses worked in silence but Mzee entertained Tom with terrible stories about people who fell into latrines; some of whom died down there, hoarse after hours of pointless shouting for help. This occurred when the pit was given a wooden cover, which happened in most of the homes in the village. Termites ate away at it from beneath, until one day it became so thin that the unfortunate person above fell right through. Mzee also told him stories about murderers who had thrown their victims into the latrine, where they had lain undiscovered for long enough for the perpetrators to escape justice. He had even hinted that one such murderer was still at large, and lived somewhere in the village. Tom hoped that the old man was teasing him, but he couldn't be sure.

Tom pushed those awful stories to the back of his mind, and turned his attention to the chatterers. Very many of these birds had suddenly arrived in the tree at the far end of the veranda. Large brown quarrelsome creatures, they were remarkably human and very entertaining in the way they organized their affairs. They would scold each other furiously and then quite suddenly fall silent. But some bird always had to have the last word, and would make a quiet remark that set them all a-chatter again.

So absorbed was Tom, trying to work out what they might be concerned about, that he didn't notice Megan on her bicycle turn into the garden. She brought Jessica with her, travelling in a basket attached to the back of the saddle: a mode of travel that seemed not to please the cat, to judge from the alacrity with which she sprang out of it when Megan brought the bike to a halt beside the veranda. Tom's face lit up when he saw his visitors.

"Look," said Megan, waving some papers in the air, "magazines from Canada. They were at the Post Office when Daddy went into town this morning."

Handing a pile to Tom, she settled down beside him.

It was hot in the garden as the sun climbed relentlessly to the zenith. Moses and Mzee continued to dig. Both wore nothing but ragged shorts, not even shoes. Megan marvelled at the taut muscles of their backs and arms and legs. There were no flabby bits like Daddy had. She watched the beads of sweat run like raindrops down their backs. She shouted a greeting in Runyankore to which Mzee replied cheerily. She tried, in vain, to engage Moses in conversation.

As she idly watched the men digging, she stroked her black and white cat lovingly.

She was smaller than when a sparkat, and her fur was rougher. In a way, she preferred her in this guise – the sparkats were so very clever and prickly.

Percival was on her shoulder as usual, happily chewing on the sunflower seeds she had given him. Megan did wish he wouldn't drop the shells down the neck of her t-shirt.

"I don't trust that parrot," Lucifer had said. "Parrots that can shift so easily are usually up to something." But Megan would have none of it.

"It's because he comes from Rainbow world," she replied. "They're better at magic there."

"Let's go to the bike track," said Tom suddenly. Coming to the end of the magazine he was reading, he tossed it to one side.

They found Alex and some of the others already there. Asiimwe was not with them. By doing jobs around the village, he had saved hard to buy his old black bike, but he visited the track rarely. Endless chores on the farm meant he had little time for such pursuits.

The boys on the track were setting their bikes at a jump made more outrageous by placing logs on the far side, so that they had to soar some way through the air from the launch lip to clear them. Megan and Tom watched Mutungi, a big boy from Alex's class – so perfectly positioned on his bike that he and the machine seemed to be one – fly high in the sky and clear the logs by a good two metres. He took his hands from the handlebars, raised them in the air and roared with delight. His bike struck an obstacle in the ground and skidded sideways, throwing Mutungi into the dirt and landing on top of him, wheels spinning. Mutungi got up laughing, in spite of the blood pouring down his arm.

Tom joined in the fun with enthusiasm. Megan would have done so too, were it not for the animals. Lucifer, Jessica and Percival all registered their disapproval of the activity. Lucifer got in the way of the bikes and snarled and spat when he was pushed to one side. Jessica tried to scratch her coat against the tyres and was in grave danger of being run over. Percival perched at the top of the jump and squawked at the competitors just at the point when the bikes took off from the launch lip.

"Megan, could you get those animals out of the way," protested Alex.

She scowled at him and called them to her. Percival on the handlebars, and a cat on either side – Jessica quite refused to be put back in the basket – she left the track.

Descending the hill towards her home, she saw a group of boys coming the other way. They were carrying the milk from their farms to the dairy in the small town. This they did in spotlessly clean silver churns, held onto the backs of their bicycles by lengths of broad black rubber. She noticed that Asiimwe was among them.

Freewheeling down the rest of the hill to join them, she then turned round and accompanied them on the climb back up. Asiimwe gave her one of his broad smiles that lit up his whole face but didn't slacken his pace. It was heavy work and, once stopped, hard to get going again. Watching the boy in front, Megan remarked how doggedly they moved, in silence, reserving all their strength for the effort of pushing. The boys were bent over at the waist; their arms, smooth and shiny, strained at the handlebars; muscular black legs pushed against the murram road. Most of them were bare-foot although a few wore flipflops.

Determinedly they crested the hill, and then work turned to fun as they wheeled into the road that led to the dairy. They leaped on their machines and bowled down for the bottom. Some took both hands from the handlebars and feet from the pedals, their shirts flapping in the breeze they created that cooled their burning faces and soaked away the sweat.

Outside the dairy, they queued in an orderly fashion, waiting for their milk to be processed. Megan helped Asiimwe unstrap the heavy churn, and he lifted it from the back of his bike.

Percival had ridden with Megan, tucking himself cosily into the basket behind so that her body sheltered him from the wind. The sparkats found themselves outpaced and, arriving at the dairy after everyone else, protested loudly at their treatment.

Once the first hill was surmounted, the journey back was one of fun and laughter for all of them. Asiimwe and Megan raced, neck and neck, down the big hill, turning to laugh with each other as they did so. Percival, in daring mood, returned to his position on the handlebars. He hung on tight and crouched low to lessen the drag of the wind, his happy squawking proclaiming his enjoyment. Jessica and Lucifer, tired of being left out, went off about their own business, in disgust.

The cyclists passed more sedate travellers; pedestrians, and boda boda boys who made money by carrying pillion passengers on their bikes – very often ladies wearing elaborate traditional dress. Many of these machines were fancifully decorated to attract more custom. To this end Ateka, one of Asiimwe's young uncles, had painted the crossbar and mudguards of his bike and added a sign, declaring the name Batman.

So much speed did Megan, Asiimwe and the others acquire in their flight that they cornered at the bend and raced up the slope without having to pedal at all. Then, as one, they turned off for the bike track.

"Cool! Brilliant!" croaked Percival in relief as Megan's hectic cycling stopped.

"Want a go?" yelled Alex, his tanned face gleaming with sweat beneath his tousled brown hair. At once, all the farmers' sons dropped their own black bicycles and made for the mountain bikes; and then they were away, whooping and laughing along the race track.

Tom flopped down happily beside Megan. He began stroking Percival who had come to sit beside him, and tried to encourage the bird to talk. He wanted to extend his vocabulary beyond those two words he already knew.

Together, children and bicycles arrived at Asiimwe's home.

Asiimwe had work to do, feeding and watering the two dairy cows that belonged to his uncle. Tom went to help him.

It was Asiimwe who suggested that they use the water in the bucket he was holding to find the next clue. Tom looked down at the water, muddied now that the young cow's nose had been in it. She was licking the remains of the liquid off her soft lips with a long rough tongue, and already looking for more.

"It's a bit mucky," he said.

"Never mind. Let's see if it works anyway."

Tom took the mirror from one of his ample pockets and both boys peered into it. The screen savers were still busy, and another jewel, a red one, had appeared in the frame. Tom pressed this to bring the disc into view and set it spinning. Now there were only five segments remaining. Around it the screen savers floated wraith-like, silent and active. Asiimwe was pleased with himself that he guessed correctly the third hieroglyph, the curly nine, which Tom told him was the number one hundred. Carefully, he dropped water from the bucket onto that piece.

As they expected it would, that segment expanded and the others disappeared under the frame. Again the hieroglyph appeared clear at the top, and underneath were the eight dots with the spirits moving among them. This time the dots were arranged in an almost regular pyramid that had a

130

three dimensional look to it. The spirits danced in and out of these dots, seemingly at random, until the boys realized what they were doing.

"They're filling in blocks of colour between the points. Like tiles?" wondered Asiimwe, trying to make sense of it all.

"Hardly colour," frowned Tom. "Every tile is sludgy brown and the lines between are almost black."

Megan and Alex came up behind them. Megan peered over Asiimwe's shoulder and bit her lip, thoughtfully.

"It's a tortoise, a very old brown tortoise!" she exclaimed.

"That could be because the water's old and brown," laughed Tom.

"Seriously, I wonder if that makes any difference." Asiimwe was thoughtful.

"We need the sparkats," declared Alex. He laughed. "I don't think they're best pleased with us."

"Miaow." Lucifer was behind him, expressing agreement.

"Ah, there you are, Luce! Snap out of it," he teased.

Lucifer gave him a sharp nip on an exposed toe to indicate he didn't wish to be called Luce.

"You should learn to control those fangs, you bad-tempered moggie," muttered Alex, ruefully rubbing his toe.

"We're sorry," said Megan. "We're sorry we left you out. We didn't think."

"Miaow," repeated Lucifer. The tone told them that the apology was only grudgingly accepted and that only for the sake of the mission.

Jessica, on the other hand, rubbed herself round Megan's legs in a gesture of forgiveness.

"Jess, can you help with this?" asked Alex. "Megan thinks it's a tortoise."

"I'm not sure just what it signifies," she puzzled, "but I don't think it's good."

She laid her ears back, flat on her head.

Lucifer wasn't pleased either.

"Oh, I know what it means well enough. I went there before Jess was born. It wasn't a pleasant place then, and I don't suppose it's improved. But I think we should have expected this." Lucifer's good humour was returning now he had his audience back. "The 'ody' is bound to cover all kinds of worlds. There has to be at least one bad one among them. And so far things have been pleasant enough."

"What's the world called?" Tom wanted to know.

"I think it lost its name along with everything else," surmised Lucifer.

"Just call it Lost world."

Percival chunnered quietly to himself. He didn't like the sound of this.

"How do we get there?" Asiimwe, at least, was ready to go.

"We find the murkiest puddle we can. And Tom, we're going to need some provisions. Bring your rucksack. Pack a torch or two, some food and plenty of water."

On their bicycles, Megan and Tom returned to the Andersons' house by the path through the tea estate.

There they filled Tom's rucksack with kabaragara and groundnuts and bread, and several bottles of water from the filter. They added two big flashlights and a miner's lamp. The very special torch from Grandma that shone different colours in different positions Tom stuffed into one of the deeper pockets of his jeans. Megan laughed as he struggled to heave his load onto his back and helped him by pushing from behind.

They found puddles in plenty behind the cookhouse where washing-up water had been thrown out.

These were unpleasant and smelly but visited by exquisitely beautiful swallows of many kinds. They sipped up tiny bits of mud to use in the construction of intricate nests for their young.

Standing as close to the puddles as they could without actually getting their feet wet, the sparkats invited the children to log on and get surfing. Their hands became warm with the effort of stroking.

"There's very little pulling power left among the ruins of Lost world," Lucifer explained.

But at last sparks began to fly, and then they came thick and fast and covered the children, blocking them from outside view.

26 Lost World

Megan's hand fled to her nose. The others reacted likewise. A smell that seemed to combine all the rottenness and decay they had ever experienced or could even imagine, assailed them. It stung their eyes and turned the whites red; it crept between their teeth and left a coating of vileness on their tongues. Everything around them was covered in a foggy haze that gave it a ragged outline. It was with relief that they noticed the sparkats with them. They had kept their Bioworld moggie garb although their fur was dull and had lost its hidden lights. Only Percival had significantly changed. He had shifted into a ragged brown crow type bird; he had dusty feathers and his voice had sunk to a croak.

They were standing at the end of a promontory that jutted out into a brown and evil-smelling lake. Everything in this world was brown, or dull green, or grey. The land they stood on was slimy and insubstantial. All around them were pieces of plastic and bits of broken bottles, piles of twisted crushed metal and rotting things; they didn't want to guess what these might have been. The water beside them was covered in yellow foam and dank green weed. From it arose a smell of decay and a yellowish steam. Occasionally bubbles of putrefaction would burst from whatever lay below and stir the foam for a while, leaving behind on the surface oily purple streaks. Huge pieces of metal stuck out above the water: giant girders and pipes, wheels and the hulls of submarines. They could taste the stench that forced its way down their throats, and feel the slime of it on their arms and legs. The air was warm and almost suffocating; their breath came in choking gasps. They looked in vain for help to a sky thick with yellow vapour that blotted out a brown-rimmed, blood-coloured sun and mustard-hued clouds.

At the far end of the promontory were some stricken trees, their blackened limbs raised imploringly to the sky. On the topmost branches were birds, some species of vulture; they had black and brown bodies and naked raw pink necks. They communicated in ugly grunts. There was a hum in the air: the sound of whirring machinery, accelerating cars, but all at a distance in time and space.

As they watched, an animal – what species they couldn't make out – floated past them belly up. Two vultures swept on the carcass and brought it to land. Their companions joined them and together they ripped apart the now bloodless, evil-smelling cadaver.

"Why is this world the way it is?" Tom demanded to know.

"Because it's dying a horrible death," replied Lucifer sourly. "Once it was beautiful, but that was many thousands of years ago. In those days it was not unlike your Bioworld," he added meaningfully.

Megan paled. "So what happened to it?"

"It was the people," explained Lucifer casually. "They stood on two legs, like you do, but were generally thicker and shorter. They had no hair and small, sunken, squarish eyes. They had very big heads because they had lots of brains. For many years they used their brains for good. They invented and they created and they discovered. Their world was regarded, throughout the universe, as a model one, something to be imitated.

"But then they started to get too clever for their own good. They had invented and discovered so much, they became thoughtless and over-confident; they were sure they could never fail; they declared there was nothing they couldn't tamper with and improve. And the generations threw up evil men who thought they were invincible, and some, just a few at first, wanted to explore the bad as well as the good. Greed and power became passions for them, and some exploited others for their own ends. Finally, those who had been exploited rose up against their masters, and war and genocide were rife.

"The land did recover from the desolation that followed, and the disease and hunger and poverty that blighted it, but it seemed a new breed of people came through it. There was no faith in a future that might not be there, and every person strove for him or herself alone. They derided each other and sneered at people they called friends; everything was laughed at and made fun of as each one strove to come out on top."

Tom felt chill clutch his heart as Lucifer told his story – he recognized the bullies back in Bioworld.

"Across the entire world, there was prejudice and hatred towards others who were different from oneself; even against those who were just there, where you wanted to be. Pollution was everywhere: from factories and power stations, from vehicles and even people's homes; and no one cared to prevent it. In this chaos of evil, some became very rich, climbing on the backs of others. They didn't care that their wealth was made by poisoning earth and sky and sea.

"And pollution continued to pour across the world, from ever more numerous and ever bigger factories and rubbish tips. On land and sea, stinking noxious gases oozed from where people disposed of all the waste materials they had produced; and the 'things' they had acquired and finally tired of, and thrown away to replace with other 'things'. The rivers no longer flowed; they heaved slowly like vile yellow mucous in a festering

134

wound on a land blighted with plastic and rusting metal. The sky lost its stars and sun in a blurred green obscurity that sent stinging shafts of the very essence of pollution into eyes turned beseechingly up to it.

"The disease that arose from this ruination took the form of a hacking, rasping cough and breathing difficulties, a certainty of corrosion in the throat. And this corrosion caused sores, raw and red and painful; they refused to heal; they exuded pus and made it all but impossible to eat. The victims became thin and weak. As their lungs were eaten away and destroyed, finally, coughing up blood, they died in agony. And it seemed that this scourge changed its form and was no longer caused by pollution alone. It became contagious. Having started in the rich countries, it quickly spread to the poor where it destroyed whole communities almost overnight.

"People were suffocating in wealth and greed all of their own devising. They thought they were making money, but they were stuffing their wallets with poison. Invincible, destruction spread its arms wide, and crops and animals and people inhaled the stench of mortality and died." Lucifer levelled emerald eyes at the surfers, pleased with the impact his tale had made.

"And so now there are no more people," said Megan solemnly. She was shifting from foot to foot, not wanting to leave one down too long in the slime.

"No, and very few plants and very few animals. Just those that thrive on decay like those vultures in the blackened trees over there."

"What caused the trees to go black like that?" Tom wanted to know.

"That was acid rain, carried from a factory half way round the world. The acid rises and collects in the clouds which the wind carries where it will, finally depositing it on some hapless land thousands of kilometres away."

Asiimwe stopped trying to scrape off the deposit that settled everywhere on arms and legs. "This pollution," he asked, worried, "is it at all like the pollution we have in Bioworld?"

"Exactly the same," said Lucifer solemnly.

"Wherever we're going let's get there and get back," suggested Alex impatiently, having tried in vain to find something firm on which to stand. Jessica, her ears laid well back, miaowed her agreement; the smells were even more offensive to a sensitive feline nose than they were to a human one.

"Where are we going?" protested Megan as they started off. She was wearing sandals and hated the slimy feel of the ground where loathsome, smelly mud oozed between her toes, and her feet rubbed up against she didn't want to know what. She could feel Percival's anxiety in the claws gripping her shoulder tightly through her thin t-shirt, and was grateful for his reassuring presence.

Alex, having the same problem, wished he had brought his boots. "You never said anything about footwear," he protested to Lucifer.

"I can't mollycoddle you over everything," was Lucifer's caustic reply.

He didn't like visiting Lost world, and the necessity of doing so was making him grumpy. He didn't like the slime that crept between the pads on his paws any more than the humans did. Alex opened his mouth in angry reply but something struck his lip. He shut his mouth again in horror and quickly knocked whatever it was away with the back of his hand. He pushed his hair out of his eyes and found it lank and greasy and full of grit. Looking back at the unhappy faces behind him, Lucifer mellowed.

"In Frost world," he explained, "we could arrange appropriate food and clothing because we have contacts there, but in this blighted land there is no one capable of providing such things. But I did tell you about the food," he finished triumphantly.

Alex scowled at him and looked back down to his feet. Only Tom was fortunate enough to be wearing trainers.

"Not far now," said Jessica encouragingly over her shoulder. She wiped away something unpleasant that landed on her nose.

They passed through what must once have been a forest, full of scorched trees like those they had seen earlier.

They look so sad, thought Megan. They stretched out tortured arms towards her in a gesture that seemed to beg for the help she could not give.

Among the trees were pools of stagnant water. Oil floated on the surface, giving a metallic sheen to the hidden depths. Occasionally, bubbles of gas rose to the top and exploded, sending their putrid smells towards the surfers. Here, a few plants struggled to thrive, but all were malformed and crept low to the ground: flowers had petals that curled in on themselves, leaves were covered in black spots and rust marks, and stems were thin and insubstantial.

As they moved deeper into the forest the trees, still blackened, became larger, and there were more birds, fighting and squawking and gazing down on the travellers. Percival looked up at these distant cousins and a flash of recognition passed from eye to eye. Mostly the animals were heard rather than seen: the crack of a broken branch, the slosh of a foot in a puddle. Occasionally there appeared a large hairless face with bloodshot running eyes.

"What are they?" asked Alex, appalled.

"Some kind of mutant, I expect," replied Lucifer nonchalantly. "The place is full of them. They're harmless."

"That was a baboon," exclaimed Asiimwe suddenly, noticing movement among the branches. "It was just like those in Bioworld, but it was huge!"

The others looked where he was pointing, and they too saw the large animal with gleaming eyes and unkempt fur. In this leafless environment it was difficult for it to find cover.

"Anything evil in this place grows and grows," explained Lucifer. "That's why he's so big. I expect there are others around." Some thought amused him and he gurgled a catty laugh to himself.

To the weary surfers it seemed like hours before they finally emerged from the forest into a huge clearing. Again the almost hot, stifling air, full of the bitter sweet smell of decay, hit them like something solid, trying to push them backwards. Here there had clearly once been some kind of settlement; there were several houses, now no more than piles of rubble. Megan peered round a broken down door and drew back at the mouldy, stale, damp smell that assailed her. There were pieces of rotten wood that were decayed furniture, and sludge on the floor that had probably been carpet – its fibres long dissolved – and was now home to brown slithering things. On a broken brick wall a picture of an old man hung crookedly: an old man with a large round bald head and sunken eyes that even now bored into the soul from the faded old picture. Broken pots were the only other signs of past habitation. Whatever people had once lived here were now long gone. Megan shuddered. Percival, on her shoulder, squawked miserably and attempted vainly to preen his ragged feathers.

Lucifer led them unerringly to the centre of the settlement.

"I'm sorry," he said, "but it's down here we have to go. We need to raise this cover."

Alex and Asiimwe helped Lucifer and Jessica pull away the few weeds and stones from the edges and lift the rusty metal lid from the manhole. The thick warm smell that assailed them almost knocked them over. Once it had settled, they peered cautiously over the edge and down into the hole.

"Are you sure this is the way, Luce?" asked Alex.

Lucifer glared at him.

"Yes."

"How do you know?" added Asiimwe.

"Because this is the way of the mirror."

"And that explains it all," declared Alex flippantly.

27 Tortoise

"I'm not going down there!"

Megan was adamant as she peered below her where an ancient, rusty ladder sank into the dark, smelly abyss of the drain. Alex shot a grateful glance at his sister. It's always reassuring to know someone else is at least as scared and reluctant as you are. Asiimwe was anxious to console her.

"I'll go in front of you," he said, "and you can keep really close."

Jessica pushed herself along her legs, nuzzling her gently. She looked up, purring softly.

Only Tom and Lucifer seemed completely focused on the task before them.

"This is where we'll need the torches," Lucifer said to him.

Tom handed the flashlights to Asiimwe and Alex. Megan took the miner's lamp that she could wear on her head; she wanted to keep both hands free for the ladder. Tom kept for himself the coloured torch that was now giving out a warmly reassuring yellow light.

"What about you two?" Megan was concerned for the sparkats.

"Did no one ever tell you that cats can see in the dark? Now, follow me. Jess, you bring up the rear."

To the children's amazement, Lucifer set off down the ladder head first, reaching for every rung with cat precision, using his strong tail to balance himself. Alex was next to place a foot on the rickety ladder, and soon he was shouting encouragement from the bottom.

"I'm here already. It's not too bad."

Carefully the others made their way down, feeling in the dark for every foothold. Percival fluttered round their heads, complaining incessantly.

Soon they had all joined Alex and Lucifer in the dirty, ice-cold water at the base of the ladder.

"This way," said Lucifer. "If I remember correctly, there's an old pipe at the side. Yes, here it is. You can sit down for a while if you like."

The surfers declined the offer and stood close together, shoulders hunched. Jessica suggested food but no one was hungry; indeed all felt slightly nauseous from the stench. It was chilly down here, too, and they kept near to each other for warmth.

Alex looked at his friends in the artificial light.

"Hey, Asiimwe, Tom, look at me!"

They did so.

"You've grown old," he exclaimed. "Your cheeks have sagged, and your chins and necks; and there are lines at your forehead, mouth and eyes, and …"

The surfers gazed at each other in horror.

"Look at our hair!"

All had hair showing streaks of grey. Alex's full wavy locks had grown bushy so that he resembled an eccentric professor, and Tom had a bald patch right at the back. Megan put a hand to her face; her skin felt saggy; she recoiled in horror at the grey curls that hung round it. Only Asiimwe, she thought, looked rather distinguished, as if he were wearing an iron grey judge's wig.

"Don't worry," Jessica purred, "the effect is only temporary. Perhaps we ought to get on before we lose our nerve. Which way, Lucifer?"

"First of all, it's this drain," said Lucifer, almost apologetically.

He indicated a giant pipe leading off to the right. It oozed with sloppy mud and gave off the now all too familiar stink of sewage. None of the surfers moved. To encourage them, Jessica stood in the dark brown water at the entrance. There were lumpy bits at the bottom. She wasn't at all sure what they were and wisely decided not to mention them. She lifted one of her front paws and shook the filthy moisture from it with distaste; it was already stained and brown. She slowly swung her head in despair. Megan was still fingering her face with dismay.

"Thinking about it isn't going to help," announced Tom, and he and Lucifer splashed forward, past Jessica.

"Come on," said Asiimwe to Megan kindly, taking her hand. "I don't suppose this'll take long."

The warm words were enough to put Megan back on course, and she and the others waded on down the huge drain.

There were eyes in the darkness, curious eyes. By the beams of their lights they could see these belonged to large grey rats.

"Even the baboons have more sense than to come down here," muttered Alex under his breath. Or have they shifted? he wondered.

"Splash as hard as you can," instructed Lucifer. "That's the only way to keep them from getting your toes."

Soon they were covered from head to foot in the murky water. The travellers felt shivery as the iciness of it crept up to their knees, and the unpleasant dampness penetrated their thin clothes; but it wasn't really cold; the gases from the rottenness kept the air warm.

"Oh well," said Asiimwe optimistically, "at least with all this movement we can't feel anything nasty that we tread on."

The remark was intended to raise a smile from Megan but instead he

140

got a scowl that brought out the ridges across her forehead. Asiimwe grinned at the dry, lined face with its silver curls. There was the same intensity in the grey eyes and Asiimwe realized that, for him, Megan would always be beautiful, even when old.

Apart from her legs and feet Megan felt warm enough, but she wished heartily that she had her hooded jacket with her, to keep the slime from her unruly grey hair. She felt she had never been more uncomfortable in all her life.

The water became deeper and then shallower and then, miraculously, they were on firm ground. The low ceiling of the tunnel that had been so claustrophobic gave way to a high, cavernous roof. They were standing on sand, and the sand was yellow.

Thankfully, Megan took off her sandals and rubbed them and her feet in the deliciously gritty cleanness. The others followed her example. Lucifer and Jessica settled down to give their coats the thorough feline beauty treatment.

"Here is where we'll find all answers," explained Lucifer mysteriously.

No longer afraid, Megan's anger took over.

"This is the worst experience I've ever had in my whole life," she snapped at Lucifer. "You could at least have told us which clothes to bring. Jackets would have helped keep all the nastiness off our skin. We don't have fur coats, you know. Or why couldn't you magic us some?" she complained.

The boys were privately thinking the same.

"Why are you being so mean?" Megan finished, her anger subsiding now it was out of her system.

"My apologies," drawled Lucifer, now more relaxed on reaching the sand. "The worst is over. But you have to understand. If a creature isn't mean, as you call me, in Lost world, he very easily becomes confused. The meaner you are the faster you pass through it. It's a very mean place."

"So, what now?" asked Megan, slightly mollified.

"We dig away this sand."

"What with?"

"Now I *will* use a bit of magic. Look behind you, Alex. Shine your light into that recess."

The beam revealed a number of ancient tools, most rusted away, but a few suitable for use.

"Did you really magic those?" asked Megan, impressed.

"Well, it's pretty magical to know they're there," Jessica answered

Megan. Lucifer frowned at her.

Asiimwe and Alex selected a number of spades that were still usable. Having spent so many hours digging at home, Asiimwe was quite an expert in the matter. As the boys searched their way through the pile, they noticed tiny green ferns growing from cracks in the rocks above.

"This part isn't quite as bad as the rest," Asiimwe ventured.

"No," agreed Lucifer. "Here you'll find the only grain of hope in the whole of Lost world. That's why I brought you here. There couldn't be anything worth taking anywhere else in this unhappy place."

"So there is hope for this world?" Tom seized on the word Lucifer had used. "Things could get better for Lost world?"

"Indeed they could. Hope is always there; hope never dies. But it would take a long time," he sighed, "many thousands, maybe millions of years. Perhaps better to have a big bang and start again." Lucifer shook himself. "Back to the present," he said. "Now that we seem to have recovered some of our good humour, shall we have something to eat before we start work?"

Tom wriggled out of his rucksack and unpacked the bread and the kabaragara and the nuts. Percival immediately seized a kabaragara. With delighted squawks he daintily peeled back the skin. Lucifer and Jessica looked with disdain at the proffered meal. They scrambled lightly over the rocks to an opening way above.

A few minutes later the children heard screams and snarls and scuffles. Bits of stone and twig and moss rattled onto the picnickers hunched below. Then there was silence but for the odd crunching sound, until Lucifer and Jessica returned, licking blood from their furry chins. They lay down beside the surfers and fell asleep, their distended tummies displaying sated hunger.

The surfers soon finished their meal and began, again, to examine each other's old faces, this time seeing the funny side of things.

"You look just like Amos," Megan laughed at Asiimwe. "And Alex is much more like Daddy than I ever thought he was."

Alex pushed his thick hair behind his ears, imitating his father, and they all laughed. Tom felt his bald patch uncertainly and wondered if that really would appear in later life. They amused themselves pinching the skin on their hands, and noticing how very long it took to resume its former position.

"But I don't have any aches like old people have," exclaimed Megan, waving her legs and arms.

"Maybe the decay of this place hasn't penetrated our insides yet,"

142

declared Tom cheerily.

Eventually they tired of discussing old age, and the cats still slept.

Irritated by their contentment, Alex pushed Lucifer roughly awake.

"Come on, Luce," he said. "You're meant to be leading this expedition."

Lucifer gave a menacing growl and struggled grumpily to his feet.

"There's something underneath this sand," he said. "Let's start digging for it."

Alex noticed that neither of the cats seemed inclined to lend a hand. When he mentioned the fact, Jessica patiently explained that cats don't belong to the digging variety of animals and quietly continued to lick her paws.

The surfers heaped the sand against the surrounding wall. It was damp from the atmosphere of the place. They quickly became coated in it. Megan laughed to see it standing in the wrinkles of the boys' old faces. She was aware of the grittiness of it on her arms and legs and in her hair; she could feel great wads of it in her sandals beneath her toes. Percival, much excited by the whole undertaking, tried to help by carrying sand in his beak and squawked with frustration at his total inability to do so.

Asiimwe was the first to strike something hard. He put his spade to one side and began to brush away the sand with his hands. Excitedly, the others helped him. Percival leaped, screaming with delight, from one of Megan's shoulders to the other, entangling his long claws in soft grey curls as he did so.

"It's some kind of shell," exclaimed Tom.

"A mighty big one," agreed Alex.

Their hands were rubbed red and raw, and were sore and tingling from friction, by the time the mighty shell was revealed in its entirety.

"Is it a tortoise shell?" wondered Megan.

"It's colossal," declared Tom as the full extent of the shape became clear.

The shell formed a huge but shallow hump, segmented into a number of separate pieces; this done by ridges that stood slightly proud of the rest. It covered almost the entire cavern.

"We saw a brown tortoise shell in the muddy water," Tom remembered.

"And this was it," exclaimed Lucifer triumphantly. "This creature is an important symbol in this waste land.

"Tortoises, as I am sure you know, live extremely long lives. This one was the very last creature who remembered his world's former, happier state to survive in the poisoned atmosphere. In his despair, he came down here and buried himself in the sand, where he died at the age of three hundred and forty five, leaving the land he loved to scavengers. It is on his shell that we shall find the clues. We must look hard at the patterns."

Tom and Asiimwe fought to remember what they had seen in the mirror.

"I've got it!" shouted Tom. "It's a maze!"

"What do you do in mazes?" encouraged Lucifer.

"Get to the centre," said Tom, without looking up. His feet and hands were already tracing the lines of the ridges. "Look," he said, "there are gaps to pass through. Let's find our way to the middle."

He knelt down and started to mark a route. There seemed to be many dead ends. Alex soon became tired of the search. I mean, he could see where the middle was anyway.

"Look, here it is," he declared derisively, stepping over the ridges. "I'm standing on the middle."

"Surely something should happen when you get there," said Megan, looking at her brother expectantly.

"Not if you don't take the right route," pondered Tom.

Asiimwe was deep in thought.

"Some of the ridges," he said, thinking aloud, "are a slightly different colour; they're a paler brown. There's another pattern that overlays the first. Perhaps we have to follow that. Do you see it, Megan? I'll try this way. You go the other."

Carefully, Asiimwe picked his way. It was actually easier just concentrating on the lighter ridges. And then he stood in the very middle.

The earth began to shake so that the surfers hung onto each other to keep their balance. The sparkats opened sleepy eyes to watch what was going on.

"Look, there's a gap all round the centre section. We could pull it up by that ring." Tom was full of excitement.

"When did that appear?" objected Alex. "It wasn't there before."

Jessica explained. "The ring was certainly there all the time, but hidden from your five senses until you solved the puzzle."

Another manhole, thought Megan suspiciously. I hope it doesn't reveal a rusty ladder. Percival hung his head in dread and Megan caressed him sympathetically.

They were both relieved to see the solid stone steps, leading ever downward. Nobody mentioned the putrefying body that must have lain under there for some time, beneath its giant shell.

They passed down the short flight of steps, Alex leading now while the sparkats – both still too full of their recent meal to be capable of real action – brought up the rear.

To their surprise the air smelled fresh and the steps they trod were rough and dry, uncluttered by the slime and muck they had learned to anticipate.

At the bottom was a stretch of clear water such as they had not yet seen in this world. A pale glow of light rose from the depths and illuminated the pool eerily. They switched off their torches to save the power. In the shallow water were many shells in soft colours – pink and blue and yellow – and on each shell was depicted a tiny maze. Tom warmed to his discovery.

"We must take the shell with the maze that matches that on the tortoise," he declared.

Megan picked them up and turned them in her hand; they were beautiful and smooth and clean and pure. Barefoot, the surfers paddled in the clear fresh pool. Even the sparkats, normally so shy of anything wet, dabbled their paws in the sparkling liquid.

Megan cupped her hands to fill them with water. She poured it onto her sand-filled, gritty face, and then more down her arms and legs. She felt her flesh warm and smooth and young again, and she laughed.

"Megan," shouted Tom, "you're not old any more!" They all started splashing each other, and they dunked their heads beneath the surface to remove all traces of grey hair.

"We're making the water murky," shouted Asiimwe. "We won't be able to see the shells."

They stood still, the water swirled a little, and then all was as clear as when they first arrived.

Conscientious now, they examined the shells one by one, laying those they had already looked at in a pile by the side of the pool.

"There must be thousands of them," Megan declared wearily. She sat on a rock, her knees hunched to her chest, her arms tight round them, and looked despairingly at her pile, the smallest of all.

"I wish those cats would help," complained Alex.

He pushed a foot at Jessica, fast asleep on a warm rock. A shell of a pretty pale violet shade rolled out from under her fur.

"Good on you, Jess!" shouted Asiimwe. "That's it! Look!"

He held out the shell to the others. It was shaped just like the tortoise they had uncovered; on its violet base stood out purple ridges with a lighter patterned overlay.

"You had it all the time," challenged Alex.

"Did I?" yawned Jessica.

"I wonder what kind of animals lived in these shells?" mused Megan.

"Maze fish, of course," replied Jessica, superciliously. She nudged Lucifer who pulled himself awake.

"Ah," he said, "so we have the third item." He examined it approvingly. "You're doing well. Put it away carefully, Megan."

Megan held the shell in front of Asiimwe's flashlight.

"There it is," she said triumphantly, "the little purple heart."

Megan opened the money purse at her waist to reveal the crystal and the queen. She placed the beautiful shell with them and zipped it shut.

"Now, I suppose we have to go back," she said, dreading the journey.

"Indeed we do, but not the way we came."

They all sighed with relief. Somehow bad things that you don't know about are never as fearsome as those that you do. Although Megan wasn't sure that was true; her imagination could work exceedingly well.

"All we have to do is regain the open ground and then our electricity will work," Lucifer assured them.

The sparkats swayed from side to side as they left the pool of shells, their tummies still full of lunch, and they belched occasionally as they waddled along. The surfers plodded wearily behind them. As the tunnel they were following led gradually upwards, it became smellier in the air and full of more unpleasantness underfoot. They used only one flashlight as nobody particularly wanted to see the strange, slimy creatures that sucked their way along the walls.

I wonder what they are, thought Megan, just as something spiralled through the air to land on her leg.

"Ugh!" she exclaimed, and put her hand down to strike it off.

It wouldn't budge. She yelled as another landed on her right leg. Both hung on tight. Hearing her cry, Jessica made her way back along the tunnel to a frantic Megan who was splashing up and down in the muddy water.

"Leeches!" declared Jessica.

With her sharp teeth she pulled them away from Megan's flesh, and spat them against the wall. Megan pulled Jessica to her and, muddy as she was, buried her face in her fur. Back on her shoulder, Percival squawked sweet reassurances into her ear.

"Walk with me now please, Jess," she begged.

"Better turn on all the flashlights we have," said Jessica. "Leeches hate the light."

They swung the torches up and down the walls, and watched the balls of blubber flee for cover.

It was a silent party that finally reached the over-world and again put hands to noses and eyes, to shield themselves as much as possible from the reeking smell and stinging acidic air. Darkness had fallen; there were no stars; a smudged moon hung like a purple bruise in a sour yellow sky. They made their way across a patch of boggy land to a rocky outcrop on the edge of a dead forest. They sloshed through mud, not looking down to see what evil things they might be treading on – there were some things it was better not to know – and clambered among the rocks covered in green slime. Ashen-faced from her brush with the leeches, Megan slumped down on a clammy stone.

"Tom," she said, "can I put my lamp back in your bag? I'm tired of wearing it."

Tom sank down beside her and opened his rucksack. He put in his hand to fetch out a kabaragara, and touched something furry. He recoiled for a moment and then brought out a tiny frightened brown mouse.

"What've you got there?" demanded Lucifer.

"A mouse," said Tom. "I don't know where it came from."

"There are others," declared Alex. He fetched out more shivering bundles of fur.

Lucifer advanced towards the rucksack.

"No! Go away!" protested Megan. "They're mice, you're a cat." She put her arms protectively round the rucksack.

"But just think for a minute why the mice are there," said Jessica patiently.

"I know," said Asiimwe. "They want a lift to a better world."

"Exactly," said Jessica.

"Well, that's OK," said Megan. "They can have one."

"Undoubtedly they are diseased," said Jessica. "Think what damage a strange disease could do in your own Bioworld."

"That's true," said Alex. "We can't take them, Megan."

"Well, those two aren't eating them," said Megan. "I hate this world.

We'll just let them go."

She passed the rucksack to Tom who tipped the furry inmates into the mud. There were six of them. They set off at a run towards the distorted trees. Megan stared warningly at Lucifer and Jessica who assumed indifference. Suddenly two huge baboons swung down from the bare branches above them, picked up the trembling rodents and devoured them whole. Megan stared aghast into gleaming red eyes. She felt at her waist for her pouch of treasures.

"Don't worry, Megan," reassured Jessica. "Their time is not now."

Megan wasn't so sure. There didn't seem to be any limit to the badness of this world.

"Will they search for a shell of their own?" she asked.

"Maybe."

Megan was thoughtful. She didn't like the idea of baboons swarming around that beautiful pool and treading on those delicate shells.

"Come on, let's get away from this lost world," suggested Jessica.

Everyone agreed with that idea. At the other side of the rock on which they were sitting was a large, murky pool.

"Stand in that and get stroking," instructed Lucifer.

28 Time to Think

"Why are we all standing in this muddy pool?" complained Alex. They looked at each other's grubby faces and laughed.

"Ugh! Quick! I want to be clean!" shrieked Megan and fled to the house.

Once there, she grabbed a large, fresh towel from the cupboard, threw her clothes to the floor and made for the washroom.

This was a tiny place with a concrete floor that sloped to a hole at the bottom of the outside wall; through this water could pass into a gully below. There were two crude shelves for soap and shampoo and toothpaste. Under the shelves were three jerrycans and two washing-up bowls. There were strings along the inside wall and across the doorway, to carry towels and face cloths. Megan quickly checked the jerrycans and was relieved to find them all full.

She poured herself a basin of water. She soaped herself from head to toe until she was completely covered in frothy white bubbles. Spying Daddy's long-handled brush in the corner, she used that to scrub her back and arms and legs until she was tingling. She then tipped the basin of water all over herself; and then another, and another, and another. Next she turned her attention to her hair. She poured shampoo all over it and rubbed it in firmly with the tips of her fingers, before rinsing it with yet another bowl of water. Finally her teeth; she cleaned those to gleaming whiteness. For good measure, she tipped the remaining water over herself, before rubbing her body dry with the towel.

"Megan, what are you doing in there?" Holly, hearing so much splashing of water, was curious.

"Washing," came the reply.

"Well, I guessed that, but what's taking you so long?"

Holly was suspicious. Her daughter didn't usually go in for such furious bathing.

"I was dirty," Megan shouted back.

Opening the door, she appeared wrapped in a towel, her face glowing with cleanliness.

"Well, I'll certainly vouch for that," agreed her mother, picking up the discarded clothes from the floor. "These things are filthy, and they smell."

"Put them to soak please, Mummy."

Megan sidled past her to the bedroom. When she emerged in clean skirt and t-shirt Holly was waiting for her.

"Megan," she complained, "you've used all the water. Three whole jerrycans."

"I'm sorry," said Megan. "As I told you, I was dirty."

"Now Haj will have to go back down to the well. He won't be pleased. He has other work to do."

"I'll be sure to apologize."

"You certainly will! And oh, Megan, look at my best shampoo! You've finished the entire bottle, a month's supply. You know I can't get any more until I go to Kampala again. It's too bad of you."

"Mummy, I'm sorry, please don't be angry. I've had a difficult day."

"*You've* had a difficult day!" her mother exploded.

But Megan had gone, to the rabbit hutch, to tell Snowball all about Lost world.

She looked for Percival but he was down at the lake, sorting out his beautiful feathers. From there, he travelled to Rainbow world to spend time with Klara and Plato, and scoff slightly roasted sunflower seeds.

"Three down, four to go," said Lucifer, lazily. "It's your turn to report back to Control."

"Is it?" asked Jessica.

But Lucifer obviously wasn't going to do it, never mind whose turn it was. Full of contentment and self-satisfaction, he stretched out on the veranda, pleased that the brief visit to Lost world was over, and had been successful.

So Jessica rubbed the bald patch behind her ear and took hold of her mobile phone. She searched for a signal from the spot where she knew the star was hidden by the magnificence of the sun, and passed on the message of success. The voice at the other end confirmed that this had been registered, and then signed off. As far as Control was concerned there were no problems or questions with that particular mission.

Lucifer smiled smugly to himself. He spent some time straightening out his fur. This tabby coat with its orange highlights was beginning to look quite respectable, thanks to the care he lavished on it.

That done, he paid a visit to Simone. She was waiting for him in her beautiful garden, with a huge bowl of freshly caught fish with which to win his heart.

Alex strummed his guitar lazily.

"What's the matter, Megan?" he asked kindly. Usually the sound of the guitar cheered his sister, but not this time. "You haven't smiled for hours. That's not like you."

"I'm just thinking about our world, Alex. Will it go the way of Lost world in time?"

"I don't see why it should." Alex strummed to a different tune.

"But what's going to stop it? Remember all those cars and factories belching out their pollution when we visited Canada. And look over there. Look at all that smoke, all that burning."

"That's just a small bonfire."

"That is, maybe. But we know what happens at the end of the dry season, just before it rains. Then the farmers completely scorch the earth to clear it for new crops."

The alternative of digging took too long in an unmechanized farming system.

Megan cast her mind back to the scene and could visualize it as if it were before her that very day. Those dry nights that preceded the rain. The whole countryside ablaze for miles around. Bushes, trees, plants crackling into oblivion, and who could count how many birds and animals burning alive in screaming agony. Flames leaping and curling into the hot, brittle air; ashes and smoke drifting into homes to lay the evidence of destruction at the occupants' feet. She remembered the dry heat that caught in eyes and throat, leaving a burning cough behind, and the vision spoke to her of the blighted land she had so recently visited.

She sat with Alex and his music into the evening. She gazed out at the glory of the stars in a sky of the deepest blue, and she held Jessica and Snowball close. She listened to the myriad insect calls; she watched the fireflies darting in the undergrowth, and wondered at the piercing brightness of their dancing diamond lights. Was all this in danger? For the first time in her life, she truly understood how its seeming strength might cover a deep fragility that needed to be treasured.

Later, as she lay in bed in the waiting night, she could hear the baboons gibbering in the forest on the other side of the garden. She knew they were keeping watch over the house, but she wasn't concerned about them. She was working out what she, Megan, could do to save the world.

"Because," she confided in Jessica, "everyone leaves it to everyone else, and so nothing gets done. When I grow up I'm going to be an environmentalist," she told her pet.

This DNA we are trying to protect, she wondered, does it really matter? Certainly not if Bioworld is doomed. But we can't let it be spoiled. This is DNA for new animals or birds or insects or plants. As in all things, it's the little pieces that make up the whole jigsaw. You have to work on the small things to make a success of the big ones.

Still trying to work out ideas in her mind, Megan fell into a deep sleep and left the night to the owls, and the bats, and the baboons, and the richness of African life.

Tom stood at the bench in his father's workshop. The rabbit box was coming on well; he was proud of it. He looked forward to the expression on Megan's face when he finally gave it to her; he would have to think of a special occasion for that. He'd never had a girlfriend. It'd be great to have a girlfriend, and Megan would be the one he would pick. But he knew Asiimwe liked Megan, and she liked him. They always chose each other for partners in class, had done for years the other children told him. He glanced at his pattern to make sure he had the details right.

"You must think a lot of that young lady," ventured Mzee, grinning.

He and Duncan were working on a set of chairs for Priscilla's remodelled dining room.

Tom flushed, involved in the delicate work of making the wooden tail look furry.

Duncan asked Mzee for his opinion on the arm of a chair.

But Tom replied. "Yes, I do think a lot of her. She's a good friend, and so is Alex."

As if on cue Megan's cheerful, freckled face, framed by its burning curls, appeared in the doorway.

"What's that you're making?"

"Oh, just practising," said Tom quickly, and hid the rabbit box away.

Fortunately, Megan was far too excited to be curious.

"We need all the help we can get with the shade for the fundraising," she said. "We're miles behind time."

The two friends cycled off in the direction of the secondary school.

29 Fundraising

What an enormous shade! Well, didn't it have to be to accommodate so very many people, thought Tom. There were several uprights and many crossbars, and then poles over the top to hold the waterproof sheeting. It was erected on the spot where the 'big' people would have their seats. It had taken a team of young men with many helpful children several hours to set it in position the evening before, and decorate it with large gaudy flowers. None could tell how many would come when the Vice President was to be guest of honour, and she accompanied by many distinguished colleagues.

The occasion was a fundraising in favour of the local secondary school, the one attended by most of the children in the area. The exceptionally good results of its scholars in recent years had attracted the attention of the authorities who had given a significant contribution towards a science laboratory. The plan today was to raise a like sum, and so have the full amount that would allow building to commence.

A number of boys set out chairs in rows, with tables in front of them. Girls laid embroidered cloths on these and added small posies of colourful flowers, and large bowls of yellow lupins on the ground before them.

Suspended from the cross poles hung a host of banners displaying the red, black and gold of Uganda – the beautiful crested crane standing proud in the middle of each – and the shield and motto of the school.

All through the morning parents of those attending the school, and other well-wishers, arrived with their gifts – cows, goats, rabbits, chickens, carpets, baskets, cloth, carvings, furniture – the gift depending on the circumstances of the giver.

Tom watched Amos arrive with his ducks: they had minds of their own and didn't take kindly to being confined to the crate that Amos had built for them, nor did they like the way Lucifer and Jessica prowled round the edge of the field. The school itself contributed a large Friesian bull from its own herd.

Refreshments were brought in: crates of soda, and, to eat, an enterprising catering group had fixed small, individual parcels of food – a few pieces of meat and some cabbage – that would be for sale.

The opening time arrived with no sign of any guest. But the military band from Kampala was punctual, and entertained the crowd that had already assembled. Dressed in camouflage fatigues, black berets and boots, their highly polished instruments shone and flashed in the sunlight. And then they began to play.

Tom knew it just had to be the best band he had ever heard. While punctiliously adhering to the required military precision and rigid formation, they yet gave the music a genuine African swing that had the audience swaying and clapping in rhythm. Tom couldn't take his eyes from the soldier with the huge double-sided drum; the fluffy beaters twirled and spun in the air and always struck just at the right moment. The soldier leaned back, seemingly transfixed by his own playing, his rubbery face unsmiling and looking at no one. When the music stopped all of them, the drum soldier included, immediately stood still and straight and to attention. What a contrast from the life of a few moments before. Such control and rhythm in combination.

Only the sparkats remained unimpressed. They laid back their ears and viewed the poultry from a distance.

And then she was there. The Vice President, flanked by other notables, took her place. Everyone stood to sing the national anthem, after which the school choir, smart in freshly pressed uniforms – blue skirts and trousers and gleaming white shirts – moved forward to sing their message of welcome while the invited guests took refreshment.

The speeches were short and to the point. Ruboroga was a good school that could name many distinguished leaders who had started in its ranks. It could look forward to a great future and, just at this moment, a science laboratory was what it needed most of all.

Then came the bidding – the chief purpose of the day. Every item gifted was held up for auction, for the benefit of the education of local people as the Vice President put it. A goat could bring 30,000 shillings, a cow 500,000. All those invited were expected to bid, and bid high.

Tom felt somebody grab his arm. Megan was behind him, Percival clinging tightly to her shoulder; he couldn't risk separation from her in this dense crowd.

"Come with us," she urged. "Alex and I have found a good place."

Megan took his hand and pulled him over to where the refreshments were being served. Sitting on the crates of soda, they had an excellent view of what was happening. The young man in charge seemed disinclined to send them away, especially when Alex bought a bottle each for all three of them.

"Cool," whirred Percival softly.

Tom could see Priscilla and his father and the twins at the front of the crowd. With them were Steve and Holly Martyn. The engineers from the tea estate would be expected to join the bidding. Tom wondered what his father would come home with that night. Asiimwe was busy helping Amos with the ducks. Alex kept his eye on Toppie who had charge of some chickens. So too did Lucifer who crept closer to watch. Jessica had decided to give the fundraising a miss, and had returned home.

"Watch out, Luce," said Alex. "I might decide to auction you."

Lucifer curled his lips in a mock snarl.

"On second thoughts, I don't think I'll bother. Manky old moggies don't fetch much."

"Don't tease him," said Tom who knew how he hated to be teased himself.

Lucifer was angry and struggled from Tom's grasp. He made for the open road, the tip of his tail vibrating in fury.

Alex laughed. "I'm going to give Amos a hand."

Toppie more like, thought Megan, who saw that Toppie was now helping her grandfather with the ducks.

As the day wore relentlessly on, the prices obtained rose beyond all reason. A cow fetched a million, a goat fifty thousand as each 'big' man or woman strove to be more generous than the next. Nobody actually handed over any money for these things, Tom noticed, rather they wrote notes of promise to pay. Each sale took place in the fullest possible glare of publicity. The onlookers cheered on the participants to make ever higher bids and broke into rapturous applause as a price was fixed. Some even jumped on and off their chairs in excitement and hugged those standing beside them. A member of the local committee was detailed to check that all expected dignitaries were present. Should anyone be found absent, a runner was sent to his home, to demand either his presence or his money.

The two muzungu from the tea estate entered into the spirit of things. Duncan tried for a couple of Amos' ducks but was outbid by Mr Katembe. He bid high for a beautiful carpet which he gave to Priscilla for her dining room. Between them the twins carried this home in triumph. To Alex's great delight, his father acquired a set of drums.

The school bull did not take kindly to being tied in a small space among crowds of shouting, restless supporters but it was with him that the bidding really left the ground! He was bought for four million shillings! Tom gasped. Others cheered.

The army major bid for a carved stool which he presented as a gift to the Vice President. She bid for a large chair which she gave to the headmaster for his office.

By the end of the day promises of fifty million shillings had been collected. The science laboratory was a reality.

No sooner had the 'big' people departed, than the party began. The adults drank too much and became happy, so that the children did as they pleased.

Alex, Megan and Tom accompanied Asiimwe back to his house where his uncles were distributing omuramba, a drink made from sorghum and millet flour, and had roasted a goat to feed any visitors they might have. They brought out the drums and led the guests in energetic dancing. Alex and Asiimwe, stripped to the waist, joined in with enthusiasm, Alex thrilling to the look of approval on Toppie's face. Traditionally, African girls look for the best dancer when choosing a boy friend. There was no question who was best in Toppie's eyes. Later, Alex fetched his guitar and he and Toppie found themselves a quiet corner. Tom didn't have the confidence to join in the dancing, nor did he have the same sense of rhythm, but he was happy enough watching with Megan.

30 Science or Magic

On Monday morning all the children of the area were still excited by the success of the fundraising of the weekend. Some imagined that they would see the science building already erected when they walked past the secondary school.

Undoubtedly, it would be a long time indeed before young scientists in the primary school could ever think of using science laboratories. However there had recently been much improvement in schools in Uganda, thanks mainly to a massive injection of American money. All the teachers in the whole country went on courses to help them make their lessons more interesting so that their pupils might learn more successfully.

For over forty years Mr Karumu had taught over-sized classes in inadequate rooms, sometimes not in a building at all but outside under the trees, even for two years in a school without a roof. Alternately burned by the sun and lashed by the rain, he had taught without books, without pencils, even without a chalkboard. And he was weary of the endless grind. But even he, old man that he was, summoned up the strength to be inspired by the new ideas; and the children all agreed that his science lessons were among the most interesting they had ever had. Formerly he had written everything he knew on the board; and those among the children who had books and pencils had copied it all down and learned it. Tom had been most impressed by the Ugandan child's capacity to learn and remember page after page of notes by heart. Looking back over his own schooldays so far, he realized he had never been asked to actually *learn* anything except a few times tables and spellings, and two lines for last year's Christmas play.

But now things were different. Now the children did experiments.

This Monday morning, they had been asked to bring bowls and small objects from home. Mr Karumu himself had been down to the well to fetch water. The lesson was to be 'floating and sinking'. Tom considered this rather elementary; he reckoned he knew pretty well what floated and what sank. Mr Karumu must have anticipated his scepticism because he fired his first question at the new arrival.

"Tom," he said, "what do you think makes a battleship float?"

So, I have got something to learn after all. Tom grinned at Mr Karumu and said, "I'm sorry, sir, I've no idea." And the kind, perceptive old man grinned back.

He then poured some water into a bowl and asked the children approximately how many drops they thought were there. By now he really had Tom's attention, and that of all the others.

"Don't pour it away yet, Megan."

Tom was beside her at the end of the lesson when she made to empty the bowl of water onto the flowerbed outside the classroom.

He took the mirror out of his pocket and polished it on his jeans.

"Not here," hissed Asiimwe, "too many people around."

Megan picked up the bowl and took it to the flowerbed on the far side of the playground, slopping water as she went. Mr Karumu had said they could have five minutes.

Carefully, Tom pressed the violet jewel that had appeared, lodged in the frame.

Only four segments left. The screen savers swam into place.

"Quick," urged Asiimwe. "We haven't got long."

"Is it that one?" guessed Megan hopefully. She pointed to the crooked finger.

"That's ten thousand. We need one thousand first, the lotus flower." Tom indicated the one next to the finger.

Carefully, he flicked a drop of water onto the lotus flower. As before, that segment increased in size to fill the entire mirror.

"That's strange," remarked Asiimwe, "all the dots are in a pile at the bottom."

The screen savers moved in amongst them and began pulling and pushing them into some kind of order.

"They're drawing with them."

"The colours keep changing."

"It's alive! It's a tiny animal. What is it?"

"It's a little lizard," marvelled Megan. "And it's got wings!"

"Ah, cool!" exclaimed Tom, delighted.

"Cool," echoed Percival nonchalantly, from the roof above them.

"It's shrinking, it's disappeared."

"Let's take the water down to the stream," suggested Megan.

"Why?" asked Tom.

"Well, the creature might still be in there, and be invisible. It won't want to be stuck in a school flowerbed."

She did her best to scoop the water from the mirror back into the bowl, and set off across the grass. Down at the stream she watched the water splash, shining, into the pool trapped between two rocks.

"There you are," she said. "I'm sure you'll be more at home here."

158

Percival, perched in the tree above, cocked his head on one side and listened.

With a squawk Percival flew to his favourite place, the top of the flagpole in the playground. From there he could see right over the village and the tea estate, and the mountains beyond.

Percival liked coming to school. At first some of the children had thrown stones at him but now everyone accepted him, especially when he joined in their games lessons, and shouted 'brilliant!' at their efforts. Best of all, Percival enjoyed playtime: all that screaming and running excited him.

He would have liked to join Megan in the classroom for the lessons, but Mr Karumu had made it clear he wasn't welcome there. On one occasion the teacher had chased him with a broom and beaten him on the tail with it. That was when he decided not to bother with lessons.

Megan scrambled up the short hill and crept into her seat, pushing apologetically past Tom and another child. Mr Karumu was writing something on the board. She hoped he wouldn't notice the late-comer. He turned and scowled at her. He always noticed.

After school the children gathered together in the Martyns' garden.

Megan described the tiny creature they had seen in the mirror in great detail to Jessica and Lucifer, while Tom drew an amazingly accurate picture of it. But the sparkats took no notice. They lay in the sun, on their backs, their eyes closed.

Exasperated, Megan resorted to her homework. She pulled her social studies book from her bag. I never wrote down the names of all the rivers, she remembered. I missed that part of the lesson when I was at the stream.

"Asiimwe ...." she began.

Lucifer opened one eye. He rolled over, stood up, stretched as long as he could, forwards and then backwards, and then the same again, and yawned as wide as he could. He shook all his four paws and turned to look at the children, busy over their books. I'm glad I don't have to do homework. He laughed deep inside himself. After all a sparkat was surely the very best thing to be in the entire universe. He nudged Jessica to her feet. He knew she would have been listening too. Sparkats sleep with their ears open.

"So, what about this lizard then?" His voice was more gravelly than usual, being still full of sleep.

Tom and Megan looked up.

"Perhaps you can identify that one, Jess?" Lucifer suggested to his partner, testing her.

"That's not too difficult," she replied. "It must be a quazor. Yes! That means we're off to Technoworld."

The children gathered with relief, from the cats' enthusiasm, that both had been there before, and that it was a good place to go.

"You know, Jess," purred Lucifer thoughtfully, "I think it's time you tried part of a mission on your own. You'll have no problems in Technoworld. I'm going to sit this one out."

He rolled over onto his back and waited in vain for someone to tickle his tummy.

Jessica looked decidedly wrong-footed.

"Well yes, I suppose I can manage it, but what are you going to do?"

"I think I'll just lie here in the sun," replied the lazy voice.

"Let's get going soon," said Megan. "I hate the way the baboons keep peering at us."

"Just an irritation," said Jessica. "For now," she added.

"Why do you say that?" Megan was concerned by the hints the cats kept dropping, of difficult times ahead.

"Well, eventually they will bring in reinforcements, possibly hyenas or jackals; they always seem to be on the wrong side of everything. And then .. but the time is not now."

"Jess, do we need boots or jackets?" asked Alex. He had no wish to be paddling in sewage in his sandals again.

"Anything needed will be provided in Technoworld," said Jessica. "It's a positive place. Only in Lost world is there no hope and no help, nothing but despair."

"Are there people there?" asked Tom. He was disturbed by the lack of his own kind in these worlds. Maybe people aren't as important as we think, he wondered.

"Sort of," said Jessica mysteriously.

"How do we get there?" Alex was impatient for action.

"Think about it. Technoworld is very scientific. How do you think we'll get there?"

The children looked at each other, seeking inspiration.

"Something scientific, but natural too," mused Tom.

Asiimwe leaped to his feet. "Something that changes colour like the lizard in the mirror. The ruined settlement at the edge of the forest. It's

160

full of chameleons. Let's go there."

"You're getting the idea," smiled Lucifer, awake once more.

He watched the four of them cycle across the grass and out onto the road, Jessica by their side, Percival flying from the bushes to join them.

Alone on the veranda, Lucifer pointed his nose to the sun in ecstasy and concentrated. He grew in size. Orange spread up his long fluffy tail, mingled with green on his legs and body. His face turned orange, his whiskers white, and green crept to the tips of his ears. And then he was home.

Simone ran across the lawn to meet him. A smile lit up her amethyst eyes; she pushed her long purple hair back behind her ears. She pretended to reproach her darling.

"You keep abandoning me, Lucy." She stamped her dainty foot in its dark blue slipper.

Lucifer sidled up to her and rubbed his face along the back of her slender legs, and then curled his orange body round them. Simone stooped to caress him and rubbed her face against his. The two, reconciled, made their way to the house.

Klara sat on the floor, drawing, her loose green hair hiding the paper.

"Lucy's home again," Simone announced to her sister.

Klara put her arms round his furry neck.

"We do miss you and Jess when you're away," she said.

"That's sparkats for you," declared Simone. "They're the most intelligent of all creatures. You can't expect them to sit idle. Like Plato," she finished, rounding on the unfortunate little dog who was standing guard over Klara's paper. His coat was white and glossy and his spots gleamed with colour where Klara had brushed him earlier that day. He was a beautiful little dog but he knew Simone and Lucifer despised him. He, in his turn, had contempt for the big, aggressive sparkat, and would always annoy him whenever he could. Right now he stood close to him and barked full in Lucifer's face. Lucifer leaned back, whiskers and ears both laid flat; he glared his distaste.

"Oh go away, Plato," said Simone.

"Come to me," said Klara. "I love you just as much as I love Lucifer." She wrapped him in her pale arms. Simone looked at her with derision.

"What are you drawing?" she asked.

"I don't really know," said Klara. "I like to let the pencil take me where it wants."

Simone walked over to where her sister's work lay on the floor.

"It's some kind of lizard," she said suspiciously. "We don't have them in this world."

Lucifer examined the drawing. He stared straight at Klara, his emerald eyes unnerving her. It was clear, he decided, that she knew nothing. Klara looked up and saw, behind her sister, Percival, also peering intrigued at her drawing.

"I was just scribbling," said Klara, defensively to all of them.

"What are *you* doing here?" Simone directed the question at Percival.

Percival squawked loudly, started when he saw Lucifer glaring at him, and flew out through the open window. Lucifer, too, wondered what Percival was doing in Rainbow world. Hadn't he set off for Technoworld with the others? And Simone wondered why Klara had drawn a quazor. Was her Lucy going to tell her about that? She started to wheedle him. Did he know what the creature was? Did he know where it lived? Had he been to its world? Where did he go when he wasn't with her?

Lucifer wished she wouldn't question him so. Did she know the details of his mission? How could she? But then she always seemed to know more than he thought she did. Anyway he couldn't possibly tell her. But he didn't like to displease his beloved mistress. If only she would be patient. But Simone possessed endless patience and endless powers of persuasion.

"Has anyone seen Percival?"

"He was here a moment ago," said Asiimwe.

"Maybe he doesn't want to come to Technoworld," suggested Tom. "He didn't much enjoy the last one."

"Forget Percival," advised Jessica. "I think he'll be working for us wherever he is."

"I love this place," enthused Megan.

The abandoned compound had six round, mud-walled buildings that had once sported thatched roofs, now long fallen in. When she was smaller Megan had used to love playing house here with her Ugandan school friends. Holly had given the girls a few old pans and dishes to make the place more realistic but these had quickly disappeared, taken by poor peasants who had few such things of their own. So the girls learned to improvise with sticks and stones and leaves. Megan explained all this to Tom as they wandered in and out of the ruins.

But now was not a time for playing games, as Alex pointed out. Now was a time to look for chameleons, and these were easy enough to find.

Many scuttered away at their approach or quickly turned colour so as not to be recognized. But one seemed to be less nervous than the rest, a small fellow with bright eyes. Megan was sure he was smiling at them. He ignored the children and fixed his gaze on Jessica who stared back. Then he set off through the forest, Jessica and the children following.

The trees became fewer and fewer, and the land became rocky and hard. After some time the little chameleon stopped.

"Now is the hour," declared Jessica. "Let's log on and go surfing. Start stroking."

Sparks flew quickly this time; they noticed they didn't have to stroke very hard.

31 Technoworld

"I think we must have arrived!" declared Tom. "Just look at Jess's fur!" The sparkat's coat had taken on a silver, metallic sheen. "Looks as if it's made of shiny iron filings." He rubbed his hand along her back. "It's all spiky and stiff, just feel it!"

The others needed no second bidding, exclaiming in surprise until Jessica grew tired of the game and told them to give over.

"Never mind me, take a look at yourselves!"

The surfers had a silver sheen to their skins and their hair had turned wiry. Megan's curls had become coiled springs. The boys enjoyed tugging them and watching them leap back into shape, until Megan distracted them by pointing out their bicycles. Every trace of mud and dust from Bioworld had disappeared; they gleamed as new and the colours had taken on a metallic lustre.

"What a pity you couldn't do something about our clothes," laughed Alex.

"You want fancy clothes?" smiled Jessica. "Then fancy clothes you shall have."

At Jessica's bidding, the chameleon that had accompanied them, stepped forward. With his long curled tongue, he licked the surfers' shoes and their clothes, and suddenly they were dressed completely in silver leather. Short boots, long trousers and jackets for the boys, all three of whom turned to gaze at Megan. She wore high boots and a skirt that finished just above the knee. Over the leather of this, in a separate layer, hung strands of real silver, set with diamonds. The short tunic that completed the outfit seemed to be made of woven foil. The surfers ran their hands over their new finery, soft and smooth to the touch. Alex tossed his glittering hair from his eyes. If only Toppie could see him now.

"Happy?" asked Jessica.

The smiling faces provided her with the answer.

Megan fingered her skirt. "What are the clothes made of?" she asked.

"Moon dust or moon ore," I expect answered Jessica. "Maybe a bit of both; they are slightly different colours."

The chameleon, too, had changed. Not just his colour which was now metallic with a purple lustre, but his shape also. His head was more pointed; his feet became webbed; his tail grew long and straight with an arrow at the end; and out of his back arose two huge leathery wings.

"You're just like the creature in the mirror," exclaimed Megan.

"He's a quazor," said Jessica. "A quazor who shifted into a chameleon in Bioworld for the purpose of the mission."

"A quazor?" queried Tom.

Jessica explained that quazors are lizard like creatures that are equally at home on land, in water or in air. "But their preferred element," she said, "is the water where they can breathe under the surface as easily as above it. These creatures," she went on, "are immortal. The quality of their sleep is such that it constantly renews with youthfulness every cell of their bodies. The only cause of death is accidents."

Megan observed the little creature in amazement.

The boys surveyed their surroundings. They were in a bleak landscape with but a few stunted trees. The ground on which they stood was solid rock, and that rock had the colours of many minerals running through it. Tom bent down to run his hand over the threads of iron and magnesium that he recognized.

In places cushions of moss clung to the rock. Amongst it tiny earth-hugging plants with beautiful daisy shaped flowers shone like metal – gold, silver and bronze in colour. The small trees were full of bright red and maroon berries that hung in great clusters from every branch. Above all this a small pale sun shone in a purple sky.

The air was fresh to breathe so that they were filled with a boundless energy, and had such clarity that they could see over vast distances. The place seemed to be the total opposite of Lost world. Full of anti-pollution, as Megan later put it.

There were animals everywhere, none of them afraid, all of them small: mostly reptiles and amphibians – frog-like creatures and lizards – and a few mammals with metallic fur such as Jessica had acquired. There were small rodents and, inevitably, tiny baboons with sparkling coats.

Jessica told them to follow the quazor.

The quazor set off at top speed, using his wings so that his feet just skimmed the ground. As he ran his breath came in tiny bursts of smoke and fire.

"He's a little fiery dragon," marvelled Megan in delight.

The children leaped on their bikes and followed him, Jessica loping by the side of them. They thrilled to the power of their upgraded machines and the smoothness of the ride as they bowled over the rock on tyres that made light of unevenness.

As they moved further into the depths of Technoworld, so the terrain gradually changed and became harsher. It began to drizzle, silver and white drops. Like the tails of many fireflies. The ground was unrelentingly rocky and moss gave way to lichens in every shade of green. Just a few bright copper flowers made splashes of light in an increasingly dark environment.

As before, the trees were small, but here they had no berries and were stunted in their growth. This was partly due to the sparsity of soil and nourishment to be found among the rocks, and partly to the prevailing wind that forced them to bend, always in the one direction. The leaves they bore were supple leathery needles that allowed the wind to pass among them, and they gave off a fresh energizing smell as they moved.

Far in the distance, Megan thought she could make out the upright figures of people. She drew her bicycle alongside Jessica.

"You did say there were people in this world, didn't you?" she asked. "Over there, are those people?"

"Looks like it," said Jessica, glancing in the direction Megan was pointing, but uninterested.

"What are they like?" Megan persisted. "Are they like us? Will we meet them?"

Jessica looked round and sighed. The boys, too, had brought their bicycles close. They also had noticed the figures on the horizon and wanted to hear all about them. Jessica called ahead to the quazor to slacken his pace. The quazor looked puzzled but did as he was asked.

"I think it would be easier to talk if we walk for a while."

Feeling slightly claustrophobic with all the bicycles huddled around her, Jessica began.

"Like our friend the quazor," at mention of his name the little creature turned and bowed his head happily, "these people are immortal. Well almost," she qualified her remark. "They have studied human science to such a degree that they have conquered disease and so don't die in that way any longer. But their body parts still wear out and these are replaced with metal spare parts. Some of them are more metal than flesh, and some are entirely of metal and are thousands of years old. They are rather strange to look at." She paused thoughtfully. "They have machines to do all their work for them and so they spend their days doing science experiments to make more machines." A puzzled look crossed Jessica's face. "That's all I know about them really. Some of the machines they make look like people and so you can't always tell which are people and which machines." She fell silent, thinking about what she had just said.

Alex and the others strained their eyes in an attempt to see more clearly the stick people in the distance.

"So, what do they do with their extra hundreds of years?" Tom wanted to know.

"Much the same as they did with the first hundred, I suppose," said Jessica.

"It must be wonderful to live for ever," exclaimed Megan who enjoyed every minute of her life.

Alex wasn't so sure. "I think it might get quite boring, after the first couple of centuries or so."

The quazor nudged Jessica impatiently and they were on the move again.

And then, suddenly, they rounded a large rock and came face to face with a group of people. They looked human but, as Jessica had explained, they were only partly so. Some had metal ears or eyes, or hands, or legs, and some were made entirely of metal. They moved on cushioned platforms, like snowshoes, that carried them smoothly over the uneven ground.

It would be difficult to say which party was the more surprised. But it was the leader of the technopeople who spoke first. His voice sounded like a badly strung guitar. He bade the surfers welcome and asked where they had come from. Alex was the first to recover his wits sufficiently to explain. Even as he spoke, it all sounded hollow and unconvincing and he felt his voice tailing off. But it seemed there was no problem. These technofolk were perfectly aware of other worlds that shared their planet and not unused to visitors from them.

Great age had given them some wisdom and kindness, and they insisted the children accept their hospitality before carrying on with their mission. Jessica was of the opinion that it was an excellent idea for the surfers to learn about other worlds and quickly agreed to their taking a break.

They wheeled their bikes down an iron road towards a huge house built entirely of metal with plastic windows. Tom decided it had exactly the look of a Lego house. It was completely square and had a flat roof. It was four storeys high. There were six windows on each level, all regularly spaced. Whoever built it didn't have much imagination thought Megan. She was walking behind a woman with metal feet and hair.

Once inside, they found themselves seated at a table of steel, on plastic cushions that shifted comfortably to every movement of the body. On metal plates before them were rolls made of plastic that tasted like hamburgers. They ate in silence, too overcome to speak.

A technowoman, with a voice like a metal spoon in a teacup, leaned over the table, and said,

"Come on, don't be shy. Surely you have something to ask us? We know a great deal about your world. Maybe you have some interest in ours?"

Tom had the first question.

"Why don't you make your spare parts from flesh instead of metal?" he asked. "They would look more realistic," he added, glancing round the room at the mixtures of flesh and metal. "We do that in Bioworld," he finished.

"Ah, but how long do those parts last?" queried a man with a completely metal face. "A single life-time. No longer." He answered his own question and continued. "Whereas this metal we have perfected, now that lasts for ever. See this face of mine. How old do you think it is?"

"One hundred and fifty." Tom hazarded a guess.

"My face is six hundred and eighty five years old," declared the technoman triumphantly.

"And how old is the rest of you?" Megan asked.

"This leg is three hundred and eight," he began, "and my left hand is .. it's very new actually, it's only one hundred and sixteen. But my heart ...." and here he paused for dramatic effect, "... my heart is nine hundred and ninety seven! And what a party we will have in three years time." He clapped his metal hands with a deafening clang, and ground his metal teeth.

The other technopeople all nodded their enthusiasm.

"So what do you do all day?" Alex wanted to know. He looked up from his hamburger.

"We don't actually *do* very much," replied a technoman who was all metal but so well oiled that he didn't clank at all. "We have machines that do things for us. We have computers that think for us."

"We take exercise, sometimes," said a technoman, metal from the waist up, yawning.

"We do experiments to try and find out about other worlds."

Alex looked round to see if Jessica would contribute to this conversation, but Jessica had disappeared.

"What about children?" Megan wanted to know.

"What about them?" The technowoman's voice was defensive.

"Well, do you have any?"

"Goodness gracious no! Think about it. If we had children and no one ever dies, there would be far too many of us."

"But surely some of you must have fatal accidents?"

There was an intake of breath around the room. Then an answer.

"Yes, some of us do perish in accidents. That is why we are getting fewer in number. But we don't have children. We are all too old to have children. There are some bits of a body we just can't renew." The technowoman's eyes became hard as steel.

Alex was suddenly wary. "I suppose," he began, "I suppose you could take children from other worlds."

"Exactly so. When we meet children we bring them here and, when we have spoken with them, we invite them to stay."

"And if they don't want to?"

"If they don't want to stay, then they are free to go. We are people of peace, not violence."

"Well we don't want to stay," said Alex firmly, scraping his chair back across the metal floor and getting to his feet.

"That's quite all right. But you came with bicycles. Perhaps you would like to see what a bicycle can do in this world before you leave us?" wheedled the tiniest technowoman of all.

Reassured by the gentle tone of the voice that was like a sonorous church bell and sat strangely alongside the tiny form, but mainly because he was curious to discover what a bike could indeed do in this world, Alex spoke for all of them when he said they would stay for a while.

Megan was pleased to see that Jessica had reappeared and was nodding her head in agreement. After all she had been here before on another mission and must know about the place.

"Bring your bicycles into the yard behind the house," instructed a technoman with a voice like a well-oiled chain.

They picked up their bicycles from outside the front door and made their way to the back.

"Now," snapped a breezy sporty looking young man who, on first sight, didn't appear to have any metal parts at all, "look over there at that large computer screen." He flashed a smile at them that revealed two rows of perfect metal teeth. "Use the mouse by the gate to flick through all the forms of transport that I've set up for you. When you come to one that appeals, pedal straight towards it and see what happens."

Alex went first. He stood with his bike by the huge mouse that had long metal whiskers and flinty grey eyes, and clicked his way through cars and trains and planes and then through motorbikes.

When he came to Suzuki 500 he pedalled as hard as he could towards it and straight into the screen. He felt a surge of exhilaration from the machine beneath him, and then he was speeding and roaring over open moorland. The smell of petrol was in his throat and the vibration of the machine sent pulses of adrenalin fuelled sensation throughout his body. And then he was back, and it was Tom's turn.

Tom chose a speedboat and felt the thrill of it crashing into waves and riding over them, showering him in spray as it did so, and jolting under him as it steadied itself for the next bout of surf.

Megan was in a rocket soaring among the stars.

On the most glorious BMX he had ever seen, Asiimwe raced towards a jump, rose many metres into the air and met the ground with a satisfying thud before speeding on over bumpy turf, and through gullies thick with mud that spattered him from head to toe.

"Now," coaxed a completely metal man once all four were reunited with their bicycles, "how would you like to do that every day? You could if you stay here," he finished encouragingly.

"Nice try," said Alex. "I expect you go through that with all the children who come here."

The metal man looked so crestfallen Megan was almost tempted to offer to remain, at least for a while.

At that moment a technowoman appeared with a tray of drinks, a grimace on her metal lips that was meant to be a smile.

"Now this is where we must leave you," said Jessica firmly. Stifling the surfers' protests she led them, wheeling their bikes, through the gateway to the open countryside beyond. "Remember, I've been here before. I know about those drinks."

"I suppose they're drugged?" asked Tom.

"Let's put it a bit more kindly than that," suggested Jessica. "Let's say they make you feel very comfortable where you are."

Megan thought she would never forget the hurt look on the face that held the drinks beseechingly out to them. And suddenly she was angry with the sparkat for putting those people through the hope and the despair.

"You've brought other children here, haven't you?" she said accusingly. "Did you really think we'd stay?"

"No," said Jessica defensively, "but some do. Suppose you were a child from Lost world? Then you might very well decide to stay."

But Megan hadn't finished. "You deliberately deceived those people." She confronted the sparkat angrily. "I'm surprised at you Jess. That's the kind of thing Lucifer would do." Jessica laid her ears flat in dismay. "You let us bring our bikes on purpose. You knew we'd meet them."

"I knew they'd come looking for you," corrected Jessica. "You were in no danger. They are the most peaceful people I know. And surely you enjoyed the rides?" There was a note of real hurt in her furry voice.

Megan looked into the pleading amber eyes. "Of course we did, Jess," she said, sorry now for the offence she had given. She put down her bike to give the sparkat a reassuring hug.

"There must have been more to it than that," said Alex suspiciously. "Why did you let us go with them? It wasn't just to give us a fun ride. Sparkats don't work like that," he added wryly. "Why did you do it?"

"Well, they do make uncommonly good game pie," replied Jessica, licking her lips. "The best I've tasted in any world." And she fixed inscrutable amber eyes on Megan who was tickling her behind the ears.

The quazor led them on again, over land that was flat and made for easy cycling. The thoughtful party made good speed across it and then, suddenly, things changed once more.

the plans

32 Tooth

Where there had been silence, now there was noise. There was a dampness in the air that fell soft on their faces as they approached the mighty river. Boulders strewed its rocky banks, and among these grew larger plants than before, and taller trees that still were covered in the same leathery needles. Birds with heavy blue wings and cruelly curved beaks and shining black eyes perched on the tops of these trees and quarrelled and chattered in loud raucous voices, watching the river for any sign of the many varieties of fish that swam there. Megan's gaze searched in vain for a shifted Percival among them.

At the point where the surfers met the river, it ran into a gorge. It was here that they were forced to leave their beautiful bicycles in a small cave the quazor showed them, covered by foliage from a nearby tree. Jessica called on the watchfulness of two silver-furred foxes to ensure their safety but, even so, Alex wasn't too happy with the arrangement. Red-eyed baboons with leaden fur, smaller than normal but still vicious, were taking note of the whole exercise.

"These foxes are tougher than they look," laughed Jessica, reading his thoughts, "I've never known a baboon get the better of one yet."

There was a narrow bridge spanning the gorge. It was made of metal and clanged to the sound of the boots on their feet. Only as wide as was needed for travellers to pass in single file, it was easy to look out over the low rail to the rushing, boisterous torrent below. To the right was a tremendous waterfall. The broad, shallow river reached an edge just upstream from the bridge, and then it fell straight over it with a thunderous roar, hundreds of metres to the bottom. And the spray from that fall rose higher than the original plunge, and spread rainbows in wide arcs. From there, the water crashed on down the gorge in a series of rapids, its colour reflecting the sky above, purple and dark blue and filled with stars.

Once on the far side of the gorge, they turned right towards the bottom of the great waterfall. And then the quazor led them in behind the crashing spray. The roaring was so loud they couldn't hear each other speak, and they were quickly drenched in the droplets of a fine, cold mist that completely engulfed them. The quazor stood on his hind legs and flapped his wings. Then he jumped clean off the edge into the whirlpool below.

"Gone to fetch supper," explained Jessica with satisfaction.

The surfers proceeded cautiously along the slippery narrow path, running their hands along the wet rock behind them for support. Above their heads waved the tendrils of climbing plants that rooted in the crevices and were constantly swayed this way and that by the ever-moving water. Just past the centre of the massive fall they reached an opening in the rock behind. A large lizard with a surly look guarded the spot. His gaze swept the surfers from head to toe, suspicion writ large on his leathery face, but he recognized the sparkat and shuffled to one side to let them pass, his eyes on them until they moved beyond his sight.

The surfers continued down a short tunnel and found themselves in a vast cave. The roof was impregnated with streaks of ore that created metallic colours, the same colours that ran down the heavy solid granite walls that were pocked with recesses and dotted with ledges.

In each of these recesses and on every one of the ledges were creatures that sat quite still and fixed unblinking eyes on the surfers. There were owls with silver feathers, moles with wiry fur, badgers with glinting coats and even tiny baboons with bright red eyes. And from the ceiling hung bats with metal wings. The starers showed nothing but mild interest, but the surfers still found them slightly unnerving.

The floor was crafted from compressed slabs of rock, all carefully placed together in geometric designs that displayed, to best advantage, the different kinds and colours of stone. The place was lit by a strange silvery glow that came from just beneath the surface of the beautiful floor.

"How does that work?" wondered Asiimwe, kneeling to examine the stone more closely.

"The light is in the heart of the rock itself," explained Jessica. Asiimwe looked puzzled so she elaborated. "As rock can be impregnated with colour, so it can be with light. You will notice that the light varies in intensity and colour, depending on which type of rock it comes from."

There was a scuffling at the entrance and Jessica ran to help the tiny quazor with its burden of fresh salmon.

"We need your help," Jessica called to the stunned surfers.

They carried in armfuls of wood and a stone bowl full of berries. Megan marvelled at the beauty of the bowl that was so thin it was translucent.

With his tiny hands the quazor heaped the wood together and, using his dragon fire, breathed crackling life into the pile.

"Over to you," smirked Jessica.

She and the quazor curled up together, making a strange ball of fur and scales.

174

The surfers set to work. Asiimwe chopped off heads and tails and gutted the fish, a job he had done many times at home. Tom sharpened sticks so he and Alex could hold the fish in the smoke from the fire and so cook them. Megan crushed the purple berries to make a thick juice.

Jessica and the quazor watched them lazily from half closed eyes.

"Leave the big one raw," instructed Jessica.

Megan suppressed a shudder, remembering the fate of other animals in other worlds.

Soon the great cave began to fill with the delicious smell of smoking salmon, to the apparent astonishment of the owls and the moles and the badgers and the bats and even the baboons, all of whom blinked uncomfortably as the acrid smoke drifted their way.

The surfers sat on the stone floor and bit into the smoky chunks of fish held in their hands. The flavour was full and delicious; the soft flesh fell from the bones with ease and they soon found themselves happily sated. The drink gave them energy and filled them with good cheer. They had to share the one bowl and all enjoyed lifting the great vessel to their lips so that juice poured from the sides of their mouths.

They were determined that the gnawing sounds coming from where Jessica and the quazor lay, who tore at the rich pink flesh with a sideways shake of the head, wouldn't put them off their own meal. They turned their backs when Jessica demolished the pile of heads and tails and guts that Asiimwe had put to one side. They pretended they didn't hear the tremendous burp that followed.

Not knowing how to dispose of the fish bones that were all that was left from the meal, they piled them into a corner.

As they stood to leave one of the owls hooted loudly directly above them. They looked up but could see no hint on any of the large, staring faces as to which one it was. The noise had a shattering effect in the echoey hall and reverberated round and round the stone walls. The vibrations struck the neatly piled fish bones; they clattered to the floor and spread out across the geometric designs, sliding over the smooth surface. Megan was about to run forward and pick them up again, when Tom put out a hand to restrain her.

"Look. They've fallen into three patterns. Let's take note of how they're arranged. Could be a clue."

They all tried to commit the designs to memory.

Jessica was busy licking bits of salmon from her furry paws.

"She's lost interest now her belly's full," thought Alex cynically.

The quazor was on his way again. They followed him through an opening at the back of the cave and along a short tunnel that grew into another space, this time so extensive that they couldn't see either walls or roof. Still there was the strange glow from the floor. And here there was vegetation. Tiny plants grew beside a small underground stream, no more than a trickle that would eventually join up with the mighty waterfall.

Tom inspected the surprisingly regular rock structures that bordered this stream, but it was Asiimwe who made the connection first.

"Is there any paper in that rucksack of yours, Tom?"

Tom handed over a torn piece of paper and a blunt pencil.

"Each of these boulders is different." Asiimwe began to draw and spoke more to himself than to anyone else. "Remember the patterns of the fish bones." The others listened to him, concentrating. "They made three different flat shapes on the floor. Suppose each one of those showed a different elevation of one of these three dimensional boulders. Then all we have to do is find the boulder that matches one fish bone shape from the front, another from the top and the third from the side." He held out his drawings for the others to see. "Look, they're like plans for a building."

"That's *all* we have to do?" asked Alex sarcastically. "There must be more than a hundred of them."

But Asiimwe was already searching, Tom with him.

"How come you know so much about surveying?" demanded Alex.

Asiimwe was busy and didn't reply. Alex joined him.

Their search took them further and further along the course of the little stream.

Looking up from the fish that she found more interesting than the rocks, Megan was attracted to a reddish boulder overhanging the water. It was somehow out of keeping with the others.

"Look at this one, Tom." She called him over.

And then things happened very quickly.

There was a piercing shriek that came from high up, somewhere in the roof that they couldn't see. Stones and gravel fell from the same spot. There were more shrieks and the sound of running feet all around them.

Then it came – a growling, rumbling, crumbling, cracking sound. And the earth trembled beneath their feet. Huge rocks slid down from somewhere above and bounded across the floor, crushing the stone structures beneath them. More and more exploded after the first wave, filling the cave with dust. The surfers put their hands over their heads and crouched, waiting and coughing, the sting of earth and stone on their faces and in their hair, the shocks of the quake resounding through their bodies.

A few more rumbles and all was uncannily still, particles of dust floating in the air the only movement. At their feet the floor was wet where the landslide had diverted the small stream; the dust of the fall had mingled with it to make sloppy mud.

"Everyone all right?" It was Jessica's uncertain voice.

Beside her, Alex and Asiimwe shook themselves and ran their hands through their grime-filled hair.

"Where are the others?" wondered Alex, wiping the dust from his face.

"We're here," shouted Megan, excitedly, "and we've found the treasure. It's a metal tooth. It's a sort of dark blue colour. I suppose you could call it indigo. It's just like the metal the technopeople use. It must be one of their teeth." Her voice sounded hollow and far away.

"We found the right boulder, and the landslide split it open for us," declared Tom amazed. "The tooth was inside." His voice was a reverberating echo.

"But where *are* you?" shouted Alex.

"Just the other side of the landslide," replied Tom uncertainly, realizing that they were separated from their companions by a gigantic fall of rock. "We'll have to climb over the top."

And then Megan and Tom heard a familiar sound above them, the gibbering of baboons excitedly calling to their friends. They looked at each other in horror.

They caused the slide.

The gibbering echoed hollowly around the empty space.

Megan and Tom clawed desperately with their hands at one side of the fall while Alex and Asiimwe did the same at the other.

"Have you got the tooth safe?" asked Tom.

"Course I have," retorted Megan. "It's in the money belt with the other treasures."

It soon became clear that the landslide had been a very big one. Megan and Tom stopped scrabbling uselessly at the fallen boulders. They realized with a chill that the baboons had them just where they wanted them.

Jessica was distraught. "Now I'm for it," she wailed. "Lucifer will say I messed up. He'll say this wouldn't have happened had he been here."

"Stop whinging," snapped Alex unsympathetically. "It's his fault he isn't here. Get moving these rocks."

With hands that rapidly became raw and bleeding, he and Asiimwe struggled to move the impossible pile of stone before them.

On the other side Tom pulled away a large chunk of rock to reveal gleaming eyes that stared at him; hot smelly breath blew into his face. Quickly and averting his gaze, he heaved the rock back into place.

Doing their best to shrink into the pile of stone, he and Megan looked around them, above and below. The baboons with the leaden fur had them surrounded. Megan clutched the money belt at her waist and shouted at them defiantly. Tom's anxious eyes searched dark recesses for a means of escape.

"Come on. In the shadows over there. It's the opening to a tunnel. Let's take it."

Pulling his torch from his pocket, he ran, sloshing through the mud that swirled on the rocky floor, Megan close behind him. The dirty water splashed up to their knees as they blundered headlong down a damp tunnel until, panting and breathless, they emerged into another cave. This one was much smaller than the first; they could see all the sides and the roof above.

They looked behind them and saw the creatures massing in the entrance through which they had just passed. They were small and wiry. They were fluorescent white with long thin hands, tiny pin-prick eyes, large round ears like saucers and curved noses, the ends of which met their pointed chins. They had huge flat feet that made a sucking sound as they walked on the wet rock.

From their position behind a rock that rose from the centre of the cave Megan and Tom noticed that these creatures weren't looking for them; they were smelling and listening and feeling for them. Megan shifted position and a loose stone rolled across the floor. Dozens of sharp noses pointed in their direction, and they came on.

Making for a small entrance on the other side, the surfers ran again.

"They can't see us," hissed Tom, breathlessly. We must find somewhere where we can remain very quiet. And somewhere where we don't smell. If we could find some water .."

They came to a Y junction. One path was full of loose rock, the other sand.

"This way," said Megan, pulling Tom to the left. "The sand will deaden the sound of our feet."

And so it did, but it also hampered their progress, and the creatures were able to pick up the vibrations, and their smell.

"I wonder what we smell of?" muttered Megan inconsequentially.

As they stumbled on, they realized they were being coaxed by their pursuers at every choice of direction. And then they saw why. There were other goblins, coming from the tunnels opposite, gliding over the sand that so clogged their human feet, cutting off all hope of escape. They hissed as they came, and spat, and flexed their muscles, and coiled the ropes they were carrying.

"Back to back," said Tom. "I don't think they like the torch."

He shone light into the evil faces. With their hands the goblins covered their useless eyes and other parts of their bodies onto which the light fell.

Tom's torch flickered and went out. They heard a coarse laugh, saw gleaming eyes and leaden fur, and were aware of harsh ropes coiling round them. They felt themselves begin to lapse into a dreamy unconsciousness.

And then, suddenly, they were wide awake. The space was filled with blinding white light. Screwing up their eyes and shielding them with their hands, they looked above to see a huge tiger's head rise in the rocky ceiling. And, behind that awesome presence, as if out of the very rock itself, came the rippling, muscular body and the heavy padded paws. Megan and Tom took in the beauty of the symmetrical head, bronze white and black in perfect reflection, the fire of colour along the back, the dazzle of metal, the heat of flames. The golden eyes glowed fiercely from the proud face and the low voice was a menacing snarl.

"Get back where you belong, low life of the underworld." And his breath was hot and sweet.

Some ran, gibbering, others stood rooted to the spot. The great tiger stepped on them with his massive paws, and where he had stepped there was nothing left but footmarks in the solid rock. The baboons had more courage. They flung themselves at the tiger. He picked them, one by one, from his velvet fur to which they clung, with his huge jaws, and spat out only bones.

Megan and Tom cowered towards each other, presuming the tiger friendly, but not certain.

Megan recovered first. "Who are you?" Her voice was faint and unsure.

"Who I am doesn't matter," the great beast replied. "This mission is none of mine. But I have an interest in Zero Six Six. It is for her that I set you free. Now let me take you home."

Tom and Megan scrambled gratefully onto the broad handsome back. The roof fell away as they rose towards it. They rushed out into the open air through a storm of shards of metal and heavy grey drops. Until the drops turned to watery rain and they were in a sudden shower in the ruined compound where the chameleons lived. The tiger tossed them off his back and dissolved into a pool of golden light.

"Cool!" squawked Percival, and flew to Megan's shoulder.

"What do we do now?" demanded Alex, his hands torn and bleeding, looking to Jessica for help. "Where have they gone? Will they be all right?"

The shouts from the other side of the rock fall had ceased.

Jessica's reply was unsatisfactory. "The baboons were at work in this," she said. "And I fear others put them up to it. There's nothing we can do right now. We must return to Bioworld, and plan."

The little quazor, realizing that something had gone desperately wrong, wanted to ask the owls and bats to help. But Jessica was adamant. They must return to Bioworld immediately. She needed to get in touch with Control, but she wanted to consult Lucifer first.

"Why?" Alex was angry. "Why wait for him? He should be here anyway."

Jessica hung her head.

"You're protecting him, aren't you," said Alex. "You don't want Control to know he didn't come to Technoworld. Are you sure he's worth it? I don't think he is."

"I can sort this," said Jessica, suddenly showing her old confidence. "But we must return to Bioworld first."

In her mind she had the idea that she would come back alone when she had Alex and Asiimwe safely home.

It was a sombre group that bade farewell to the sparkling waterfall and its friendly quazor and clattered back across the metal bridge. They came to the cave where they had left the bicycles. The little foxes bounded to greet them, blood pouring down their silver fur, from wounds to side and neck. Inside the cave, lying next to the bicycles, were three dead baboons, their coats matted and dulled from the fight, their dead red eyes devoid of menace, in a face set forever in a hopeless snarl that displayed white and even teeth.

Alex and Asiimwe patted the foxes their thanks and, with wan smiles, taking two bicycles apiece, Jessica loping beside them, head and tail hung low, they made their way through the stony countryside and into the ruined compound.

33 Explanations

"Alex!" It was Holly. "Where's Megan?"

Alex was taken by surprise. "I don't know, Mum."

"Well find her for me will you? I want her to add something to this e-mail for Grandad before the power goes."

Alex looked at Asiimwe and shrugged his shoulders. He scowled at Jessica.

"It's all right Alex, she's here!"

Alex and Asiimwe leaped to their feet and made for the house, but Jessica got there before them.

"How did you get back? How did you escape? How ..?"

Megan held the shiny tooth aloft. In the light of the strong sun it glowed with an indigo heart.

"We returned on the back of a beautiful tiger," she said.

Jessica looked up, startled.

"He seemed to know you."

And every bit of Jessica's fur that was normally white went pink, even the tip of her tail.

Megan watched lazily the lizards run across the whitewashed walls of the latrine, their quick tongues flicking in and out in search of some hapless insect. They always emerged in the brightest sunlight. She wondered idly if they were able to shift into quazors; she wondered what they might know and understand of the mission.

As darkness fell it was the turn of the geckos. On silent, splayed feet they chased each other over walls and ceilings. Moving in jerks, they made frequent stops to look behind them, waving their tails expressively. Megan found these little creatures very endearing although she did think that perhaps they weren't very good-tempered: they spent a lot of time chittering at each other, driving imagined enemies from their territory. Maybe they too could become quazors at will; maybe they too knew more than mere human beings could ever imagine.

Lucifer stirred uneasily in Simone's lap. He could feel a distinct itching in the orange fur behind his green ears. He stood up, concerned.

"Ouch! You're digging in your claws," protested Simone. "Off you go then," and she pushed him angrily to the ground.

Lucifer made for the thick bed of large golden lilies that almost surrounded the circular lawn. He looked up to the sky where evening was changing from indigo to violet and the strong-coloured stars were rising in the purpling heavens. The bright red were always the first to appear and it was one of those that Lucifer sought. He rubbed with a soft paw behind his left ear, reached for his mobile phone and almost immediately raised a signal on the clear wind free night.

Someone up there in Control was not pleased with him. He was flustered and raised his fur on end so that he became twice his normal size. So he had been caught out! But he would wriggle his way out of trouble, he always did, his quick wits would not desert him. He calmed himself down and his fur settled. He must think this out. How did they know he hadn't joined in the fourth quest? Jess wouldn't betray him; she was too soft to do something like that. Anyway, he had deliberately stayed out of it to give her a little independence. He now said as much over the phone. Back came the answer.

"But your motives were devious. End of story."

Well, that was true enough. But how did Control know anything about his motives? Only Double O Three could read his mind, and Double O Three was with him. And he supposed Double O Two and Double O One could too. But, he'd never had anything to do with them – yet. They were outside and above the Intelligence Service. What about Double O Four? It must have been Double O Four? But who made him suspicious?

"Stupid cat!" said Simone spitefully, smoothing out the creases in her dress.

"Why do you say that?" objected Klara, fondling Plato. "He's an intelligent and beautiful sparkat, and he loves you."

Simone's face softened. "Yes, he does love me, doesn't he," she said. "But he keeps secrets from me. I *will* know his secrets." And she stormed out to find him. But Lucifer had returned as fast as possible to Bioworld to get himself out of trouble.

"Well," he said to Jessica whom he found licking her paws that had become scuffed and bruised on the harsh rocks of Technoworld. "How did it go? I believe you messed up," he added, answering his own question. "Have you reported back yet?"

"Well, no," explained Jessica. "I was waiting for you to do that."

Of course you were, thought Lucifer. Jess was so naïve, she could never be devious. She'll never make a top secret agent, he thought scornfully.

But she did have enough subtlety not to mention the tiger when recounting the events of the past few hours. Tom had no such scruples and described the animal in great detail.

Now who could that have been? wondered Lucifer. Who could have shifted into a tiger to help Jessica? But he knew he was fooling himself. He knew it wasn't a shift at all. His suspicious gaze rested on his partner, now dozing lazily in the sun.

34 Mbarara

An expedition to town was always a treat for Megan. Every month
or so, Holly went to Mbarara in the pickup, Haj driving. It was the
nearest place to get food and other supplies beyond the mere basics for
her family. Alex decided to remain at home with his bike this time, but
Megan persuaded Tom to accompany her. Tom always liked to be with
Megan and he needed new batteries for his torch that had let him down at
the critical moment in Technoworld. Percival decided to stay with Alex;
he didn't like the noisy pickup. And the cats certainly weren't having
anything to do with it.

Holly climbed into the cab beside Haj, and Megan and Tom jumped
into the back. They weren't alone. No vehicle ever left the village with
any room to spare. As soon as it became known that one was departing,
it seemed that the entire population decided it had business somewhere
along the route, and leaped up behind.

First there was the long journey down the murram road to Ishaka. It was
raining and, on the part where a hill rounded a corner, cars and pickups
began to skid and slide, engines revving, wheels slipping. A group of
boys and young men waited by the roadside in the downpour, arms folded,
shoulders hunched, knowing they could make a few hundred shillings
pushing motorists out of trouble. They glanced with distaste at the four-
wheel drive from the tea estate that took the hill in its stride, and denied
them their earnings.

Megan judged Haj a wonderfully clever driver, the way he managed
to negotiate the potholes and ruts, and avoid other vehicles. Public transport took the form of cars and minibuses. Always packed to overflowing
with passengers, they openly raced each other, shouting and jeering and
laughing as one outdid the other.

Beyond the bustling little settlement of Ishaka there was a tarmac road
all the way to Mbarara. Even Haj didn't tangle with the big buses that
plied up and down that route. They approached with a crablike gait. They
travelled at break neck speed and it was not at all uncommon to pass an
upturned vehicle on the verge, a group of curious people gathered round it.

Sometimes Haj would stop in Kabwohe to do some business of his
own. Sellers came to the window of the pickup to offer roasted bananas
to the occupants.

Always there were crowds of people on the road, both pedestrians and cyclists. They passed many boys with bicycles, laden down by three or four huge bundles of matooke. Matooke was a rich harvest from this area and every vehicle headed for Kampala had its bunch of matooke strapped on somewhere.

Mbarara is something of a boom town. President Museveni is one of its sons and it basks in his glory. The pavements are broken and the roads much in need of repair – pedestrians fight squelching mud in the wet season, flying dust in the dry – and the buildings need a coat of paint. But, in spite of all this, there is an air of prosperity and busyness and jauntiness about the place.

Megan and Holly enjoyed the market. The stalls huddled close so that it was sometimes difficult moving between them. The selection of fruit and vegetables was vast, and most of it good quality. There were peppers and carrots, pawpaws, avocados, big water melons and much more, all colourfully heaped side by side.

Tom was intrigued by the piles of quite ordinary bottles for sale, and old tins and plastic cartons: items that would be re-used or recycled into something completely different. A tin would be given a handle and so become a drinking cup, a metal container for cooking oil cut down to serve as a baking tin.

All around the stalls were tiny shops, mere cubby holes, but each one packed full of goods. Some sold tea and coffee and other basics at very reasonable prices. Others displayed rolls of material and colourful braid and beads. Still others had quantities of nails and bolts and screws and lamps and wicks. Piles of charcoal stoves were stacked at one end of a row of stalls. Everywhere lay heaps of sacks containing all types of flour.

Neither Megan nor Holly was interested in visiting the meat market with its discouraging smell of offal and dried blood. That was one part of the shopping that Holly willingly left to Edith, her housekeeper.

Holly and the children made for the supermarket, the size of a village shop in Britain. It was run by Indians and was a treasure store of luxuries. There you could buy packet soup and tins of baked beans and jars of jam. Megan brought out her shopping list and started taking items from the shelves.

"I want to do that experiment again," she explained in answer to Tom's question. Holly was interested too.

"What experiment?" she asked.

"The one Mr Karumu showed us. He made a volcano out of vinegar and baking powder. It really erupted. It was brilliant. And Mr Karumu's a wonderful teacher."

Tom grimaced. Megan laughed at him.

"Come and see the best part of Mbarara."

Her shopping finished, Megan pulled Tom from the store.

"Meet you in the Coffee Shop in an hour," Holly called after them.

They made their way to a stretch of road just outside the market, where the red murram turned to black. On a piece of waste ground were boys with bicycles loaded with charcoal for sale. Everything about them was black – skin, bicycles, clothes and wares – everything except the flashing whiteness of the teeth in their bright smiles. Megan would have liked to take a photograph of them with the camera she had been given for Christmas, but they wanted her to pay five hundred shillings to do so, and Holly wouldn't give her the money. So she contented herself with passing the time of day with them which she always did, and this time she introduced them to Tom.

One of them had a paper bag full of small mendazi which he offered to the children. Each took one and sat down on the sooty grass to eat it. The boys seemed to find everything they said amusing which made the children laugh too.

Watching them was a group of maribou storks. From their vantage point at the top of an enormous rubbish tip they were able to survey the whole street. Huge untidy birds. Like grey vultures, Megan thought. They scavenged through everything that was thrown away and played their part in keeping the town clean. Now their interest was focused on the children and, more particularly, on the mendazi they were eating and the crumbs that might be left behind.

And then the colour drained from Megan's face. She spotted a small black baboon by the fire the boys had lit to boil their kettle. He was smirking at Megan and holding up his two little hands, and in those hands he clutched a silver tooth.

"Look," hissed Megan at Tom. "He's laughing at us, and he has a tooth like ours."

"It can't be like ours," said Tom, reassuringly. "We have the real one. He's just teasing us."

"Well, I find him *so* irritating." And she put up two fingers to the baboon who did the same back. Then she stuck out her tongue, and so did the baboon, and his was much longer than hers. She waggled her hands beside her ears. The baboon imitated her and gibbered with glee.

"Don't let him get to you," grinned Tom.

Peals of laughter rang out behind them as they made their way back to the market. Megan looked over her shoulder and waved.

On the other side of the market was the bus station, a busy, noisy, dusty, smelly place. The reek of diesel was choking. The drivers constantly revved their engines, trying to persuade passengers they were about to leave, hoping that would make them leap aboard their bus, rather than another. Every time a bus arrived – from Kampala, or Kasese, or Kabele – sellers rushed to the windows, and held high in the air their offerings – bread and biscuits and chapatti and roast bananas and kebabs. When it came time to leave, crowds of young men banged on the sides, gesticulating and shouting; about what the watching children had no idea.

Holly liked Mbarara. It was smaller and more manageable than Kampala, and there weren't so many of those distressing beggars with missing arms and legs who crawled along the pavements.

The Coffee Shop, with its alluring aroma of freshly ground coffee, was a pleasant oasis from the drenching heat. Holly always finished the trip to Mbarara by calling there. She treated herself to two cups of real coffee while Megan and Tom sipped fizzy lemonade.

"I won't be a moment," said Holly. "I need to have a word with Mrs Singh." Mrs Singh was the mother of the young man who ran the little restaurant.

Fizzy lemonade was a treat in rural Uganda, and the two made the most of it. They bent their heads low over their glasses to listen to the tiny explosions and feel the bubbles break on their faces.

"Water is the element that magnifies and reflects and clarifies," intoned Megan sonorously, imitating Lucifer. "Tom, have you got the mirror?"

Tom pulled it out of his pocket. The screen savers were swirling as ever. There was a new jewel on the frame. It was deep indigo, just the colour of the tooth.

"Shall I?" he asked.

"Yeah," said Megan. "Why not?" She smiled impishly across the table at him.

Tom pressed the dark new jewel. Immediately the disc came into view, now only three segments left. Tom picked up a drop of lemonade with his straw and let it fall on the crooked finger. As they had known it would, that segment grew larger until it filled the whole screen. Beneath the hieroglyph appeared the eight dots. They watched the screen savers move in among the dots exploding them so that there seemed to be hundreds of tiny points, moving at random, seething and bubbling over each other, and leaping up and raining down. And the screen savers drifted between and around them, painting them red and orange and yellow.

"A volcano," exclaimed Megan. "Quick, put it back. Here comes Mummy."

"Come on you two, drink up. Haj will be waiting."

Megan and Tom found themselves sharing their space with a number of live chickens destined for the pot that night, and one boy even had a young goat on a string.

"All right," sighed Alex indulgently, "let's see how Mr Karumu teaches science."

"It might show us the way to the next world," ventured Tom who explained what had happened in the Coffee Shop.

Lucifer pricked up one ear.

"It really was pretty good," Asiimwe assured him. "We read the story of the lost city of Atlantis, and started talking about its destruction. Then Mr Karumu showed us how to make a working model of a volcano."

"Tom and Asiimwe, help me please," requested Megan. "And you watch too," she said to Jessica and Lucifer.

The sparkats pricked up lazy ears and pretended concentration, while both lay buried in their own thoughts, and each watched the other suspiciously.

Tom went down to the field where the cows had been watered and brought back clay which he and Asiimwe fashioned into a volcano with a gaping crater. This they set on the cookhouse floor.

Megan dipped into the bag she had brought back from Mbarara.

"First, in goes the baking soda."

With an exaggerated gesture, she tossed it into the mouth of the volcano.

"And now the food colouring."

With a flourish, she added that too.

"But just watch this!"

She poured in far too much vinegar.

The mixture bubbled and hissed and spat, and gunged itself over the rim of the volcano in seething red froth. Out of the door of the cookhouse it went, and into the yard where, far from lessening as it had done in the

188

science experiment at school, it became a mighty flow of molten lava. With a yowl the cats stirred themselves. In the quickest shift they had ever made their fur seemed to burst into fire. They ran to join the children. Percival circled overhead, squawking,

"Brilliant! Brilliant!"

Watching in horrified fascination, Tom absentmindedly stroked Lucifer until sparks flew from his coat and hissed as they met the lava. Lucifer shook him off and he and Jessica began to run, showering sparks over the children as they too ran beside the great flow, all losing the battle to keep up. Megan's excitement turned to fear as the soles of her feet began to feel uncomfortably hot. She could see only lava in front and to each side, and the smell of sulphur became overpowering. Great rocks were hurled into the air. They came back to earth with a grinding crash and were eaten up by the snake of lava that was making its way down the path. A hot wind hurled itself into Megan's face. She choked as burning ash settled on her body. She looked despairingly across the lava for somewhere to escape. And then it seemed to her that she saw tiger stripes in the molten stream. Lucifer noticed them too. For a moment he was taken aback, but quickly recovering his composure he yelled among the mayhem,

"Time to log on, surfers. Get stroking." All together they grasped the sparkats and stroked.

35 Youth World

Megan looked around her. The noise of the volcano had gone. She was on a wide ladder hanging in the middle of nowhere; she could see neither top nor bottom. Fear made her grasp the rung in front of her so tight that her knuckles turned white. She could feel her bare feet slipping.

"Here," a voice said gently. Asiimwe's strong black hand bent down to grasp her own and pull her up beside him. His presence restored her courage. She looked about her to see Alex and Tom on the ladder above, and the two sparkats below.

The ladder itself was made of ever moving gas and yet it was solid to hold. Through each rung and the two sides ran coloured threads lined with small barbs that interlocked with the threads on either side.

"Just watch," said Lucifer, "and hang on tight. Watch the birth of a world."

Below them the stream of lava they had travelled beside rolled and roared its way into blackness. And with it went the sulphurous smell and burning air. And then there was nothing. The darkness was total. The surfers felt neither hot nor cold, neither happy nor sad. There was no wind, no smell, no noise. Emptiness was absolute. Megan closed her eyes and even Percival was silent. Alex thought he had never felt so powerless. It was as if the capacity of thought had also disappeared. He shifted his feet on the rungs. He wished he had taken his guitar from his neck before they left; it was a difficult object to control on the ladder.

Then, far away, a speck of softness appeared, a hint of lightness. It grew and moved and changed shape into a thin horizontal line of twilight, cutting away part of the blackness. With it came a crooning that was more a vibration than a noise, and a fresh coolness in the air that was full of purpose. The surfers felt confidence and joy course through them.

The line of light became an engulfing sheet. It rolled and boiled and lifted waves from the middle of itself, and had substance. The gas became liquid; great chunks of this liquid solidified and formed rocks and land.

"This is how worlds are made," said Jessica who had moved to the rung beside Megan and was caressing her hands with her long orange tail.

"No, it can't be," said Alex. "Worlds take millions and millions of years to form. Things have to evolve gradually."

"Perhaps time itself has to be created to make evolution work?" wondered Asiimwe.

190

"Exactly," said Lucifer, looking appreciatively at him. "And time has not yet been generated in this world, so everything comes together. Sometimes time is created first, and then you get all the evolution stuff. Personally, I think it's more fun this way round."

"So do I," agreed Megan, watching the explosion of earth and water around her.

Their ladder of gas became solid and hovered above a stretch of shingle by a rocky piece of newly formed land.

"Here's where we leave the ladder."

Lucifer and Jessica were the first to spring from their perches, quickly followed by the others who threw themselves onto the gritty sand. They rubbed sore feet and hands, turned numb from the clinging. The ladder itself curled in on its centre; it withered like an old leaf, collapsed and disintegrated into yellow powder.

"Have you been here before?" Megan asked, hoping for reassurance.

"No, of course I haven't," laughed Lucifer indulgently. "It's a new world, isn't it?"

Alex stretched out his hand and ran shining particles between his fingers.

"Sand?" he queried.

"Not exactly," said Lucifer. "Sand is made from rocks that have been weathered by time; it is the end of a process. This substance is at the beginning. These particles will be welded together by heat to form solid rock. Probably that is, all worlds are different of course."

Their attention was caught by a blast of hot air that stood their hair on end and wafted heat into their faces. A jet of water surged from the surface of the lake beside them, carrying with it rocks and fire. The water belched again, and then again, and so an island was formed that hissed and steamed as it cooled. A narrow trail of rock linked it to where the surfers sat. As they watched, spell-bound, the rocky path cracked with a deafening roar, splitting it into myriad tiles, all of which had six regular sides.

"Magnificent," breathed Tom. "A causeway! A causeway made of hexagons for giant feet."

"Cool!" Percival echoed his sentiments.

While they marvelled the ground beneath them started to rumble. Piles of sand rearranged themselves, carrying the surfers with them so that they fell together in a heap.

"Come on," shouted Lucifer. "Follow me."

His fur shining with fire in the glow of the elements, he bounded towards the causeway, leaving the shifting sand behind. Asiimwe looked back to see cracks appear in the bed beneath it. Particles poured into the resulting crevices to be hurled back up again amid a heat so intense that they congealed together into small boulders. The quakes and the underground eruptions continued. More cracks appeared to let out smoke and fire and gushing water.

From the comparative safety of their island, the surfers gazed in silent wonder. Megan crawled to the edge of the rock and dipped her hand into the water.

"It's hot."

She gazed down into the soft sulphurous depths. And then she fell quiet before the immensity of it all.

The surfers sat in awed silence to witness the creation unfolding before their eyes.

The land across the causeway was still shaking although the massive earthquakes had subsided. The island on which they sat shook too, but less fiercely. Everywhere, the shaking crumbled rocks to soil. And then tiny mosses, grasses and humble plants grew among it.

In one direction the sky became lighter until it was pearly white just above the intense orange glare that remained near the horizon. On the other side it was deep indigo, pitted with golden stars.

As if in response to that perfect renewed light, the grasses and other plants shed their seed and became more.

And the soil divided and spread. Water poured between the divisions and made rivers. It collected in great pools to form lakes.

Small trees began to sprout and put out exploratory arms into the heavens, and blossom appeared on branches, and leaves.

And the air was filled with the buzz and whirr of many insects that alighted on the trees; the blossom fell away and fruits grew.

The water began to seethe with life – scaly creatures and large mammals – and some of these made their way to the land.

"Come on," said Lucifer. "Let's join in."

He set off, stepping stoning back across the causeway. The rest followed his example. They left their rocky vantage point, jumping happily from hexagon to hexagon. They felt a deep joy inside them and a feeling of weightlessness so that they stepped as if on springs.

And then the whole of creation burst into song as a small, pale, perfectly round sun leaped from the horizon and stationed itself in the zenith. From there finger rays poured down on all the land and bathed it in warmth and light. The sparkats' fur took on a golden tint, as did the surfers' hair. And the animals, big and small, spread themselves over the land, fur and scales and feathers amid a cacophony of noise. And, amongst them all, tiny gibbering baboons with glittering fur.

Lucifer led them up a grassy hill brimming with colourful daisies, and down the other side into a half-hidden dell.

"Look at this."

The valley was full of insects and tiny birds and mammals that constantly changed their shape and colour.

"This is the cradle of it all," he said smugly.

"But how did you know it was here?" asked Alex.

"I just followed my nose," replied Lucifer unsatisfactorily. "I've been surfing the worlds for a long time and have seen many created. Often most of the creation takes place in secluded dells like this one. It's the multiple of these tiny lives that makes a world, and you get a nose for where they are. They often play a more important role than the larger mammals, and are always more abundant."

Moving amongst them, Megan was fascinated by the bright butterflies and the beetles. They kept changing colour and shape and pattern.

"They haven't settled down yet," explained Jessica. "They're deciding which colours are best, the same with shape and size. Do you see how the wings move from squares to triangles to octagons? I think there is going to be something geometric about this world. Would you like to help them?"

"You mean create them?" Megan was captivated.

"Rather, suggest or encourage."

So Megan watched the butterflies and, when a pattern appeared that was particularly pleasing, she stroked it gently signifying approval. But it didn't always work. Sometimes the butterflies responded to her suggestions, sometimes they didn't.

"So, what difference am I making?"

Jessica shrugged.

Down by the stream Tom and Asiimwe watched fish-like creatures that were also investigating shapes and colours. The shades here were more subtle, for life in the gloomier rivers that received only pale rays from the new sun.

Alex was interested in the dragonflies, spinning like helicopters; iridescence glowed in the transparency of their wings. They too experimented with shape and size and colour.

"They respond to music, Alex," whispered Jessica.

Intrigued, Alex took his guitar from round his neck and now sat to play for the newborn insects. As he strummed, so they answered with their shapes, becoming angular when the music was jerky; and circular when it was quiet and smooth.

"Will the shapes fix?" Megan wanted to know, as she watched her brother absorbed in his playing.

"Maybe. Maybe not."

Megan was used by now to these kind of unsatisfactory answers from sparkats, and carried on watching. Percival, on her shoulder, was absorbed and so unusually silent.

One of the dragonflies seemed particularly taken with Alex's music. And then, quite suddenly, its wings lost power and it fell abruptly to the ground. Unconcerned, as if he sensed what would happen next, Alex played on. The dragonfly body became shorter and wider, the tail longer. Legs grew, just four, while the spindly insect legs disappeared.

"Almost like a dragonfly going back to its nymph stage," marvelled Asiimwe who had left the river to listen to his friend.

The head grew larger; a nose and ears emerged; out of the open mouth came fire and smoke. Scales ran all along the back down to the tip of the tail that grew a pointed arrow.

"A little dragon," breathed Tom.

And then came the colours – yellow and blue and red, and mixtures of all these – until the tiny dragon fixed on purple and looked up to Alex for approval. Finally, the transparent wings that had hung so loosely at its sides filled out and grew strong and leathery. Without a backward glance, the tiny dragon took off vertically and disappeared from view, welcomed by the wideness of the sky.

For a few moments Alex continued to play, totally absorbed in his creation.

"Alex, you created a dragon!" breathed Megan at last.

"Not quite created it," corrected Lucifer. "Influenced it would be a better description." But he was impressed none the less.

"Amongst it all there must be a clue," reasoned Tom, bringing everyone's attention back to the mission. "We must be led somewhere."

His eyes searched the nearby trees to rest on a tiny, gibbering baboon that held its hands to its mouth in amazement. It had witnessed the whole event.

36 Seeds

All eyes joined Tom's in scanning the surrounding environment. In the end it was Percival who made the breakthrough. He spied a group of colourful birds among the lower branches of a freshly formed tree. Their new feathers shone in the light of the young sun – orange and gold and brilliant shades of blue and green. Although they resembled parrots they had no long tail feathers; and their beaks curved up rather than down, to enable them to feed on the buds that grew underneath the leaves and close to the trunks of the trees they favoured. They caught Percival's attention; he looked them up and down with as much curiosity as they did him. He left the security of Megan's shoulder and flew to join them. But they, tantalizingly, moved to the next tree at his approach. And so they led him into the forest, keeping one tree ahead.

"Percival, where are you going? Wait for me," shouted Megan. Leaping to her feet, she ran after the parrot.

"You'll get lost," protested Alex, remembering how near they had come to losing his sister in Technoworld. He too set off in pursuit.

"Are we all going to follow those birds?" asked Tom

"Anyone got a better idea?" shrugged Lucifer.

They all made for the forest.

After a while it really did seem to the surfers that the birds were bent on leading them, not just on a chase through the young forest, but somewhere in particular. Their way took them ever downward. The rocky slopes on either side of them became steeper and bereft of vegetation until they found themselves entering a canyon that narrowed with every step. Light streamed from above where sunbeams danced over the rocks, but it had little impact on the track they were following. The birds, shining with some inner light, led them ever deeper.

"Hang on, I've got my torch." From one of the copious pockets in his jeans Tom pulled out the torch with the coloured lights and switched it to brilliant white.

"Look at that." He played the light up and down the cliffs.

"What?" asked Alex. "Those wretched baboons?"

"No, not them." Although there were very many of the tiny chattering creatures caught in the beam of light. "The pictures. Look. What creatures made them? Humanoids?"

They all turned to look for explanation from the sparkats who were teasing the baboons, making feigned lunges at them that sent them skittering for cover.

"They're like cave paintings from the Stone Age," marvelled Tom. "But how can that be in a new world?"

"You're forgetting about time," declared Lucifer exasperated. "It hasn't been created yet, so everything is muddled up." He resumed his teasing of the baboons.

"Oh yeah, right, of course," said Tom. He turned back to the paintings. "The colours must have been made from vegetable dyes," he observed.

"Look at the story they're telling," said Asiimwe. "It's all mixed up but it's the story of creation – the light and the water and the trees and the birds and the fruits." Asiimwe moved along the rock face as he spoke, while Tom illuminated it with his torch.

"The fruits are glowing," observed Megan, "just like the birds' feathers, and they're the same colours as the birds. So it must be the fruits that are important?"

"Of course," Asiimwe agreed with her. "The fruits are the source of life because they contain the seeds. And this is a new world."

"But it must be a special seed." Megan was thoughtful. "Let's look more closely at the fruits."

The birds circled their heads encouragingly as if to assure them they were on the right track. Percival was with them, paying particular attention to a golden female. The two of them swooped and soared and looped the loop together.

"Oh, leave him," said Megan to Tom who was trying to catch his attention. "Let's look at these paintings."

The pictures of the fruits were crude and primitive. There were large juicy ones like pears and melons, thin ones like bananas and cucumbers, and hard woody seedpods. These last had flat, circular tops and under the discs were holes. Coming from these holes the painter had drawn a series of dots representing seeds flying in all directions.

"They're just like the 'ody'," exclaimed Tom.

"Then those are what we must look for," declared Megan. "But we won't find the real thing in this dark place."

The birds had already escaped back to the light. Their task accomplished they rose to the sun, taking Percival with them. The surfers, more prosaically, made their way back up the canyon on foot. They retraced their steps through the forest to the spot where Alex had created the dragon. The way was hard to follow; it was greatly changed, the vegetation much denser because the creation was still in progress. There were a number of baboons on the spot they had vacated. They were eating fruit and throwing away the seeds. Seeing the surfers return, they scattered.

"I'm sure they haven't realized which kind of seedpod they should be looking for," laughed Jessica.

"Well, we know which seedpod," said Megan. "But where can it be?"

Her eyes searched despairingly through the vegetation that was thickening with every minute that passed.

"The 'ody' is a bit like a poppy," she said, trying to narrow the area of search. "So, it'll be down in the grass."

"Careful," said Jessica warningly. "You're thinking narrow again. You're thinking Bioworld. This is a different world. It is not in our gift to name worlds, but let's call it Youth world for now. There is no reason why things in Youth world should be the same as those in Bioworld. Maybe your so-called poppies grow on trees here."

"So it could be absolutely anywhere!"

Megan threw up her arms and twirled round in mock despair.

Their search became increasingly difficult because as they covered one area so it became re-covered with yet more created plants, and they had to search all over again.

Finally, tired and sticky from the sap of new growth, they flopped despairingly beside the snoozing sparkats who had found a sunny spot in which to spread themselves out.

"Hey you two, we need some help."

Alex shoved Lucifer with his toe. Nothing happened so he shoved harder. Ears twitched, a face twisted round and said,

"Yeah? What is it?"

"We need some help. We can't find this seedpod."

"Surely it would be sensible to ask someone who lives here."

The face twisted back and the eyes closed.

"Of course," said Tom. "Percival," he shouted, and tiny baboon hands flew to their ears as he shattered the peace.

Percival and his new friend flew down to join them.

The problem explained to Goldie and a drawing made in the loose earth, she cocked her head to one side and flew to the top branch of a bush just behind the sleeping sparkats. There, with her upturned beak, she stripped off seedpods and dropped them to the ground below.

"Yess!" Asiimwe was triumphant. "We've found them, or rather Goldie has."

The pods were round and golden; they had flat tops with frilled edges; underneath were holes from which the seeds would escape. The circular discs at the top were divided by lines into segments.

"But which one do we take?" asked Megan. "There are lots of them."

"Perhaps we need to look for one that's a bit different."

"Here then," said Alex. "This one has eight segments and the extra one is raised like a pie-crust."

"Let's look under it," suggested Asiimwe.

With the small knife he always carried in his pocket for jobs about the farm, he prised it open. Inside there was but one seed. Surely too large to escape through a hole; but then it had another purpose. It was black and brown and knobbly, certainly nothing special to look at.

"It's like a piece of cinder from a volcano," declared Tom excitedly. "A volcano was our original clue."

Asiimwe dropped it into Tom's hand. As he held it to the sun it caught the light and turned orange, as if still fresh from some eruption. And deep inside glowed a tiny orange heart.

"So what's in the other segments?" wondered Alex.

Asiimwe opened them up to reveal small black seeds, so tiny they resembled dust, hundreds and thousands of particles of life. He shook them into his hand and threw them into the air.

"Now grow!" he commanded, and laughed.

He tossed the remainder of the seedpod into the fast flowing stream that fed the lake. A small baboon leaped after it but it was gone. And then, behind them, a crescendo of noise broke out as the baboons stripped pods from the trees and shouted and quarrelled. Chasing each other, they made for the density of the forest.

"Never mind them," said Jessica, stirring at last. "They are helping to spread the seeds."

Asiimwe handed the fifth treasure to Megan and she carefully stowed it away in her money belt with the others.

"Let's stay a while here," suggested Megan. "I don't think I've seen a more beautiful place."

She dabbled her feet in the stream. The stream gurgled in reply; it seemed to have fingers that caressed aching toes. Megan watched some small furry animals with huge eyes that played and gambolled with much larger ones with long thin legs. It struck her that none of the animals seemed at all afraid of each other. So this must be a good world, she thought. But then her attention was taken by the baboons pelting each other with seed pods, ducking and hiding to avoid the missiles and thoroughly enjoying the game. What about them?

The stream before Megan became a lake. She saw the terraced hillsides and the boy in the dugout canoe, and knew she was back.

How would you colour the sections
of the shield, according to the rainbow?
Where would you place the creatures
Mzee mentions in his story in Chapter 37?

37 Islam

Megan's fingers slid into the money pouch at her waist to check the treasures. Only two to go. Lucifer lay asleep in the sun. Had he actually returned from Youth world without waking up, she wondered. Maybe Jessica engineered it all. She stroked the black and white cat who sat beside her. Jessica reached out a paw and gently touched Megan's chest, to show her appreciation. The boys idly tossed stones into the water, watching the ripples widen into nothingness.

"Percival! Where's Percival?" Megan jumped to her feet. "Surely he can't have decided to stay with Goldie. Oh, Jess, he wouldn't do that, would he?"

But she couldn't be at all sure that he hadn't done just that. So it was a despondent Megan who idly wandered home with Jessica, in thoughtful silence.

Tom left Alex and Asiimwe beside the lake and made his way back too, leaving Lucifer to his slumbers. He crossed the garden to his father's workshop and cautiously opened the door. Mzee was there finishing off a cupboard for the baby's room, but he allowed the boy to take out the rabbit box he was working so lovingly for Megan. Tom studied it. His own creation. He couldn't make it alive, but he could make it more life-like. With a small tool, he worked on the ears; the insides had to be beautifully smooth, just as Peter's were. The work was tedious but the results pleasing. This was going to be something of which he would be really proud.

One of Asiimwe's young uncles, Ateka, was a boda boda boy. He had decorated his old black bicycle lovingly and labelled it Batman. Ateka sometimes offered Megan a free ride, and then both of them would let their imagination run riot as they sped up and down the many hills. So, when she heard that Ateka had business at the mosque, she was already clambering on the back. Maybe the activity would take her mind off Percival's betrayal, she hoped.

Megan knew the mosque. She knew the Muslims went there. Very often, in the early morning, she was awakened by their call to prayer. She loved to lie in bed and let the sounds drift over her – unfamiliar but inviting, mysterious and beautiful. She had seen the Muslims approaching and leaving their place of worship: the men in long gowns, the women in colourful dresses that covered them completely, the children shining with cleanliness. But she didn't know anything about their beliefs.

Happily, they freely bowled down the two long hills and, sweatily, dragged their way up the other sides, until the golden roof came into view. Megan examined the building with interest as they slowly covered the last bit of the journey, Ateka straining at the pedals, determined not to get off until they reached the gate. She marvelled at the shape of the roof and the domes, at the colours in the elaborate paintwork, and the colonnaded steps leading to the entrance.

While Ateka spoke with his friend, Megan crept cautiously round the door of the mosque. She wondered at the vaulted ceiling, the archways, the beautiful stonework richly decorated with Arabic calligraphy, the bright red mats on the floor. She was awed by the hugeness and the emptiness and the warm welcoming lightness of the place. The quietness was shattered by the muezzin who began the call to prayer from the elegant circular minaret. His high insistent voice penetrated the cares of those he summoned, and released them, for a while, from the heavy responsibilities of their lives.

"Megan! Come on! You shouldn't be in here!" Ateka pulled her out into the sunshine. "We're going back now."

All the way of the return journey, Megan thought about the mosque and the Muslims, only pausing for other thoughts when the wind was in her hair as they sped down the hills. She supposed Ateka's friend was a Muslim. She knew Haj was a Muslim. She knew there were Muslim children at school. I expect they have a creation story, she thought, taking her imagination back to Youth world. I'll ask Haj about that.

Her thoughts were interrupted by a thump on her left shoulder. A golden face nuzzled her cheek, and a long green tail caressed her neck.

"Percival, you're back," she shouted with delight. She quite forgot her anger at his defection. She looked round for Goldie.

"So you left your newly created girlfriend behind." She smiled and put up a hand to stroke him.

The stars ruled alone that night; the moon was new and offered no challenge. Lucifer held up his mobile phone and quickly picked up a signal. He passed on the news of the mission's continued success, and knew that both he and Jessica had approval for work well done.

Smugness and confidence enabled Lucifer to make a visit to Rainbow world soon afterwards. As he lay in Simone's warm embrace, he prattled of creation and seedpods and treasures. So secure did he feel that he didn't even glance around. If he had done so he would have seen Klara

202

out in the garden. Her smooth moss green hair glowing under the bright night sky, she bent low over her drawing, a parrot with a golden head and a long green tail guiding her hand.

Megan had hoped that the book she had found would tell her about the Muslims but, disappointed, she put it down beside her. Her attention was taken by wings, wings coming from the ground, from the edge of the flowerbed of scarlet poppies right beside her. Winged creatures were erupting from the depths of the earth, emerging in droves, faster and faster as she watched.

"No, Jess," she said, putting a restraining hand on the cat beside her. Percival chattered with curiosity and looked questioningly at Megan.

Tiny things with overlarge transparent wings, silently they spiralled upwards in a great swirling column. Reaching the height of the tree, they split and veered away in different directions. Freed from whatever dungeon had held them, they flew into the gathering darkness. Those that escaped the birds. The hatching of the flying ants had been witnessed by a flock of hungry chatterers that gathered them as quickly as they left the underground prison. They crammed their tiny stomachs with the easiest meal that had come their way in a long time. Megan began to wonder about the hole they must be leaving in the ground and imagined some vast cave down there. They came on and on – hundreds, thousands, millions of them.

"Flying ants!" Haj was beside her. "Good to eat, Megan. I show you tomorrow."

Very early the following morning, Megan saw Haj take a sack to the security light that had shone all night in the corner of the front garden. She went after him.

"Oh Jess," she breathed. "Oh look at that!"

On the grass, underneath the light, was a beautiful, rippling, quite regular fan shape, created entirely from the wings of flying ants.

"That's magical!"

Unimpressed, Haj was about to gather them all up into his sack. Megan put a hand on his to prevent him.

"No Haj, please, just wait a bit. Let me fetch Alex. I want him to see the ants."

Haj was impatient, but he waited. He told the children that the tiny creatures had killed themselves by flying into the light to which they were irresistibly drawn.

"Good to eat," he added as he shovelled them into the sack. "Come after school and I show you."

Megan and Alex and Tom made themselves comfortable on the floor of the small hut behind the office of the tea estate in which Haj lived, and learned how to cook flying ants.

First, Haj put them in a pail of water and stirred them until the wings floated to the top. Then he fried the wingless, chunky little bodies over the fire, in a little cooking oil.

The old man placed a kettle on the heat.

"They taste better with chai," he grinned.

"And here's the matooke." Asiimwe appeared in the doorway with a covered dish.

Haj took a spoon and scooped some of the ants from the pan. He lifted them to his mouth and swallowed.

"Delicious," he declared, licking his lips and grinning.

Megan and Tom took small portions of the ants and spread them sparingly on the matooke. But Asiimwe and Alex tucked in with relish, and happily washed down second helpings with mugs of chai.

Now could be a good time, thought Megan, when all the ants and matooke had disappeared and Asiimwe had brewed another pot of chai.

"Haj," she ventured, "do you know any creation stories?"

Haj laughed. "Very many," he replied. Then he fell serious and looked intently at the little girl with the searching eyes in a face surrounded by curls that were a deep bronze in the dull light of the fire. She came from a land so far away, and he was pleased that she should be interested in his culture.

And so began the storytelling. Haj's young visitors learned tales that were a mixture of African tradition and Islamic influence.

They learned that the Creator made things out of light, and the first light that he made was the rainbow. Haj told them about the four classes of animals – those that swim whose king is the whale; those that creep whose king is the python; those that fly whose king is the eagle; those that walk on four legs whose king is the lion. And he told them that the Creator made four classes of creature gifted with intelligence: the angels made from light; the wind spirits made from air; the evil spirits made from fire; human beings made from earth.

But of all of the things she heard that evening, Megan enjoyed most the story of the enormous cockerel with many-coloured feathers that stands in Heaven and crows every morning before dawn so that the cockerels on earth can hear him.

"After the cockerel crowed for the first time," said Haj, "the sun rose and the first day began on the earth."

Megan thought that cockerel must be just like the muezzin at the mosque.

It was Haj who broke up the little party; he had other things to see to.

"Thank you so much," said Megan. "We'll come back to hear more."

And Haj knew they would.

He set off towards the office, leaving the children to clear up.

Megan gathered the cups and plates together and took them outside to wash them. Tom swirled the tealeaves in the bottom of the pot.

"I wonder." He took out the mirror from a pocket.

He pressed the orange jewel that had appeared in the frame. The two remaining segments of the original disc spun among the screen savers. Tom poured a drop of tea over the sixth hieroglyph, the bird representing one hundred thousand, and that segment grew until it filled the frame. The dots formed a pattern which the screen savers were perfecting. The colours were earthy as if made from natural dyes.

"It's a series of symbols," mused Tom.

The screensavers pushed and pulled at the design that was based on nine small rectangles within a larger one. Each dot that the screen savers moved filled one of the rectangles with a different colour, except for the bottom rectangle on the left; that remained blank. And then the colours took on shapes. Tom noticed a whale, a snake, a bird, a lion ...... and – in the middle at the top – a multi-coloured cockerel.

"The Creation story Haj has just told us," he exclaimed.

"Which one isn't there?" Megan demanded.

"The angel," whispered Asiimwe. "There is a bead missing from the angel on the shield." He felt his skin go clammy.

"I've seen that design before. It's on a shield hanging in my house."

"Where did it come from?" asked Alex. "Is it special in any way?"

"I don't know. I'll have to ask my grandfather."

Asiimwe looked shaken. He didn't want to involve his family in anything to do with other worlds which they would see as magic. But he knew he had to find out more about that shield.

Amos was amazed by his grandson's questions. The shield had hung on the wall of the sitting room all his short life; and he had never asked after it before. Nevertheless, he was pleased that Asiimwe should show an interest in his ancestors.

The shield had come to his house with his wife when they got married. Amos thought back to the time of their wedding. He remembered how hard it had been for his young bride to settle in among the Banyankole whose culture was different to that of the Masai where she had grown up.

Her family had given her several items to bring with her to her new home, and her uncle's shield had been one of them. Amos suggested that Asiimwe ask his grandmother; she would know more about it than he did.

Asiimwe found Perpetwa in the cookhouse. Beans had been plentiful this harvest, and he drank in the smell of their cooking that spoke to him of prosperity. Perpetwa wiped her hands on her apron and stepped outside into the sunshine to join her grandson.

She was happy that Asiimwe should be interested in any aspect of her family's history. Although, in truth, she knew very little about the shield: just that it was beautifully made, and had been of great importance to her uncle.

"Uncle went hunting in the bush," she said, "like many a young man before him. He was away for several days which wasn't unusual. But when a whole week passed, we began to think something dreadful must have happened to him. Then suddenly he re-appeared, looking happy and well-fed and bearing gifts from a strange tribe he had met. The most important of the gifts, he said, was this shield with its design of beads, depicting part of the Creation story. Uncle was to keep it, the chief story-teller had said, and do with it what his heart told him. And I suppose his heart must have told him to give it to me. Maybe it now has something to do with you?" She looked hard at Asiimwe who was beginning to feel uncomfortable. "Uncle and his friends went out on several occasions to look for the strange tribe but found no trace of it. I think maybe Uncle did find it again, but only when he was on his own. I'm not sure about that. He would never say. The whole business became too mysterious for anyone to really want to find out."

All this Asiimwe related to the others as they sat together in the shade of a poincettia.

"So we visit the Masai," said Jessica. "This will be your mission, Asiimwe, this is your territory."

Asiimwe looked uncomfortable but took the lead.

206

"It's several days walk from here, unless we take the bikes. We'll need provisions."

"That won't be necessary," said Lucifer lazily. "We can be there in less than a minute."

"But we don't need to go by magic," mumbled Asiimwe nervously. Knowing how Africans felt about such things, he didn't want to arrive at the home of his relations in a flash of electricity.

"Don't use that word," Lucifer purred deeply in mock severity. "It's not magic, it's science, and it's a lot quicker."

"You must at least let me go home and fetch gifts." Asiimwe was adamant. "It would be most rude, in my culture, to arrive empty handed."

It took Asiimwe and Alex less than half an hour to gather what they wanted. Because of the good harvest, Asiimwe didn't feel at all guilty about taking the matooke and the beans and the precious millet, but he was still startled by the voice of his younger brother.

"Where are you going, Asiimwe?"

"Just visiting," he replied, and fled the compound.

Laden with rucksacks full of gifts, they made their way to the bush. Very soon, they felt the undergrowth become more tangled, it sought to pin down their feet.

"Here," said Lucifer. "Here's where we log on. Start surfing."

"You will keep clear, you cats, won't you?" said Asiimwe anxiously. Pets were not part of his African culture.

Lucifer grimaced. "Get stroking," he said.

They pushed their way through the tangled growth and there was the land of the Masai.

38 Masai

Asiimwe was desperately worried about how he would explain his muzungu friends to his relatives. He needn't have been concerned; Africans are far too hospitable to cross-question visitors. And the cats weren't going to embarrass him. Two magnificent leopards with dark gleaming spots on golden coats rested in the tree above their heads – all four limbs draped limply over the branches – and watched them lazily from hooded sleepy eyes. And in the foliage above them was a gorgeously apparelled parrot.

Asiimwe heard the shouts as they topped the rise. A small girl ran towards them, a crowd of other happy, half-naked children racing behind her. Their hands were clasped and they were dragged, almost running, into the compound. There, his cousin's children whom he hadn't seen for more than three years fought to arrange seats and bring out soda. And then his cousin appeared, and his wife, and many more relations including his great uncle, now white-haired but still walking tall and straight. There were greetings and hand-shaking and introductions and laughter.

The life of these Masai had changed very much in the last few years. They still lived in the same mud built huts with thatched roofs. They still cooked their food outside on great cooking stones. They still herded cattle, and lived on their meat and blood and milk. And they still wore the red patterned cloth about their shoulders and decorated their bodies in rows and rows of colourful beads. But now they had schools for the children and radios in the houses. Many of them went to town on their bicycles; their cloaks flowing out behind them they resembled enormous red bats.

The Masai meal was very different from that served by the Banyankole. In Asiimwe's home meat was a treat, reserved for special occasions. Here it was the main ingredient; huge chunks of it were piled up in the middle of the table. To drink, there was blood mixed with milk. Tom and Megan sipped at this half heartedly. Asiimwe and Alex downed it with relish. Megan thought, not for the first time, how good an African her brother was.

As they sat round the remains of the meal and spoke of family affairs, Asiimwe brought up the subject of the shield. The face of his uncle's wife drained of all colour. She had been told by her husband that he visited the tribe from which the shield had come but, deep inside, she wasn't sure that was where he went when he strode into the bush on his own. She asked him to take her with him but, whenever he agreed to do so, somehow they couldn't find the place, and she returned home more disgruntled than ever. Now, she said to herself, either witchcraft is at work here, or he is lying. Maybe he has another woman. She had convinced herself that the latter was true. But why the secrecy? Many Masai men had several wives. But she knew that she herself would never tolerate such a situation, and she knew that Kasiro knew that too.

"The children are interested in the shield, Motesa. Let me take them to the tribe. We won't be long."

Even though he was hardly likely to take a crowd of children to a secret rendezvous, it was with a scowl that Motesa watched them go. She clattered the pots loudly as she cleared the table.

Uncle Kasiro led the children along a rough path beside a dried-up river, the banks of which were lined with bones bleached white by the sun, the pathetic remains of animals that had perished from thirst in the recent drought. There was a sharp bend in the river and, beyond it, an encampment of grim mud huts. In front and between them were cooking circles and brightly dressed people.

"There!" said Kasiro. "Can you see the settlement?"

"Of course we can," exclaimed Megan.

"No one else that I have brought here has been able to." Kasiro was puzzled. "So, in the end, I stopped bringing them. I think they thought I was involved in witchcraft, and many people avoided me and were afraid of me. But now I have met others who see what I see." He smiled gratefully at the children and told them his tale.

"The first time I met this tribe, the chief storyteller gave me the shield. He told me nothing about it. Even so I felt it was precious in some way. But it caused friction in my house, Asiimwe, so I gave it to your grandmother. She is very dear to me and I knew she would take it far away and yet still treasure it."

"But why do you come back here, when it so upsets your wife?" Asiimwe asked him.

"I don't know," admitted Kasiro. "Something keeps pulling me here. As if there's unfinished business, and the bushmen want to know if they may yet rest from it."

"So these are bushmen?" asked Asiimwe doubtfully.

"No, these are Masai, of a different era. But the bushmen are near, in the trees. It was from the bushmen that the shield first came. Come."

209

He suddenly smiled. "I feel the rest of the story is ready to be told, and Anotchi will be the one to tell it."

It seemed they had arrived in the middle of a party of some kind. Undoubtedly a wedding they decided. The whole of the tiny village was in a state of high excitement, and this centred around two young people in traditional dress. They carried wide and colourful beaded bands on their heads, large beaded rings hung from their ears, huge heavy collars of beads encircled their necks and they wore many bracelets at wrist and ankle. They had made up their faces with red ochre mixed with animal fat. The bride was clothed in a bright red cloth that fell from her armpits and almost covered a dark blue skirt below; the young man wore a robe of red and yellow checked wool.

More visitors were clearly welcome and the five were ushered without question into the family circle. The ceremony was over. It was party time. The drums encouraged dancers into the central area that was used for meetings of all kinds. Many of the dancers, men and women, wore grass skirts and grass bands below their knees that swayed and shivered with every movement. They had bells at their ankles and held shakers in their hands that added to the excitement of the rhythm.

But there was also work to be done. Megan noticed children on the edge of the village with long sticks, driving the wide horned cattle across the dried up land to the one place in the river where there was still a muddy pool. Once they had quenched their thirst, the cattle were herded into pens to be safe from predators during the hours of darkness. Cat-like shapes in the distance watched the activity; Megan knew that among them were two very special leopards.

As the sun slipped down the sky, the whole company of the villagers sat round the dying fire, drinking some heady smelling home-made brew and telling stories in their own language. The muzungu understood not a word but enjoyed the rise and fall of the gentle voices.

There was the distant roar of a lion and the sound of disturbance from the pens, cattle stamping their feet and lowing restlessly. Two men with lanterns left the party to investigate; they found only a solitary fox that slunk off into the night. But the noises of the bush were close: animals calling in affection and hatred and warning.

Anotchi, father of the bride, had raised his head at sound of the lion and now looked across to the five visitors to his home.

Anotchi was chief storyteller of the clan. A child brought him his personal stool that was kept for these occasions. The top was beautifully decorated with Masai warriors, and Masai warriors formed the legs that held up the seat. Now he spoke.

"The three things have come together at last: the call of the lion, the wedding and the arrival of strangers from afar. Now I can put other stories aside for a while and tell the story of the shield that has been a source of worry to me for so long. And so, by the telling, I will pass the burden to you." He looked long and hard at the visitors. And then he began.

"Many years ago, our ancestor, Makenyi, heard the distant roar of a lion in the night. Fearing for our cattle, he left the hut. To his horror he saw the lion, not in the distance, but right up close, so that he could feel the breath of the great beast on his face. It was a magnificent male animal with a huge, shaggy mane. Makenyi thought his end had come when the lion knocked him to the ground with a single blow from one heavy paw. But it didn't kill him, or even hurt him. Instead it turned and left, padding slowly into the morning sun.

"Shakily, Makenyi got up and looked at the paw prints of the lion in the soft dirt, to remind himself of what had happened. In each paw print was a bead, but a bead such as he had never seen before, made of some unfamiliar, almost transparent material. He bent down to pick up the first one. Then, following the trail, he picked up all the beads until the footprints finished at the base of a large and ancient tree in the forest. In the topmost branches was a tiny bushman. He beckoned to Makenyi, who climbed the tree, taking the beads with him.

"The bushman was crouched on a platform of wood. His body was small and skeletally thin. His face was a death's head covered in leather that stretched over the bones like parchment. His eyes were sunk deep down into their sockets. Across his shoulders he wore a monkey skin and, around his neck, was a long monkey's tail. Makenyi thought he must have been hundreds of years old. He was terrified and sought to climb back down the tree. But the old man held him with a bony hand and with his piercing eyes, and his voice was gentle. From behind his back he brought out a shield. The edges were decorated with red and white beads but the symbols from the centre were missing. 'Use the beads from the paw prints,' he instructed our ancestor, 'and make the symbols, according to my instructions.'

"Makenyi did as he was told and created the wonderful design you have already seen. The shaman, for so he was, asked Makenyi if he noticed anything. Makenyi replied that one bead was missing, which you too will have observed.

"The shaman now spoke earnestly to our ancestor. 'When you find a boy who can explain the pattern of the beads bring him to me and I will pass the remaining bead to him and at last be released from my earthly bonds. In the meantime no one in your tribe must know what has happened, except the chief storyteller. Your tribe will know when the time to speak has come for the roar of the lion and the beads of a wedding will come together with guests from afar. For, to find this boy, you will need to pass the shield to a visitor from another world.'

"And so, Kasiro, the shield descended through the ages to you, while the story passed down the generations to me as chief storyteller. Now I pass on that also to you."

"If we can explain the pattern," exclaimed Tom excitedly, "the shaman will give us the final bead, the sixth treasure. But the shield's at home!"

"I can remember the pattern." Asiimwe's voice was husky. "I see it every day."

He started to draw it in the dust at his feet.

"Have you any spare beads?" he asked the curious faces, now still and silent, around the fire.

A pot of coloured beads was immediately laid before him. In the bright glow of the flames, and under the watchful gaze of the moon, Asiimwe built a replica of the shield.

"Now," he said to the others, "where's the pattern?"

Tom concentrated.

"A bead is missing from the angel in the bottom left hand corner," he thought aloud. "The angel is yellow, so it's a yellow bead? That would fit; we haven't got anything for yellow yet."

"But we need to work out the pattern if the shaman is to give us the bead," Asiimwe reminded him.

They all stared down at the clever design with its nine symbols of different colours. The whale was blue, the lion red and the cockerel was all the colours of the spectrum. The devil was indigo, the wind turquoise …

"It could be a rainbow sequence," suggested Megan.

"It's based on squares," said Alex thoughtfully.

"Magic squares," said Tom

"Not that word again," sighed Asiimwe.

"Yess!" shouted Tom. "Yess! Got it! I've seen magic squares before. All the columns, rows and diagonals must add up to 15. Give each colour a number. Red will be one, orange two, yellow three, and so on."

"But there's nine spaces, and only seven colours in the rainbow," protested Megan.

Asiimwe was joining in the enthusiasm. "The extra ones are turquoise like we had in Rainbow world, and multicoloured like the first jewel in the frame of the mirror. That must come first, that's the cockerel. *That's* number one, now red is two ……"

"That's it!" shouted Alex, delighted. "Now, where's this shaman?"

"Not so fast," cautioned Kasiro. "It's already dark."

"But look at the moon. It's full."

Asiimwe shuddered. "But it was new back home. So we *are* in a different world?"

"Of course we are," said Tom. "It has to be a boy from another world who solves the problem!"

Asiimwe wished Lucifer or Jessica were here to explain.

As they spoke five leopards approached the fire. The wedding party didn't notice them, nor did they notice when the five visitors disappeared. It was just as if they had never been there in the first place.

39 Beads

The surfers and Uncle Kasiro each sat astride a crouching animal which then got to its feet in one graceful movement. In silence they crossed the parched land in a flood of dreamy moonlight that hid the stars. The pale light shone on the fur of the splendid creatures, sending shafts of silver before them, deliberately defining their route. On either side of the party were two further leopards with green tints in their rich fur. Megan was reassured to recognize Jessica and Lucifer. Occasionally she caught the glint of bright feathers above them, and knew that Percival too was with them. All around were noises: hyenas and jackals called to each other and crept as near as they dared to the strange group. Reaching the trees, they were met by the querulous gibbering of many baboons. And here the leopards stopped.

From the undergrowth came the crash of some great animal moving nearer, and then into the moonlight stepped an enormous gorilla. He was a great silver back, in the prime of life. The fur on his arms and legs and round his face was thick and glossy and very black. He moved slowly, swaying gently from side to side, the hands of his long loose arms curled as he walked on them. Quietly he approached the children who gazed at him silently, awe and fear written on their faces. Reaching the first leopard who stood still like an animal carved from stone, he raised his great head. Under the heavy black brows were dark eyes that glowed with intelligence and knowledge.

"One only will enter the forest," he intoned in a deep voice that commanded instant respect. He looked straight at Asiimwe. Transfixed by his gaze, Asiimwe slipped from the leopard's back and moved close to the gorilla.

"No!" shouted Alex. "We'll all come."

The gorilla said nothing, nor did Asiimwe.

Alex paused, confused.

The gorilla took Asiimwe by the hand and led him into the forest. Tom and Megan looked to the sparkats for help but they lay unconcerned at the side of the path. Kasiro, too, seemed content and smiled reassuringly at the others who now sat still on their magnificent mounts and waited.

Asiimwe clung tightly to the hand of the powerful gorilla who led him unerringly deep among the trees. And then he stopped, patted Asiimwe's face reassuringly with a large rough hand and pushed the boy in front of him.

"Climb the tree."

The tired voice came from somewhere above them. Asiimwe could just make out the wooden platform of the storyteller's tale.

Asiimwe took a deep breath in an effort to conquer his fear and swung himself onto the lowest branch. There were many branches and footholds and he quickly made his way up to the platform. He was unprepared for what met him there. The skeletal thinness, the death's head, the leathery skin he had expected, but not the stench of decay. He put a hand over mouth and nose. The shaman didn't look surprised, and his voice was gentle.

"Yes," he said sadly, "I am far gone since last I was seen by your kind." He pulled the monkey skin more firmly about his shoulders in an effort to hide his decomposing body from his guest. "But I am confident that you will be my release. You know which bead is missing? You have understood the pattern?"

Asiimwe took the borrowed beads from his pocket, spread them out on the platform and redesigned the symbols in front of the shaman.

"The design is in nine parts," began Asiimwe. "It represents the work of the Creator. The colours used describe the first light that the Creator made. These colours stand in the rainbow in a certain order. If we give each colour a number we get this pattern. One of the beads is missing. It's a yellow one."

"The prize is yours," gasped the shaman and his hollow eyes were filled with relief and thanks. "Take it."

From the part of the skin that had been the monkey's armpit, he pulled out a yellow bead and handed it to Asiimwe in his bony hand. Asiimwe looked down at the tiny bead that glowed yellow in his palm. As he watched it grew to the size of the nail of his little finger, and a paler yellow surrounded the deep gold of the heart inside.

Once the bead had reached its full size, the shaman let out a long sigh of contentment. There was a rattling in his lungs and a further sigh. His body fell in on itself, and he and the monkey skin crumbled to dust on the platform. A slight breeze blew through the trees and the dust was gone. Only the long monkey's tail remained swinging from a high branch.

The boards of the platform splintered and cracked and fell from the tree in tiny pieces, scattering the pattern of beads as they did so and leaving Asiimwe hanging onto the branch below. Subdued, he climbed back to the ground and held out the yellow bead to the waiting gorilla. The gorilla curled Asiimwe's fingers around it and gave him a big gorilla squeeze. He guided the boy back to the edge of the forest and quietly disappeared.

Asiimwe walked out into the moonlight. Megan slid off her leopard and ran towards him to give him a quick hug of relief.

"Here, take this." He handed her the yellow bead. Megan opened the money pouch at her waist and placed the bead with the other treasures. Hand in hand they joined the others.

They returned to the scene of the wedding but there was nothing there. No people, no cattle, no huts, not even a mark where the fire had been. And suddenly they found themselves sitting on the ground; the leopards had disappeared. The hot sun blazed from a clear blue sky; it was day once more.

They rounded the bend in the stream and Asiimwe's young cousins ran to greet them.

"Well, did you find anything?" Motesa asked her husband querulously.

"It's over, Motesa," Kasiro replied. "The children have solved it. I shall never go there again." He put an arm round his wife's shoulders and she, smiling, snuggled into his chest.

Nobody seemed to know anything about the large joint of meat that arrived in the cookhouse at Asiimwe's home, but the family enjoyed eating it nevertheless.

Sometimes I'm really glad we don't have phones in our village, thought Asiimwe, crunching on a juicy piece of bone. He looked up to the wall above the table where the shield hung as it always had. The yellow bead from the angel was still missing. It was just the same as it had always been.

40 Where Next?

Lucifer raised eyes to the sky, searching for a signal so he could tell Control of the latest part of the mission. Jessica sat idly beside him swinging her heavy tail. Both animals were becoming very careless about showing their sparkat reality, thought Tom. Out loud he said to Lucifer,

"Asiimwe should be sending the report. It was his mission. He did all the work."

"Oh, don't be too hard on them, Tom," said Alex. "They did a great job of prancing around as leopards."

Lucifer's emerald eyes glared at Alex and, for a moment, a leopard face snarled. He quivered his raised, fluffed out tail and moved to another part of the garden to find a signal there. Alex laughed.

Asiimwe watched the stars appearing. They were exceptionally clear tonight because the moon was a tiny sliver of white. He remembered the full moon of their journey with the leopards.

"Jess," he asked, "were we in a different world?"

"Not exactly. We were in Bioworld all the time but in a different time zone, that's why the moon was different and the little village disappeared."

"I see," said Asiimwe doubtfully.

"So, where are we going next?" asked Alex.

"We're up to number seven. The last one will be the hardest of all, it always is, and the most dangerous," she added.

"And once we have all seven items, the baboons will be after Megan and Tom," said Alex thoughtfully.

"It's not so much the baboons we need to worry about; it's what comes with them.   Let's take it step by step, find out where we're going first. I expect it'll be off-planet, the final ones usually are."

"Aliens?" wondered Megan.

"I don't think you'd recognize them as that," laughed Jessica.

"I hope we don't go to Dranstorn." Lucifer had returned and was in teasing mood.

"Don't remind me of such things." Jessica shuddered from her whiskers to her tail.

The pickup roared into the yard. The twins leaped off the back and came running towards them, each waving a plastic toy they had bought in Ishaka. The sparkats did a quick shift and bounded from the garden; neither of them was very fond of the smaller children who liked to pull their tails.

"Tom," came Duncan's deep voice. "I've found some beautiful mahogany from a tree that came down over the other side of the estate. Do you want to help me unload it?"

Tom leaped to his feet.

"Six treasures, my darling," crooned Simone. She thought she was speaking to herself but Lucifer heard and stirred uneasily in her lap. Plato heard her too, and left in search of Klara.

Megan sat in her bedroom. She had closed the shutters tight. She took the money belt from round her waist and tipped the treasures onto her bed. Holding each one in turn before the light of the lamp to catch its heart of solid colour, she admired the beauty of it. She arranged the treasures in the order they had collected them and then rearranged them in the order of the rainbow. There was one for each colour, but the crystal from Rainbow world had both blue and green in it. So which colour was left for the seventh one? Probably it would be a mixture of colours like the cockerel on the shield? She would ask Tom what he thought.

She found Tom sorting through pieces of wood in his father's workshop. He was looking for something suitable with which to repair her rabbit hutch.

"What about these bits?" he asked her. "Dad said I could take anything from this pile."

Megan reckoned those bits would do very well. Together, they loaded the wood onto their two bikes and cycled the short way to Megan's house. While Tom got busy with saw and hammer and nails, Megan looked after the rabbits. She confided to Snowball the problem of the colours. He appeared disinterested but Percival, on the corner of the roof, cocked his head to one side and listened.

Megan's gaze wandered, as she idly stroked Digger's soft coat. Digger was a brown rabbit with flecks of grey in her fur. Megan liked to stroke her backwards to bring out the different colours, and Digger didn't seem to mind.

At the far end of the lawn were a couple of sacred ibis. These birds fascinated Megan. They were so full of contrasts. Their dress was of black with a sheen of purple and green, elegant and expensive; and yet, when they opened their long curved beaks, the sound they emitted, coarse and loud and rough, perhaps betrayed their true character? Beyond the bougainvillea, at the edge of the grassland, was a group of crested cranes. Of all Uganda's wonderful bird life, for colour and majesty and grace,

218

these were surely the winners, thought Megan. It was easy to understand why the people of this country had chosen that particular bird to adorn their national flag.

And then the baboon sprinted across the lawn and completely spoiled her reflective mood.

She got up to inspect Tom's carpentry. He really is good at working with wood, she thought, running her hand approvingly over what he had done. From one of his many pockets, Tom pulled a rather ragged piece of paper and passed it to her awkwardly.

"I did this for you," he said.

Megan looked into the face of Snowball, drawn beautifully in pencil and coloured lightly with crayons. She admired the nose and whiskers that seemed almost to twitch on the paper as they did in life, the beseeching blue eyes and the pretty black-tipped ears.

"It's just like him!" she exclaimed. "Tom, you are *so* good at drawing. I'm going to put this picture in my room."

Tom beamed with pleasure. He fought to control the redness that crept up from his neck and across his cheeks, and that only made it worse.

"Let's get these rabbits back in their hutches."

Once the rabbits had taken up residence in their upgraded home, the children fetched obotunda from the kitchen and sat on the veranda.

Megan told Tom about her thoughts on the colours, and about the baboon she had just seen.

"I think we should complete the mission as soon as possible," she said.

Percival, still perched on the roof, nodded his head in enthusiastic agreement.

"Let's use rain water for the last clue."

Megan set off across the compound to collect a jugful from the great barrel, fixed permanently in the open so as not to miss any drop of moisture that the skies might send.

As she bent over the jug, Alex and Asiimwe, on their bikes, swept into the yard.

"You're just in time," said Megan. "We're going to look at the last clue."

Lucifer and Jessica, guessing what Megan was up to, appeared from the bushes. Their plaintive yowl articulated what the two boys didn't.

"You might have waited for us."

Tom took out the mirror. Six pairs of eyes watched the screen savers swirl around. In the frame of the mirror an extra jewel had appeared. Tom pushed the yellow stone. The final slice of the circle became clear, with the seventh hieroglyph at the top. It was an astonished man that represented one million.

"Megan, you do the last one."

Megan poured a little of the water from the jug onto the symbol and the segment grew to fill the whole frame. The dots on it seemed to be placed at random.

"Look, the screen savers are turning them all into coloured stars," exclaimed Tom. "Megan, just look how beautiful they are!"

Megan watched entranced as the screen savers pulled at the edges of each dot to urge it into a star, and then filled it with colour.

"So stars it is," said Tom.

As he uttered the word 'star', the screen savers faded and the whole of the mirror turned deep purple. Something of a lighter colour was about to emerge from its depths, as if the mirror still had something else to show them. Lucifer came up behind Tom and placed a large paw onto the purple glass. It cracked from side to side and blood oozed round the edges. But Lucifer held his paw steady.

"We've finished with that now," he said gently. The mirror shattered into a thousand fragments that fell from Tom's hands and disappeared through the cracks in the boards of the veranda to the waiting earth below. Four questioning faces looked at the sparkat, all too astonished to speak.

"Star world it is indeed." Lucifer nodded approvingly. "Let's wait until dark for this most important of journeys," he added pompously.

The night sky waited for them and they for it. Their eyes fixed on the heavens above willed the sun to take its leave. First to climb over the horizon were the four bright stars of Pegasus that made a square; they rose into the growing darkness that encompassed the universe. Other stars trailed behind them, and more and more, searing the blackness of space with bands of brilliant points of white and silver.

"Somewhere in the middle of Pisces I think we have to go. Isn't that right, Jess?" said Lucifer.

"Yeah, yeah the fish, I think so," replied Jessica in what she hoped was a convincing voice. Her map reading skills had never been able to match those of Lucifer.

As always in Africa, the stars grew rapidly in intensity and number. But this night, they increased beyond their normal size and brightness and seemed to come nearer and nearer; and with them came a wind and a moaning and an exhilaration.

"Make for the gap," shouted Lucifer to Jessica. "Stroke like fury, surfers," he roared at the children. Their fur standing on end all around them, Lucifer and Jessica leaped to the sky, dragging the others with them. Some unseen force held the hands of the surfers to the sparkats' coats.

"Both hands," howled Jessica urgently. "We need to keep the circuits."

Megan looked down at her fingers and saw, revealed, all the bones and nerves and tendons beneath the skin like in an x-ray. She looked across to Asiimwe on the other side of Jessica. His hands, too, glowed with radiation, to the very bones; and his bones were startling white like her own.

Megan had the feeling she was being propelled through a shower of silver meteorites, faster and faster, hardly time to draw breath. She hung onto Jessica's orange coat.

Percival's claws dug deep into her shoulder as he tried to shrink against his mistress and so away from that searing wind.

41 Banquet

The hall was very grand indeed. The massive floor was the shape of a five pointed star. It was made of a silver coloured substance that was alien to the earthlings, and had configurations of black within it. From each point and indentation rose a thin silver pillar that extended so far up into the sky that it was lost in thick angular pewter coloured clouds, and its summit could not be seen. The walls were white and opaque, and smooth like marble. At the far end of the hall was a table and, above it, a huge and deep five pointed recess in the wall. This was filled with red and yellow glass that shed coloured light onto the floor.

"You are most welcome," said a tinkling voice.

They looked to the left from where the sound came and there, just waist high, stood a small yellow star. It stood on two of its points, yet two more were arms and the final topmost point sported a series of yellow spikes like some punk haircut. In the middle part was a face, just eyes and mouth, no nose or ears were visible.

"Welcome to the party."

"Party?" asked Megan. "What party?"

"Follow me."

And the little star set off across the floor. The earthlings looked at each other. Alex stepped out behind the star, mimicking its stiff gait, the others following, and Jessica bringing up the rear.

Lucifer waited until the others were well out of the way, and then slunk off towards the door. His stealthy cat movements went quite unnoticed by those whose attention was sufficiently taken with so much that was new. His large paws padded gently and firmly, filled with determination. The door was a single slab of stone that moved under the slightest touch from one within but was quite immovable to anyone outside, and therein lay its security.

Once on the other side of it, Lucifer lifted his white whiskers to the sky, searching for the path by which they had come. The watching star-let opened its tiny mouth to raise the alarm and Lucifer absentmindedly silenced it with a soft, heavy paw. He turned his paw over to examine the creature he had broken, bit into the side of it and hurled it away in disgust, nauseated by the saltiness that filled his mouth.

Then Lucifer sprang with all the pent-up power in his cat coils, and leaped into space. Travelling backwards in time, he made his way unerringly to Simone's feet in Rainbow world. He purred encouragingly, held his tail high and pressed his sleek orange body round her slender legs.

"So, my Lucy, where have you left them?"

Lucifer looked up into that lovely pale, questioning face. The purple hair, smooth and shining and smelling of allure, brushed tantalizingly against him as she bent down to caress his back and searched his emerald eyes with her deep violet ones.

She was beautiful, she was powerful, she would serve him well. With his paw he drew in the sand a five-pointed star.

I don't think it'll mean anything to you, my darling, but maybe it'll keep you happy. And indeed it did.

It meant a great deal to little Plato sitting inconspicuously in the corner of the room, and he ambled off to find Klara.

"You sit there," said the star, indicating four stools arranged round one of the points of the star shaped table. Megan opened her mouth to ask a question but their small guide had disappeared.

"What do you make of this, Jess?" asked Tom.

Jessica shrugged her luminous coat. "Never been here before."

"Where's Luce?" wondered Alex. "You know, that cat's never around when he's needed. I suspect he has his own agenda. What do you think, Jess?"

Their conversation was interrupted by a semi-musical noise so loud they put their hands over their ears. Then, as suddenly as it had started, it stopped. The earthlings peered down the hall to see where it might have come from.

"I don't much care for the music they have around here," laughed Alex. "I wouldn't let it anywhere near *my* walkman."

Percival squawked his agreement and continued squawking long after the noise had ceased, so deep was his distress.

Megan examined the star shaped table at which they sat. What was it made of? Some kind of precious stone? It was white but there were dots of silver and gold, tightly packed all over it and into it, as if it were formed from the motes of sunbeams pressed together. She ran her hand over the surface; it was smooth like satin, as was the stool on which she sat. Jessica leaped onto her lap and started to purr. Megan was immensely reassured by this casual attitude and began to relax and enjoy herself. Sensing the easing of tension in Megan's shoulders Percival, too, became calmer, and no longer tried to stitch his claws into her t-shirt; he made a soft whirring noise in her ear.

"Look, there they are."

The noise had started again, but softer as if the players had at last sorted themselves out. Asiimwe pointed to the band that was approaching.

There were twelve players – star shaped creatures just like the one that had welcomed them – only the bandsmen were slightly larger, and they were white except for the spikes of their hair that were pale blue. Each one had a metal instrument, circular or square, which it banged with a cylindrical hammer. The sound was insubstantial and haunting, the music of infinity.

But they're not getting it quite right. Alex listened carefully. Some of them aren't keeping time. He looked more closely and noticed that two stars in the second row kept banging their instruments in the wrong place. Their little leader scowled at them but it made no difference. Quite without thinking, Alex left his seat, crossed over to the two stars that were having trouble, took the instrument from one of them and showed them both how to keep time. Megan looked on, horrified by her brother's audacity, but the leader smiled his gratitude at the improved playing. Alex returned to his seat, grinning smugly at the others.

The star band approached the table where they made a guard of honour on either side of the aisle. Between the ranks of players moved bigger stars, mostly silver but a few black ones among them. All had spiky hairdos slightly brighter than their skins which, even from a distance, appeared rather knobbly and horny. The thin mouths didn't smile; the eyes were fixed straight ahead. They're a bit like starfish, thought Tom, as a faint but distinctly salty, seaweedy tang assailed his nose.

At a signal from Mawgram, a big black star with short curly spikes, they arranged themselves around the table and sat down. Then began a clamorous chattering in a strangely brittle language that slowly turned to English. But what an unusual accent; each word started high and finished low, and all the vowels were long.

The earthlings concentrated hard and caught the words, but the meaning of the strange conversation escaped them: names of people and places they didn't know, and talk of some great discovery in an ancient wood.

More stars appeared, yellow, like their first guide, and laid star shaped plates on the table, some filled with steaming food that smelled of seaweed.

Mawgram leaned over the table and addressed the visitors.

"Thank you for agreeing to join our meal," he said formally.

"Did we?" whispered Alex.

Mawgram had unusually quick hearing and said, rather testily. "Well, you didn't disagree, did you? So you must have agreed, mustn't you?"

Alex didn't exactly follow the logic of this, but was sufficiently taken off his guard by the star's exceptional hearing when it didn't appear to have any ears that he judged it wiser not to pursue the matter.

Mawgram carried on. "We knew you were coming. We were informed by Control to expect a party from Bioworld. So, what part of your mission brings you here?"

"The end of it," Alex answered cheekily. He was having difficulty taking these stars seriously.

Mawgram scowled at Alex and coughed in his direction, sending the smell of rotting seaweed into the boy's face. Alex wrinkled his nose.

Tom came to his aid. "We've really just come," he explained, "to find the seventh treasure to complete our mission."

He looked hopefully at Jessica for help, but Jessica was still purring, with her eyes closed, on Megan's lap.

"Well, I don't think it's very polite to expect us to help if you only tell us the end of the story. We want it all." The grey star folded its arms; its mouth became a straight line of disapproval.

"OK, you asked for it."

And so, little by little, with all four earthlings adding their bit, the story came out: the 'ody' with the DNA, the seven treasures, the mirror, the baboons.

"You have treasures for six colours of the rainbow already," stated Mawgram irritably, when they had finished. "So the next step must be easy. Which colour is missing?"

"Well none really. Because both green and blue were in the first one," puzzled Megan.

The stars moved into a huddle. Some became heated and turned quite red, and hot air rose from their spikes. But eventually a consensus was reached. Mawgram dusted himself down.

"As I indicated," he said, "the solution is obvious."

"That's a relief," said Alex in an aside to Tom that the stars ignored.

"Surely you can work it out for yourselves."

Alex scowled at them.

"I suppose," said Tom, "we need something really special for this last one."

"With all seven colours," suggested Asiimwe, thinking of the cockerel.

"And like the first jewel in the frame of the mirror," added Megan.

Jessica, on Megan's lap, nodded her head in encouragement.

"A seven pointed, seven coloured star!" exclaimed Tom.

There he goes again, thought Megan. That cryptic mind of his!

"Yes!" declared Mawgram, his grouchiness quite gone. "And this will indeed be a very special star, crafted in our workshop here. It will be made especially for this mission. It will be made of materials found in Bioworld. I have been looking forward to this particular event for several millennia." He tossed his curly spikes in self congratulation.

"Now, let us eat."

The food was still steaming and still smelling of salt and seaweed. A team of stars spooned a different substance onto each arm of the star shaped plates already laid before the visitors.

The earthlings were pleased that the stars had obviously understood their explanation, and grinned at each other.

"Of course we knew all that anyway," declared Mawgram, picking a red berry from the side of his plate.

"Then why did you make us tell it all over again?" objected Alex angrily.

Mawgram laughed. "Just to see if you got it right." He stuffed his mouth with food as he spoke. Alex was aware of a thin black tongue and sharp black teeth.

"*We* got it right!" he exclaimed indignantly.

"But how did you know?" Jessica, alert now, was genuinely worried that some security leak had occurred.

"That's easy," said Maradoc. Until now the bright silver star who sat beside Mawgram had kept silent. Not looking at the earthlings as she examined the food on her plate, she added casually, "We read your minds."

"Read our minds?" The earthlings were outraged.

"Can you tell everything we think?" Tom wondered anxiously.

"No, just simple things, and, of course, things you are thinking in the moment. You have to want us to know what you are thinking, as you wanted us to know the details of your mission."

Alex was relieved. So probably they hadn't read his initial opinion of them – rude and self-important, and stinking of salt and seaweed.

"But if a thought should be very harmful to our environment, then the vibes come across very clearly."

Luce! Alex suddenly understood the cat's motive. You daren't stay here in case you can't control your thoughts. I bet that's it!

The earthlings watched the stars to see if there was any particular order in which they should tackle the food. Indeed there was. They started at the top and moved clockwise. They noticed that the stars shovelled their food into their mouths with amazing speed using retractable pincers at the end of their points. They realized that they would have to use their fingers. Jessica watched, fascinated, the pincers flash in and out. Almost as good as the claws of a cat.

The top arm of the plate contained small black and red berries. These tasted sharp on the tongue and gave off a kind of zizz that resounded through the head and took away any hint of tiredness or dissatisfaction. Percival enjoyed sharing Megan's food but when she tried to interest Jessica in the berries the cat miaowed in protest, leaped from her lap and disappeared down the aisle towards the door.

The next arm was full of a green jelly-like substance; aquamarine flowers floated inside it. The stuff was gooey and clung to their fingers. It tasted like sweet apples, with the flowers adding tartness. Once swallowed, the jelly went straight to their arms and down to their hands and fingers until they could hardly hold them still. Asiimwe scooped the last bit of jelly into his mouth and, leaning his elbow on the table, he spread out his hand. Megan did the same and the tips of their fingers touched and pressed against each other. They laughed. The stars took no notice; they were all far too busy tickling each other and shrieking with laughter.

On the third point was a solid, yellow substance.

"Looks like cheese," said Megan. "But it tastes much fresher," she announced, biting off a second piece.

The earthlings grasped the idea. This would refresh their legs and feet. And they followed the lead of the stars, tapping a catchy rhythm under the table.

The fourth arm contained hard round objects that resembled nuts. These were crunchy and salty and set their hearts racing.

The last point held a thick, transparent liquid with dark specks in it. They stuck in their fingers and carried them to their tongues. As the cool liquid slipped down their throats a tingling sensation ran through every part of their bodies. They felt refreshed all over and full of energy.

"You enjoyed your meal?" Maradoc asked them.

The looks on their faces answered her question.

"The food energizes us – all over – for the party, your 'welcome' party."

Mawgram raised his hand and a hall full of stars got to its feet and began to sing. There must be millions of them, thought Megan. They sounded like all the choirs she had ever heard rolled into one.

"Join in! Join in!" they urged. "Don't worry about the tune and the words; we'll put them into your minds."

And all the earthlings sang with enthusiasm, even Tom who was usually shy when faced with anything musical.

After the songs came the dances. Star dances, they learned, started slowly but quickly speeded up. As the stars revolved ever faster in circles and figures of eight, so they left the ground and whirled upwards until only the clouds at the top prevented them leaving the room.

"Join in! Join in!" came the shouts again.

The earthlings began to rotate in time with the thrilling music. Taking his cue from the stars who joined pincers, Asiimwe took Megan's hands and they spiralled round and round together. As they whirled they felt their feet leave the ground, they rose up and up until their heads reached the clouds and they could feel the dampness of the moisture on their faces. They laughed, the music changed and they found themselves spinning down again.

"That was wonderful," sighed Megan.

She turned to watch Alex and Tom spinning too, Percival perched on Tom's shoulder. But the music altered unexpectedly and they landed in a laughing, tangled heap on the floor. Percival, thrown from his perch, squawked his displeasure and flew back to Megan to rearrange his ruffled feathers.

"What kind of dancing do you do?" It was a white star this time.

Asiimwe answered. "We dance to drums. An African drum is made of wood with the skin of a cow or a goat stretched over it. They're not like the metal instruments you have here."

"We don't have those drums, but we can make the sound. If you think about it we can read it in your mind."

And, miraculously, up from the floor came the deep vibrant sound of Ugandan drums.

Asiimwe and Alex took the floor and began to jump and twist in time to the music. Shortly afterwards they were hidden from sight by prancing, swaying stars. Tom grabbed Megan's hand and they too joined the frantic movement until the drums suddenly stopped and they sank to the floor. Tom pulled Megan to her feet. She felt something warm and furry round her legs.

"Oh, Jess, you're back." She knelt to rub faces with her friend.

"You will stay in the hall tonight," announced Mawgram. "Gemma will show you where to sleep."

The smallest yellow star they had yet seen led the earthlings, now weary past imagining, up the spiral staircase. As she bounced up the steps her

228

exceptionally long thin spikes bobbed up and down with her. At the top they emerged into a large star shaped room.

"I'm beginning to feel these stars have a one track mind," remarked Alex.

"No more than we have." Megan was amazed how quickly she rose to their defence. "All our rooms are either square or rectangular."

Alex smiled at his sister. "I must say, they're growing on me. That was some party!"

Tom was thoughtful. "The different colours and sizes seem to mean they have different roles in the community."

"Yes," agreed Asiimwe. "The black and silver ones are clearly the bosses, and the white ones are the entertainers."

"And the little yellow stars are the servants," observed Megan. "I wonder how they hear so well when they don't appear to have any ears?"

"I expect they're hidden, like they are in birds," decided Tom. "And they must be related to crabs. They have pincers, and there's that smell of salt and seaweed everywhere. Starfish?"

"I think the small ones look rather cute," said Megan.

"I don't know about that," grimaced Alex. "Cool hair though!"

The huge bed in the centre of the room was star shaped; it clearly slept five people. The earthlings lay on four of the arms with their feet together in the middle. Jessica spread herself out on the fifth. Megan moved over to join her and they cuddled up together. Percival stationed himself by the window where his sharp eyes searched the night sky.

42 Journey Begun

Sleepily, Megan looked across to the next arm of the star where her brother had lain down the night before. He wasn't there. Neither were Tom and Asiimwe who had been opposite. There was no large orange furry ball beside her. Panic seized her for a moment – she was alone. Then she noticed Jessica. The sparkat had moved over to a spot where the morning sun streamed through the star shaped windows and was soaking up warmth into her beautiful coat.

"Come and see this." She heard Asiimwe's soft voice call Tom to the window, and got up to join them.

Where's Alex? she wondered. Alex had woken and made his way downstairs long ago.

"Look." Asiimwe pulled Tom's arm.

Megan crept up behind him and Tom. They drew apart to allow her between them and all gazed at the spectacle below.

The paved courtyard was full of reddish yellow light that flooded from a pale blue sky. The yard was large and bordered on all sides by luxurious flowerbeds from which wafted enticing perfumes. The colours of the flowers were shades of red and orange and gold, and some climbed the wall to the window where the earthlings stood. Megan put out her hand and pulled towards her a golden starry bloom.

"Smell that." She held it up to the others.

But the boys weren't looking at the flowers. Their attention was taken by the figures coming over the green hills beyond the courtyard, bringing with them a number of frisky horses.

"Just look there, Megan," urged Tom, distracting her from the flowers.

The horses were all the same creamy white colour, they had rainbow manes and tails, and each one had eight legs.

"Like Sleipnir," Tom whispered.

"Sleipnir?" queried Asiimwe.

"The horse that belonged to Woden, the god of the Norsemen. He used to ride Sleipnir down the rainbow when he wanted to visit Earth."

"And look," breathed Asiimwe, "some of them have horns. They're unicorns." He'd read of unicorns in stories in those very British books that still provided the backbone of school textbooks in Uganda.

Yellow stars were busy bridling five of the prancing horses. The reins were gold, there were no saddles. Once prepared, each horse was tethered to a carved pillar at the end of the courtyard and given a bundle of hay.

"I could do with a wash," yawned Megan, turning from the window at last.

As if reading her mind, Gemma pointed to a door that was, uncannily, the shape of a raindrop. Everything inside the room beyond was lemon coloured. There was a shower that worked on a lever principle, a bowl with silver taps and a flush toilet. What a treat for us Africans!

Once washed and refreshed, Megan wrapped herself in a huge soft lemon towel and sat down on one of the psychedelic cushions scattered on the lemon coloured carpet. Beyond the carpet was a cupboard. It was full of clothes. Megan gazed in astonishment.

"Choose which you like," instructed a small star with long droopy spikes on its topmost point. It was busy collecting towels. It had its name written on its chest. 'Horatio,' Megan read.

"You need to wear Star world clothes when you travel to the moving forest. They blend in much better than your kind."

"But," Megan wondered aloud, "who do all these clothes belong to? They certainly wouldn't fit a star. Anyway, stars don't wear clothes."

In response to her question, Horatio explained.

"Creatures come here from all over the galaxy to fulfil missions." He paused while he carefully unfolded fresh towels. "The Master has some kind of understanding with Control. They never bring a change of clothes with them." He scowled at Megan. "Anyway, as I said, you need special clothes in the moving forest."

"Master?" asked Megan. "Who's the Master?"

"You've met him already," Horatio answered patiently. "Mawgram, he's the one we call Master, and Maradoc is second in command. But come on, don't spend all day choosing your clothes," he added, as Megan carefully inspected each garment.

Finally she settled on a pair of jeans with flowers and butterflies embroidered round the bottom of each leg, and a green shirt with a gold belt. She tied back her unruly red curls with a green ribbon that matched the shirt, and finished the outfit off with golden trainers to match the belt. Before she left, she doused herself in the perfume that stood on a shelf inside the cupboard.

When she emerged she found the boys sitting on the window seat eating star shaped biscuits made from some kind of seed.

They, too, had found fresh clothes in an equally well-equipped washroom in which everything was a different shade of green. Alex, she noted, looked very smart indeed in his black leather jacket which he wore nonchalantly over a red shirt. Asiimwe and Tom discarded the jackets;

they wanted to show off the garish patterns of the sports shirts that they had chosen for each other.

Jessica showed her admiration of them all by rubbing herself across the backs of their new jeans. And then she amazed them by doing a quick shift into a starkat that caused her fur to stick out in hundreds of spikes all over her body and gave her face a halo of spines. The earthlings' curious hands felt their furry, rubbery firmness until Jessica shook her head and moved away to call a halt.

Megan sat on the window seat with the boys and picked up one of the biscuits. Percival took one too, held it firmly in his claws and used his strong beak to prise the seeds out of it. Gemma stood beside them with more food and a jug brimful of liquid. The sparkles from it jumped clear out of the jug and tickled their noses, which made them all laugh.

Out in the sunshine, they made their way over to the horses. They stroked the colourful manes and ran their hands down the soft noses. The rasping of their teeth against the hay was loud in the cool morning air, and their breath warm and white.

"You like the horses?"

Mawgram was standing behind them. The looks on their faces answered his question.

"They live wild in our world. We do not force them to serve us. They do so freely."

Megan picked up some hay from the ground and held it out to the nearest horse who tickled her hand with his soft muzzle as he took the food. Tom tangled his fingers in the long rainbow mane, marvelling how each colour merged gradually into the next. Then he ran his hand along the single horn – hard and smooth with grooves spiralling all the way up to its point.

Alex was thoughtful. "How did we get here?" he wanted to know. "It's such a very long way."

He had become used to moving easily from world to world on the planet Earth. But to travel across space?

"It can only be done by a matter of will," explained Maradoc, packing a bag as she spoke, "outside time and space, fuelled by some kind of energy, a form of electricity in your case. But freedom of movement, as we know it, exists only within our own galaxy. We have, as yet, no means of travelling beyond that."

Knowing he wouldn't be able to grasp the matter any further, Alex changed the subject.

232

"Where exactly are we going now?"

"To the workshop. We'll find it in the moving forest, where it is safe from prying eyes. There we will fashion your final treasure. We'll travel on horseback. We'll take these five horses, three of which as you can see are really unicorns. You four will ride Pegasus and Chiron; they are the most fearless and intelligent. Maradoc and I will ride Moonraker, the third unicorn."

"Pegasus is a magic horse in our world," Megan told him, "and he's also in the stars."

"He's pretty magical here too," laughed Mawgram. "You and Tom may ride him, and Alex and Asiimwe Chiron, named after the centaur who divided the stars into their constellation groups. Two guards will accompany us," he went on, gesturing to a pair of white stars. Megan was almost sure she recognized the two bandsmen of the night before; they were not quite white, almost grey, and their spikes were very short and thick.

"Albert and Edred will ride Samson, the larger of the two horses. On Sunflower, the smaller one, will be Cuthbert and the luggage."

At mention of his name, a small yellow star swaggered forward, looking very self-important. He had long stiff spikes that he had dyed in bands of red, blue and yellow. He bowed to the Master and nodded to the earthlings who thought him most comical.

"Alex and Tom will ride in front," said Mawgram with authority.

Once they were mounted, Cuthbert reached up to give both pairs of riders a small flat bag made of shiny leather. Inside each was a map, a small notebook and a pencil.

"Why do we need a map?" asked Megan. "I thought you knew the way."

"But the way keeps changing, as our enemies seek to confuse us and the forest keeps moving. The first part will be easy. When we dismount for refreshments we will study the map. Until then keep it in the bag, and the paper and the pencil. Cuthbert will explain about those when we stop."

Tom wasn't listening to the conversation taking place beside him. He was trying to come to terms with his new situation. He was a little nervous at being on top of such a very large horse.

"I hope you know more about this riding business than I do, Pegasus," he confided. Sensing lack of experience in his rider, Pegasus whinnied his encouragement.

Alex had ridden horses before, but Chiron was rather larger than anything he had mounted in Canada. He could sense the power of the animal under him.

Asiimwe had never seen a horse in reality and was awed by all that quivering flesh beneath him. But he had ridden a cow; he and other boys in the village sometimes played at rodeo riders. Surely this horse couldn't be that different, although it was a great deal further from the ground.

The Master and Maradoc left the earthlings and mounted Moonraker. Albert and Edred were already atop Samson; they carried spears and knives and bows and arrows. Other stars helped Cuthbert load up Sunflower with bags and sacks and then, to the astonishment of the earthlings, he mounted himself by taking a huge standing jump. As if he's on springs, thought Megan.

"What's in the bags and the sacks?" she asked Edred whose horse was now level with Pegasus.

"We have food in there, and cloaks; it sometimes gets cold in the mountains and the forest. And we also carry equipment for the workshop, materials from Jupiter needed for another mission."

They set off along the track leading from the courtyard in a direction away from the sun. Megan looked back to the huge building they had just left. As they moved further from it, it appeared more and more like a massive rock on the skyline and no longer as something made by hands. She turned her eyes forward and saw they were passing through a valley, gently rolling hills on either side, their slopes covered in bright petals.

"Look at the flowers, Asiimwe," she said. "The white ones glow like stars."

Pegasus and Chiron walked slowly together, so that she and Asiimwe were on a level. Asiimwe found himself sliding from side to side on Chiron's broad back; there didn't seem to be any ridge to sit on as there was on a cow; he couldn't bring himself to look sideways. He caught sight of Jessica at his feet who grinned up encouragingly.

The party moved slowly to give the earthlings a chance to become used to their mounts. How smooth it is, thought Megan. Perhaps that's because Pegasus has eight legs instead of four? Or maybe we're not even touching the ground? Hanging on tight to Tom, she twisted herself round to try and look down at the golden hoofs, and indeed it did seem as if they might be flying.

"I wish you'd sit still, Megan," hissed Tom.

"Look, look ahead Tom!"

234

Tom raised his eyes from Pegasus' ears. A small village lay in front of them. Still moving slowly, they approached the cluster of star shaped buildings, each one but a roof balanced on five pillars; there were no walls.

As they neared the houses, they noticed that you couldn't actually see inside. So there must be walls but our eyes don't register the material?

Their attention was diverted by a host of tiny stars that came running from the largest building. They danced and laughed and clapped and jigged up and down on their two points, almost falling under the huge horses as they did so.

"They're children," laughed Megan. She bent down to try and shake hands with one but the distance was too great for both of them. The Master smiled and waved, and then they were behind them.

Soon after that the road became narrow and rocky and began to climb steeply. It was when they were nearly at the top that they saw him. A young white star, probably from the village reasoned Megan, appeared to have turned one of his points in a hole and sat whimpering and rubbing it by the roadside. Megan called down to him as Pegasus passed by.

"Do you need a ride? Give me a point."

But, before the little star could reach up to the offer of help, Edred leaped from Samson and put a sword clean through the poor little fellow. Yellow liquid oozed all over the path.

"Why ..?" Megan began to protest.

Then, horrified, she watched. As the shape of the star lay in the dust, its shine became dulled and the five points writhed and curled. All covered their noses to keep out the nauseous odour that rose from it and passed them by with a spine-chilling shriek. Until all that remained in the dust was a pair of gleaming eyes, and then they too faded and were gone.

"A demon," announced Edred casually, and remounted. Megan's face had become quite ashen. She said nothing. They all wondered at how the stain of the yellow liquid from the star had completely disappeared from the ground.

"Demons take many forms," explained the Master. "That's why they are so dangerous. It's the same in your world. It's the same in all worlds. You must learn to read creatures for what they are, not what they look like."

"But how could you tell it was a demon?" Asiimwe wanted to know.

"By its eyes. Did you not notice how they gleamed?"

No, I didn't, thought Megan, but next time I will. Gleaming eyes?

"Baboons?" wondered Alex.

Soon after this encounter, Mawgram called the party to a halt. The earthlings rolled off the unicorns' backs. Asiimwe fell in a heap on the road. Laughing, and staggering herself, Megan pulled him to his feet. When he tried to walk, his legs bowed.

"Like a cowboy," she giggled.

43 Maps and Giants

Cuthbert took down one of the sacks from Sunflower's back and began to unpack it. He pulled out a bright yellow cloth which he spread on one of the rocks, doing his best to ease out all creases with his pincers. On top of this he put a large plate of food and a tiny posy of the starry flowers they had seen on the way. Then he stood back to ensure everything was just right.

It's a big orange pie! Megan looked on fascinated while Albert sliced it into several pieces with his sword. It tasted hot and spicy and vaguely fishy. The earthlings nibbled cautiously at first and then tucked in hungrily, pronouncing it delicious. Jessica smelled the pie, thought about it, and smelled it again before disappearing to hunt on her own.

"Go far away," shouted Tom after her, not wanting any crunching noises to spoil the enjoyment of the meal.

Percival casually stripped the heavy purple berries from a nearby tree; he didn't fancy the fishy smell.

The portions of pie quickly disappeared. Edred accurately cut up the remainder into four and offered it to the visitors. Asiimwe stole the last piece from under Megan's nose and, giving her a cheeky grin, took a large bite out of it.

"That's mine," she protested but, before she was able to restrain him, he had jumped to his feet and run over to where the Master was unfolding a map. He and Maradoc began to pore over it.

"Bring your maps."

He called the other earthlings to join them, and they all crowded round the three maps laid out on the ground. Large orange spiky paws stepped onto the contours and rivers and trees. Alex put out a hand to push them away. They refused to budge. Alex looked up into Lucifer's emerald eyes.

"So you've come back at last, Luce," he said. "Got your thoughts under control then?"

Lucifer let out a peevish miaow and moved to Megan and Tom's map, where Jessica was already peering at the details.

"I don't know what you had for lunch, Jess," complained Tom, "but it sure doesn't smell too good."

The two starkats, both offended, moved to the side and lay with their backs to the others, waving their spiky tails in disapproval. Now only Percival's claws obscured the scene.

"Just decide where you want to be and stay there," protested Tom. So Percival jumped to the collar of his bright shirt and peered over his head.

"Your maps are both the same as mine," explained the Master. "I wanted you to have them in case you become separated from us." The earthlings looked up at him. "But that won't happen, of course" he added hastily. "Pegasus and Chiron are intelligent unicorns. Stick with them and no harm will come to you. Now let me talk about the maps."

The earthlings concentrated on the unfamiliar scene.

"See, here is our home, our castle." The Master pointed to a large star on the map. "This is the road we have followed, and there is the village through which we passed. Now here," and he indicated the opposite corner of the map from the castle, "is the workshop for which we are heading."

This was marked not with a star, but with a cross. Round about it, the map was coloured dark green and someone had drawn very artistic trees all over it.

"The workshop is in the moving forest," continued the Master. "We keep it there, underground, so it cannot be penetrated by prying eyes from the sky. We all have our enemies, Megan," he said, seeing the look of anxiety cross her face. "This is the road we will travel." He indicated a clear line leading to the edge of the forest. Once amongst the trees the line became very indistinct; the earthlings could hardly make it out.

"The path in the forest is constantly changing," Mawgram explained. "That is why it is so unclear. We arranged it that way to keep it safe. And, of course, it doesn't help that the trees walk about."

The earthlings looked up at him in amazement but he and Maradoc kept their eyes on the map, not realizing that there was anything strange about moving trees.

"In the forest," Maradoc took over, "we journey more by compass than by map and each time we travel this way we ride a different route." She pulled an eight-point compass from her saddlebag to check the bearings.

All this time Cuthbert had stood coughing at the Master's shoulder to remind him of his presence.

"I'm sorry, Cuthbert," he laughed. "We've kept you waiting. Cuthbert is in charge of the maps," he explained.

"Did you draw all the trees?" asked Megan.

Cuthbert bowed. "I most certainly did."

He beamed with pleasure and straightened the spikes on his point.

"Now, earthlings," he began bossily, "you have an important task. As we make our way through the forest, you are to note down or draw any landmarks we may pass. Later, we'll add the new landmarks you notice to those already there and so improve our map. Also, more importantly, we'll be able to mark in our route. Then, when we are able to see the way we have been, we will be able to see the way back. We always return by the same way as that by which we went."

"Why?" asked Megan.

"Never mind 'why', just do it!"

"But why do you need two lots of observations?" Tom wanted to know.

"And why do earthlings ask so many questions?" Cuthbert's short fuse was running out, and the red dye from his spikes seemed to suffuse the rest of him. "Because everybody notices different things of course."

He turned to fetch a sack from Sunflower's back.

"You'd better do the writing and drawing," Alex grinned at Asiimwe. "I need my hands for the reins."

Asiimwe laughed; he needed both hands to hang on. But he took the bag with the map and the pencil and notebook. Megan took the other bag, equally unsure as to how she was going to manage.

Cuthbert unpacked the sack.

"It will be cold up in the mountains and in the forest," explained Mawgram. "You will need something to keep you warm."

The earthlings found themselves draped in long fine cloaks of the palest green, light in weight and almost transparent.

"Those will do very well," remarked the Master, surveying them approvingly. "They look as good on you as they did on …. never mind," he finished. And Megan was sure she detected tears in the star's eyes.

She fingered the delicate material, gossamer to the touch, it was spider web thin.

"What are they made of?"

"We make them from the long grasses that grow at the foot of the hills behind the castle. Our weavers make them into a cloth that is very fine and light, but also immensely strong and warm."

"You stars don't wear clothes at all?" Tom was curious.

Maradoc laughed. "Nor do most creatures," she said. "You are the exceptions, not us. Our blood is different from yours. We feel neither heat nor cold. Now, time to remount."

The earthlings wondered again at how the stars managed to spring onto the backs of the great horses, even the Master and Maradoc who were big and heavy.

Part sparkat, as well as part crab …?

The terrain gradually changed and it did indeed become very cold. The flowers disappeared and here grew lichen and mosses, shining green and gold in the now pale sun. Jagged rocks stuck out from the sparse soil.

Level for a while, the road then wound steeply upwards. The steady plodding of great shaggy hoofs almost lulled the riders to sleep. Only the cries of the birds of prey kept them awake. Great eagles soared overhead, eyes wide for small animals and birds that had nowhere to hide. Lucifer and Jessica padded behind, making occasional leaps off the path to frighten some unwary creature. Percival, in his customary position on Megan's shoulder, nodded his golden head to the beat of Pegasus' feet. At the very summit was a pillar of granite, marking the highest spot.

"Can we stop?" urged Megan.

"What for?" asked Tom.

"I need to mark that pillar in the notebook."

"We can't stop now. You'll just have to remember it." He was keeping a close watch on Moonraker out in front who was beginning to slip down the other side among the loose stones.

"Anyway, you don't have to start noting landmarks until we reach the forest."

"Don't I?" Megan couldn't remember exactly what Cuthbert had said.

"You were too busy getting annoyed at his bossiness to listen properly," teased Tom.

"Well, I'm going to remember it anyway, just in case." I hope we don't pass too many landmarks before we stop again, she thought. "Pillar, pillar," she repeated over and over under her breath.

The horses glided rather than walked on the down slope.

Just as well, thought Megan, or their eight hoofs would get all tangled together in the loose shale. It really was harder going down than it had been climbing up. Tom leaned back against Megan to balance himself.

At the bottom the Master called a halt.

Megan hurriedly took out the notebook and wrote 'pillar'. Then, spotting a mountain on the left completely bare of vegetation of any kind, she wrote 'bald mountain on the far left'.

"Now," the Master was saying, "we must be wary here. Giants live in the caves along the way, at the tops of the slopes to the right. They will probably throw things at us. If they do, let the unicorns have their heads. They have dealt with them many times before."

"Are they evil?" asked Megan, with curiosity.

"No, just stupid," sighed the Master. "They are mostly stars of low intelligence who think it is fun to throw things at travellers."

"Why?"

240

"I wish I knew. They just do it."

"Yobs," said Megan.

"Yobs?" queried the Master.

"Yes, yobs. We have them in Bioworld. People who do all sorts of wrong things for all sorts of wrong reasons. Often they're not very intelligent and don't seem to have anything else to do."

"Well, we have yobs here too," laughed Maradoc. "I think every world has them."

"Have a care for the yobs then," shouted the Master. "On we go."

They had advanced no more than a couple of kilometres further when it happened. It seemed as if the whole hillside exploded. Huge stars of all colours stood silhouetted against the skyline, their massive bulk blocking the sun. Their spikes were long and thick and made haloes round their topmost points.

They hurled things right into the path of the little party, huge dangerous things, rocks and logs of wood and chunks of metal.

Pegasus rose up on his four back legs. He began to plunge and rear his way through the debris. He jumped over the branch of a tree, skirted round a chunk of iron, changed direction to avoid a flying stone and, in between, he galloped and dived and snorted his way along the road. Bending down right across Pegasus' neck, Tom hung onto the reins until his knuckles went white. He had handfuls of the unicorn's rainbow mane in his fists. Megan's arms were tight round his waist. She lay along his back and buried her face against the soft green of his cloak, but she couldn't shut out the grinding, crunching sounds of the missiles landing all around them. Amongst all the mayhem could be heard the high-pitched squawking of Percival as he tried in vain to creep in between Megan's arms and Tom's back. Then they felt Pegasus leave the ground completely. Although none of the three dared open their eyes, they knew they were soaring upwards.

After the initial shock, Alex and Asiimwe realized that Chiron had the whole thing quite under control. They began to delight in the frantic ride as the unicorn deftly evaded the missiles hurled onto them. He was far superior to the giants in intelligence and had no trouble at all in keeping himself and his riders out of harm's way. Sensing their enjoyment, he added a few thrills of his own and took them on a helter skelter ride several metres above the road. The boys forgot to be cautious and responded with shouts of laughter and waving arms.

When the rocks started to move, Jessica and Lucifer laid back their spiky green ears and watched for a while. They awaited the right moment to leave the others and make their silent way along another path. They moved quite unnoticed by the giants who were totally preoccupied by the horses and their riders.

After what seemed an interminably long time, the shouting of the giants and the crashing of heavy objects ceased. The horses, at last, stood still. The earthlings looked around them. The road behind was littered with rocks, like the aftermath of a landslide.

"Who will clear the road?" Megan wondered as they stood at last at the entrance to the forest.

"The giants will," laughed the Master. "They always retrieve the best of their missiles so they can use them again." He held up his pincers in despair.

Having satisfied himself that all the horses had survived the ordeal unscathed, he smiled broadly.

"They're no match for the skill and intelligence of these horses, eh Pegasus," he said, patting the big unicorn's nose.

"Well done, Pegasus," whispered Tom.

"Well done, Pegasus," repeated Megan, stroking the rump behind her.

Then she remembered her notebook, pulled it out and wrote, 'small pond on the left, mountains in the distance on the right'.

Alex and Asiimwe congratulated Chiron and thanked him for the ride. The unicorn snorted in appreciation and turned his head to look at his riders.

"I enjoyed that," said Alex.

"So did I," agreed Asiimwe.

"So that must make us as bad and irresponsible as the giants. Do you reckon, Asiimwe?"

"Undoubtedly," he replied provokingly, and they both laughed.

242

44 Moving Forest

And the Master led the party into the moving forest, into a land alien to their bright spirits. It was eerie among the trees. They stood close together and very tall, reaching desperately for the light. Their lower branches, denied the sunshine, were dead and brittle and brown. The ground below yielded nothing; all life strangled by the brooding darkness. The silence was uncanny, broken only by the rustling of the travellers and the occasional snort of a horse. There was a dank smell of decay that stung the nose; it came from the damp, grey mist that curled its fingers everywhere – even into Megan's hair. She tucked that into the hood of her cloak to keep them out, and pushed Tom's hood over his head too, where he sat in front of her. Percival crept round and squeezed between them. Icy drops of water fell from the branches above and struck bare hands and faces.

They proceeded slowly, bowing their heads now and again, to avoid the low arm of a tree. The gloomy murk increased with every step. Megan noticed the ruins of a star house on the right and started trying to remember it for the notebook. The way was long. The earthlings felt themselves rocked soothingly by the steady thud of the horses' hoofs.

Alex and Asiimwe worked hard on the landmarks, determined to beat the others. Alex, in front, called them out, and Asiimwe, balancing his notebook on Alex's back, wrote them down. A ruin, a distinctively shaped boulder, a fallen tree, a cairn, an old tower. Jessica called up to them to watch where they were going, but neither took any notice.

All of a sudden Alex pulled on Chiron's reins, all senses alert.

"Asiimwe, I can't see the Master or Moonraker."

Asiimwe looked round. "There's no one behind either."

Spotting the starkat at their feet, he asked her. "Where are they, Jess?" Jessica miaowed and shook her spikes.

"What about you, Chiron?" Alex stroked the unicorn's mane. "Do you know where we are?"

Chiron snorted and swayed his head; he was as mystified as they were.

They peered into the gloom. Nothing but swirling fog and that dreadful stench, seemingly even stronger now. They put their hands over their noses but couldn't block out the reek of it. Jessica laid back her ears and mewed plaintively.

"How did we lose them?" Alex was baffled. "If we just sit still they're bound to come looking for us soon."

They sat without moving for an unbearably long time, with only the smell and the fog and the constant dripping from the trees to comfort them.

"What's going on?" Alex was alert. "We haven't moved, but that tree wasn't there before." He pointed to a small broadleaved tree, struggling for growth among its larger neighbours. "And where's that one with the broken branch? It's gone!"

"But the Master said that the trees walk around," Asiimwe reminded him.

"I didn't *see* any of them move."

"They probably only walk when we're not looking. Let's watch one very closely and see if we can catch it moving. That one over there, with the large bracket fungus growing on the trunk."

The two boys stared fixedly at the tree but nothing happened. Finally, Alex could stand it no more and looked away.

"Look, Asiimwe," he shouted. "Those three that were so close together, they've gone!"

Asiimwe turned to agree with him, and then looked back.

"Now *it's* gone too!"

Where the tree with the fungus had been, there was just a patch of rough grass.

"And that one with yellow leaves, it wasn't here before!"

"They're not going to let us see them move, we might as well give up," laughed Asiimwe.

"Never mind the trees. Look, there's a light over there."

Alex pointed to where a very pale and uncertain light shone in the greyness, turning the air a dirty yellow.

"And there's another one. There're lots of them. They're moving off. Quick, let's follow them before they disappear."

Chiron set off at a trot but as far as they followed so the lights moved away in front of them.

"I wish they'd stand still," grumbled Alex.

And then they did. Chiron stopped also. The earthlings watched mesmerized as the lights, at least a dozen of them, moved around the unicorn and its riders and the starkat, spitting and snarling, all her spikes on end, completely encircling them with an eerie glow. The lights were cold and white and, strain as they might, they couldn't see what lay behind them. But the vile smell wafted towards them and the fog, thicker and darker than before, crouched close to the ground so that they couldn't even see Chiron's hoofs. Jessica was quite hidden from view; they knew she was there only from her fierce growling that was somehow reassuring. The haze and the smell were all pervading, rottenness and decay everywhere. Alex and Asiimwe said nothing; they sat as if frozen to stone. Jessica's deep-throated rumbling growl was the only sound. Then a voice, a language neither of them understood, harsh and guttural and menacing. Fear chased the dampness through their bones.

Suddenly a golden arrow flew over their heads. There was a shriek and a gurgle from the direction of one of the lights and the others took off through the forest, with them the fog and the smell. Alex's face was ashen and Asiimwe's quite grey as the other horses came up to join them. Edred had his bow in his hand; it was he who had fired the arrow.

"What were those?"

"They were muskadons, evil mischief makers. Their power is little but sometimes they join forces with others and then their power is great."

"What were they trying to do?" Asiimwe asked, dreading the answer.

"They wanted to stop you reaching our workshop and completing your mission. They have no power to harm you, not on their own; they can only delay. There are many evil creatures in this forest. Each group can achieve little individually. Only when they unite need we fear them. And our soldiers see to it that they do not unite. While the soldiers cannot possibly destroy them all, they can and do keep the separate bands apart and so render them harmless. For a long time this was not the case; and we stars suffered badly. But these days we have the upper hand. We would not have brought you here were we not quite certain of your safety."

Some of the colour returned to the earthlings' cheeks at this reassurance. Tom brought Pegasus alongside Chiron and he and Megan heard exactly what had happened.

Megan leaned down to stroke Jessica who, still alarmed, reached up to rub her face against the outstretched hand. She looked at the ground. It was green, greener than anywhere they had been so far in the forest. There were even small flowers, greenish white in colour. They were in a clearing. There was sky above them. And all around where they stood were great boulders, making a circle.

"We're in a stone circle," she murmured. "Stone circles are signs of magic in our world too."

"Yes. They brought you to the stone circle, hoping to increase their power. I should have thought of that. They are not very clever, and very predictable."

"Are stone circles evil then?"

245

"Like most things, they are neither evil nor good. It's what creatures do with them that makes them one or the other."

"What do they look like, those muskadons?" Alex asked the Master.

"They don't look like anything; they are just smell and fog. I failed to recognize them because the forest is full of mist and darkness anyway. Sometimes they carry white lights, but only for luring purposes; generally they prefer darkness."

"We were lost for hours," said Alex, indignantly. "Where were you all that time?"

"You were gone but a few minutes." The Master laughed. "That is part of their confusing tactics. They play around with time."

And you claim they're not very clever, thought Asiimwe.

Before they left the light of the clearing, Megan pulled out the notebook and wrote 'second star house' and 'clearing with stone circle'. It was difficult writing with Percival in the way; he insisted on keeping so close, and she had to lean over him to reach the paper.

The horses plodded on steadily, through the darkness and the wet.

Drops of water could be heard, pattering much more heavily now, from one branch to the next.

It must be raining above.

Megan kept her eyes wide open for landmarks. They passed a mine on the left, little stars busily pushing trucks full of some bluish coloured rocks along rails. Others rang bells, signalling the end of the shift to those below ground. And beyond them, on the right, was what looked a bit like a chapel, certainly a meeting place of some kind.

The trees began to thin and they were in another small clearing. The Master pulled Moonraker to a halt.

"Time for a rest," he said. "We are now about halfway there."

Megan took out her book and wrote 'mine'. She drew a picture of the chapel-like building as she didn't know what to call it.

45 Weevils

Once more the darkness of the forest absorbed them. They moved again among those eerie trees across the lifeless floor below. The air was damp and they could feel moisture gathering on their faces; tiny droplets stood in a fine sheen on the silkiness of their cloaks. For some time they plodded steadily on, Alex now keeping his eyes firmly on Maradoc in front, whose silver covering thankfully shone a little in the gloom. Moonraker swayed his rainbow tail as if to give Alex something to watch, and thus hold his attention.

Then they smelled it – that evil, rank, fetid odour of their meeting with the muskadons. Megan was alert, searching with eyes and nose in every direction. She could see nothing but she knew they were there. Just to her left her gaze caught the shape of a large stone statue looming out of the fogginess, dampness glistening on the rock made it shine. It's some kind of animal, she thought, surveying its weathered shape, a bit like a griffin. A griffin, she knew, had an eagle's head and a lion's back. It's just a statue, she reasoned, nothing to fear, and it looks well here in the forest. I must put it in the book. She observed it more closely to try and decide how she might draw it. As she did so, she caught sight of its eyes, and they gleamed.

"Oh, Tom, there's something over there."

Even though she spoke in a whisper, the Master heard her in the stillness of the forest, and stopped Moonraker. Megan pointed to the griffin-like creature.

"That's just a statue. We erect them in memory of our heroes who visit other galaxies. So far none has returned and it is our way of remembering them. It is only stone, it won't harm us."

"But it has gleaming eyes."

"No, Megan, I think not," said the Master kindly. He looked intently at the statue. "Star Andros was a much respected star."

Why a griffin? Megan wondered, but the question would have to wait. She looked closely once more; there were no gleaming eyes, just stone ones, quite unseeing. Maybe she had imagined it? She knew she had not. And when she drew it in the notebook she added gleaming eyes. Percival chuntered his approval and nuzzled her chin. Megan stroked him gratefully.

A little further on her attention was caught by another statue, this one almost like a sphinx, yet not quite for it had horns.

"Tom," she whispered, "Tom, look at it, don't its eyes gleam?"

Tom looked hard but could see no gleaming eyes.

"They do gleam, don't they," she turned to Percival and received a confirmative nod.

"And they're going in the notebook too," she told him. I wonder if Asiimwe has noticed the eyes. But the eyes on Asiimwe's drawings were dead and stony.

Alex was studying the way ahead. He saw that it was usually barred by a dense band of trees but, when they got there, there was always a path. Obviously the trees make way for us, he explained it to himself, but why can't I catch one of them moving. He determined he would do just that before their journey ended.

The dankness and the smell grew as they penetrated more deeply into the vast forest. Suspense was in the air as if even the trees themselves tensely waited for what must surely come. It was silent save for the gentle thud of horses' hoofs and the snapping of small branches.

Megan looked behind her, to the sack resting on Sunflower's broad back, the sack with the cargo of rocks from Jupiter.

"It's moving," came her cry, "it's moving. There's something inside it."

All stopped and were still but for the swishing of magnificent tails. Edred and Albert dismounted and cautiously made their way towards the sack, all other eyes upon them. In one quick movement they dragged it to the path and tipped the contents on the ground. Lucifer and Jessica stood watching, spiky fur on end, tails bottle brushy in expectation of the unknown.

"Weevils!" snarled the Master. "Their cunning knows no bounds. The purple bottle!"

Cuthbert turned on Sunflower and sought among the contents of a small brown case. He found a bottle of purple liquid that he tossed to the Master. The Master caught it with unexpected dexterity.

It was clear to all just what was happening. The little creatures, quick moving and dark green with very many legs, were chewing the stones with sharp teeth that flashed in the darkness.

"They're breaking the rocks," shouted Tom. "There'll be nothing left but bits."

He and the other earthlings jumped to the ground and desperately tried to brush them away with their bare hands. As they did so the robbers turned those jaws onto them, like wasps and nettles all at the same time.

"No, not that way," intervened the Master, and he poured the entire bottle of liquid over the stones. Sizzling and squealing immediately followed, and those weevils that were not quick enough to run lay dead in the dust, on their backs, flashing jaws agape, teeth biting at nothing, numerous legs thrashing the air.

For a while the travellers busied themselves gathering the scattered stones, not noticing until they heard rustling movements in what little undergrowth there was, that they had allowed themselves to become surrounded. Creeping had been the approach, smelly and almost noiseless, drawing with it a stale choking stench that now rendered breathing almost impossible. Rolling back and forth, there advanced clouds of dense grey fog that tantalized the eyes and caused one to see what was not there and miss out on what was.

"A clever ploy," whispered the Master, gasping for air. "We allowed ourselves to be distracted by a mere irritation from the real danger. Cuthbert, ensure the rocks are safe! All of you protect the horses. Earthlings, take these torches, they don't like light and ..."

The rest of his words were lost as all evil fell upon them.

From every direction came shouts and cries and cackles and a faint wind that brought with it the foulest of reeking odours. But there was nothing at all that the earthlings could see of their attackers. Arcs of light from flourished swords. Decay creeping into nostrils.

Totally disorientated, foul noises and noxious smells pushing up against them, the earthlings swung their torches round and round, hoping the moving rays of light would destroy anything that might be out there.

The horses were even less affected by all the activity than the earthlings. They waited patiently throughout. They're not aware of any of it, marvelled Tom, looking up into Pegasus' patient face, just as we are only aware of the sounds and the smells, not the sights.

Percival too, seemed to be shielded from all that was going on. He had taken up a position on Pegasus' rainbow mane, between his ears, having found Megan's shoulder too full of movement for his liking. From there he watched fascinated, the unexplained activity around him, occasionally shouting out, "Cool! Brilliant!" above the din.

The starkats, in contrast, were in the thick of the fight, both snarling and leaping with claws unsheathed at enemies unseen by the earthlings. Horrified, Megan watched a great gash appear on Lucifer's back and blood pour among the orange spikes. Lucifer didn't flinch and lunged again. More blood spurted from a wound in his neck, and still he continued to fight. He arched his back and pounced. His strong jaws found their mark. Something fell with a great thud to the ground and let out a piercing scream. Jessica was wounded in the shoulder and Megan ran to help her, protecting her with light from further attack.

The stars, too, were fighting hard and receiving wounds. They fared less badly than the brave starkats. Perhaps they were more practised in facing whatever weapons were threatening them. Tom ran to help Cuthbert. He was wielding a sword far too big for him but, judging from the cries that arose around him, it was finding its mark. Asiimwe kept his torch focused on a point in front of the Master and Maradoc who seemed to be working their way methodically through a pack of something that groaned each time one of its number hit the ground.

Eventually the lunging and the shrieks and even the smell began to lessen.

"Now!" shouted the Master. "Now's our chance! Mount up and let's get out of here."

Tom helped Megan onto Pegasus' back and she pulled him up in front of her.

Alex and Asiimwe heaved the wounded Lucifer onto Sunflower where he clung onto the sack of rocks, and then leaped onto Chiron. Jessica, although wounded, was still strong enough to run by the side.

Then began a furious gallop through the forest. Tom gathered fistfuls of mane and bent forward, to avoid the branches that hung low above him. Megan clutched his soft green cloak in both hands and leaned against it. Pegasus held his head low as he charged along the path behind the Master, his golden hoofs drawing sparks from the ground below. Alex and Asiimwe hung on tight; they gave Chiron his head and bent to watch the earth fly away under them. They thought the ride would never end, but eventually the pace slowed and stopped.

They looked up to gaze on a pool in a clearing. Plants grew around the edge of it and dragonflies hovered among the reeds that bore, at the very summit of their stems, huge apricot blooms, their centres filled with thick stamens laden with golden pollen.

"Here we can tend our wounds and become refreshed," announced the Master.

"What did we meet back in the forest?" Alex questioned Maradoc.

"All forms of evil," replied the star, too exhausted to say more.

All the stars had scratches and some quite deep wounds on points and

250

faces that oozed dark red blood.

"Come on," said Asiimwe to Megan, "your hands are covered in bites and stings."

It was warm in the glade. They took off their cloaks and made their way to the water.

"Your hands too, Asiimwe, they're worse than mine."

Cupping the fresh liquid in her palms, she bathed Asiimwe's sore fingers. As she did so, every trace of bite and sting disappeared.

"Magic water," she said, speaking to his reflection in the mirror that the clarity of the water created. He smiled back at the image, studying the slightly moving face, the serene grey eyes concentrating on his own reflection.

Beside them were Tom and Jessica. Tom bathed the deep wound in the starkat's shoulder. She licked him gratefully as it became whole again.

Alex carried Lucifer from Sunflower's back to the edge of the pool. Tom turned to help him set the wounded animal down on the bank. The starkat had lost a lot of blood; his back was completely soaked with it; blood and spittle oozed from his mouth; he lay quite still where the boys had put him. Gently they bathed him all over with the healing liquid. For a while nothing happened and then, miraculously, the great starkat stirred, his wounds closed up and he stood shakily on all fours. As Tom stroked him tenderly the spikes that had lain flat on his back sprang erect again. He made his own way to the water's edge and submerged himself three times before returning to the shore. Alex went to him and fondled him in admiration.

"Well done, Luce," he whispered into the green ear. And Lucifer purred under his caress.

"Lucifer, you're a star!" murmured Tom, smiling proudly. Settling beside him, he ran his hands up the spikes along his friend's back.

"You're a star." Percival experimented with the new words.

All around the small lake, the stars were bathing each other, and each experienced the same miracle of healing. The Master bent down and gulped long draughts of water that soothed the rasping cough that had been with him since the encounter in the forest.

"Brilliant!" squawked Percival.

"Did you note all the landmarks, Megan?" Cuthbert was at her shoulder. Megan pulled out the book.

"Hmm, your writing is not very tidy."

"You try writing when you're riding a horse and your fingers are cold," retorted Megan.

"Asiimwe did better," said Cuthbert, ignoring her. "More landmarks and better writing."

Asiimwe was behind her, smirking. Megan scowled at him and, when he continued to smirk, she thumped him.

"Do you feel better for that?" he asked laughing, and he pulled her hair until she laughed too.

"So what do you do with the landmarks now?" asked Asiimwe.

"Put them on the map of course. Then we will be able to see the way we came and so we will know the way to go back."

"But why do we have to go back the same way?"

"Not 'we', 'you', that's what you should have said, not 'we', 'you'. You are not coming."

"All right, why do *you* have to go back the same way?"

"All these questions! I am not telling you."

"OK, but why aren't we coming with you?"

"I do not wish to tell you that either."

Cuthbert stuffed the maps and notebooks back into the bags and moved away, his colourful spikes shaking violently from side to side.

Asiimwe and Megan looked at each other and burst into laughter.

Tom sat a little way off with Alex and the starkats. He was annoyed that Asiimwe and Alex had done better than he and Megan with the landmarks. But, more than that, he was annoyed that Megan didn't seem to care, and had made it up with Asiimwe so quickly. He relieved his tension by stroking Jessica fiercely, quite oblivious to the rough spikes bruising his hands. Jessica seemed to understand and didn't complain.

"No time to linger here further," declared the Master. "Not far now. They will have refreshment for us at the workshop."

The ripples in the water disappeared and the smooth surface of the skin of the lake itself was once more healed. The crab that had taken refuge under an overhanging bank plunged down deep, to the reassuring murk of his home.

46 Workshop

Wearily, the earthlings helped lead the horses the last few metres to the entrance of the cave workshop. The orange in the sky was deepening, turning the land to purple. It would soon be dark. What time would it be at home, or even what day?

A small red star with flaming spikes stood in the wide doorway. He called somestar to take care of the horses and ushered the party inside. He clapped his hands officiously. Three more red stars with the same fiery spikes entered carrying cushions that they tossed onto the floor of a small recess next to the door. The earthlings sank down gratefully into the softness that enveloped them. It was warm in here and they took off their fine cloaks. The starkats curled up together and were immediately asleep, resembling, in their spiky coats, large orange hedgehogs. Percival, restless as always when out of the sunlight, bounced his claws up and down on Megan's shoulder until she moved him gently to a piece of rock protruding from the wall.

Another star brought in a tray with glasses of liquid.

"This will refresh you enough to do the night's work."

The glasses were of crystal and covered in stars that caught the soft light coming from the roof. The drink inside was clear, like water. All through the liquid were bubbles, and the bubbles were stars.

The Master came to sit beside them.

"Try it," he urged.

They all took a sip. Immediately they felt the liquid flow through their bodies, bringing energy and warmth to every limb.

"Cool!" exclaimed Alex.

"Cool!" whirred Percival. "Cool!"

"What is this?" asked Asiimwe.

"Stardust soda. Stardust falls to the world from the constellations. It is full of latent energy. We mix it with mineral water to make a powerful drink. The stars here work day and night. They don't sleep. They revive themselves with stardust soda."

The earthlings said little, content to lie back on the cushions and feel the energy surging through them.

The cave was suddenly filled with a rattling roar. Out of the gloom and into their view rolled a skateboard, riding it an orange star with thick golden spikes. He skidded to a halt just in front of the earthlings. His board was made of a transparent material with stars of colour embedded into it.

"Wicked!" exclaimed Percival.

"Wicked!" repeated Tom, delighted that Percival had remembered his lesson.

"Time to move on," announced the breezy orange star. "I am Fireball, the official guide," he added importantly. "I will show you everything and explain everything. Any questions, I am the one to answer. We don't like creatures disturbing the workers. So remember, I am the one who knows it all." He preened himself with well manicured pincers. "We have a long way to go; these tunnels and caves stretch for many kilometres, so we have transport."

He put a pincer to his mouth and whistled long and shrill. The ground rumbled and a whole herd of skateboards exactly like his own roared down upon them, coming to an abrupt halt at their feet.

"Wicked!" exclaimed Tom again.

"Wicked!" mimicked Percival.

"Wicked!" repeated Fireball. "Wi-cked! Wi-cked!" He had found a new word to his liking. Shouting it over and over again, he leaped onto his board and set off.

"Don't lose him," urged Maradoc. "We will wait for you here."

The earthlings and the starkats jumped onto skateboards and rolled off in pursuit. They could hear Fireball shouting, "Wi-cked! Wi-cked!" in front of them.

Alex and Asiimwe laughed. Tom wasn't quite sure the orange star wasn't making fun of him and Percival, and scowled.

They rolled at great speed through a series of tunnels, up and down slopes and round corners and even over a number of jumps that set Percival squawking on Megan's shoulder. The earthlings laughed with the thrill of the speed and the noise of the boards on the stone floor and the air rushing past their faces. Not so enthusiastic were the starkats. Unused to this form of travel, they wailed constantly. They stood with all four paws together, backs arched high and all their spikes erect, tails out straight, longing for the hectic ride to be over.

The maze they first travelled through opened out into a large hallway. Fireball twisted his body sideways, turned his board and skilfully tipped it to a halt. The earthlings followed his lead. Lucifer and Jessica had no idea how to control their racing boards and shot past the others into a distant tunnel. Fireball set off after them and returned with two bad-tempered starkats. Lucifer snarled at the earthlings as if daring them to laugh. Not even Alex did.

"Wicked!" exclaimed Fireball and led them to a large alcove in the wall. In it a number of red stars were busy with whetstones, sharpening knives and other tools.

"This is the repair room," he announced. "Knives quickly become blunt with all the carving that must be done."

"Carving?"

"We carve many items from stone."

"What items? What for?"

"Items that are needed for missions like your own. Many such are requested from different parts of the galaxy."

The place was incredibly noisy once they moved inside, but from the main hallway they had heard nothing at all, even though there was no door.

"The sides of the opening are constructed from sound deadening material," explained Fireball casually.

Sound deadening material? Asiimwe caressed the soft green rock with long sensitive fingers. It was porous so that the holes could lap up the sound.

At the back of the hall was another alcove, again the sound within cleverly muffled. This was a forge. A huge vaulted room. Fires blazed all around. The smoke was channelled into a massive vent to one side so that the air was quite clear. A team of large red stars with short purple spikes was shaping hammers and other tools on anvils, while smaller red stars worked the bellows of each of the five fires.

In neither room did any star pause to look up at the visitors.

"There is much work to do," explained Fireball, "and few to get it done."

Back on their skateboards, they rattled down a shorter passageway into a large open space. Even though their arrival was noisy, none of the stars there looked up at their approach.

"Welcome to the planning area," proclaimed Fireball proudly. "This is where we work out what to make for the missions."

As far as the eye could see groups of two, three or four blue stars with short black spikes sat on the tiled floor that was a riot of bright colours, in deep discussion over various plans.

"Come," encouraged Fireball. "Have a look as you go. But don't expect the stars to speak to you. They are far too busy for that."

Beyond the open space they passed through a narrow glass door. The ceiling in the room they entered was about twenty metres high and from it hung great star lamps that gave brilliant illumination to those reading below. The room was as wide as it was long. Around all sides were shelves, and on the shelves were hundreds of books arranged in alphabetical order, according to the names of the worlds.

"The library," declared Fireball with pride. "There is no entry for Bioworld at the moment. But once your mission is accomplished we will write a book about it and add it to the shelves." His golden spikes nodded enthusiastically.

Neither Tom nor Asiimwe were concentrating on what Fireball was saying; they were gazing in amazement at all the beautiful books with gold printing on the covers. Tom pulled one out and leafed through the pages of designs and decorations and diagrams.

Beautifully presented, like the manuscript of a medieval book.

"Look, here's one from Rainbow world." Asiimwe held out a book to the others.

They scanned the list of names on the front. Simone and Klara were both there.

"They never said," protested Megan, peering round Asiimwe's shoulder.

"Things didn't go quite right," explained Fireball. "It was a successful mission but there were problems along the way. Some creature was trying to obstruct what we were doing."

Alex glanced at Lucifer who was looking decidedly uncomfortable in his effort to control his thoughts and prevent them from being read. His emerald eyes caught Alex's gaze and he quickly looked away. Alex said nothing; he had a new respect for Lucifer since the fight in the wood.

"I wish I could read the book," said Megan but there was lots of small writing and Fireball was restless.

"Who writes all these books?" Alex wanted to know, thinking what a long and tedious task it must be.

"We have scribe stars. Look."

He pulled back a screen at the far side of the room to reveal a row of stone desks, each with a stone bench attached. Seated at every one was a green star with spikes that looked like young plants, painting intricate designs and letters into a book. One, Megan noticed, was decorating a T with violet flowers.

They retraced their steps across the planning area where the stars were still deep in thought. They passed along a short corridor and through a tall arch at the back of it. The archway was decorated with carvings of stars, the faces of them so intricately worked that they caught the light from the star lamps swinging above, and radiated a mass of colour in all directions. Some had comic faces with silly cheeky grins; some were grotesque with huge protruding tongues; some had squint eyes that leered at the earthlings; and all had brilliantly colourful spikes. Like gargoyles on an English church.

They walked under the arch into a lofty hall that receded in every corner into thin silver mists. There were no star lights hanging here. Large standing lamps with shades made from real bats' wings illuminated all.

"They are given freely," explained Fireball, "when the bats have no further use for them."

Hanging in some vast roof, lost in obscurity above, as if keeping watch on these remains of their ancestors, were huge bats with glittering eyes. They shuffled and jostled in an endless wave of movement.

"Guards," explained Fireball. "Their radar systems combined together can detect any unwanted activity on the floor below."

"And here," he said, "is where we must choose the ingredients for the final item to complete your mission."

All around the room were huge alcoves that stretched back into unknown territory.

"This is the Earth section." Fireball led them to one side. "We have other alcoves for each of the planets. As you can see it is full of rocks and stones and pieces of soil. These all come from the planet Earth. You will need to find material from Bioworld only, not the other parallel worlds. Then, from whatever you choose, we will fashion the final treasure. The planners you saw are working on that as we speak."

The earthlings stood surrounded by great piles of rocks: shades of deep red, dull yellow, black, white, brown, many tones of grey and blue. Asiimwe picked one up and weighed it in his hand, and the others followed his example.

The starkats left them to complete the task alone and retraced their steps to the library where they had noticed a green star munching something that smelled curiously like venison. Percival perched right at the top of the highest pile of rock and watched.

The earthlings heard the rumbling of a skateboard and a shout of 'wicked!' and Fireball disappeared from view.

47 Star

"How are we going to choose among this lot?" Alex seated himself wearily on large boulder. "I suppose we could take the very precious stuff." He tried in vain to break off a piece of ore that had specks of gold shining within it.

"No, I don't think so." Tom was thoughtful. "Surely we need the kinds of rock that can be found all over our world, and those that are useful, and each one should be as different as possible from the others. That is if they are to be totally representative." The others looked at him, expressionless.

"So, where do we start then?"

"We need to have examples of all three main kinds of rocks: igneous, sedimentary and metamorphic," Alex said knowledgeably, remembering what he had read in the science encyclopaedia his grandparents had sent him for Christmas.

He smirked knowingly at Megan's questioning face.

"Carbon is most important," said Asiimwe, not wanting to be outdone. "Carbon is in every living thing. I think we should start with that."

"Good idea," agreed Tom. "And then we could find two examples of each – igneous, sedimentary and metamorphic."

"That would make seven," observed Megan. "And seven is the special number!"

"Coal is a good example of carbon," declared Tom.

"Or charcoal," added Asiimwe.

Their search was helped by light that moved and glowed among the piles.

"Underground fireflies!" marvelled Megan.

Their Star world clothes seemed impervious to the dust they raised; not so their hands and faces that were soon covered in sooty blackness. They clambered over the heaps until eventually Tom came upon some charcoal. He laid it by the opening to the alcove, just as a rattling sound and the word 'wi-cked!' echoing from the walls announced the arrival of Fireball. Jessica had also returned. She purred and arched her back under the touch of Fireball's heavy caressing pincers. Both sat down to watch the earthlings.

"Now the igneous rocks," said Tom.

"How about granite? There's lots of that in Uganda." Asiimwe climbed over a heap of pebbles to reach a large chunk of granite that he heaved back to the entrance. He showed Megan the colours hidden within it.

"Basalt could be the other example," said Alex. "That's found in volcanoes."

For the sedimentary rocks, Megan suggested rock salt.
"It's used so much in cooking and to preserve food, and everyone in the world has to eat."

So rock salt was added to the growing pile.

"Limestone is sedimentary," said Tom, and explained to the others how it is formed.

"And so is sandstone," added Alex. They found examples of both and finally decided on the limestone because it had some fine fossils embedded within it.

"The last group is metamorphic," reminded Asiimwe.

"I suggest slate and marble," said Alex authoritatively. "Slate because shelter is a basic necessity and it is used for the roofs of houses in many countries; and marble because grand buildings and monuments are constructed from it – it marks our history."

And so all seven samples were laid at the entrance. The earthlings tried in vain to rub the dust and soot from their hands and faces but surveyed the collection with pleasure.

Something was bothering Megan.

"They're not exactly colourful. How are we going to make a rainbow star out of them?"

"That is for the planners to decide," breezed Fireball. "Don't you worry about that."

"Come on, Jess, time to go," said Alex. He poked the starkat with his foot.

Jessica rolled over onto her back but when no one bent to tickle her tummy she jumped up and followed the rest to the archway. The earthlings placed the rocks that were heavy and cumbersome in a small miners' cart that Fireball found. Alex took the handle; they mounted their skateboards and rattled back to the planning area.

After what seemed too long a time, the blue stars put their work aside and came forward to examine the rocks laid out on the beautiful floor. They stood in a circle looking thoughtful, running heavy pincers through stiff spikes. And then they started scratching lines on the floor.

Occasionally a star would shake his head and an alteration would be made. Once they were completely satisfied with their design, a red star brought in a large piece of parchment which he laid on the floor where the marks had been made. The blue stars danced a little jig on the parchment and then lifted it up and laid it before the earthlings.

The earthlings gazed amazed at the intricate pattern that had been transferred from the floor to the parchment, of lines and circles and angles, all based on the double spirals of a helix.

"What does it mean?" Tom asked the question for all of them.

"It is all about DNA and chromosomes. Just take it to the powder hall," was all the answer they got.

Tom scowled at the stars but they took no notice; they were already busy on another project. He and Asiimwe rolled up the parchment.

Fireball guided the cart of rocks, and the earthlings and Jessica and Percival, to the very centre of the planning space. Then he put his pincers to his mouth and gave a piercing whistle, so high that the others covered their ears and grimaced in pain. There was a dull roar and the whole of the centre section of the floor, like an immense elevator, was lowered into a huge underground chamber. Into this flooded soft, pale, moony light from hundreds of star lamps. The walls, floor and ceiling were decorated with millions of tiny stars.

"A three dimensional map of the Milky Way," Fireball announced proudly, indicating the stars. "It took hundreds of years in your time to produce and still it is not quite finished."

Red worker stars ran up to seize the plan which they laid on the floor, right over the constellation of Orion. Full of chatter and smiles and friendliness, they explained to the earthlings exactly what they were doing.

They brought to the centre of the room hammers and chisels and a huge pestle and mortar. With hammer and chisel, they split some of the rocks into wafer thin slices, all of an exact thickness.

"How did you do that?" Alex was intrigued.

"Want a go?" teased one of them.

Alex picked up the offered chisel and struck it with a hammer. The rock cracked far from where he had struck it and the chisel snapped in two. The little red stars stood with their points crossed; they shook their heads and then collapsed into giggles, their spikes shaking furiously. The earthlings laughed with them.

Next, with a pestle and mortar that was a metal version of that used in Ugandan kitchens, they ground other parts of the rock into fine dust.

"Anyone want a go?" chortled an unusually plump star.

All had a try but found the work groaningly hard on the arms and shoulders. They contented themselves with watching.

260

Followed by their audience, the stars carried the slices and the powder to the far side of the room. They spread out the plan on the floor. They sprinkled the dust from the rocks along the lines that the planners had made, and then laid the slabs of stone on top.

"Now watch this. This is the best part."

The smallest of the stars, who was clearly also the leader, swelled with pride. All the other stars giggled uncontrollably and looked at the earthlings in anticipation. The leader sprinkled some grey powder over the stones, and laid a fuse from them to the other side of the room. She called everyone to join her behind a rock where she kept a large box of matches. Dramatically, enjoying the effect of every gesture on her audience, she took out an over sized match, struck it and put it to the fuse.

Horror and fascination swept the faces of the earthlings as fire raced across the floor along the fuse. BANG. A terrific explosion rocked the whole room. The earthlings were momentarily blinded by the light and instinctively fell to the ground, covering their heads with their hands. Percival squawked his distress. Jessica wrapped her spiky tail round her ears. A strong smell of gunpowder wafted over them.

They heard the giggling of the stars, a hissing from the pile of stones and shouts of, "Look! Look!"

There before them was a fantastic firework display. Stars shot up to the ceiling and sizzled to the floor, more and more, all colours and sizes. Some of the larger stars split to give out smaller stars. They lit the room like day. Some drifted over to where the watchers crouched, and even fell on their outstretched hands where they disintegrated into oblivion. The faces of the earthlings broke into smiles of wonder. Only Percival declined to watch and hid his face in Megan's hair.

"Science, not magic," Asiimwe reassured himself. He had seen fireworks before.

And then the show was over. The stars scrambled from behind the rock and rushed to the other side of the room. They clapped their hands in undisguised glee.

"It has worked!"

They embraced each other and danced round and round, for a few moments completely forgetting the presence of the earthlings who were right behind them.

"So just look at that," declared the leader, swelling to twice her normal size.

"You're a star!" said Percival, who had recovered his voice at last.

There, on the floor, lying on the parchment plan that had miraculously survived the firework display, was a mighty seven pointed rainbow star. Each point was a different colour of the spectrum and had all the shades of that colour intertwined within it, from very palest to very deepest.

"That's wonderful," enthused Megan.

"Awesome!" exclaimed Tom, winking at Percival. He was trying to teach the parrot that one.

"Don't you mean 'wicked'," teased Alex. Tom fought to ignore him.

"But how's it going to fit into Megan's money purse?"

"Aha!" The tiny leader assumed an attitude of great importance.

"Bring on the wand."

In pattered a minute turquoise star carrying a star-tipped wand. Coming from the top of the utmost tip of this was a flame gun. With it the tiny creature touched the exact centre of the rainbow star. Immediately all the points shrank, sizzling, until the entire star was no more than the size of a large coin. Megan scooped up the prize and held it to the light oozing from the cracks round the elevator that now hung near the ceiling. In the centre was the moving heart of light: this time a tiny ball in which revolved all the colours of the spectrum. She passed the last treasure to the others. Joy and triumph shone from their faces. Megan added the star to the collection at her waist.

"The library," said Fireball, taking up the plan in his pincers.

He whistled for the elevator. They all scrambled onto it and waved goodbye to the friendly worker stars as they moved up to the planning space above.

In the library they left the original design to be copied into a beautiful book and set out on the shelves with the rest. All regretted that they would never see it completed.

"You never know," said one of the green stars mysteriously.

"Back to the Master!" shouted Fireball.

He set off on his skateboard, yelling 'wi-cked' as he rounded each bend, the others following close behind. Even Jessica was beginning to get the hang of things.

And then Fireball started to show off. Laughing aloud and every so often shouting 'wi-cked', he stood on his board on one point alone, waving the other in the air. He stood on both pincers and then on one pincer. He bounced from one pincer to the other. Finally, he turned a somersault and a back flip, landing with perfect precision on the board below him.

The earthlings tried to copy the expert. Alex stood on one foot and made himself into a star. Tom and Asiimwe, behind him, did the same. Megan tried to be even cleverer, jumping in her star position to face the other way round. So doing, she cannoned into the back of Asiimwe. Both tumbled to the hard floor but got up laughing. Fireball stood over them, pincers on hips.

"Tut tut," he said, helping Asiimwe to his feet, who then helped Megan to hers. Then he was off again.

"Wi-cked," he whooped, roaring round the bends. He came to a halt centimetres from the Master's feet.

The Master and Maradoc were relaxing on the cushions. Sipping something from a glass that had sent their short spikes into rubbery coils, they looked relaxed and happy. Lucifer was with them also slurping from a glass bowl; his spikes no longer stood out straight but resembled tiny corkscrews. He had returned another way. Lucifer didn't like to be laughed at and had no wish to trust himself to the skateboard again.

You're like me, thought Tom. You find it hard to laugh at yourself, and you get angry quickly when people make fun of you. He gave Lucifer a hug and Lucifer purred with contentment.

A small red star appeared with a tray bearing glasses of stardust soda. The earthlings felt again the fizzes on their noses and the strength flowing through their bodies.

"Drink deep," encouraged Maradoc. "You will need much strength for the tashk that is to come. For now you must return to your own world. It is nesheshary that the final journey begin from the planet you are helping. But, be for ever washful. You are now in great danger. You have all sheven of the treashures. The evil ones would steal those, and you too, Tom and Megan. Come, don't look sho worried. You have good on your shide, and Jesh and Lushifer to help you."

Was it her imagination, wondered Megan, or was Maradoc having problems with her words? She's tipsy, thought Megan, and tried hard to stifle a giggle.

Mawgram looked at her sternly. There was a serious message to get across. His face tried to convey that but didn't succeed. His cheeks were flushed, his bright eyes bleary.

The earthlings took second glasses from the jug on the tray, drained them and set the empties down.

"Now ish time to return." The Master stumbled over his words. Alex tried to smell what was in his glass but he moved it away. Not stardust soda, that was for sure.

Home, thought Megan. Home! I wonder how much time has passed.

Reading her thoughts, the Master replied. He struggled to control his voice, and succeeded where Maradoc had not.

"It is difficult to say how much time will have passed," he began unsatisfactorily. "Maybe five minutes. Maybe a hundred years. Probably just a night. Even in your world, time is not exactly constant, you know. Sometimes it seems to go quickly, sometimes slowly. Now pick up your cloaks and let us go."

They moved outside into the night sky.

"The stars, they're so near." Megan put out a hand to touch one right above her head.

"They're further away than they look," laughed the Master. It was with great relief that he felt the clear night air sharpen his brain, and the woolliness caused by the drink leave him.

"And there's no moon," observed Megan. "Just stars."

"We have no moon," explained the Master.

"They're stars from the centre of the Milky Way. That's why they're so close together," added Asiimwe, enjoying the spectacle with her. "We're in a different part of the galaxy."

Pegasus and Chiron whinnied, demanding their attention.

"They wait," said the Master. "They will take you to the far end of the forest. There you will see a rainbow – a special rainbow studded with stars. That will be your route earthwards."

Megan's eyes widened with excitement and she gave the Master an impulsive hug. His skin was stiff and coarse and knobbly, and smelled of the sea and of crabs.

"Come on, things may not be so much fun when we reach home," laughed Alex.

"Why couldn't we have *come* by the rainbow?" asked Tom curiously.

"Because others were watching, and now they are not," replied Maradoc enigmatically.

Helped by the stars, the earthlings mounted the unicorns. Jessica leaped up on Pegasus, and Lucifer on Chiron, both taking great care to keep their sharp claws well sheathed. Percival, as usual, clung securely to Megan's shoulder.

The powerful horses set off at a gallop, leaving the ground and the stars below them. The earthlings had assumed that they would be the masters of the great unicorns, but it soon became clear that the situation was quite otherwise. It was as if Pegasus and Chiron had decided to take them on a splendid tour of wonder before dropping them home. They soared up among the stars. Asiimwe and Megan stretched out hands to try and catch one as they sped past, the glitter from them confusing their eyes. Alex, hanging onto golden reins and rainbow mane, sought a constellation he might recognize, but the race was too fast for that. Tom peered over Pegasus' head to yet more stars below them. Percival and the starkats kept their eyes firmly closed and hung on tight.

The wind roared around their ears, and they laughed aloud from sheer joy of the experience.

Eventually the unicorns turned and plunged downwards. The earth-lings felt themselves slipping forward onto their necks. Lucifer couldn't prevent a desperate yowl escaping him. A rainbow was rushing up to meet them, but such a rainbow as had never before been seen. All along the parts where the colours joined were silver stars, and the whole arch looked so solid that all instinctively covered their eyes as the unicorns galloped straight into it. The rain spattered all over them like a cold shower and quite took their breath away. Down they went – red, orange, yellow, green, blue, indigo, violet.

48 Tension

The sun's rays felt their way over the curve of the world, disturbing the thick white mist that lay cool and refreshing on the land, and revealed the tops of trees that sailed in dignity, cut off by tendrils of cloud from their roots below. It was already morning. Megan looked up into the rapidly paling sky. There were no unicorns, no rainbow, just the vanishing stars and the rising sun. The four children looked at each other, still wrapped in soft green cloaks and wearing their smart clothes, and the two starkats with spiky fur.

"Megan, Alex, where are you?" Holly's voice sounded anxious.

"It's the next day!" Megan was appalled. "We've been away a whole night!"

Hurriedly, the starkats shifted to moggie shape. The children paused for a moment to watch the spikes disappear from ears to tail; they certainly looked most comical when just half done.

Then, remembering the urgency of their situation, they threw off their beautiful cloaks. Asiimwe gathered them all together and hid them under a low-lying bush. Tom and Asiimwe set off for home and Alex and Megan made their way to the back of the house, hoping to slip in undetected. Megan removed her Star world clothes and stuffed them into a suitcase on top of the cupboard, replacing them with an old pair of jeans and a faded t-shirt.

"Ah, there you are! Where've you been?" Her mother was in the doorway, relief and anger in her voice.

"We've been so worried about you. Look at your face!" Megan's face was still covered in grime and soot. "Where have you been?" her mother asked again.

"We were with Asiimwe." Megan was thinking fast. "We were sort of camping. We had a charcoal stove, it got out of hand."

Holly looked doubtful. "Was Alex with you?" she asked.

"Yes, and Tom."

Holly began to relax, especially when she caught sight of her son with an equally dirty face in the hallway. That seemed to confirm the story.

"Holly, have you seen my briefcase?" Steve's voice came from the kitchen.

"Next time you go camping, perhaps you'd be good enough to let us know. Now go and get cleaned up," finished Holly. She disappeared in search of her husband's briefcase.

Alex and Megan grinned at each other. Percival looked dejected. It was hard to preen the sticky soot from his feathers. He refused to allow Megan to cheer him.

Nobody questioned Asiimwe, and Tom crept in unnoticed. In Priscilla's culture, boys of ten were old enough to look after themselves. She wouldn't have checked his bedroom last night, and it would never occur to his father to do so. Not for the first time Tom found himself grateful that children were allowed so much freedom in this paradisal land, and plagued with so few questions.

"We can't go during daylight," Lucifer explained to Jessica. "But, on the other hand, we can't afford to hang around here too long. We'll leave as soon as it gets dark. Keep close to Megan and I'll make sure Tom's safe."

Lucifer looked up to the heat-filled sky, took out his mobile phone and searched for a signal. He reported to Control that all had gone well in Star world and the final move would be made under cover of darkness. He decided not to wait for a reply. He switched off and replaced the phone. If anyone up there had noticed he wasn't at the banquet, he certainly didn't want them to mention it.

Lucifer found Tom in his father's workshop, his usual place of refuge. This morning he had it to himself. He picked up the rabbit box, but today it didn't interest him. He was feeling out of sorts and irritable. That was why he had come in here; he needed to get himself back together before he rejoined the others.

Why was there so much tension inside him? Why couldn't he laugh his way through life, like Alex did? Why was he so easily irritated by little things? Why did he care that Asiimwe and Alex had noted more landmarks than he and Megan had? Why did that star annoy him when it shouted 'wicked' all the time? Why did Megan like Asiimwe so much?

Tom reached for a wooden lamp that he was also working on. This was for Priscilla. As he rubbed down the smooth surface, he felt peace remove the tightness from inside him. Something furry rubbed against his legs and miaowed. He stooped down to pick up the beloved tabby cat.

"Yeah, Lucifer," he said. "You and I are so much alike. We have the same problem, don't we?"

Suddenly Tom realized how wonderfully reassuring it is to have a soulmate. And that's exactly what Lucifer was to him, and always would be. He sat down on the rough wooden bench and cuddled his pet and confided his difficulties. Lucifer relaxed in his arms and put out a paw to touch his chest, to show he understood and sympathized with all that was said.

When Duncan entered the workshop, Tom was busy once again on the rabbit box. His father stopped to admire it, and then asked for his advice about a bowl he was turning for Mrs Katembe. Tom swelled with pride and suggested making the edges slightly thicker to give the bowl a lip.

The baboons circled the house in a way that completely disorientated Megan. They were restless and fractious and quarrelsome, as if they knew, as they surely did, that an important moment was at hand, one on which much, including their very lives, might depend.

With Jessica and Percival she shut herself in her room and closed the shutters. She insisted that Jessica take on her sparkat form, she felt so much safer that way. She laid out all seven treasures on her bed and checked them; the crystal, the queen, the shell, the tooth, the seed, the bead and the star. She counted them and admired them. She noted the colours and the hearts deep inside them; then returned them safely to her money pouch.

"Well, Jess, what are we going to do all day?"

Percival chose that moment to emit a loud squawk.

"That's it! We could teach Percival some more words!"

Everyone was growing a little tired of his limited vocabulary.

"Come on, Asiimwe," suggested Alex, "let's join the others at the bike track. I've had enough magic for one day."

"Science," Asiimwe corrected him.

"And what about the baboons?"

"They're not after us. It's Megan and Tom they want."

The two sped off down the hill to the race track, heads in the wind, shirts flying behind them. Following, gambolled six large baboons with gleaming eyes. These settled in the stunted trees around the race track while the boys tore up and down, and spurred their friends to horrendous jumps.

"What's with those baboons?" wondered the African boys when the group of six became ever bolder and crept nearer and nearer.

Alex took his machine to the far end of the track, eyed the jump and pedalled for all he was worth. Rising from the saddle, he and the bike soared over the launch lip and landed with a satisfying thud on the other side. The back wheel touched the ground first, quickly followed by the front, and then he was in the saddle again and pedalling along the other side of the track to the cheers of his friends.

As he passed the trees, approaching the second jump, the baboon leaped, all four limbs spread-eagled, landing on the back of the saddle behind him. It put both arms round Alex's waist and squeezed.

"What the ...?" shouted Alex, weaving from side to side, doing his best to shake the creature off.

The bike, with its own momentum, reached the second jump and hurtled over the top. The bike flew in one direction, Alex and the baboon in the other. They rolled over and over, each, in fear, trying to break free of the other. The remaining five baboons advanced, to be met by a crowd of boys who beat them with sticks, pelted them with stones, and shouted obscenities. Finally, they gave up and took off into the bush. Alex stood up, shaken, and bruised and bleeding from a deep cut on his cheek and scratch marks on his arms. His clothes were torn and dirty. He was surrounded by a circle of questioning faces. Baboons can be dangerous, they all knew that, but ......

"Time to go home, I think," said Asiimwe. "Come on, Alex." He handed his friend his bicycle that had fortunately survived the crash intact.

"Why did they attack *me*?" asked Alex aggrieved.

"Well, they're not very bright. I suppose they couldn't tell the difference between you all. Just wanted two muzungu children."

Night falls quickly in equatorial Africa. Yet it was impatiently that the four children waited for it on the veranda. On Megan's shoulder Percival shifted restlessly from one foot to the other. In a pile beside them were the fine green cloaks from Star world that Jessica had suggested they take with them.

"We'll go as soon as the stars come out," she promised them.

"Go where exactly?" Megan was unsure of this last bit. There was something unclear about it that made the collection of the treasures straightforward by comparison.

"Creation world of course," said a gravelly voice behind them.

They all turned round in recognition of Lucifer. None thought to question where he had been, although Alex was very curious.

"Perhaps I'd better take the treasures, Megan," he said softly. He put out an entreating paw. "If they should capture you we don't want them to gain the treasures as well."

Megan could see the logic of this, and yet it was still with some reluctance that she unfastened the money pouch from her waist. She checked through the treasures one final time, before clipping it round Lucifer's neck. No longer a moggie, Lucifer stood proud in orange and green finery. The mission in Bioworld was almost over and caution was a thing of the past. The pouch was completely hidden in his long glossy fur. Megan felt strangely naked without it. She trusted Lucifer completely so why did she feel unnerved when she looked into his haughty confident eyes.

Even now they were gathering, waiting for their chance. The children peered into the increasing darkness of the African night. Knowledge of its dangers marred for them the feeling of achievement and security that their success so far had given them. At the edge of the lawn, where Moses had grown tired of slashing and the grass remained long, were the familiar fireflies, the lights in their tails like a diamond in each one. Beyond them, in the denseness of the bush, were red, gleaming eyes that they knew belonged to baboons; and they could hear the hungry bad-tempered snarl of hyenas. Something else was out there too. They thought back to the grim encounters in Star world. When the stench drifted hazily across the grass, they knew that evil had shifted that night.

"We're waiting for clearance from Control," said Jessica.

Lucifer was somewhat taken aback by this information. He hadn't expected Jessica to get started without him. He had thought to be in complete command of the final push.

"Yeah well, what's keeping them?"

"I think they were waiting for you. And they wondered why you weren't at the banquet in Star world."

That was what he had feared. But how did they know? Lucifer questioned himself. Of course Jess wouldn't tell them.

Lucifer's fur rippled impatiently.

"Surely they realize that when you achieve the rank of Zero One Zero you are expected to use a bit of initiative. I was finding out what the other side know."

"And what do they know?" asked Alex suspiciously.

Lucifer scowled. I don't have to answer for my actions to a mere earthling.

"I'll take over now, Zero Six Six." He rubbed behind his ear to release his mobile phone. He moved off the veranda, out of earshot of the others.

A few minutes later, after some fiery exchanges over the phone, Lucifer informed them that they were waiting for the black hole to be brought into correct alignment. He showed them the screen of his phone that now depicted a tiny map of the nearest constellations.

"Why?" asked Megan.

Lucifer was calmer now. He clearly had himself more under control. "Because that's how we enter Creation world."

"But isn't a black hole negative energy?" asked Tom.

"Not if you approach it positively." There was a bleep from the phone. "One's coming up on the screen now. There it is, just passing Venus. Have you got your cloaks? Star world clothes will suit you better for this final adventure."

The beam of light that descended to Bioworld was so searingly bright the children couldn't bear to look at it. The heat that emanated from it made them sweat under the cloaks they daren't remove. The gleaming eyes around them began to close in. As the sparkats led the children in the jump onto the beam that extended into space, they hurled themselves from the trees and clung onto the sides.

It was like being on a metal escalator in the metro, but it moved much faster and went up at an angle that was almost perpendicular to the ground. Their own speed was added to that of the beam as they struggled to race up the steep incline after the bounding sparkats, their fur glinting in a halo of golden light. And then the big cats stopped and the earthlings stopped too, and let the escalator of the heavens carry them along.

And it became like a ride at the funfair, soaring high and then dipping down to miss a star. As they approached them, the stars lost their spikes and became balls of fire it strained the eyes to gaze on. But mostly they were away from the stars, ascending through the deep blue black of space.

The way was relentlessly up. Megan hung onto Jessica's tail and looked beyond her to see where they were going. She could make out the silver road of the beam ever climbing and she could see the end. It finished in nothing.

And at the end there *was* nothing. There was no movement of air – none at all; Megan's hair was quite still about her face.

"Where's Percival?"

"He didn't jump with the rest of us," explained Tom.

Lucifer looked round at them. There was anger in his eyes.

A perfect calm descended in the complete stillness that now enveloped them. Gone the frantic climb and the roller coaster ride, and a suspension of time and space took its place. Megan felt that she was at the beginning and end of time, in the same second that it began and ceased to exist. She and Asiimwe exchanged glances in a smile that would last beyond a lifetime; her wide grey eyes met his deep brown ones in complete understanding and their two pairs of hands searched for each other.

Alex and Tom surveyed the scene now laid before them – the great, silent masses of the planets suspended in time. Deep in the subconscious they all recognized that such serenity would not be found in any moment in Bioworld, and tried to hold onto it forever.

They couldn't see it but they could hear it, a shrieking and a twirling, as of a distant tornado. Particles of space dust and debris assaulted them from all sides and tangled in their hair and clothes and stung their faces. They tried to turn away from the onslaught and pulled their cloaks more tightly around them. The dust became thicker, the noise became louder and they felt themselves whirled round and round. With one hand Megan clung tight to Asiimwe, with the other to Jessica's tail. Jessica lost awareness of the earthlings behind her, so engaged was she on the task in paw.

The mouth of the black hole came roaring to meet them. Megan finally lost her grip on Jessica's tail, torn from her hand by the buffeting roar at the entrance. Asiimwe too was wrested from her grasp.

Then they were all falling in silence and stillness. Like being a parachutist: but tumbling over and over, sometimes flying, sometimes floating, sometimes all in a ball, on and on through nothingness.

And Tom knew at last what nothingness was. He felt it but afterwards could never describe it: it was nothing to see, nothing to hear, nothing to smell, nothing to taste, nothing to feel, but everything to think. But at least the nothingness had time because, just when Tom was becoming used to it, it was over. He felt himself falling across rather than down, with scenes above and below and to left and to right, all merging into each other.

He passed through everything that had ever been in his world or any other, but his own senses were only able to pick out things relevant to him, that he knew in his own consciousness. And so he saw Rainbow world and the other worlds he had visited, and he saw Africa and the bullies on the cliff-top in England. Megan saw her own Rabbit world where all the rabbits had black tips to their ears just like Snowball. And Alex saw his land of dinosaurs with the friendly giants and the terrifying raptors; seeing their vicious talons and blood dripping jaws, he realized at last what it was that had so frightened him all those years ago. Asiimwe saw Africa, and the thousands of ancestors who had brought him to what he was.

A floating motion carried them all to a halt on a dank hillside under a leaden sky heavy with rain.

49 Creation World

Before they had time to take in their new surroundings, there came an urgent instruction from Lucifer.

"Hide here, quickly!"

They bundled themselves into a narrow cleft under an overhang of rock. Following Lucifer's lead they crept as far underneath it as they could.

There was something shining in the corner.

"Percival!" shrieked Megan. "How ...?"

"Shh!" snarled Lucifer.

From this inadequate hiding place the earthlings looked out to see baboons and hyenas and large dogs land softly, just where they had done a few moments before. The animals paused for a short while to shake themselves and sort out their fur and test the air with questing noses. Then they fanned out. Some leaped over the top of the sheltering rock; others rushed past it; still others made their way down the hill in the opposite direction. Sounds of grunting and panting and the smell of sweaty fur attacked the hiding earthlings.

As soon as all had passed, Lucifer crept out from under their hiding place. He twitched two green ears to ensure nothing lay in wait for them and then gently rubbed the left one to release his mobile phone. A few moments and he had the information he required.

"The only way to the rock of the cauldron for us is by the river. The ferryman is expecting us."

That's strange, thought Jessica. But somehow it was comforting to have an instruction direct from Control. If indeed that was what they did have. She looked hard at Lucifer, but he wasn't looking at her.

"Come on," he said, "follow me."

The earthlings prised themselves from their refuge and dusted themselves down. Megan rubbed ruefully at the smarting red dents in her knees where she had been crawling on gravel. Alex waved his head slowly from side to side to get rid of the crick in his neck. Tom and Asiimwe soothed away the cramp from their aching limbs. In his delight to be free, Percival emitted a loud squawk; Megan clasped a firm hand over his beak to silence him. He continued to squawk in a quietly nasal way.

"Keep low to the ground," instructed Lucifer. He shifted quickly into a lithe black panther, only the emerald eyes betraying who he was. Jessica followed his example. The earthlings' cloaks took on the grey green colour of their surroundings and only Percival was bright. Megan covered him with her hood when he took up his usual position on her shoulder.

They ran bent double, over rough moorland covered in low growing plants that grabbed their passing feet and scratched their bare ankles. Every so often Lucifer shouted, 'down!' and they all flung themselves onto the springy undergrowth, pulling cloaks around them to claim invisibility. Then he shouted, 'now!' and they were on the run again.

A lone baboon on a solitary rock was about to give a warning cry. Jessica silenced him with one blow of her powerful paw. A whimper and his limp body lay on the moor.

"Cover him," ordered Lucifer. "We don't want others to find him."

After what seemed like hours of 'now' and 'down' instructions, they reached a huge boulder sticking up from the moor. Using his long black tail, Lucifer tapped it three times. With a low rumble it swung to one side, revealing steps behind.

"Quick!" urged Lucifer. They hurried down the steps and along a rocky tunnel. Megan stopped to pick up something that glinted on the floor. Asiimwe cannoned into her. Lucifer scowled for concentration. Megan and Asiimwe grinned at each other and went more carefully. Megan looked at the tiny key that lay in her hand. It was made of bleached bone, a skeleton key. She put it in her pocket.

They made their way along a narrow corridor, the air in it becoming increasingly damp.

"No creature saw us," said Lucifer to the ferryman who stood by a stone footbridge that spanned an underground river. The ferryman was covered from head to foot in a deep grey cowl that denied all view of his features. He was tall and thin, but nothing more about him could be discerned.

Megan looked in distaste at the brown river before her; she couldn't see its depths and imagined it to be bottomless. She could make out shapes in the murkiness that looked slimy and mud coloured and unloved. The boat itself was long and narrow; it was of wood and polished brass; some creature obviously cared for it lovingly.

Megan shuddered as the ferryman helped her on board. Now why did I do that, she wondered. He's on our side. The others refused help, Alex recoiling at the gloved hand held out to him. Something wasn't quite right, of that he was sure, but he couldn't put his finger on it. A smaller creature, also cowled, appeared out of the shadows, untied the boat and climbed into the back. Percival shrank against Megan's neck. He didn't like the dark, sunless places, and he didn't like these boatmen at all.

The ferryman took the single oar and poled the boat out into the middle of the stream. It slowly gathered speed as it entered the blackness of a tunnel. The only light was glowing eyes in the stony walls, and flaming torches held by repulsive looking toads and lizards.

Why are we in such an unpleasant place? Alex asked himself. It doesn't seem to have anything at all to do with creation. He looked at Lucifer but the emerald eyes were expressionless. Jessica moved over to him and purred gently round his ankles in a reassuring way.

The earthlings were silent. The cold dankness of the place struck under their cloaks and chilled their hearts. Megan studied the walls and the roof. No gleaming red eyes. They had clearly managed to evade the baboons and their friends. For now. She felt at her waist for the money pouch and remembered she had given it to Lucifer. As she did so she noticed the ferryman's head turned towards her. She looked down avoiding his gaze, preferring instead to face the small guard at the other end of the boat. She caught sight of his feet. They were green and each foot had six long toes ending in a sharp red claw.

What are you? she wondered, horrified. But Lucifer and Jessica are here, she reminded herself. They have everything under control.

Lucifer was sitting at the feet of the ferryman, an expression of contentment on his face. Jessica, beside Alex, looked uncomfortable, unsure, her whiskers twitched unhappily.

The slap of the oar was the only sound in that desolate place. The boat went round a bend. Here they passed strange plants growing in the rocks, hanging on where there seemed to be no nourishment at all. They had tiny fern-like leaves covered in dark brown spots. They crowded as close as they could to the lights, a reassurance of life in this dead place. The creatures under the surface of the water glided silently, malevolently, as if accompanying the party; and Megan preferred to look up at the bats in the roof. They watched the passing boat keenly from their upside down position and Megan felt there was no malice in their involvement.

They floated through a large hall populated by many toads. These were huge and bloated and had surprisingly friendly faces. They reminded Tom of middle-aged gentlemen with beer bellies. Asiimwe tried to make sense of the expression in the eyes that passed them by. Is it pity? he wondered. Now why should they pity us? He became more and more uneasy. Lucifer's gravelly voice interrupted his morbid thoughts.

"Not much further now," he said with a beaming smile.

Why does that cat's smile always become a grimace? wondered Alex.

There was daylight ahead. The boat glided from the damp and the darkness into the open air. The ferryman allowed it to drift to a stone landing stage on the left bank. The small guard leaped from the back and made fast with a rope to a bollard. Watching him, Megan noticed that his hands matched his feet. They were green. Each hand had six long fingers and these ended in red claws. The ferryman poled the other end of the boat to the side and held it there with gloved hands while the others stepped out. Megan was relieved to note that each glove had only five fingers. Finally the ferryman climbed out also, and he and the little guard made to join the party.

Why do they need to come with us? wondered Alex.

"Now," said Lucifer, "this I know you'll enjoy."

They climbed up steep iron steps to a hilly terrain made entirely of metal. There were hills, there were trees, there were plants, all of metal. Quite beautiful in a strange shiny sort of way. The sky was silver, and in it floated a dull bronze sun that cast long shadows from the trees and hills.

"They're not really metal," laughed Jessica. "That's just their colour, not their substance."

Tom was intrigued by the shadows. He had never before seen his own shadow so long. It marched away across the hills to the distance. How could that be when the sun was high in the sky? Was the light bent in some way? His thoughts were interrupted by Lucifer.

"We travel fast along these roads. Take one each." He indicated a rank of gleaming silver mountain bikes. The earthlings needed no second bidding.

The sparkats had smart motor scooters: Lucifer a Yamaha Slider and Jessica a Maluguti Madison 125. These machines were clearly much more suitable to the requirements of the four footed feline shape but even so both looked strangely uncomfortable. Alex and Asiimwe had great difficulty hiding their mirth at their uncharacteristically ungainly appearance. Lucifer quelled their laughter with a look. Percival knew about mountain bikes and decided that this time he wasn't interested. While Megan was engrossed in choosing hers, he slipped away.

"This is the last lap," shouted Lucifer as they crested a hill. He was now in wonderfully good spirits. He and the ferryman raced into the lead, the latter taking care not to reveal what there was of him under the cloak.

They all found the going easy as they sped down the metal road. Tyres hummed on the surface and a pleasantly fresh wind blew in their faces. They raced towards the horizon and the silver sky. Rain began to shower down on them, lead coloured spots that dampened their faces but didn't disintegrate.

"Not rain, not hail, but asteroids," shouted Lucifer, turning his head. "Tiny liquid ones, they won't hurt."

As they cycled, the shower of shining drops became heavier, but they did no harm, just as Lucifer had assured them. They fell on their faces and clothes, and each drop ran down their bodies and trickled off the edge still complete.

Like a drop of mercury? wondered Asiimwe.

The little globules fell thicker and thicker.

Are they trying to hide our progress? worried Alex. He couldn't shake off that feeling of unease that had overcome him in the boat.

As they rounded a corner Jessica, bringing up the rear, felt herself pulled from behind by invisible hands or paws. Her scooter fell with a crash to the ground, wheels spinning; but so geared up with excitement was the rest of the party, and so thick were the asteroids, that no one noticed her disappearance.

Something or some creature had hold of a large chunk of Jessica's thick black fur.

"Shh..!" whispered Klara, and fixed a green hand over her mouth.

Percival was perched on Klara's shoulder. He fluttered down excitedly to greet the sparkat.

"Come with us, quickly," urged Klara.

Jessica looked up dazed. It was Plato who had leapt from the bushes and brought her to the ground. But now she needed no second bidding. Something was very wrong with the group she had left. Maybe here was a chance to put it right.

Flanked by Percival and Plato, Klara's slender figure set off at a swift trot down a bronze coloured path, the tall trees on either side of which made a protecting tunnel overhead. And then they were out in the open.

Here was Creation world as Jessica had always understood it, alive with animals and bright birds and insects and flowers. Soft springy green grass, a gently warming yellow sun in a fresh pale blue sky.

50 Betrayal

This was the essence of exhilaration decided Alex as he spurred his bike onwards. Faster and faster, he rounded the bends leaning at an angle that only just kept him out of trouble. What a superb track! The downs were quite brilliant in their smoothness. The ups that followed them were spaced exactly right. Just as you thought you were sure to run out of steam and have to start pedalling again, there was the top and another down. He sped ahead of Tom and Megan and Asiimwe, just behind Lucifer and the ferryman.

None of them noticed, in the dense asteroid storm, that the crowd of bicycles was becoming ever greater, and they were progressing as if flanked by outriders. And these outriders had gleaming eyes, and some had spotted backs and some were birds with long naked necks and powerful beaks. The baboons gibbered with glee and the hyenas barked with excitement and the vultures laughed raucously as they all sailed down the final slope and into the rocky valley below. The earthlings came to a sudden halt at the bottom of a high stony cliff, panting with exertion and high spirits.

And then their joy turned cold as, ringed around them, they saw the baboons and the hyenas and the vultures gradually creeping nearer, silent and confident and full of purpose. They knew the hour was theirs.

The ferryman threw back the hood of the cowl from his face; he tossed the cloak and gloves to the ground. There stood Simone in splendid purple beauty, her hand resting on Lucifer's head, and he was purring. Simone was every inch the queen. She had a crown of amethysts on her long, shining purple hair. A robe of maroon and gold fell from her shoulders to her feet, leaving bare her slender arms. Her amethyst eyes burned with triumph. The guard from the boat also cast off his cowl, revealing a tiny raptor that licked its lips and glared at the earthlings and blew on its red nails.
I've seen him before, Alex's blood ran cold.

Simone bent to whisper something in Lucifer's ear and, from his tail to his whiskers, he left the black panther behind and shifted into his glorious sparkat form.

For a moment none of the earthlings said anything as the enormity of the betrayal entered their sinking hearts. Megan looked round wildly for Jessica. She wasn't there.

Then a deep voice growled.

"You have something for me?"

"Indeed we have, Leader." Simone and Lucifer bowed low, and indicated where the earthlings stood.

Onto the scene padded an enormous cat, the largest the earthlings had ever seen. In shape he was a puma, but his colouring was otherwise. His coat was a rich dark brown and on it, all over, were rings of jet black. His fur stood on end; there was so much of it none of it could lie flat. He trailed behind him a long heavy tail, patterned with black rings like the rest of his body. He had pointed ears with tufts rising from the tops, and a wide mouth that revealed sharp fangs. His eyes were black coals that bored into Simone who returned his gaze unflinching.

"Do not fear," he purred, addressing the earthlings, "I come only to take what is mine. Hundreds of years ago, in the depths of time, I sent Monkey to fetch it for me, but Monkey was a traitor and I never received my due."

"It wasn't yours to take," shouted Alex, amazed at his own audacity. He was the first to get a real grasp on what was happening. "You wanted to turn the DNA to evil to make diseases like AIDS and so destroy our world."

"Now why would I do that?" purred the great cat, lifting a heavy paw and alternately showing and retracting his claws. "Of what use is a destroyed world to anyone?"

"Because that way you can get power over it. You can offer to cure the disease if the creatures give their souls to you."

A wave of anger crossed the mighty face. The cat snarled and his black whiskers twitched. How could such a scrap of an earthling see through his plans so clearly? He batted Alex with a sheathed paw in warning. Megan nudged her brother to keep quiet. There was no point in angering the beast. But the cat was in an excellent mood, he wasn't going to let this best of days be spoiled.

"And you, my two faithful followers," he crooned to Lucifer and Simone, "yours shall be the highest status of all in the land that is to be ours. But let us not waste time. Where is the 'ody'?"

A large baboon stepped from the surrounding crowd. In his hand was the 'ody', still intact. He waved it towards the earthlings, giving them a toothy grin, before he laid it at the paws of the massive puma.

"Well done! You and all your tribe will be rewarded for this. No longer will Man be the greatest of the primates in the new Bioworld. The Baboon will take his place, and he the baboon's."

The whole tribe of baboons burst into rapturous applause.

"And now the treasures?" went on Cassius, for it was he who stood before them.

Simone bent down and unclasped Megan's money belt from around Lucifer's neck. She placed it with the 'ody'.

"No," shouted Megan. "No, you traitor!"

Cassius' lips curled in a grimace just like Lucifer's. "I believe I have you to thank for these items, Zero One Zero," he said. Lucifer bowed.

"And now we have new life to forge," he went on. "And two of these must be the ones to do it. Where are those that will release the power of the 'ody'? Take them!"

Simone pointed with her long nails, one finger at Tom, another at Megan.

The raptor sprang and caught Megan by the arm while two baboons leaped on Tom's back.

"No," shouted Megan, struggling and kicking to free herself.

"Help her, Luce," pleaded Alex in desperation.

"She will not be harmed," said Lucifer. "She merely has a job to do."

But he didn't look at Alex, and the puma scowled at him.

"Let them go," shouted Asiimwe, trying to grab the raptor from behind. The raptor bellowed and struck at him, drawing blood from his forehead. A baboon flung itself against his chest and the two fell to the ground. Alex tried to pull it off but more joined the fight.

Writhing and protesting, Megan and Tom were dragged away. Megan used her teeth, the only bit of her left free. She wanted to tear the raptor's tough limbs but her bite made no impression at all on his leathery hide. She spat at him but he didn't even feel the spittle through his tough skin. Tom tried to flex his arms and break the hold of the baboons but their sinewy strength was too much for him. Megan screamed and carried on screaming because the screams blew away the foul warm smell of the raptor's breath down her neck. Finally worn out, she looked across at Tom, his hands now tied behind him, led by two baboons. He smiled encouragingly at Megan but she didn't respond; the foulness of the raptor's scaly arm round her was almost more than she could bear.

Realizing that matters had now moved on, Asiimwe's and Alex's attackers flung the boys to the ground – they were no longer needed – and joined the triumphal group that clambered up the rocky cliff and over the hill.

Alex and Asiimwe scrambled to their feet. Now what do we do? They were quite alone. There wasn't a creature in sight. The valley was strangely quiet after the gibbering of the baboons and the snuffling of the hyenas and the shrieking of the raptor. They looked at each other in disbelief. Did it really happen? Asiimwe sat with his head in his hands. Alex scanned the horizon for signs of life.

"I knew there was something unreal about that sparkat," he said.

"Over here," a cackling voice called to them. "Over here. Over here. Over here."

They made their way to a clump of bushes where they saw a green and blue parrot with a golden head cocking its eye at them.

"Percival!" exclaimed Alex.

"Come with me! Come with me! Come with me!"

Asiimwe looked at Alex who shrugged his shoulders.

"Any better ideas?" he asked.

Percival fluttered from tree to tree along a pleasant jungle path that became more colourful with every step. He paused now and then to ensure the boys were following him.

Eventually they reached a clearing where Klara and Jessica were poring over a map, Plato sunning himself beside them. Relief shone from the two boys' faces as they stroked Plato who had leaped up to greet them.

"You know?" Alex addressed Jessica.

"Yes, Klara told me. She and Plato have been watching Simone and Lucifer throughout the mission; they knew they were planning something treacherous. And Percival has been helping too, hopping between worlds with information."

The parrot bowed his head and made a whirring noise deep in his throat.

"I sent a message to Control. They passed us this map. It tells us how to reach the rock of the cauldron by many different routes. They've gone the long way round through the valleys. If we go over the top, we may yet beat them to it."

"I don't see what good that would do," said Asiimwe derisively. "Us few against those hordes. And they've got the 'ody', and the treasures."

"We need to call on Gabriel," said Klara.

"I am Gabriel." The velvet voice was behind them. "There will be no need call me. I suspected treachery and have been waiting my time. Double O Four kept me informed." Jessica started at mention of Double O Four.

They turned to face a magnificent shimmercat. His colours – bronze and silver and gold – shone like metal in awesome symmetry. His fur was silver velvet, and on it were large star spots of bronze and gold. At rest they were bronze, in movement they became gold. His silver face displayed bands of gold, as did his swinging tail. His voice was deep as the ocean and soft as the clouds. Jessica's fur stood on end at sight of him; she seemed to melt before him.

"We will get there before them. They have a head start, that is true, but they quarrel along the way. Lucifer and Simone want power for themselves. They have stolen one of the treasures, the star. They plan to double-cross Cassius. And so they delay. And that gives us our chance. The star is now hanging round Simone's neck, and she will not give it up easily."

"First," said Alex, speaking his confusion, "I'd like to know something about this Creation world we've arrived in. It seems a very strange place."

"You have indeed reached Creation world," began Gabriel patiently. "It's a world of differences, because it reflects many worlds: worlds of jungle, desert, ice and much that you could never dream of. That is why you seem to move through so many different places in such a short space of time.

"As you have surely been told, I work for the Creator. I take care of the forest that grows the new life for all the worlds on the planet Earth. Cassius, the puma you just met, is my soulmate, the other side of myself. It is his treachery, of which our agents have told you, that gave rise to our present mission. But come, let us reach the rock of the cauldron before the quarrelling mob."

And the shimmercat crouched low.

51 Final Act

The journey was a splendid one. High on the back of the great spirit, their hands deep in the thick fur, the earthlings set off at easy speed to leap over trees and bushes and soar above rivers and valleys. They passed over just a small portion of the terrain of Creation world: the metal part with the bike road, the jungle they had just left, icy plains, mighty oceans.

They came to rest on a mountain peak, on the top of which a large rock stood alone. Only if viewed in a certain way was it shaped like a cauldron, and therein lay its strength and anonymity.

Behind them was a plateau, in front a sheer drop.

"See, we have beaten them to it. They do not realize they have need for urgency."

A nagging question burned in Alex. "We've been betrayed once. How do we know you're the good and Cassius the bad?"

"How indeed?" Taking pity on Alex's exasperated expression, Gabriel continued. "In the end, it's all a matter of faith. So who are you going to put your faith in? Me or them?"

He pointed below to where Simone and Lucifer were racing across the valley, flanked by hyenas and vultures, and a raptor and baboons holding struggling earthlings. All were pursued by Cassius demanding to know where the final treasure was.

At sight of Megan's plight Percival squawked his distress. Klara stroked his head to calm him. Plato snuggled up to Jessica seeking reassurance.

Gabriel purred, a gentle throbbing that very slowly became louder.

At sound of this there came cats from every direction, as from the very ground itself, all sizes and all colours: there were domestic moggies, leopards and cheetahs and panthers and jaguars and lions, tigers and pumas and sparkats, lynxes with stubby tails and tufted ears, servals with pretty patterned coats, fierce wildcats, strange cats the earthlings had never seen before with luminous coats patterned with squares. Jessica knew that, among them, were Jasper and those other leopards that had helped them, that had passed information to Double O Four. In front of them all were two jet black moggies with blazing green eyes; every hair on their backs erect they exuded courage.

"Now let the battle begin."

The instruction was no more than a rumble in the shimmercat's throat. He let out a mighty roar that shook the rock of the cauldron. All movement and noise below stopped and every eye looked upwards. As if at a signal, the creatures in the valley bottom melted into the landscape.

"They will regroup," warned Gabriel. "They will come round the back and attack from the plateau, hoping to drive us over the edge."

"Well, we have all these cats on our side." Alex looked round approvingly.

"Don't underestimate the baboon," warned Gabriel. "Never underestimate any creature. And they are superior in number. But do not be worried. Good is always stronger than evil."

"But what about my sister? She could get killed in the fight."

"She could indeed," said Gabriel unsatisfactorily. "But remember Cassius needs her alive for the final act."

Alex had forgotten that and was somewhat reassured.

Asiimwe seemed to remember being told that a baboon could perform the final act if the earthlings no longer lived, but he pushed that thought to the back of his mind. He couldn't bring himself to believe that Lucifer would actually allow Tom and Megan to die.

"What do you want us to do?" he asked the shimmercat.

"What you can. There are weapons under the cauldron."

The boys searched under the rock and armed themselves well with knives and swords, all marked with runes it would have been interesting to examine more closely in other circumstances.

"Let's stand back to back," suggested Alex.

Jessica and Plato took up positions at the boys' feet. Klara struggled to calm Percival.

Then hate and treachery were upon them. Screams and snarls came from the cats. The fur of every one stood up straight so that they grew to twice their normal size and their tails, bottle-brushy, were held erect. They sprang, claws unsheathed like scythes. Baboons fell at the first charge but there were more and more and more, and the hyenas slunk wide and crept in behind the ranks of the cats. The vultures encircled them all, waiting patiently for the meal.

Out of the corner of one eye, Alex was aware of a magnificent red bronze cat being set upon by a group of hyenas and baboons that tore him to pieces. But he had no time to dwell on such things. He and Asiimwe slashed in every direction with their knives and swords. Clawing hands scored their faces and arms and their cloaks dripped red. Jessica and Plato made it their task to save the earthlings from the fiercest thrusts. They leaped at the throats of their enemies and paid no heed at all to their torn coats and broken claws.

Gabriel heard Cassius open his mouth and issue a challenge. He raised his mighty head. He turned to his soulmate and saw, pinned beneath each massive front paw, the forms of Tom and Megan.

"If you want to save them, you will have to kill me," he growled. "Or maybe I will kill them right now. They are of no further use to me. Baboons can perform the final act."

Before Cassius' thoughts could travel any further along that line, Gabriel sprang. Cassius leaped at him, so releasing Tom and Megan who ran the short distance to where Alex and Asiimwe stood fighting. Megan put her back to the rock and took a knife from Asiimwe. She was immediately reassured to feel the furry caress of Jessica's body against her legs. Tom armed himself with a sword and stood beside her. They were grateful to notice the little dog Plato at their feet, biting at the ankles of those that stood against them, so that the earthlings could take careful aim with their weapons. He was quite fearless and seemed not to care that his white coat became spattered with more of his own blood than any other creature's. Klara, too, was with them, displaying a courage that sat incongruously beside her delicate beauty. Only Percival wanted no part of any of this and flew in distressed squawking round Megan's head.

But the thrusts and punches lessened as all eyes turned to the mighty battle between the two great cats. It seemed that the whole world joined in that fight. Thunder raged in the sky. Waves swelled in the ocean. Wind tore among the branches of mighty trees.

The sky darkened. Nothing could be seen but the light of life in the struggling forms of two powerful phantasmal cats.

The glow of Cassius dimmed. Evil conceded the day. Good prevailed.

Thunder rumbled into the distance. Waves became calm. Wind drifted into a light breeze. Darkness descended to the horizon.

The powerful shimmercat, his jaws red from the battle and his magnificent coat stained with blood, stood in triumph over the form of his soulmate. He tore the 'ody' and the purse full of treasures from the fur round his neck. The wounded Cassius stumbled to his paws and limped across the plateau. The exertion proved too much for him. He sank to the ground, gasping for breath. Baboons and hyenas turned tail and ran. Vultures continued to wait.

"Stop them," boomed Gabriel as Simone and Lucifer sought to flee also. Alex and Asiimwe were onto them immediately and rugby tackled the pair to the earth.

Megan looked around. All the dead animals had vanished into nothingness and those wounded had fled. Blood no longer stained the ground. The pale sun shone benevolently. The vultures grew bored; the meal had somehow disappeared; they flapped away. All that remained was a ring of cats, silently watching.

Gabriel moved over to where Cassius lay, the life ebbing out of him. As he drew his last breath there was a flash of light and his body became liquid. Rich brown and velvet black it formed a pattern of stars on the ground that rose slowly to the sky and placed themselves in the heavens.

"So has the Creator dealt with him," said Gabriel. "I am satisfied."

He picked up the 'ody' and the purse of treasures from where they had fallen and mingled with Cassius' liquid fur.

The earthlings, stunned by these events, sank down by the rock of the cauldron and lowered their battle scarred knives to the ground.

"Now for the last act," said Gabriel. "Here are your treasures, Megan. Show them to me."

He handed the money belt to Megan who laid the treasures out on the ground and told Gabriel about each one.

"Simone has the star," she explained.

Alex pulled it none too gently from Simone's neck, ignoring her pouting look.

Gabriel turned to Simone and Lucifer.

"The baboons and hyenas will not be punished. They know no better, they do their leader's bidding. But you two were given positions of understanding. You used your superior intelligence to gain power over more trusting creatures."

"Yeah," muttered Alex. "One group shouldn't dominate another."

What an extraordinary thing for a human being to say, thought Lucifer.

"And you shouldn't fiddle with DNA," added Asiimwe.

What another extraordinary thing for a human being to say.

"What you most desire will be taken from you," Gabriel went on. "You, Simone, will go to Bioworld where you will stay for as long as it pleases me. There you will become an eternal schoolgirl so that others may direct your actions as you once did theirs. And you, Lucifer, will also spend very many years in Bioworld. There you will remain an ordinary moggie, unable to shift, unable to speak, but very able to think and relive your past deeds.

"Now the cauldron. Which of you has the key?"

"Key?" queried Alex.

"I didn't tell them about the key," said Lucifer, hardly able to conceal his smirk in spite of Gabriel's hard words.

"But I knew about it," said Klara. "Percival took it from Simone's jewel box and I left it by the river for Megan to find."

"This key?" asked Megan, incredulous. She took the tiny skeleton key from her pocket.

"Under the rock," said Gabriel, "there is a small gap which guards the secret of your key."

Megan felt in the gap with her fingers and turned the key in the lock. From the keyhole wafted warm amber light. The earthlings gazed around full of awe as the swirling amber engulfed them and drew them into a mighty forest where the trees were so tall they couldn't see the canopy. Fierce light was all around, flickering and welcoming. They moved not at all, but the forest moved around them. The kaleidoscope of branches and leaves and flowers spun before their dazzled eyes, and brought to their feet a tree of such antiquity its very presence filled them with frightening wonder. Among its gnarled roots was a tiny hollow full of radiant glow.

"This," purred Gabriel gently, "is our forge. Now, Megan and Tom, take each treasure, hold its heart in the light, lick it to pass on existing DNA, and then place it in the forge."

The moment was too solemn for questions and the earthlings did as bidden.

As they performed the final act, so the treasures dissolved in a multi-coloured liquid, and the face of the shimmercat was overcome with a formless source of light and power.

Gabriel closed his eyes and began a silent prayer. A strange, compelling smell arose from the forge. From its depths there climbed a slim pillar, itself transparent but within it tiny points of light. Then around the pole spiralled a double helix. In the spiral of light the earthlings saw very many images of animals and plants: all the created life of their own world climbing upwards in two great coils.

"DNA. Science, not magic," muttered Asiimwe to himself, finally convinced. Gabriel took the 'ody' and held it above the pole. The DNA spiralled up the pole and embedded itself among the seeds in the 'ody'. So great was the pressure of it doing this that the seeds crumbled into dust. Gabriel held the 'ody' in place until the spiralling ceased and the pole died back and the forge disappeared among the grass at the base of the mighty tree.

"Take this," said Gabriel holding the 'ody' towards Megan and Tom. As you return to Earth, scatter the dust through the atmosphere. Jessica will see you home."

And suddenly Gabriel was gone, taking with him Klara and Plato. Alone on the hillside stood four earthlings, one sparkat and one parrot.

"You're a star!" squawked Percival.

Tumbling they passed through the black hole. Racing they sped down the silver escalator. As they recognized Bioworld below them, they felt themselves leave the path and begin to float. Megan shook out dust into the atmosphere and handed the 'ody' to Tom to do the same. Tom handed it to Alex who passed it on to Asiimwe.

Empty at last, the 'ody' disintegrated and became so much dust itself.

52 In the End

Jessica felt an irritation behind her ear. She uncurled herself from the end of Megan's bed and went to the window. She took out her mobile phone and searched the skies for a signal. Control had a message for her. Zero Six Six was needed for another mission immediately. Jessica looked back at the sleeping girl on the bed, the pillow covered in wild red curls. She had grown very fond of Megan and her friends and family, and had enjoyed playing at being an ordinary moggie during the past few weeks. But she wasn't an ordinary moggie, she was a sparkat. And she wasn't even an ordinary sparkat. She was a member of the Intra Galactic Intelligence Service. Her life and her movements were not her own; they belonged to the Service. And now she must go. She took one last look around the room and leaped through the window. Under the light of the watching moon, she ran across the grass turned black by the darkness. Once on the other side of the lawn, she shifted from her black and white coat and, from her tail to her whiskers, became a sparkat. She glanced up to the stars and leaped into the sky.

Megan felt the bottom of her bed.

"Jess, where are you?"

She got up and went to the open window. The sky was paling in the rapidly encroaching dawn. Barefoot, Megan ran out into the garden.

"Jess, where are you?"

But Megan knew that Jessica had gone and that she would not return. She sat on the veranda, pulled her knees up to her face, and sobbed. Percival flew gently onto her shoulder and nuzzled her neck. He would stay, he tried to tell her.

The last day of term was given over to a party. In Uganda, the primary school year ends in December and it is traditional that those leaving P7 be given a good send-off. Most would be attending the local secondary school where building of the new science laboratory had already begun. Alex was to be a weekly boarder in Mbarara. He was pleased about that. He had worked hard to pass the entrance exam. It would be much better, he thought, than being sent off to Canada or England.

And so the day was taken over by singing and dancing; all the entertainment organized by the children themselves. And, of course, there was a great feast. Each child had arrived that morning with some gift from home. The older girls and a few of the mothers helped with the cooking and set the food out attractively. The teachers mellowed that day. Mr

Karumu even allowed Percival into the classroom where he amused the children by shouting out his most recently acquired vocabulary.

"Over here!" he repeated endlessly and, "Come with me!" But favourite of all was the word, "Wi-cked!"

"I wonder where he learned that?" laughed Asiimwe.

Half way through the afternoon the children began to drift home.

Unknown to Alex another party had been arranged for him, back at Asiimwe's place. Megan and Tom slipped away early to help with the preparations. Asiimwe ensured that the guest didn't arrive too soon.

Alex was amazed to turn the familiar corner and see before him strings of bunting and a great banner that read GOOD LUCK ALEX. The younger children, laughing, almost carried him into the compound where a bottle of soda was set before him. The family had prepared an entertainment of singing and dancing that included the very oldest and the very youngest. There was a sumptuous meal followed by the usual speeches. And so Alex had the opportunity to say how much this particular family meant to him and how glad he was that he would not be going any further than Mbarara for his secondary education. Thoughtfully, Megan had brought his guitar to the celebrations and now Alex, as she had known he would, picked this up and began to play and sing. Toppie fixed admiring eyes on him, and all could tell his music was only for her. Gradually the others drifted away to carry on drinking and talking and playing elsewhere, and left the two young people alone.

Megan sat under a purple bougainvillea and looked up to the sky.

Where are you Jess?

Tom joined her.

"I've got something for you," he said gently, and handed Megan a roll of paper.

Megan smiled, questioningly. She took the paper from him and slowly unrolled it.

"Oh," she gasped. "Oh Percival, look at this!" Percival craned his neck to admire a beautiful painting of an orange cat with green ears.

"It's Jess, it really is Jess," breathed Megan in delight. Indeed the likeness was quite uncanny. The amber eyes were surely alive.

"Did you do it yourself?"

"Yeah," said Tom self consciously, blushing. He had had the idea only a few days ago when Jessica had disappeared, and had been surprised at how well the painting had gone, almost as if an unseen hand had been guiding the brush. He was completely unprepared for the spontaneous hug that Megan now gave him.

Back home, he made straight for the workshop where the rabbit box was nearing completion. That was to be for Christmas, he decided happily, as he carefully carved a star into the bottom.

When Megan showed the portrait to her parents later that evening they both agreed it was beautifully done and that the eyes were quite striking, and definitely Jessica's own.

"But the colour's all wrong," declared Holly.

"What do you mean?" Megan was indignant.

"Well, she's orange. She should be black and white!"

"Oh yeah." Megan started to giggle and just couldn't stop.

Steve took the picture into Mbarara where a friend put it into a metal frame for his daughter. A frame just like the one that had surrounded the mirror, thought Megan, as Alex hammered a nail into her bedroom wall for her to hang it on.

Asiimwe rode into the Martyns' garden. Megan ran to greet him.

"Look what I found in the market."

From the inside of his jacket he brought out a tiny grey kitten that mewed plaintively.

"Oh, she's gorgeous!" exclaimed Megan, taking the tiny animal from him.

"Whereabouts in the market did you get her?"

"I bought her from a man I've never seen before. The strange thing was, he was quite determined that I should buy her, and no one else. He only wanted a hundred shillings for her. I knew you'd like her," he added, smiling at her enraptured face. "She's yours to keep."

"Oh Asiimwe, thank you." She put a hand on his shoulder and kissed his cheek.

The little kitten, nestled in the crook of Megan's other arm, looked up at them approvingly from deep amber eyes.

"Mummy," Megan shouted, running to the house. "Asiimwe's brought me a kitten. May I keep her?"

There was a television in the living room of Tom's home. Just sometimes they could receive programmes from overseas. Duncan switched it on for the BBC news. Tom, Lucifer at his side, was working on a design for a go-kart.

"First for our big story," began the newsreader. He sounded so excited that even Tom and Lucifer looked up.

"Professor Jackson, perhaps you'd like to tell us about it."

"Certainly would," declared the enthusiastic young man, from behind his spectacles. "This must be one of the most important finds of the millennium. It all happened in the centre of Africa. We were busy with routine research when this friend of mine came across a kind of plant we had never seen before. Now that was incredible enough, but then we found this bee-like insect that was equally unknown to us. And on the third day," the young man seemed as if he was about to explode with enthusiasm, "we discovered a new species of butterfly. And then they just came on, thick and fast, more and more new species!" His voice rose high with excitement.

Tom and Lucifer were riveted to the television screen.

"That really is a most unusual occurrence," agreed the newsreader. "We will now go over to Uganda to join Dave Barnes at the site."

The scene switched to a forest in Uganda, and a bronzed young man in shorts and t-shirt and bush hat.

"So Dave," asked the interviewer, "what do you make of all this?"

Dave threw his arms in the air, a broad smile on his face.

"Just don't know what to say really. Never seen anything like it. All these new species in just a few days. Wow!"

"What do you think might be the reason for their appearance now?" Dave shrugged his shoulders happily. "Search me," he laughed. "It's one big mystery."

The scene switched back to the studio.

"So, Professor Jackson, what are we to make of it all?"

"Well of course," the Professor was thoughtful, "we don't know whether all of these are completely new species or whether they are species that we simply haven't come across before. But when so many species are disappearing off our planet for ever this is indeed a wonderful happening."

"So what do *you* make of all that then, Luce?" teased Tom, drawing Lucifer to him. Lucifer miaowed and struggled free.

The newsreader hadn't finished.

"We're getting reports of problems in a British boarding school. They have a pupil, a girl, whose misdeeds are so extreme that they frequently hit the headlines. It seems that no school can contain her, but this one school is determined to persevere."

"We have a good record of dealing with difficult pupils," declared the very large and fierce-looking headmistress.

"Wanna bet," laughed Tom. "Now I wonder what her name might be!"

He hugged Lucifer to him. His loved his moggie dearly, after all he was a soulmate. He stroked the tabby fur with its orange lights and looked into the emerald eyes, angry now at being held against his will. He miaowed his protest and Tom put him down.

Lucifer ran to the door and out into the garden. He rubbed behind his ear to reach his mobile phone but it wasn't there. His fierce emerald eyes searched the stars. They twinkled at him but sent no messages. Lucifer howled his complaint.

The Sparkat Trilogy

BOOK 1 ~ THE PUZZLING MIRROR

Runner up in the recent WOW competition organized by Waterstones Booksellers.

The thoughts of some young readers ...

I think this is one of the best books ever. I'm not just saying that. In Year 5 I read Nina Bawden's Carrie's War and up until now I thought that was the best book ever.

The Puzzling Mirror is a great book. I can't say that enough times. I am lost without it. It doesn't seem right reading another book. It's true.

The Puzzling Mirror is a fantastic book. I loved the originality of it and the descriptions were perfect. It was a really good read.

The descriptions are brilliant. I could see clear images in my head.

I think it would make an ace film. I would happily star in it.

The characters felt like my friends.

I like your ideas for books.

All the different worlds are interesting. The land with the robots is best.

... and of some slightly older ones ...

Especially enjoyable is the Ugandan background with all the authentic details of everyday life and culture. It really brought the place alive for me.

As well as enjoying the story simply as a story I saw several themes running below the surface.

I liked the idea of science versus magic and how the two fit together. You made me think of science in a new way. The natural world and the way it works *is* magic in a sense, but nothing to be afraid of.

I loved all the imagery and the use of contemporary ideas and themes – from pollution to skateboards.

I adore the child characters and the sparkats (especially bad Lucifer) and I think you get a perfect balance between the child adventure story (a bit reminiscent, perhaps, of C S Lewis) and the 'other'. The baboons remind me a bit of Kipling's monkeys in The Jungle Book and the Uganda stuff is great.

The African setting is unusual and vividly portrayed.

The book grips from the start and plunges straight into a wonderland which I would enjoy sharing with children.

I enjoyed the introduction of the strange sparkats and the early unsettling feeling that anything can happen.

... and of the reviewers ...

Not only will young readers enjoy an exciting adventure, they will also have an interesting insight into everyday life in rural Uganda. They will discover that, although there are differences from their own lives, there are also similarities, and that children everywhere have much in common.
Uganda is portrayed as a positive place. That is how most of Africa is on a daily basis, far away from the tragic headlines that so often dominate the news in more affluent countries.

Herald Express

Africa is always in the headlines, often for the worst of reasons.
So, for a change, read about the positive side of everyday life in beautiful rural Uganda where people live and work, largely undisturbed by politicians and soldiers.
The story is informative, but at the same time full of adventure and excitement. It asks the reader to address some of the issues of our times, such as pollution and the changing of DNA.

South Hams Gazette

This story shows the readers that there is a different side of Africa to that presented in the news. As everywhere else in the world, most people are busy with their everyday lives. They want the same things as we do – a future for their children and a good job.

Writers' News

This is an amazing manuscript. The characters are fabulous, as is the plot. I am impressed with your imagination, writing skills and story-telling ability. The readers will truly love this material. You have a gift for writing.

Children's Literary Agency

BOOK 2 ~ THE SEARCHING STONE

Your books are full of great ideas. They are fun.

Percival is one of my favourite characters – he's great!

The book was very interesting and very different from what I expected which was good.

The book is cleverly thought out and I really liked the ending.

I love the details of everyday life in Uganda – delightful and fascinating as well as educational. It's what makes your books so special and gives them the edge over other children's books on the market.

BOOK 3 ~ THE LIVING AXE

Love the contrast between your two worlds – one of strange magic and the other of real life in Uganda.

RUNYANKORE is a local language spoken in the south west of Uganda.

GLOSSARY OF THOSE WORDS
USED IN THE STORY

boda boda	bicycle used as public transport, the passenger sitting on the back
dukha	small shop
eskari	watchman
kabaragara	small sweet banana
kanga	large piece of cloth, used by women as a wrap around skirt or dress
matatu	minibus – a much used form of public transport
matooke	plantain, large green banana, often boiled and mashed
mendazi	doughnut
muzungu	white person
mzee	old man
obotunda	passion fruit juice
posho	maize flour, used to make porridge or a kind of dough
shamba	small farm
agandi	a general greeting
nimarungi	the reply to the first greeting
murram	red shale, used to surface roads

international law, international relations, and international political economy; the red volumes allow further reflection and investigation in these and related areas.

The books in the series also provide a segue-way to the foundation volume that offers the most comprehensive textbook treatment available dealing with all the major issues, approaches, institutions, and actors in contemporary global governance—our edited work *International Organization and Global Governance* (2014)—a volume to which many of the authors in the series have contributed essays.

Understanding global governance—past, present, and future—is far from a finished journey. The books in this series nonetheless represent significant steps toward a better way of conceiving contemporary problems and issues as well as, hopefully, doing something to improve world order. We value feedback from our readers and their role in helping shape the ongoing development of the series.

A complete list of titles appears at the end of this book. The most recent titles in the series are:

Post-2015 UN Development (2014)
Edited by Stephen Browne and Thomas G. Weiss

Who Participates in Global Governance? (2014)
Molly A. Ruhlman

The Security Council as Global Legislator (2014)
Edited by Vesselin Popovski and Trudy Fraser

UNICEF (2014)
Richard Jolly

The Society for Worldwide Interbank Financial Telecommunication (SWIFT) (2014)
Susan V. Scott and Markos Zachariadis

The International Politics of Human Rights (2014)
Rallying to the R2P Cause?
Edited by Monica Serrano and Thomas G. Weiss

Private Foundations and Development Partnerships (2014)
Michael Moran